The Walk of a Queen

by
ANNIE M.P. SMITHSON

> *'Did you see an old woman going down the path? I did not; but I saw a young girl, and she had the walk of a queen.'*
> — CATHLEEN NI HOULIHAN

THE MERCIER PRESS
CORK

The Mercier Press,
Cork.

First published by the Talbot Press

This edition 1988
© The Mercier Press, 1988

British Library Cataloguing in Publication Data
Smithson, Annie M.P., *1873 - 1948*
  The Walk of a Queen
  I. Title
  823'.912 [F]

  ISBN 978-1-78117-928-4

Transferred to Digital Print-on-Demand in 2024

CHAPTER I

MINGLED THREADS OF DESTINY

Rain—rain—rain. It was simply pouring from the skies above, running in tiny rivulets along the footpath, while the streets glistened and shone in the lamplight as horses and motors and struggling pedestrians splashed along. Geraldine Moore, in waterproof coat and cap and with umbrella held aloft, walked as quickly as she could along St Stephen's Green. It was just eight o'clock, and the Irish language class to which she belonged began at that hour. She was rather late this evening for she had had a heavy and sordid day's work to get through in connection with her position as Health visitor, and the weather, needless to say, had not helped to improve matters—the Dublin slums always seeming to be less beautiful than ever on a wet day. She had been visiting her 'Mothers' in the district until nearly six o'clock, and then had to returned to her lodgings in Rathmines, get her tea, enter up her day's work in the Case Books, and start back into town again for her Irish Class. She was intensely interested in all that concerned the Language movement, and on principle she would have considered it wrong to miss her Gaelic hour, even though she was now in her second year and fairly well on with what should have been her mother tongue. But tonight, cold and wet and tired with the day's drudgery, she entered the class-room feeling weary and depressed. Only the more ardent spirits of the movement were there, for the night was bad enough to keep most people within doors, but Geraldine noticed, with some surprise, two new faces as she absently murmured her Gaelic greeting and slipped quietly into her accustomed place.

The Class had not commenced, as the teacher was late in arriving—probably delayed by the wet evening—and a girl from the opposite bench came across the room to speak to Geraldine.

'Oh! Jerry!' she cried, 'Anthony and Desmond are here. You know they got home for Christmas—no, no, I'm too excited to talk Gaelic'—as Geraldine spoke a few words in that tongue—'you know well that I can never really speak it properly. Look! that is Anthony—there—on the right—and Desmond on the left.'

'But—but what a resemblance!' murmured Geraldine, 'I don't believe that I would ever know them apart.'

'Oh, yes, you would,' cried the other girl, 'they are not really alike at all—when you know them.'

Geraldine laughed.

'Well, indeed one would want to know them very well,' she said, 'even for twins I think the resemblance is perfectly marvellous.'

'I'll introduce you after the Class,' said Sheila Ryan, 'they have heard all about you, of course, and—oh! here's the Professor,' and with a laughing nod and a quick whirl of skirts she was back on her own bench.

After the Class she was as good as her word and brought her two brothers up to Geraldine.

'Now, Jerry,' she said, 'here are Tony and Desmond. They know you and I are chums and you must be the same with them, too.'

Geraldine had caught herself several times during the last hour glancing with deep interest at the two young men. They had only just returned from Frongoch, and so for her they were surrounded with that atmosphere—almost a halo—of patriotism—the true patriotism which believes in deeds rather than words, and which goes to suffering or to death in that quietly determined and matter of course fashion characteristic of our young men in Ireland today.

They were both tall, rather thin, and dark, their hair indeed was of that purple black colour which is often seen in the West of Ireland, and their eyes dark grey. They seemed hopelessly alike to anyone meeting them for the first time, and as far as physical resemblance went, they certainly were very similar, but after a better acquaintance with them people soon realised that the individual expression of each was totally unlike. Anthony had a straight, direct way of looking one in the face while he was talking, a proud, rather distant manner with strangers, and the walk of a queen's son, while Desmond's eyes often shifted uneasily from the face of the person whom he was addressing, and he had a habit of walking rather quickly—furtively as it were—as though in constant dread of pursuit or arrest. Yet still he walked well, and held himself straight and upright as a dart—as well indeed he might, for both he and his brother were drilled to perfection. Both had been 'out' in Easter Week and deported to Frongoch, had been released at Christmas, and now it was early in the New Year.

It was on Desmond's face that Geraldine's glance had rested the more frequently, and as far as women were concerned this was the usual case. With the opposite sex Desmond Ryan had always been a supreme favourite, they seemed totally unable to resist his sunny smile and winning personality, for with them he was at his best, and always at home in their presence. Even Sheila, although she was devoted to both, knew in her innermost heart that Desmond was the 'white-headed boy' with her—as with others—and she knew, too, although she would never admit it even to herself, that Anthony was the stronger character and the better man of the two.

She herself was a great contrast to her brothers. No one would ever have guessed that there was any blood relationship between them, so far as resemblance went, and indeed in character also she was very unlike them, but in this respect more dissimilar to Anthony than to Desmond.

To describe her as an exceedingly lovely girl would be no exaggeration, for with her red-gold hair and exquisite colouring she made a picture not easily forgotten. She was of a very lovable disposition, too much so, for where her affections were concerned she was weak as water, and Geraldine, who loved the younger girl with a very real love, sometimes found herself wondering what sort of a man he would be who was destined to awaken Sheila's heart, and praying that he might be one of 'the right sort'.

'We have often heard of you, Miss Moore,' Anthony was saying—it was a characteristic of the twins that they always spoke in the plural when together, and they were seldom apart—'Sheila has told us so much about you that we seem to have known you for ages in the spirit.'

'And now we are tremendously glad to know you in the flesh,' supplemented Desmond, and while Anthony spoke only with grave but sincere friendliness, Desmond's caressing voice and swift smile seemed to carry a sort of chivalrous homage with them.

Geraldine flushed with pleasure as she shook hands.

'And I am glad—very glad—to meet you,' she replied, 'it—it is an honour to know those of our men who have suffered for Ireland,' and her voice faltered slightly. Anthony flushed in some embarrassment, but Desmond raised his hand to the salute as he replied with the charming ease which always characterised his intercourse with the feminine portion of humanity.

'It is easy to bear a little suffering for the Motherland—and for her daughters.'

'Oh! come on now,' said Sheila, 'remember, boys, we have to catch the train to Dundrum. Thank goodness the rain is over at last,' she added, as they emerged into the street and saw that although the lamps were shining on wet and glistening pavements no rain was actually falling.

'Oh! it must be tired raining,' said Desmond. 'But let us get the tram at the corner here, it will take Miss Moore home, and we can get out at Harcourt Street Station.'

'Yes, that will do,' said his sister, 'it's hardly worth while for us to tram it, but still we may as well see as much of Jerry as we can.'

The tram was crowded. A man near the door stood up to give Geraldine his seat, which she took reluctantly, as she smiled her thanks—being a very modern young person with an intensely independent mind she always disliked accepting these masculine acts of mere courtesy. But her innate good breeding forbade her to refuse, or to receive it, as she had often seen some of her sex do, as their mere right and hardly worthy of acknowledgement.

The twins were standing in front of her, hanging on to the strap, and Sheila had gone higher up the car. Needless to say that she would never have had to wait a moment for a seat, her beauty was of that compelling order which draws all eyes to it, and there was not a man in the tram who, after one brief glance at the face under the little fur cap, was not ready to sacrifice his seat, or anything else she might demand. But one man was quicker than any of the others, and Geraldine looking up the tram saw a young fellow in the uniform of a lieutenant in the British Army spring to his feet as if electrified, while he saluted with a smile.

Sheila gave him her hand in greeting as she sat down, and at the same moment Geraldine recognised him as a certain Lieutenant Hammond whom she had met several times at Firfield House, the Ryans' place near Dundrum. He was the usual type of the British officer with which the War has made us so familiar during the past years. Geraldine found herself wondering how Sheila could trouble or care to laugh and talk with him as she was doing, and doing so gaily too, with the exquisite colour coming and going in her face.

Anthony Ryan bent down presently and asked curtly.

'Who is that fellow?'

'He is a Lieutenant Hammond,' Geraldine answered, 'I don't know him very well, but I have met him at Firfield. Mrs Ryan thinks a good deal of him, I believe.'

'Yes, she would. He is just her style,' was the rather dry response, and then the tram stopped at Harcourt Street Station and the Ryans got out—Sheila giving Geraldine's hand a tiny squeeze as she passed, but her parting smile was sent higher up the car.

Geraldine frowned and glanced involuntarily at the English officer, a glance which he caught and answered by a smiling salute, and than, rather to the girl's annoyance, he moved down the car and took the seat beside her, which was now vacant.

'How de do, Miss Moore?' he said. 'You have not forgotten me, I hope? We met at Firfield.'

'No; I have not forgotten you,' replied Geraldine quietly.

'Miss Ryan has just asked me to take a run out there next Wednesday,' he continued, with what seemed to Geraldine a very complacent smile.

'Will you have leave for much longer?' she asked, and he glanced at her in some surprise as he replied:

'For some weeks anyway—in fact I may be left here for a longer period. It all depends on—on certain circumstances.'

'I see,' said Geraldine.

Lieutenant Hammond sensed that the girl beside him was not inclined to be friendly—'not a sport' as his vocabulary would have expressed it, but he was rather conceited, with a very high opinion of himself, and could not really believe that she was quite indifferent to his manifold charms. And certainly he was a very good-looking fellow, slender and fair with eyes of 'china blue,' and he looked his well-groomed best in his immaculate uniform.

'Who were those two chaps who were with you?' he asked. 'Jolly fine looking fellows. Are they in the Service?'

Geraldine turned her serious grey eyes to him.

'Did not Sheila—Miss Ryan I mean—tell you?' she asked.

'No; at least we hadn't time to touch on them as a matter of fact,' and he smiled again in the self-conscious manner which annoyed the other so much. 'You see, she had to get off the car so soon. But I thought that they left with her—they seemed to be together—and I was wondering if they were friends?'

'They are her brothers,' replied Geraldine, adding with enjoyment, 'Captain Anthony Ryan and Lieutenant Desmond Ryan.'

'Oh! then they are Service men,' he said. 'I guessed as much. Do you know their regiment?'

The girl smiled and lifted her head proudly as she met

Lieutenant Hammond's bland gaze.

'They are not in the Service of England,' she said 'They are Officers of the Irish Republican Army.'

'Of the? oh! Come I say. You must be joking. What?'

'I see nothing to joke about in speaking of the men of our Army, Mr Hammond,' said Geraldine flushing, 'Captain Ryan and his brother have just returned from Frongoch, where they were interned as Prisoners of War by the British, and Ireland knows how to love and honour such men.'

Hammond was silent, he literally did not know what to answer, and when he did speak a few minutes later it was only to make some banal remark about the weather, to which Geraldine vouchsafed a rather frosty reply.

He got off the tram at Portobello with punctilious politeness, but saying 'By Jove—What?' several times to himself as he reached the pavement, and Geraldine was free to indulge in her own thoughts as the car carried her further on.

And her thoughts were rather troubled ones.

She had not failed to notice that Sheila's face had lit up at the sight of the young officer, and that she had been undoubtedly glad to meet him.

'She must have been seeing a good deal of him lately,' mused the girl, 'and, of course, Mrs Ryan would be charmed to welcome him—he might come every day to Firfield as far as she is concerned. And Sheila? Well, really she is just an adorable little fool. But it will be stopped now that the boys are home again— that's one consolation. What splendid fellows they are! Anthony seems rather reserved, but Desmond is a perfect darling,' and then she laughed in a rather shame-faced manner at her own enthusiasm, as she fitted the latchkey in the door, and entered the narrow hall of No.33 Hillview Avenue.

It was illuminated by a tiny flicker from the turned-down gas jet, and a pungent odour of frying onions was wafted from the kitchen, which was situated down two steps at the end of the passage. A small furry dog ran up these steps with shrill barks of welcome, and from the kitchen itself a hoarse voice cried several times over in rapid succession, 'Wipe your feet! Wipe your feet! Wipe your feet!'

'All right, Don Juan,' Geraldine called back, and at the same moment her landlady—Mrs Brennan—looked out, saying, 'Is that you, Miss Moore?'

'Yes,' replied the girl, 'and I'm wiping my feet all right.'

'Are you wet?' asked Mrs Brennan. 'You had better leave your mackintosh down here, it will dry off better.'

And Geraldine went down the narrow passage to the rather prim, tidy kitchen, where Mrs Brennan, with Thomas, the big black cat, Fluff the dog, and Don Juan the parrot, a very disreputable old bird with a basilisk eye, were sitting by an economical fire.

Mrs Brennan was a thin little woman of about fifty-five, a martyr to 'the rheumatics,' which had indeed crippled her pretty severely, so that she had to use a stick when walking. She had married—rather late in life—a widower with two children, and she was of that prim, methodical and rather acid type of women which is sometimes designated as 'old maids spoilt'. Her husband had been the love of her youth, but some quarrel or misunderstanding having arisen between them they had parted, and he—man-like—had taken for a wife the first girl who happened to come along. It turned out a bad bargain for him, for Julia Clancy—pretty, with the unhealthy prettiness of the city factory girl, but shallow and feather-brained—developed after marriage into a lazy, untidy sloven. Jim Brennan, owned a cab and an outside car, had often to be out early and late, and he soon found that he need not expect any kind of comfort or order in his home life. His wife would lie in bed till nearly noon and then steal down to the kitchen in curling pins and soiled wrapper to sit by the hob drinking strong tea and eating buttered toast. In the evening she would 'dress herself' and go out to see the shops or go to the pictures with friends of her own type. Poor Brennan had mostly to fend for himself and bitterly regretted the day that he had fallen out with tidy, thrifty little Amelia Byrne, all for the sake of a few sharp words.

When the children came things instead of becoming better, as he had fondly hoped, became worse, for Julia by then had added the home tippling habit to her other faults, and in consequence babies and home were totally neglected. Many a night would poor Brennan hurry home, perhaps losing a good fare by so doing, just to be able to bathe the little ones or give them a warm supper.

After ten years, Julia died, leaving him with the two children—Tom, the elder, aged nine, and Nellie, a little girl of seven. Her last illness had been tedious and to Brennan it was a terrible time. He employed a woman to look after the house and the children—a nurse coming daily to see to his wife—but she robbed him and did little work. He tried others, with only similar results. Then one night in winter, coming home rather late, and letting himself in with his latchkey as usual, he seemed to feel, as it were, a change in the atmosphere. The hall was spotless, and the linoleum on the stairs shone as it had never done since its infancy. He stepped gingerly down to the kitchen to find the same conditions of cleanliness and order—the hearth swept, dresser and tables scrubbed, everything in its place. It was many a long day since Jim Brennan had come home to such a kitchen.

A small, neat figure rose from her seat near the fire. 'Your supper's in the oven, Jim,' a prim voice announced, 'tripe and onions.'

His favourite dish.

From that day on Miss Byrne came daily to 'do' for Brennan, and when his wife died some six weeks later she still continued to come daily, impervious to any talk that might arise—she had a clear conscience and was afraid of no one. Jim Brennan's comfort and well-being were the most important things to her and she attended to them well. Some months later she married him and so continued to look after him, and after the children also, to whom she was a strictly just and conscientious—if somewhat severe—step-mother.

Well! all that was many years ago now, and 'the children' are out in the world—Tom having 'joined up' in the British Army at the beginning of the War, and Nellie being in a situation as a superior maid companion to a lady in Blackrock.

Mrs Brennan helped her husband—who in these hard times had only one horse and the cab left—by taking in lodgers, and Geraldine Moore had the use of her front room as 'combined bed and sitting'. She was a favourite with her landlady, who, under all her chilly exterior and sharp way of speaking, had a very kind heart.

'Leave your mackintosh and cap on the scullery door,' she said now, 'they will dry there. God knows—for I don't—why you went trapesing off to them Irish Classes on a night like this.'

'Oh! I don't mind the wet—I'm well used to it,' said Geraldine, but she spoke without her usual cheerfulness, which Mrs Brennan was quick to notice.

'It's tired you are,' she said tartly. 'The hot jar is in your bed, and there's a nice fire, but I suppose you'll not get a chance of sleep for the next hour or more—that mad wan is above waiting on you.'

'Who?' asked Geraldine quickly. 'Do you mean—?'

'Oh! who do you think I'm meanin' but that suffragette artist. Sure no wan could deny but that it's mad she is—mad as a March hare.'

'Mad! mad! Ha!Ha!' croaked Don Juan with a wicked leer. But Geraldine was already half-way up the narrow stairs and had flung open the door of her room, to be met with a cloud of cigarette smoke and the sound of a very musical and rather deep contralto voice saying;

'Hallo! Jerry. Here you are at last. By Bacchus! but I had thought you had gone up in an aeroplane.'

'Why, you know it's my Irish night,' replied Geraldine, 'and I'm not later than usual. How are you, Jill? It's an age since you were here.'

'Barely a fortnight, my child,' said the other.

'Well it seems longer,' was the laughing reply, as Geraldine drew the second armchair up to the fire, and sinking into its comfortable, if shabby depths, contemplated her friend with affectionate eyes. Jill Devereux was twenty-five, with a decidedly clever face, which was relieved from plainness by the dark, expressive eyes. She had short bobbed hair of a soft dusky colour, and pretty hands and feet. She always dressed plainly, generally in tweed coat and skirt, and although by no means untidy, still it could be seen that she took but little interest in her appearance. She was a Black and White artist by profession and got plenty of work designing posters and magazine advertisements. Of course her ambition soared much higher in the realms of art, but as she would say herself, 'One must eat!' She was very modern, extremely unconventional in her social opinions, and in her religious views quite unorthodox—almost agnostic. Her ancestors had come to Dublin as Huguenot refugees, and she herself had studied and lived for several years in Paris—in the gay Bohemian environment of the Latin quarter—she was really as much French as Irish, and had many of the mannerisms and gestures of a French woman. In the case of her toilet alone she was unlike her Parisian friends, except indeed in one detail—her feet were always daintily and expensively shod. Many other things would Jill Devereux sacrifice before she would wear a cheap or ugly shoe.

She and Geraldine Moore had been friends for several years now, and although totally dissimilar in many ways, they had a very real and true affection for each other.

'Well! how goes the Gaelic?' asked Miss Devereux as she lit another of her eternal cigarettes.

'Oh! all right,' replied Geraldine. 'And I'm awfully glad I went tonight. Jill, I met Anthony and Desmond Ryan—Sheila's brothers.'

Jill Devereaux sat forward suddenly.

'Why, of course,' she said slowly, 'I had forgotten they were back from Frongoch.'

'Yes,' said Geraldine. 'Oh! Jill, they are such splendid fellows. Both are handsome, with an extraordinary resemblance, and yet with an extraordinary difference, too! Desmond is the better looking, and he seemed to me to be of a more friendly disposition than his brother. Anthony appeared rather distant and reserved.'

'You seem to have observed both of these heroes rather minutely,' said Jill, with a dry smile, 'however, it is as you say. Desmond is much pleasanter and some might say more easy-going than his brother.'

Geraldine looked at her in quick surprise.

'Why, Jill,' she said, 'I didn't know that you had met them?'

'Oh! yes,' replied the other, and she flushed slightly. 'I knew both, but especially Desmond, before they were deported.'

Geraldine sat in silence for a moment. She was frankly puzzled, for never before had she known Jill Devereux to change colour at the mention of any man's name. As a sex she held them in a kind of tolerant contempt.

'Desmond Ryan must indeed be fascinating,' thought Geraldine now, 'if even Jill has fallen a victim to his charms.'

'What about their step-mother?' asked her friend suddenly. 'Isn't she of the opposite way of thinking with regard to national questions?'

Jill herself never took any side in either politics or religion. She always affirmed that she regarded herself as of no fixed nationality—she was a cosmopolitan and the whole world was her country. As for religion, it was a negative quantity with her.

'Oh! yes, Mrs Ryan is a horrid type,' replied Geraldine; 'she is the typical Seoinin.'

'Who or what was she?' asked Jill, lazily. 'It seems strange that she should be so different to the others, but after all, of course, she is no real relation. And Sheila, who is their real sister, is not like the boys. She is just a pretty silly doll.'

'Oh! Jill, I don't think that Sheila is silly,' said Geraldine. 'She is so pretty perhaps her head is a bit turned, and no wonder, but she is sensible enough. As to Mrs Ryan, she was a Mrs Byrne, big dairy people, and her first husband left her well off. She was a widow, going on for forty, when she met Sheila's father. I suppose she fell in love with him easily enough, but how he ever fancied her I do not know. He was a widower of fifty, a dreamy book-lover, cultured and refined, the very antithesis of the vulgar little woman he married. And I believe his first wife was a charming woman, an Irish Irelander, too; not a toadying "Cawstle Cawtholic" trying to hang on to the fringe of miscalled Irish society like the present Mrs Ryan.'

'Oh! is that the sort she is?' queried Jill, lazily puffing at her cigarette and regarding Geraldine's flushed and earnest face with amusement.

'Yes, that's the very sort. Filling the house with British officers and such kindred souls, knitting socks and mufflers and rolling bandages for the soldiers, and attending every meeting of every old Ladies' War Committee that was ever invented.'

Jill laughed heartily.

'I wish the good, loyal lady could hear you,' she said, adding, 'but Firfield House belongs to Anthony, does it not? And does he allow it to become a rendezvous for the British Army?'

'He is placed in a rather awkward position,' replied Geraldine. 'Sheila told me that he has only a couple of hundred a year, and there is nothing for Desmond or for her. As you know, the two young men are solicitors and have an office near Dame Street, but so far the practice has been almost nil. They are mostly to blame themselves, of course, because they are so deeply involved in other work that they really pay but little attention to their profession. Mrs Ryan, on the other hand, has her own money—nearly a thousand a year—and keeps up Firfield House and grounds at her own expense. It is in beautiful order now, but if Anthony was left to his own resources he would be compelled to let it. He would hate that, and yet Sheila told me that he would prefer to do so rather than to have Mrs Ryan using it as she does at present. I don't think that either he or his brother will live there much now—they have rooms of a sort off their office, and they often used to sleep there, and I expect will do so again. His father left a written request that

Mrs Ryan was not to be asked to leave Firfield until she chooses to do so herself, and Anthony won't go against his father's wishes in the matter.'

'What sort of place is it?' asked Jill carelessly. 'I suppose you know it well?'

'Yes; fairly well,' replied Geraldine, 'and it is my own fault that I don't know it better, for Sheila is always asking me there. But for one thing it is rather out of the way, about twenty minutes' walk from Dundrum railway station—and then I know perfectly well that Mrs Ryan does not care for me. It is a good-sized square house, with a fine entrance hall which Mrs Ryan has arranged as a room; a large diningroom and drawingroom; a library with a good selection of books and a dear little morning room. The bedrooms are fairly numerous—it's a rambling place—and there is a fine walled-in garden which the present mistress makes pay well, and fields which she has let, except one, for she keeps two cows and a pony. It is really a lovely place, and in the spring when the lilac and laburnum trees are in blossom I envy those who can live there.' And her honest grey eyes swept the crabbed dimensions of her 'combined' apartment with temporary disgust.

'Well! never mind; keep up your heart,' said her friend. 'You have your Religion and your Republic. They may be only a rainbow trial, but still it is such ideals that make life worth living. Those and Art! And that reminds me that I must be off. Look at the enemy on the mantel-piece—five minutes past eleven. It doesn't matter for a Bohemian like myself, to whom all hours are the same, and who can stay in bed tomorrow till noon if I like, but you good little devotée have, of course, to be up for seven o'clock mass.'

Geraldine laughed, but she rose to her feet and stretched her hands over her head with a sudden tired gesture and Jill's keen eyes noticed the lines of fatigue on her face.

'You do too much, Chérie,' she said, 'burning the candle at both ends, though that is my fault at present I admit. No wonder old Mère Brennan didn't want to let me upstairs to wait for you. She's a queer character, but devoted to you.'

She turned towards the door, but suddenly stopped and swung round again with one of her graceful movements. 'Oh! I was nearly forgetting to tell you,' she said, 'the two rooms just across the landing in my flat are taken, and by a most fascinating little person with a most fascinating name. I'll give you three guesses—or, no, I won't. It's too late and you would never guess it anyway. But what do you think of Yvonne Delaunay?'

'Yvonne Delaunay?' echoed Geraldine. 'It's awfully pretty and sounds interesting. What, or who is she?'

'Well! I haven't spoken to her yet, but mean to do so as soon as possible,' said Jill. 'She is an artist by her paraphernalia and such like, and I imagine that she has been round the world a bit. I am pretty certain, too, that she is a mixture of several nationalities—she is just that type—but what they are I don't know. Only I think there's a good bit of my beloved Paris in her composition. She is not at all pretty when you take her to pieces—I was watching her standing at her door yesterday—but take her as a whole and she is perfectly irresistible and fascinating in some queer way of her own. I succumbed at once, and I should imagine that she could do simply whatever she wishes with the opposite sex; thanks be that I'm not a lonely male only separated from her by a landing. Well! Good-night, old girl. I'll see you soon again if the gods will.'

And she was gone, clattering down the short flight of stairs and narrow hall with her little high heeled shoes and shutting the hall door with a resounding bang that caused Mrs Brennan—already unrobing in her own room—to mutter maledictions on French hussies and their evil ways. But Geraldine smiled as she began rather wearily to prepare for bed.

CHAPTER 11

YVONNE DELAUNAY

Most people will remember how bitterly cold were the early days of the year 1917, and it was on one of those dark mornings towards the end of January that Jill Devereux, half awake, and turning luxuriously on her pillow for another sleep, thought she heard soft, stealthy footsteps on the stairs. It was a big, iron stairway and ran through the flats from landing to landing, making one giddy when mounting quickly, or if one's destination lay amongst the stars—in other words, the top landing.

Jill sat up suddenly and listened; yes, there was no chance of her being mistaken, footsteps were certainly creeping up the stairway. Quickly she switched on the electric light over her bed and listened again more intently, while she glanced at her watch. Five o'clock. Who was about so late, or so early? Then she heard the peculiar, sharp click which the door of the flat opposite to her own always made when it was opened, and knew that the footsteps must have been those of Yvonne Delaunay—that queerly fascinating personality, with whom she was now on fairly friendly terms.

'Where on earth can she have been till this hour?' thought Jill. 'Evidently she came home alone—although, of course, friends may have seen her to the street door all right. However, it's no business of mine,' and she crept down amongst the bedclothes again and tried to sleep.

But she found it impossible to do so. In spite of her endeavours to put the thing out of her mind, her thoughts would continually hark back to those stealthy footsteps on the stairs, and she could distinctly picture Yvonne Delaunay turning the key in her door and furtively slipping into her room. And yet Jill's common sense told her that she was surely making a mountain out of a mole hill. She knew that her charming little neighbour across the landing was often at dances; she remembered indeed several times having heard her return in the small hours of the winter's morning, but here lay the difference—it had always been easy to hear her at such times, she could indeed have been heard at the big door laughing and talking, and gaily calling out 'Good night,' or 'Good morning,' as the fancy took her, to her companions, of whom there were always several, as noisy and gay as herself.

But this secret, stealthy return was a different matter, and some instinct, intuition—call it what you will—seemed to tell Jill Devereux that Miss Delaunay had her own reasons for not wishing to be either seen or heard on this particular morning.

Jill dozed fitfully after a while, but by eight o'clock she was up and dressed—an unheard of hour for her. She had two rooms: a large airy one with two good windows, and a smaller one off this, which was her sleeping apartment. The furniture was her own, and was a strange medley picked up here and there, at odd places and at odd times, but the whole appearance of the flat was out of the common, artistic, and it must be admitted, untidy, but in a picturesque style.

The big room had to be used as both kitchen and sitting room, but there was little of the kitchen about it, for Jill generally had only her tea and breakfast at home—dining or lunching according to her work and circumstances at a restaurant—and in a recess off the landing there was a sink with hot and cold water where she could wash up and keep her few pots and pans and other unsightly household utensils. Her years as a girl bachelor had taught her many things, and she could light a fire—which she did in a short time on this cold morning—as well as any housemaid; and as she popped the kettle on the gas ring to boil while the fire was blazing up she thought with satisfaction of the fact that she knew how to make coffee—when she said this she meant that she could make it as it should be made—as she had learnt to make it in the dear old days in the 'Quartier Latin' in Paris.

But all the time she was drinking it this morning and toasting her feet in their pretty slippers at the fire she was thinking of her neighbour across the landing, and trying to piece together a few details which she had gathered about her.

It was nearly a month now since she had first seen Yvonne Delaunay, and it was inevitable that they should have become friendly—the only two tenants on that landing, and both women and both artists. Still, beyond the fact that the girl was studying at the School of Art, and that she evidently had enough money to live upon without having to earn her own bread, as Jill had to do herself, she really knew little about her.

But the personality of Yvonne Delaunay had a fascination for Jill, as she had confided to Geraldine Moore; and yet she often found herself trying, as it were, to analyse the secret of this fascination and finding herself totally unable to account for it.

'I am like a lovesick boy,' she thought with amusement. 'I am really so gone on the girl, and yet I don't know why.'

She had almost finished her breakfast when she heard the door across the landing give the usual click which proclaimed that it was being opened, the same sound which she had heard a few hours ago in the cold darkness of the winter's dawn, and almost immediately afterwards there was a soft knock at her own door.

'Come in!' cried Jill, and Yvonne Delaunay entered.

Small and slight, with rather nondescript features; a mouth too large for beauty, and yet how divinely it could pout and what a delightful dimple was near it; eyes neither green nor grey, but 'betwixt and between,' and a nose very much inclined to be retroussée. Her head was small and well shaped and on it she carried her one claim to beauty—her hair. It was of that uncommon colour which resembles hot ashes—dull, yet with a seeming warm light flickering through it here and there. She had quantities of it and usually wore it twisted simply into a huge coil wound round and round her head, and instead of ordinary hairpins she always secured it with quaint fasteners of amber and silver, the whole effect being one of careless beauty.

Yet in what did her fascination consist? That she had a wonderful attraction, very few who came under her influence could deny. The majority simply fell down and worshipped without question or demur, slaves—sometimes in spite of themselves—to the dominant vibrating personality, the ego of the woman. Add to this her countless little mannerisms and gestures, a voice which was music itself, to which her rather foreign intonation lent an added charm, and last, but by no means least, the art of dressing to perfection in every detail—and you have Yvonne Delaunay, Yvonne as she appeared to Jill's eyes crossing the threshold of the room and coming across to the fire.

She was wearing a pale blue satin kimono richly embroidered with flowers and strange birds, and Jill looking at it with involuntary admiration found herself mentally apprising its cost and putting it at a high figure, which, however, fell far short of its real value. 'She certainly must have money to burn,' was her thought as she said 'Good morning, Miss Delaunay. Isn't it cold—do come near the fire.'

Yvonne smiled as she slipped into a seat and extended her feet, in their quaint little slippers, to the warmth of the fire.

Jill noticed that she looked tired; there were lines of weariness and worry on the always colourless face, and deep shadows beneath the inscrutable eyes. Her wonderful hair hung in two great ropes over each shoulder.

'How cosy you are here,' she said. 'Moi, I was cold—too cold to sleep, and then,' with a little laugh, 'I smelt your lovely coffee—it was wafted through the keyhole to me, and I almost thought for a moment that I was back again in my beloved Paris.'

Jill smiled happily.

'That's where I learnt to make it,' she said, as she hastened to pour out a cup for her guest.

'Oh! but it is delicious—heavenly!' cried Yvonne, sipping it daintily with real enjoyment. 'I have a tiny headache this morning, not much, but still I can feel it just there,' touching her forehead with a rosy and well-manicured finger. 'I know that this coffee will help me so much.'

'Now she is going to tell me about last night,' thought Jill with an odd sense of relief. 'I suppose she was at a dance and in a sudden fit of virtue did not wish to waken me,' and she was just on the point of making some laughing remark about her neighbour's homecoming in the small hours when the words were frozen on her lips by Yvonne Delaunay herself as she said softly in her pretty voice, 'I always get a headache when I sleep too soundly, and last night I slept all the hours through without waking once, which is what I seldom do. Then this morning, behold! I suffer for my heavy slumbers, and—ah! but what a pity! The dear, little cup!'

For the quaint Dresden coffee-cup—one of a beloved half-dozen picked up in a curio shop on the Quays one day when her exchequer was in a flourishing state—had slipped from Jill's nerveless grasp and was lying in fragments on the fender.

She stooped quickly to pick up the pieces with her back turned towards Yvonne, trying to recover herself, to appear unconcerned, but all the time she was conscious of a horrible, dazed feeling, as though someone had suddenly given her an unexpected blow between the eyes. But she must pull herself together; she must not allow herself to think just for the present. She knew this instinctively, and by instinct, too, she suddenly felt that she must be on her guard and not allow the other to notice anything peculiar in her manner, and yet she did not really know why she felt this way, but she felt it all the same. She finished picking up the tiny fragments which had once made such a lovely whole, then turned towards Yvonne.

'How stupid of me!' she said; 'I was so fond of those cups. I really feel quite mad with myself.'

'Oh! but an accident. You are not to blame,' replied the other, adding, 'Still it's no wonder you are sorry, for they are sweet little cups.'

'Yes; I just had the six of them,' sighed Jill.

Then for the mere sake of talking and to help her to recover herself she told Yvonne about the day she had brought them. One warm June day when walking down the Quays with more money than usual in her purse she had seen those half-dozen cups and saucers in a window and had succumbed to their old-fashioned charm at once.

'I really wanted something else very badly—a pair of new shoes to be explicit,' she said, 'but I could not resist those little dears,' with a laughing glance at the remaining cups and saucers.

'I don't wonder,' replied Yvonne. 'If I was wealthy—really wealthy—I would collect old china and silver and antiques of all kinds. But as it is every penny I have has to go on food and clothes.'

As she spoke she was quick to notice Jill's involuntary glance at her rich wrapper, and answered the look at once.

'Oh! yes,' she said, 'I know I am a bit extravagant, but I can't help it. I just love pretty chiffons and glad rags of every kind. I simply could not exist without them.'

Jill made no reply. After all, what could she say. She was not sufficiently intimate with this girl to speak freely to her—as she would have done to Geraldine Moore, for instance, under the same circumstances—to say plainly that she could spend less on her frocks and yet be daintily clad.

Yvonne Delaunay seemed to be gifted with an almost uncanny faculty of reading one's very thoughts. Jill had noticed this before, and now the girl showed it again by saying:

'Of course I know I could spend less on my things, but—well, I don't. I often wish,' with a little sigh, 'that I was not inclined to spend so much on myself; perhaps if I had been brought up differently, but my mother was extravagant, too, so it may be that it is in my blood. She was so lovely—my darling mother, and my father idolised her, and while he lived we had plenty of money and so—.'

She paused for a moment and turned her strange eyes to where Jill was sitting opposite to her on the other side of the cheery fire.

'I hardly know why I am telling you all this,' she said, 'but you have the gift of real sympathy, and besides I know—I am certain—that it is destined that we should become very great friends,' she leant across suddenly and laid her hand on Jill's. 'I, for my part, would be glad of that friendship if you'—she paused, and Jill caught the little hand that seemed to be fluttering on hers—all her suspicions, her bitterness of heart at the deceit which the other had shown—all gone—vanished before the fascination of the little figure seated opposite in the brocaded kimono.

'Why, of course, I'll be delighted!' she said impulsively, her face flushing with shy delight. 'I hope we will become real friends—as we should do—being such near neighbours, with a common profession to draw us together.'

'Ah! but I am glad to hear you speak so,' cried Yvonne with, as it were, a sigh of relief. 'Moi, I am lonely. One has acquaintances, of course—so-called friends—in plenty, but they are not the real thing. But with you it is very different—with you I can talk—can speak from my heart.'

And then in her pretty low voice she began to tell Jill about her childhood spent in the sunny South of France. It appeared that her father had been a prosperous silk merchant, and had married her mother—a beautiful Russian—during one of his visits to her country. As Yvonne had said before the lovely wife was very extravagant, but her husband loved her so devotedly that he had not the heart to refuse her anything. He died when his daughter and only child was sixteen, when it was discovered that the reckless way in which they had been living had eaten away the larger part of his capital, so that he had not much to leave behind him. Fortunately the little he had to bequeath was settled on his daughter, the interest only being paid to his wife during Yvonne's minority.

'Poor little mother!' said that daughter now, relapsing into the French tongue, as she always did when moved or excited, and which Jill understood thoroughly, although she was not such a fluent speaker as the other, 'She was terribly vexed. But what would you do? My father knew her and so did what was best for us both. And then mother had friends in so many of the continental towns, and we had a good time. Oh! such a good time! We went to Russia, too. Ah! but there was the place where one could enjoy life—before the War. And now! Ah! my poor Russia.'

She paused as a wave of pain passed over her face and a deep sigh, that was almost like a sob, broke from her.

'Then—then the little mother died when I was twenty—we were in Paris then where I was studying Art. Two years after came the War and I—I found other work to do.' She stopped speaking rather abruptly, and gazed silently into the fire.

'You would want to help France—that was only natural,' said Jill, and after a slight pause she said hesitatingly, 'How is it then that you are in Ireland now? But forgive me. Perhaps I should not ask you that?'

'But of course—why should you not ask?' cried the other. 'The work in France was hard—and—I—I am not too strong, so I had to resign. I was in a big hospital just doing anything that was useful and often thinking I was only in people's way. I was ordered to go to some quiet place and to take up my Art again. Then, somehow, I thought of Ireland; it seemed quiet enough after what I had been through, and I had some friends—acquaintances—in Dublin, and so I came.'

She smiled vividly as she finished speaking, and, bending forward, kissed Jill lightly on both cheeks—foreign style.

'And now we are to be friends—is it not so?' she asked. And so Jill, all her half-formed suspicions lulled to rest, found herself back again under the old spell, and was presently talking away to this girl, telling her all about her own life and work and friends.

And amongst these she mentioned the Ryans.

An acute observer might have noticed the sudden flash of interest that showed for a moment on Yvonne's face, but Jill, full of her subject, saw nothing.

'Of course they are really more Geraldine's friends than mine,' she was saying, 'but I knew the boys, especially Desmond, a year ago and I admire them immensely. The sister is a little fool and the stepmother just a parvenu, but the boys are made of the right stuff. Not that they are really boys,' she added, 'for they must be about twenty-four; but in this country, as you may have noticed, all young men—and some old ones—are boys all the time. And then I have been so accustomed to hear Sheila and Jerry speak of them as such. But they are men—real men in every sense of the word.'

Yvonne's smile was a little strange, and the queer inscrutable look, which many of her friends knew, but few could read, hovered for a second in her eyes and around her mouth. But she only said carelessly:

'I suppose that you also are a great Sinn Féiner, and so these wonderful twins are heroes in your eyes?'

But Jill laughed and shook her head.

'No; not at all,' she said. 'I have no politics. I have knocked about so much that I look upon the world as my country—and then my forefathers were French—not Irish, and although I love the Irish nearly, if not quite, as much as the French, still some way I never took any definite side in the present state of affairs here. It is queer, I know, because I detest John Bull and all his works, yet in some strange way here I always feel like an onlooker only.'

'Well; yes, I suppose it is strange,' replied Yvonne, in a musing tone of voice, 'and yet some way that is just exactly how I feel myself. I suppose it is also because I have been in so many countries and among so many people. But I admire—ah! so much—patriotism and heroism, and I would love to meet your dear Ryan boys.'

'Well! why not?' cried Jill, 'Geraldine Moore is always asking me to go out and see Sheila at Firfield. So we will go together some day when the weather is a bit better.'

They talked for another while, and then Yvonne in her pretty wrap and dainty slippers went across to her own room.

Jill cleared away the breakfast table, and then started a new design for a special poster, for which she had obtained an order.

It was not till evening when, the work done, she was sitting once more at the fire that her thoughts reverted to the incident of the early morning hours. She tried vainly to put it from her, but always it rose up to confront her again and again. Always she found herself asking the same question—

'Why had Yvonne lied to her?'

It was not where the other girl had been, or with whom, that troubled Jill, for truth to tell she cared little, Bohemian to her finger tips, so-called respectability and conventionality meant nothing to her. But she hated deceit and lies, and she knew that she could have forgiven Yvonne many things that in the eyes of 'Mrs Grundy' would be very grave offences if only she had been open and truthful towards her.

She had been so sure that the other had understood all this.

Ever since coming to the flat across the landing Yvonne Delaunay had been in the habit of going out very often at night, sometimes to dances with a crowd of other students, sometimes to go to dinner at a restaurant with some man who called for her. For a young woman living alone these proceedings were unconventional to say the least, but to Jill it was all a matter of supreme indifference. To her men, as a sex, seldom appealed, although as intellectual comrades she enjoyed their company. Perhaps one member of the opposite sex did possess the power to quicken her heart beats in a strange way, but if so she would not admit the fact even to herself.

How other women cared to amuse themselves she considered had nothing to do with her, and she knew that Yvonne understood all this and was aware of her point of view. Why then had she—on this occasion alone—crept up the stairs and entered her own room like a thief in the night?

'It could not be just because she was an hour or so later than usual returning,' she thought; 'as if I would mind that.'

What then was the reason for her stealthy homecoming and for the lie which she had gone out of her way to tell about it?

Jill felt bitterly sorry about the whole affair—it was like a hideous secret which she would be obliged to carry around with her in future, and which she knew would be sure to poison, to some extent, the friendship which she would have welcomed so gladly between herself and Yvonne. She felt in honour bound not to confide the matter to anyone else, not even to Geraldine, and that made it all the harder to bear.

So she sat by the fire, smoking cigarette after cigarette as she tried to solve the puzzle which she was not to unravel for many a long day, and which when its meaning at length lay plain before her, she would have almost given her eyes themselves never to have understood.

CHAPTER III

FIRFIELD HOUSE

Not far from the village of Dundrum, Firfield House stood in its own grounds amidst fields and great trees, a well-kept avenue leading from the lodge gates to the front door. The lodge itself with its latticed windows and rose-covered porch was a pretty sight, and Mrs Maguire—who knew her mistress 'inside out' as she used to say—always kept herself and her children clean and tidy, while her cottage was an example to all housewives.

The country road beyond the lodge gates was very quiet. To the left it led upwards by a gradual ascent to the mountains, and by the path on the right Dundrum or Milltown could be reached. The avenue up to the house ran between two fields, and these fields were separated from the avenue and from the front of the house by barbed wire. The field on the right Mrs Ryan kept for her own use, and there her two sleek cows and her fat pony enjoyed their leisure hours, while that on the left was let to one of the farmers in the district, and was generally full of young cattle. There was only a gravel sweep in front of the house—a big, grey building, with stone steps leading up to the nail-studded oaken door—both vegetable and flower gardens being at the back.

The morning room at Firfield, designated by Geraldine Moore as the prettiest room in the house, was situated at the rear, and its French windows opened on to a smooth, well-kept lawn, which in summer was almost like an outdoor parlour, surrounded as it was on both sides with trees of lilac and laburnum, and one big cedar, under the spreading branches of which were seats and a table. At the back was the house, and straight in front a wicket gate led into the orchard, which on this May day of which we write, was a mass of pink and white blossom.

Yes, May had come at last, and the long dark winter and early spring of that year were gone at last. Gone, too, the frost and the cold which had lingered so long over their time, and here at last were spring flowers and warm sunshine again. Quite warm it was, too, on this particular evening, so warm indeed that Mrs Ryan had ordered tea to be brought out on to the lawn, where she was sitting under the big cedar tree, while her family and guests were scattered around her.

The twins and Sheila, with Jill Devereux, Geraldine Moore and Yvonne Delaunay, were all chatting and laughing, a happy, noisy group. To look at them one could hardly imagine that such things as sorrow and suffering and pain existed in the world, or that an inhuman war was devastating Europe. But after all it is surely better to laugh than to cry, and even though the laughter be only on the surface—as was the case with some of those we write about—still for that very reason it is better to face the battle of life with a smile instead of a tear. Mrs Ryan was a stout, fair-complexioned woman of late middle age, attired in the latest fashion. She was reclining in a low deck chair, but her fingers were working rapidly, for she was, as usual, engaged in knitting 'comforts' of some kind for the 'boys in France'. She was looking rather bored, as with the exception of Yvonne Delaunay the present visitors were not much to her liking.

Her stepsons ranked as guests just now, for, as Geraldine had predicted, they had arranged to live in the rooms attached to their city office, and only came out to Firfield once or twice a week, and then only for the sake of seeing their sister, to whom they were devoted. Between themselves and their stepmother a sort of armed neutrality existed, accompanied by a certain amount of constraint. Anthony especially always kept a definite distance between himself and Mrs Ryan. As his father's widow he behaved to her with punctilious politeness, deferring to her wishes whenever he could do so without sacrificing his own principles, but he often found it almost impossible to hide the very real contempt which at times he felt for her. Desmond got on better with his stepmother, his easy-going disposition helped him to pass over what he irreverently termed 'the old dame's tomfoolery!' As to Sheila, Mrs Ryan was really fond of her, and very ambitious that she would make a 'good match'—a British officer, of course, for preference, especially as she knew how furious Anthony would be at the mere thought of such a contingency. So it was with this object in view, as much as any other, that she had lately invited so many of the officers whom her 'war work' had brought within her ken to spend their off time at Firfield House. A very pleasant place it was in which to spend a few hours, and would be pleasanter still when the summer months came.

Yvonne Delaunay detached herself presently from the rest and coming over to her hostess she sank into a low chair beside her.

'Dear Mrs Ryan,' she said, 'how good it is of you to have us here, and what a lovely place it is.'

'Yes; it is quite a pretty spot,' answered Mrs Ryan, in the stilted accent with which she now strove so hard to hide all traces of the pronounced Dublin tones of her youthful days. 'Many people admire it exceedingly; it is very dull in the winter, of course, but from now on it is quite all right.'

Yvonne's eyes lit up with a tiny flicker of amusement but she was careful to keep them demurely cast down—this typically vulgar little woman always appealed irresistibly to her sense of the ridiculous.

'You must be very proud of having such a lovely home,' she murmured now. 'I know that I should be if I could boast of any such good luck.'

'Oh! but you know the place really belongs to my stepson,' replied Mrs Ryan, and she spoke with that bitter inflexion of voice which the thought of Anthony always caused, 'it is his property; but, of course, he would have had to let it if I were not living here; he is really little better than a beggar, and then his profession is totally neglected for the sake of his low, rebel ideas.'

'How terribly you must feel about all this,' murmured the girl at her side, in the wonderfully sympathetic tones she knew so well how to use.

'Oh! Miss Delaunay,' replied Mrs Ryan, 'it is a relief to speak to you. So many of the other side come here now,' casting a glance of barely veiled dislike at the gay group a few yards away, 'and naturally I cannot refuse to receive them. After all,' with a sigh, 'it is Anthony's house, in a way at least. But I really dread the people he brings here, and especially—especially on account of Sheila.' She paused momentarily, and Yvonne broke in quickly.

'Oh! yes, Sheila! And how lovely she is. But she must be quite a responsibility to you, dear Mrs Ryan, so young and pretty and not— well, not very sensible, is she?'

'Ah! no; that's the truth,' assented Mrs Ryan, 'but I would not mind her being a bit flighty—she's young still, if she would only let all this rebel nonsense alone. As you can see she is devoted to her brothers and it is their influence which is bad for her. Left to herself she would be all right—I could manage her easily—even as it is I don't mean to allow them to ruin her life with their mad ideas.'

Yvonne smiled assentingly.

'You are so wise,' she said, 'what a blessing it is for Sheila that she has such a stepmother. You would like to see her happily married to some good man—is it not so, dear Mrs Ryan?'

'Now that's it exactly,' replied the other. 'What a comfort it is to talk to you, Miss Delaunay. You are so sensible for one of your years. Yes; I want to see the child married—married to some sensible man with no silly ideas about him—someone who would see that her brothers could not lead her into mischief or go on filling her head with rubbishy, impossible notions.'

'And is it permitted to ask if this Prince Charming has appeared yet?' and Yvonne shot a quick glance at the stout figure in the chair beside her own.

'Well, there have been several,' was the complacent answer; 'you know, Miss Delaunay, that my work—it's not much, but I try to do my little bit for my King and Country'—again Yvonne's long lashes hid the amused flash of her strange eyes—'well, my work brings me into contact with many of our heroes, the dear boys who have fought for us so bravely, and I am always so glad when they accept an invitation to come and see us here, just to take pot-luck whenever they like, as I always tell them. But Sheila never seemed to take an interest in any of them until——.'

'Until?'

'Until Lieutenant Hammond came,' said Mrs Ryan. She paused for a moment, and then continued. 'Norman Hammond is a delightful young fellow, and I have reason to believe that he is well off and belongs to one of the best families in England.'

As the good lady finished speaking she took a deep breath of satisfaction, almost as if she would inhale into her very soul all the wondrous perfection of Lieutenant Norman Hammond.

'Lieutenant Hammond,' echoed Yvonne idly; 'I don't think I have met him here, have I? I don't seem to remember his name.'

'No; my dear, I don't think you have,' replied her hostess, 'but you will be sure to do so soon; indeed he will probably be here this evening,' and then she gave a little laugh as she nodded across the lawn. 'Talk of angels,' she said, with ponderous gaiety, 'here is Mr Hammond himself.'

Yvonne Delaunay had been idly digging a little hole in the soft grass with the pointed toe of her pretty shoe, but she lifted her eyes as her hostess spoke and glanced across to where the young officer was standing outside the French window of the morning room through which he had just stepped. Her foot ceased its idle movements, and her whole attitude changed; it was as though her brain was working rapidly. Then a sudden lightning flash of satisfaction showed for a bare second on her piquant face, and was gone, leaving her once more the politely interested guest. She turned to Mrs Ryan with a charming smile.

'So that is Mr Hammond?' she murmured, 'quite a nice boy, isn't he?' and her inscrutable eyes followed to where he stood greeting the others—greetings that were responded to very coldly, with the exception of Sheila, who flushed vividly as she held out her had to meet his lingering clasp. On his part Norman Hammond seemed quite content, and it did not require a very keen observer to see that he was utterly indifferent to the coldness of the rest as long as Sheila was kind to him. But the girl was acutely conscious of her brothers' unsympathetic glances and of the puzzled wonder in Geraldine's honest eyes, so partly to escape their scrutiny and partly in a spirit of defiance she cried gaily, 'Come and speak to mother, and be introduced to Miss Delaunay,' and laughingly taking his hand she led him across the grass to where Mrs Ryan with Yvonne beside her sat watching them—the elder lady in pleased complacency, the other in a sort of quiet stillness with a strange little smile around her mobile mouth.

The young officer saluted Mrs Ryan smilingly, as one sure of his welcome, and then turned swiftly as Sheila's musical voice said:

'Miss Delaunay, may I introduce Mr Hammond?' Then as the girl noticed the flash of recognition in the man's eyes she added, 'But perhaps you have already met?' and looked curiously from one to the other, for she was quick to observe the rather embarrassed look on Hammond's face. It was as though he was wondering what he should do, in doubt whether to greet Miss Delaunay as an acquaintance or not.

But his hesitation was only momentary—Yvonne came to his rescue immediately and extending her hand in frank friendliness said with perfect self-possession—

'Why, yes! Surely I know you! We met, I think, in France? You must forgive me that I had forgotten you name just at first. And, indeed, you face, too.'

He murmured a vague reply, but a look of relief had darted across his face when Miss Delaunay had spoken.

She turned now smilingly to Mrs Ryan.

'Mr Hammond and my poor self met in the hospital where I was working for some time before my health broke down. I think I told you about it, Mrs Ryan, did I not?' She glanced at Hammond as she spoke as though she were anxious to include him in the conversation to put him more at his ease.

Mrs Ryan was all smiles and volubility.

'Ah! yes, to be sure,' she cried, 'the big field hospital where you worked so hard as a VAD so that you quite knocked yourself up. So that is where you and Mr Hammond met? How wonderful it must seem to both of you to be here now after all you have gone through over there. Do sit down and tell me all about it, Mr Hammond.'

But again Yvonne came to his relief.

'Oh! please, dear Mrs Ryan, don't ask us anything about it,' she cried, clasping her hands together in pretty entreaty, 'we only want to forget it all while we can. Is it not so, Mr Hammond?'

'Oh! rather,' he replied emphatically, 'no one wants to talk, or remember, about the things that happen out there.'

A welcome diversion was caused by the arrival of tea, and Norman Hammond, as in duty bound, assisted to hand round the cups. As he bent over Yvonne's chair she murmured quickly, 'I must speak to you before I go—I must,' then aloud, 'No, no sugar, thank you, and just a little more cream.'

And so later, while Sheila was engaged with an unexpected visitor who had 'just dropped in,' Norman Hammond asked Miss Delaunay if she would care to have a stroll in the orchard.

'Oh! I should love it,' she replied, 'the apple blossoms are a perfect picture, are they not?'

'Yes, they are in full bloom just now,' he assented politely, and they moved away together. But once out of earshot of the tea-table group a strange silence fell upon them—a silence which remained unbroken until they reached the far end of the orchard, and then by a common impulse they stood still and faced each other.

The man was the first to speak.

'Well?' he asked. 'What is it? What are you doing here? And what do you want with me?'

All his languid manner—his vapid slang and 'swank' had left him, and his voice was tense with anxiety.

The woman looked at him in silence for a moment, a look, however, which conveyed nothing to him—it was inscrutable like her strange eyes, which saw so much and told so little.

'Well?' he repeated impatiently.

Then she spoke.

'Patience, mon ami, patience,' she said, in quiet, level tones hardly above a whisper, 'sit down on this convenient seat and I will tell you—as much as it is necessary for you to know. You were surprised to see me; it upset your nerves a little—is it not so?—but I was prepared to meet you. I have known for some time that you were in Dublin, and that you were a very regular visitor at this house.'

'Who told you that I was in Dublin?' he asked harshly, adding in a low voice, 'Ronald, I suppose?'

'Yes; it was your brother,' she said softly. 'Naturally he would tell me when he and I are working together.'

'But what are you doing here?' he interposed. 'The usual business? and if it's that, then what do you want with me? Our paths are widely apart, thank Heaven!'

'You are mistaken,' she said quietly, 'in this matter you can probably help us very considerably, and it is your brother's wish that you should do so.'

'And if I refuse?'

She raised her eyes and looked very steadily at him without speaking. Then—

'There was a certain episode in France——.'

He laid a shaking hand on her arm.

'Don't say it,' he said in a dry whisper. 'I'll do what you want.'

'That is all right then,' she replied tranquilly, 'so listen—.'

'But on one condition,' he interposed swiftly, and as she glanced at him questioningly he said earnestly, 'No harm must come to Sheila.'

The woman laughed softly—laughter that held a note of contempt.

'Why do you say that?' she asked 'surely as your wife—you do intend to marry her, do you not?'

'Yes; if she will have me; but I am not sure of her, I sometimes think—.'

'Ah! bah; what rubbish!' cried Yvonne impatiently.

'Why the fool is infatuated with you. Anyone can see it, and you would, too, if you were not in the same boat yourself and therefore blind. Come now and listen to me for we cannot stay here much longer for fear of attracting attention, and I have much to say.'

Fifteen minutes later they strolled back to the group under the cedars, apparently laughing and chatting like friendly acquaintances, and if Hammond seemed rather quieter and graver than his wont, no one noticed except Sheila. Poor girl! she had been suffering from a severe attack of the green-eyed monster ever since she had seen Yvonne and Norman stroll away together towards the orchard. She glanced now rather doubtfully at the latter as he came over to her side. Should she snub him or be nice to him? But when she met his blue eyes and saw the sudden flash of delight that leapt from them when he saw her she knew that her jealous pangs had been suffered for nothing.

'Come and see the daffodils,' she said shyly, 'they are just lovely now.'

And Norman Hammond, thrusting away from him the remembrance of the past half-hour, smiled, and went with her.

CHAPTER IV

THE OBSESSION OF SHEILA

It was not till the following July that Norman Hammond asked Sheila Ryan to marry him. The words had been trembling on his lips many a time, but so far he had hesitated to speak them. But one summer's evening when they were standing together in the old rose garden at Firfield—with Sheila looking exactly like a rosebud herself in her pale pink frock— he told her all that was in his heart, all that she had been waiting to hear. They talked long and foolishly, as all lovers will, and for an hour they wandered through their Garden of Eden, almost awed by their own happiness. It is a strange fact, and yet when we remember what this life means to most of us, not so strange after all, that we are astonished and often afraid when a great happiness falls to our share, while no matter how terrible a trouble overtakes us we are never surprised, nor do we wonder will it last—our instinct tells us only too surely that it will do so. But with happiness it is the other way around, and we reach out to clutch it with trembling hands—hands that fear it will be gone before it is ours—and even when it is safely within our grasp our first thought is—'it won't last!'

And so it is that we find Sheila saying to her lover, 'Oh! Norman; it is too good to be true! I feel as if I was in a dream and would wake up in a few minutes.'

He laughed rather tremulously as he bent and kissed her. The love he felt for Sheila was a real spark from the divine fire of the gods, and although only a spark—and a small one—it was still powerful enough to rekindle all that was best in Norman Hammond. He was not a bad sort by any means; not overburdened with what we call brains certainly, and not one who was capable of much self-sacrifice or who would die for an ideal. Such sentiments were simply beyond his comprehension, but according to his lights, which were not very brilliant, he wished to do his duty. Especially now was he desirous of doing the right thing and making himself more worthy to be the husband of the girl he loved.

But, needless to remark, he had the young Briton's usual complacent, cocksure attitude towards the rest of the world—and towards Ireland in particular. He understood neither the country nor its people, and regarded the whole 'Irish question' as 'bally rot' and a 'damned nuisance'. This without any real bitterness towards the Irish themselves; he simply shared in that innate feeling which seems to be implanted in the British composition, unalterable and unchangeable, although covered over at times with a veneer of 'friendliness'. So now it seems to him that the one flaw in his love ideal—as such it was to him just then, love the mighty having the power to turn even a materialistic Englishman into an idealist for the time being—was the fact of Sheila's nationality. Her religion he had not yet taken into account—religion of any kind not seeming very important in his eyes.

As for Sheila, she was not one to criticise when she loved. On the contrary she was one of those women who when they love a man do so blindly and absolutely—without question or thought—one who would love with a dog-like devotion and who would kiss the hand that struck her—if it was his hand.

There are many such, even in spite of the present status of women today; a type which seems to have come down from the stone age when the male, with the help of his granite club, dragged the unresisting female to the dim recesses of his cave, there to become his willing slave. Her type still exists, we see it in all classes, from the woman of culture who acts and lies to hide her husband's infidelities and cruelties down to the poor victim of the wife beater who begs the magistrate's clemency towards the brute who owns her. 'Let him off this time, your Worship! He meant no harm—he wouldn't lay a hand on me only he had a drop taken—sure he's the best man ever a poor woman had!'

So Sheila Ryan, being closely akin to such, thought Heaven itself had opened to her when her chosen man condescended to lift a beckoning finger.

The sun was setting, and the hot day drawing to its close when the lovers strolled back towards the house. They had had tea under the cedar, and had left Mrs Ryan sitting in her garden chair, occupied with the inevitable knitting, and now when they returned, having been nearly two hours away, she was still sitting there, but her knitting had fallen on the grass and she was fast asleep.

Sheila's happy laughter woke her, but the sleep was still in her eyes and it was a little while before she noticed anything unusual about the gay young couple who had sunk into chairs, one on either side of her. Then her perceptions quickened; she saw that Norman Hammond looked happily self-conscious, and felt Sheila's soft, little hand slipped shyly into her own fleshy palm. At once she comprehended everything and was all smiles and congratulations.

Never had Sheila felt so drawn towards her stepmother, for whom she had hitherto had, at most, a tolerant affection—and never, never had she felt so happy. It seemed to the girl as if earth could hold nothing better in store for her, her cup of happiness was full to the brim.

Mrs Ryan naturally had been charmed with the news and the happy trio had talked and laughed and everything had looked *couleur de rose*. Norman had told the elder woman quite frankly that he was not of the aristocratic lineage, such as she had fondly imagined, but he was able to tell her that he was decidedly well endowed with this world's goods, his father being a very wealthy manufacturer in the North of England.

'My grandfather started the family fortune,' he said, 'and my father doubled it. The governor is a hale old chap still, although he is getting on in years now—he married late in life and was devoted to my mother. She was much younger than he was and when she died five years ago it cut us all up terribly, and the old man has never been the same since. Hammond Hall, too, the place up in Yorkshire, has been jolly lonely lately.'

Sheila was listening with frank sympathy, but while Mrs Ryan's face expressed the most tender consideration for all that the young officer was saying, her brain was busily at work conjecturing as to the rest of the Hammond family and wondering in what exact position Norman stood in regard to the family fortune.

'Have you no sisters?' she asked tentatively.

'No; there is only Ronald and myself.'

'And your brother—is he the elder?'

'No; Ronnie is a year younger than myself, but he is much cleverer.'

Mrs Ryan smiled complacently, while trying not to look too pleased. What a lucky girl Sheila was! But she only said:

'I suppose your brother is in the Service, too?'

To the widow's surprise Norman Hammond flushed vividly and seemed suddenly ill at ease.

'Yes; no,' he stammered, 'at least he—well, he is engaged in—in clerical work.'

He spoke lamely, and even Mrs Ryan looked rather puzzled for the moment, and then her face cleared suddenly as she said:

'Oh! I understand. In the Diplomatic Service, I suppose?'

'Yes—yes; that's it. He is a diplomatist—and a very clever one, too'; and the young officer laughed in a relieved and yet rather insincere manner.

But neither Mrs Ryan nor Sheila noticed anything out of the common about him, both being too preoccupied with their own thoughts—Sheila in a happy haze which really only allowed her to think the one great thought—and Mrs Ryan full of pleasant anticipation of the time when she could speak of 'Hammond Hall—my daughter's place in Yorkshire.' But all the same she was the first to see the difficulties in the young couple's path. She spoke of them now, half-reluctant to do so in this their hour of happiness, and yet impelled thereto by the remembrance that her stepson, Anthony, was coming out to dinner that night. There was a certain matter of business in connection with the letting of some of the land which she had to discuss with him, and when he had announced his intention to come and talk it over with her she had politely asked him to dinner, and as Anthony, who had been hearing some talk about Sheila, also wanted to see his sister, he agreed to be at Firfield in time for dinner, which was at the fashionable hour of a quarter to eight.

It was after seven now, and so Mrs Ryan had to speak at once of that which was now uppermost in her thoughts.

'Of course you both know,' she said, 'that Anthony will object?'

Neither of the two spoke for a moment. Then the man, who really thought that Anthony's objections would either be soon over-ridden, or else would not count for much, said gently:

'Oh! we will soon talk him over. On what special grounds do you think he will object to me, Mrs Ryan?'

But Sheila, who knew how strong Anthony's objections would be, but who had forgotten her brother, like all else, for the time being, said in sudden distress:

'Oh! Mums; I had forgotten about Tony.'

She was the only one of Mrs Ryan's stepchildren who ever gave her any sort of a motherly title. Nothing could ever persuade either of the boys to do so, but Sheila's memory of her own mother was very faint, and to her credit it must be said that Mrs Ryan always tried to act as a mother to the girl, of whom she was genuinely fond.

'Well! I have not forgotten him,' she replied now, in rather cross tones. The thought of Anthony's quiet determination, and the cool manner in which he always managed to get his own way in spite of any opposition which she might offer irritated her beyond words.

'Oh! but surely,' began Hammond.

But Sheila cut him short as she cried:

'Oh! Mums dear. You must tell him. I would never dare. He will be furious—you know he will.'

'Let me tell him—I am the proper person to do so,' interposed her lover, 'and certainly I am not afraid to do so.'

'Ah! but you don't know Tony,' replied the girl, 'you have only met him in a casual way. Mother and I know him—don't we, Mums?'

'Only too well,' said the older woman; 'and if you will be guided by me, Norman—as I suppose I may call you now—you will at least let me mention that subject to him first.'

'No—no—by no means,' he replied. 'It might be unpleasant for you and I could not permit it. It's my business to speak to Sheila's brother and I will do so. Do you think I would have time before dinner? or,' with a smile, 'had I better wait until after he has dined? That hour is generally supposed to be more propitious.'

'There now,' cried Sheila, 'that remark shows how little you know of Anthony. He is not that sort at all.'

'Then he must be unique amongst our unworthy sex,' replied Hammond rather sneeringly. 'So I am to tackle him then before he has dined—is that so?'

'No; you won't have time,' replied Mrs Ryan, glancing at her watch. 'Good gracious! it is twenty minutes to eight. Well! Sheila, we must just dine as we are—we will say it is out of compliment to Norman,' glancing with a smile at the young officer, who, in his turn, looked down at his white tennis flannels and said 'Oh! I say. It's really awfully good of you, Mrs Ryan, to excuse me in this get up. Of course, I never expected to stay so late.'

'Don't mention it, my dear boy—don't mention it. It's quite all right,' was the beaming reply.

Nothing pleased Mrs Ryan so much as to imagine that she was a woman of fashion—lady, of course, she would have said herself—and she had sealed up in a secret compartment of her poor stunted mind the memories of other days when an Irish Stew at one o'clock formed what she considered a very good dinner. But that was long ago now, before her first husband—plain Tom Byrne—had made his fortune; days when she lived in the little parlour behind the dairy shop and measured out pints and half-pints of milk to customers, and when the milk was short would chase away waiting small boys and their jugs and pennies with a sharp, 'Away out of that wid yez! There's no more milk in the place—so off wid yez now.'

Ah! yes; the accents of 'Nancy Byrne,' as she was then called, had been very different from the 'Oh! it's quite all right!' tones of Mrs Ryan of Firfield House—yet they had been honest accents, and the woman had been a better woman then than now. But if you had said anything of this kind to Mrs Ryan she would have thought you were 'quite mad'. She was perfectly content with her present surroundings—or nearly so—the only cloud on her horizon being the tall figure which appeared at the diningroom window as they neared the house.

'There is Anthony already,' she said, while Sheila cried simultaneously, 'Oh! there's Tony.'

He came out of the house to meet them—tall and upright as usual, with his straight, keen gaze, and proud way of holding himself.

He shook hands politely with his stepmother, and saluted the other man rather coldly. But his eyes softened as he greeted his sister and slipped his arm caressingly round her shoulders. Sheila was not tall, and it was a joke between herself and the tall twins that when they held her thus her head was just 'as high as their hearts'.

'Well! Girlie,' said Anthony now—their boyish name for her. Sheila smiled back and leant against him in her old fond way, but his keen eyes noticed that something was amiss—the girl was not like herself.

'I must have a good talk with her after dinner,' he thought, 'to see how far this nonsense has gone. Anyway it has got to stop now—of that I am resolved.'

'Desmond didn't come with you?' Sheila asked.

'No; but he may drop in later and we can go back together. He is calling on some friends in Dundrum.'

'Well! I'm glad you managed to get down for dinner anyway,' she replied in the soft coaxing tones which were part of her charm. Anthony stooped and pressed a kiss on the lovely hair—the girl, who had been the spoilt baby of their boyhood, was still to them their 'little sister,' and was inexpressibly dear to both her brothers. She was also the only one of her sex who had so far caused Anthony a thought, and if this could not be said in the case of Desmond, yet even in his susceptible heart she occupied a sacred niche of her own—separate and apart from all—'those others'.

The dinner was rather a trying meal, the atmosphere of constraint was felt by all. Mrs Ryan was endeavouring to act the part of a carefree hostess, but alas! she had not yet ascended to the real Lady Clara Vere de Vere type, and so was unable to entirely hide her anxiety 'under a mask of smiling indifference' as society novels say.

Sheila was restless and evidently ill at ease, besides which she was now possessed by a sudden shyness and hardly raised her eyes from her plate. Anthony was really worried about her; that something out of the common had occurred he was certain, and his knowledge of his stepmother's foolish snobbery always made him anxious about Sheila while she remained in her charge. Yet what excuse could he have for removing her elsewhere? Would she go? After all Sheila was twenty-one and, in a legal sense, her own mistress, and the thought worried him.

'Well! I must speak very seriously to her before I leave tonight,' he thought, adding as his glance met the rather hostile look of Norman Hammond's blue eyes:

'I hope that bounder will take himself off early. The idea of having those chaps fooling around Sheila. It's intolerable!'

But Hammond had not the slightest intention of leaving early— in fact he, on his part, was just wishing that this rather impossible brother of Sheila's would soon take his departure and leave him to finish a happy evening in his own way.

'The blighter has just spoilt the whole thing,' he thought. 'I suppose he'll make himself still more objectionable when he finds how things are between Sheila and myself.'

Then as he noticed Mrs Ryan's unsuccessful attempts at conversation, Sheila's flushed, nervous look, sudden anger possessed him. He had taken rather more wine than usual—partly as a little private celebration, and partly in defiance of Anthony and his total abstinence—it may have gone to his head quickly and been accountable for the sudden idea which flashed into his mind and caused him to spring to his feet, glass in hand.

'To the future Mrs Norman Hammond! Long life and happiness to the Irish Shamrock that is going to become an English rose.'

Smilingly, he lent towards Sheila and touched her glass with his. Then straightening himself and still smiling in triumph he was just lifting the glass to his lips when it was sent spinning out of his hand and fell shattered to pieces—the red wine leaving a vivid scarlet splash on his white flannels. At the same moment a voice cried:

'You damned English puppy. Take back those words or I'll knock them down your throat.'

Desmond Ryan had stepped suddenly into the room from the wide open window, just in time to hear Norman's toast and to answer it in his own way. He stood now looking at the British officer with eyes flashing with anger.

Mrs Ryan screamed and sank back in her chair, while Sheila sprang to her feet with flaming cheeks.

'How dare you, Desmond,' she cried, and again 'How dare you!'

As she spoke she came to her lover's side and stood there looking defiantly at both her brothers—at Desmond who was standing just beside her, flaming with anger, like herself, at Anthony, who had risen to his feet indeed, but stood very quietly on the other side of the table. Clasping her hands on Norman's arm she said, 'Don't mind him, Norman; don't mind Desmond. Don't mind either of them.'

'Certainly I shall not mind them,' he replied, but the hand which held the handkerchief with which he was trying to wipe the wine stains away shook with rage. 'They are beneath my consideration, but,' and a sudden ugly look crept into his eyes and round his mouth, changing his whole expression, 'some day we will teach these Irish Rebels another lesson—and one they won't forget.'

'Will you?' shouted Desmond furiously, 'will you? Take care that we don't teach you one first.'

He was beside himself with rage and did not feel Anthony's restraining hand on his arm. But when his brother spoke he swung round to face him.

'That will do, Desmond, please say no more,' said Anthony. Then as Desmond, with a muttered imprecation, turned and stood staring out at the summer darkness with angry unseeing eyes, Anthony turned to Hammond.

'Perhaps Mr Hammond will favour me with an interview in another room?' he asked. 'The library I suppose, Mrs Ryan, is at our convenience?—thank you. Now, Sir, I would be glad if you would come with me.' He led the way from the room and Norman followed him. There was silence for several moments in the dining room, which Mrs Ryan—true to her type—was the first to break.

'Well! really, Desmond,' she began, 'I am surprised. I did not expect it from you. Such perfectly scandalous behaviour! why I—.'

But her stepson was neither listening nor heeding. He had turned and was searching Sheila's face with eyes of angry bitterness.

'How long has this been going on?' he asked. Sheila's anger had left her—and with it had gone most of her courage. But it was Anthony she dreaded, not Desmond. Who ever minded Desmond? He was like a boy beside Anthony—Anthony who was his elder by half-an-hour, which might have been five years, so much the older and more sensible did he always seem. So she pulled herself together and replied coldly:

'If you mean my engagement to Mr Hammond?——'

'No; I don't mean your engagement,' cried her brother furiously, 'because there is no engagement between you and that bounder and never will be. To allow our sister to become the wife of a British soldier. My God! Sheila. Are you mad?'

'No; but I think you are,' broke in Mrs Ryan; 'the very idea, Desmond, of speaking to your sister in such a manner. I can assure you that I feel highly honoured that such a gallant young officer has asked her to become his wife. One of our heroes—those dear, brave boys who did their bit and——.'

'Oh! for God's sake stop!' he cried, 'what are you talking about? Have you no sense of decency or—or even common sense——.'

'Desmond!'

'To talk of being honoured by an English officer wanting to marry an Irish girl. Would you think that a Belgian girl should feel honoured if a Prussian asked her to marry him? What would you think of the Belgian women if they spent their time knitting socks and rubbish for German soldiers?'

'Desmond!'

'If they asked them to dinner and tea, and petted and fussed over them, and behaved in a generally idiotic way over the Prussian invaders? Well! what would you have thought of those women? Would you have considered them loyal and patriotic?'

Going over to the sideboard he poured himself out a glass of water and drank it off, and taking out his handkerchief wiped his forehead.

'It is a wonder that you don't join your brother in the library?' said Sheila, and her voice was so icily cold that he looked at her in amazement. She was like a stranger to him. But he was getting himself in hand again, so he only said:

'If Anthony wants me he will let me know—anyhow he is a lot better able to manage an affair of this sort than I am. Tony can always keep cool.'

'However, as it happens,' said Sheila, 'I don't require either of you to manage what is my affair—and mine only.'

Again Desmond looked at her wonderingly, and again she seemed like a stranger—so hard and cold.

But before he could answer a door opened down the hall and Anthony's voice could be heard calling.

'Just come here, Desmond; I want you for a little while,' and rising hastily he left the room and made his way to the library. It was a large, lofty room, lined from floor to ceiling with books; a long table ran down the centre, and big leather chairs were scattered around, while the window sills were wide and cushioned, and from their deep embrasure could be seen the haunting beauty of the Dublin mountains. An ideal spot for the book lover was the library at Firfield.

As Desmond entered he saw that Hammond was seated in one of the big chairs looking sullen enough and Anthony was standing at the window looking out. He turned as his twin entered, and Desmond, who knew him so thoroughly, could read the pain that dwelt behind his quiet voice and courteous manner.

'Sit down, Desmond,' he said. 'I want to speak to you, to tell you that Mr Hammond says that Sheila has promised to be his wife.'

But Desmond did not sit down, he strode forward and stood beside his brother, casting a contemptuous glance at the Englishman as he did so.

'I don't see that it matters what Mr Hammond says,' he replied, 'as we will not allow our sister to marry him.'

Norman Hammond took out his cigarette case and deliberately chose and lit a cigarette. Leaning back in the comfortable chair he drew a few whiffs in a lazily insolent manner before he remarked curtly:

'As my fiancée happens to be of age and her own mistress I fail to see how either of you gentlemen can forbid her to marry me—or to do anything else she wishes.'

'What rubbish!' cried Desmond, hotly, 'as if a girl like Sheila was really responsible for her actions—or even knew her own mind. We will take jolly good care that she sees less of you in the future anyway.'

Hammond threw back his handsome sleek head and laughed.

'Indeed?' he murmured.

'Yes; indeed,' retorted the other; 'and let me tell you—.'

'Stop, Desmond!' interposed Anthony, 'it's useless to talk in that way. What Mr Hammond says is perfectly true. Sheila is legally free to do what she wishes in the matter. But still we, who understand her, know how young she is for her years.'

'Of course,' assented his twin, 'why she's like a child.'

'A child whom I intend to marry, however,' put in Norman curtly.

'I say you shall not marry her,' said Desmond.

But Anthony again interposed, putting his hand on Desmond's shoulder gently forced him to sit down, and then pulling up another chair to the table he sat down himself.

'Now, Desmond, let me talk,' he said, and Desmond, from force of habit, curbed his impatience and let Anthony speak.

'Mr Hammond has been quite frank with me,' he said; 'he is apparently a rich man and is prepared to make handsome settlements on Sheila, materially her future would be assured. Also in the matter of religion he is willing to make the usual concessions. He says that he is very much attached to her—and she to him.'

Norman nodded his head.

'Yes; we love each other,' he said; 'surely you believe that. And I really cannot for the life of me see why you object to me so strongly.'

Desmond moved as if to speak, but his brother lifted his hand for silence, and spoke himself.

'We object to you because you are an enemy of our country,' he said. 'No British officer shall ever marry our sister if we can prevent it.'

'No! by Heaven he shall not!' said Desmond.

Norman Hammond sat up straight and flung away his cigarette as he turned and looked at the two men facing him across the table. How marvellously alike they were, and yet how unlike. The features almost exactly the same, but the expression how different. Anthony's eyes were looking at him keenly and coldly—Desmond's eyes blazed at him with angry hatred and contempt. Then the mouth—that tell-tale feature in this age of cleanshaven men. Anthony's spoke of resolute determination—firmness, but, above all, of self-control; but the lines around Desmond's lips spoke of a weaker will, of an easy-going and unstable disposition. Even now his teeth were clenched on his lips to steady their trembling, while Anthony showed no such signs of emotion. Only the lines of worry on his forehead and the sorrow in his eyes betrayed what he was feeling.

Hammond, for his part, was becoming more normal, his temper was recovering, and also his brain was clearing itself from the fumes of wine. He smiled and leant forward.

'Now, look here, you fellows,' he said in more friendly tones, 'what's the good of quarrelling like this? I'm not such a bad sort, as we men go, and I mean to do my duty by Sheila; she shall want for nothing when she is my wife and I swear I'll make her happy. As for all this talk about my being an enemy and so on—why, you both know jolly well—you must know—that it's all—all bally rot and piffle.' Desmond, with flashing eyes, was on his feet again, but Anthony spoke first, very quietly and firmly.

'Excuse me,' he said, 'but that is where we differ. What may be "bally rot" to you is a sacred duty to us. Would you approve of a Belgian girl marrying a German?'

'Just what I have been saying to the old girl,' interposed Desmond.

His brother glanced at him questioningly, 'I hope Des,' he said, 'that you did not say what you would be sorry for afterwards?'

'Oh! no; I said nothing I could ever be sorry about,' was the reply. 'I only gave her a little plain speaking for once.'

'Come now,' said Norman, 'you are not serious surely, either of you? You don't really look upon me as an enemy?'

'Towards you, personally, as a man—and for the moment our stepmother's guest—we have, needless to say, no animosity,' answered Anthony, 'but you represent your nation—you are one of the enemy garrison in this country—and as such there can never be any connection or friendship between us.' And there was that in Anthony's clear, cold accents which spoke of absolute finality.

Norman Hammond rose to his feet.

'In that case I see no use in prolonging this interview,' he said, in quite a different tone of voice; 'your mind is made up and so is mine. I intend to make Sheila my wife, and as she is willing I do not believe that either of you can prevent it.'

'Well! you will see before long,' cried Desmond, furiously striking the table with his clenched fist. 'She will not be your wife. Good God! I would see her in her grave first.'

'That will do, Desmond,' interposed Anthony, and then turning to Hammond he said, 'I must ask you to leave now; we cannot stay late, and we wish to see our sister before we go.'

'You can see her and talk to her as much as you like,' replied the other contemptuously. 'I am going back to town now, and when I have said good-night to Sheila I will send her in here.' And with a ceremonious salute he walked to the door and passed out, shutting it after him.

For a moment there was silence between the brothers. Anthony was thinking hard, and as was usual when his mind was concentrated, he was staring straight in front of him, while Desmond was literally speechless with rage.

'Did you hear that?' he foamed at last; 'he will send Sheila to us! Does he think she is his slave already? To think that she would ever look at him!'

His brother made no reply. In the distance they heard voices; a door opened and shut, and then a motor came round from the back premises. So he was going—he certainly had not stayed long. Was it because he was so sure of her? Anthony shivered a little at the thought. Then the motor snorted and purred, there was a good-bye called out in girlish tones, Hammond called back, and Mrs Ryan's stilted accents joined in—the noise of the engine became louder—softer—and then died away down the avenue.

A few moments later the twins turned and faced the door as it opened and Sheila stood on the threshold.

There was a silence while one might count twenty, and then Anthony came slowly across the room, took the handle from her grasp, and shut the door. Quietly he led her to a chair.

'Sit down, Sheila,' he said, 'we want to talk to you.' She was pale and nervous, but she threw back her head with a defiant gesture and faced her brothers with the same cold expression in her eyes which had chilled Desmond in the diningroom.

'Well! What is it?' she asked.

She was sitting in a big chair at the head of the table, Anthony was seated beside her, and Desmond had flung himself down on the window-sill and was watching the other two. The light from the one shaded lamp fell on Sheila's pale but lovely face, and on the dark head and worried look of Anthony.

'I think you know what it is, Sheila,' he was saying quietly; 'we have just had an interview with Mr Hammond and he told us that he had asked you to be his wife, and that you had consented.'

'Well!' she said again.

'We want to know if it is true. We think he must have made a mistake. Neither Desmond nor I can imagine our sister giving up home and country—her nationality—every ideal which we have taught her to love, and becoming the wife of an Englishman.'

'Well! it is true,' she answered. 'I love him; he is the only man I could ever care for, and I mean to marry him.'

Desmond made an impetuous movement, but his brother

stopped him.

'Let me do the talking, Des,' he said, and turning to the girl he continued.

'Sheila, have you thought well over this? You are very young—and younger even than your years in many ways. This may be only a temporary infatuation, and if you go on with it you will probably be sorry for the rest of your life. Think well over it and do nothing in a hurry. Remember you are an Irish girl and a Catholic. What could you have in common with an Englishman—one, too, who admits that he has no definite religious beliefs.'

'He has promised to fulfil the required conditions,' said the girl.

'Yes; I know. But such promises have been made before under similar circumstances and—not kept.'

'Do you doubt Norman's word?' she broke in.

'Does our history teach us to trust the word of the English?' he answered quietly.

She was about to spring to her feet, but he put her back gently.

'No; Sheila,' he said, 'wait another while. I cannot let you go like this. My dear! My dear! Have you thought of what our mother—our own dear mother—would have felt? You don't remember her very well, I know, but we do. You were only a little thing of five years when she was taken away from us, but we were big boys of nearly twelve and we—we loved her so much. It was she who taught us love of faith and fatherland, and when she knew that she was dying she left you in our special charge. Nearly her last words were, "Boys look after Girlie."'

He paused for a moment and Sheila bowed her head on her clasped hands; she could not listen to him unmoved, but, oh! she wished he would stop. For her mind was made up, and she was determined that all the talking in the world would not change it. Softly Anthony touched the golden hair that was so dear to him, and so like that of his dead mother, then went on:

'And we have tried to be good to you, Girlie, to take care of you—haven't we? Sometimes other things—the cause of our country—may have kept us away from you. But we have done our best—and oh! Sheila, you are very dear to us.'

She raised her head and looked at him through tear-dimmed eyes.

'Yes; I know,' she said, rather brokenly. 'You have been good to me. Oh! you have indeed. But I love Norman so much. I can't give him up for anyone or anything.'

'You won't, you mean,' cried Desmond, springing from his seat and coming over. 'Good Heavens! Sheila; can you mean to really go on with this?'

She only flung him an angry glance. Because she loved him so dearly she felt his words cutting her to the heart—like Desmond himself, she was feeling what it was 'to be wrath with one we love'. Anthony could see that his brother's words were only doing harm, so he spoke again himself to the girl, earnestly but quietly.

'One favour at least I will ask from you,' he said, 'and that is that you will do nothing in a hurry. There must be no "war wedding" or anything of that sort. Will you promise that?'

'No! I'll promise nothing,' she answered. 'I'll marry Norman when and where he wishes.'

'Yes; in a Registry Office, I suppose,' gibed Desmond, furiously.

'In a Registry Office is he wishes,' she answered as furiously. 'I love him—and his people shall be my people—his God my God.'

'Sheila!'

It was Anthony who had spoken with wide open eyes of horror. Desmond could only stand rigid, staring at this stranger who was speaking.

'Yes—yes;' she went on. 'You may say what you like and call me what you like, but I am just sick of all this talk about Ireland and freedom and everything else. It's all nonsense. Norman says you could be all perfectly happy and would be well treated under British rule if you would only behave yourselves. Now you know what I think and what I mean to do, and—I'm going to bed.' She crossed the room and out of the door like a whirlwind, leaving her brothers standing gazing at the door which she had banged behind her and listening as she rushed up the stairs to her room.

A silence, pregnant and terrible, followed. Desmond was standing at the window, still in a state of dumb unbelieving amazement; the moon rose with beauty over Mont Pelier, but he never saw it; a bat flew in and brushed against him, and he never felt it. But suddenly the silence was broken by a sound that sent him swinging round and over to the chair by the table—the sound of a man's broken sobs.

'Why, Tony!' he said, slipping his arm round the other's shoulder in the old boyish way.

'Oh! Desmond!' came the stifled answer, 'what are we to do? Girlie! Girlie! Our little Girlie!'

CHAPTER V

THREE YEARS LATER

Geraldine Moore was sitting at her breakfast, one August morning just three years after that summer night on which Sheila Ryan had broken away from all the traditions of her youth, and stepped openly to the side of her English lover, marrying him a couple of weeks later—three years pregnant with history for all the world.

Like many another woman, Geraldine shows the strain of the time in which she is living; there are lines around the eyes and mouth, and grey in the pretty hair, which were not there when we first met her. That autumn of 1920 was a hard one in more ways than one. Work of every description was slack, and unemployment was a grave problem, for expense and outlay of every kind was being cut down on all sides, not only by private individuals, but also by business firms and public bodies. Amongst those who suffered in consequence of this was Geraldine Moore. Her committee found that they could no longer afford to carry on, so Geraldine for the past two months had found herself amongst the ranks of the Unemployed.

Two months and she was just beginning to feel the pinch and to look at every penny before spending it. She was also developing a nervous habit of counting and re-counting the few remaining bank notes in her purse—for these same notes were getting fewer with terrible rapidity—they might have had wings so quickly did they fly away. Once let one be changed and behold! it was gone; so that she was beginning to feel the truth of what the little woman in the huckster's shop at the corner used to say so often and so dolefully:

'Sure no wan can see the colour of their money these days, much less get anything out of it!'

The newspaper lent by Mrs Brennan was propped up before her now, and as she drank her tea and eat her bread and margarine she was diligently going through the advertisements column. She jotted down a couple of addresses, answered a few more at the office of the paper, and prepared to start out on her usual tramp for work. Although worried and anxious she had by no means lost heart: she had still a few pounds in hand, not much, but enough to keep her out of debt for several weeks yet, and she was fairly sure in her own mind that she must get employment soon.

She called out cheerfully to her landlady, 'I'm off now, Mrs Brennan!' as she went through the tiny hall, but in spite of her resolution to keep cheerful and to cling to hope still, her heart was heavy enough. It was not to be wondered at, for to the man or woman who has been used to the same routine of work day after day—be it at business or in the office, or the daily round of the professional worker—if this is taken suddenly and completely from them there ensues a blank in their lives which nothing can fill. If, added to this, there is the uncertainty of re-employment their nerves suffer still more. Geraldine, for several years now, had been accustomed to have practically every moment of her day occupied, to be able to map out her work for each day until evening. Then at night she had her Irish classes and lectures, an occasional evening at the pictures or the theatre. She had never known what it was to have an idle day; to have to look forward to long unoccupied hours stretching their interminable length before her. Not indeed that her days could be called idle now, the constant quest for employment filled a good part of them, but this was very different from the regular work accompanied by peace of mind and contentment which had been hers when she could boast that she was a self-respecting wage-earner.

She left her 'replies' at the newspaper office, and went on to the addresses which she had copied from the 'Wanted' columns. But it was no use—either she was not suitable, or they would let her know later—a vague promise never fulfilled—or the position was already taken. She called at various Registry Offices where she had entered her name only to be told 'No; nothing in your line. You might call again in a few days.'

At one o'clock hunger assailed her, for a bread and margarine breakfast does not sustain one far through the day, and she went as usual to the restaurant where she had always gone for her mid-day meal for several years now. The prices at this particular place were very reasonable and when she was earning Geraldine could afford her dinner of meat and vegetables and a sweet every day. For the last month, however, the sweet had been cut off, and for the last week the meat. Today she ordered a plate of soup, for which she paid three-pence, and that constituted her dinner. It did not by any means satisfy her healthy appetite, but she felt that if she was to hold out until work came she must husband every penny.

She knew that Mrs Brennan would let her stay on rent free for a while, and that Mrs Doyle in the shop where she dealt for her small groceries might let her run a credit account, but she shrank from owing money to anyone, especially as she did not know how long she might have to be out of employment; she might be idle for months. She shivered at the thought in spite of the warm day, and, paying her modest bill, passed out into the blazing August noonday.

She had one other address where she had not gone yet. It was a certain road in Donnybrook, and the advertisement was for a 'Nurse Companion for a delicate girl.' Not at all the kind of thing which Geraldine would have chosen, but 'any port in a storm,' and so she set off to walk to Donnybrook. The heat was intense and she found the walk very tiring, the pavements seemed to blister her feet through shoes which were getting painfully worn in the soles. Arrived at the address she found that it was a Registry Office, and the woman informed her that the situation was right across the City, at Clontarf, and added that she had just sent 'a very suitable person' there. Geraldine thanked her mechanically and left the office, trying to conceal her disappointment.

The walk back to the city was even more tiresome, and she was badly tempted to take the tram, but she would not break the stringent rule which she had made, of never spending a penny if she could avoid doing so.

When she got back to town she stood for a moment at the top of Grafton Street watching the crowd, which in spite of 'Wars and alarms' were still to be seen strolling down that fashionable thoroughfare. She watched them wistfully—envying them in spite of her wish not to do so; envying them their lovely frocks, so cool and dainty, their silk stockings and delightful shoes, their motors and their carriages, but envying above all the money in their purse.

'Oh!' she thought, 'if I had only some of their cash now. What would I not give for an ice!' She turned away with a resigned smile at her own flight of fancy—'an ice indeed!—a loaf of bread would be more in my line,' and entered Stephen's Green.

She was terribly tired and felt that she must sit down for a while, but she soon found that a seat was not easy to get, every bench seemed occupied by her comrades in the great army of the Unemployed, both men and women—but the majority were men.

It is a noticeable fact, and easily observed, that a man, once he is thrown out of his job, whatever it may be, seems, as it were, to fling up the sponge immediately. If he belongs to the 'Voice of Labour' he goes at once to help to hold up the street corners, and when tired he uses the benches of the City parks as his couch. Unwashed and unshaven he appears daily, his boots never cleaned, his clothes never brushed; but he never seems to worry— he has a grievance now on which he can hold forth to his fellow-men, and that makes up for a lot to the ever garrulous male.

A woman, on the other hand, no matter how hard the world may be using her, will still think of her appearance, only the very lowest or absolutely destitute of the sex neglect this. They do not spend hours gossiping at street corners, or sleep through the heat of the day on the park benches. On the contrary, they will trudge the city from one end to the other looking for a job—they act while men talk. Of course men will deny all this, but it is absolutely true, as everyone knows in experience. It is women who are doing the world's work today—and often keeping an idle husband as well—and if men don't bestir themselves there will be no work left for them to do.

Geraldine was meditating in some such fashion as she passed the many recumbent forms of masculine beauty which were lying on the benches around, illustrating in different poses—'ease before elegance'.

So tired did she feel that she could have found it in her heart to shove one of them off and to sit down herself. At last she espied a bench on which there was room for her. A man was leaning against the back, half asleep, his cap pulled over his eyes, and the only other occupant was an old woman, very poor and shabby, with a mushroom-shaped hat of unknown antiquity tied under her chin with a boot-lace, while a piece of twine held her gaping boots together. She had a paper parcel on her lap from which she was eating—or rather nibbling—crusts of bread, and taking snuff alternately. Geraldine recognised her type at once; she knew as well as if she had looked into it that the brown paper parcel, tied and re-tied with knotted cord, contained, besides food and snuff, all its owner's earthly possessions. She knew, too, that these would probably consist of a few coloured handkerchiefs, a rosary beads and a couple of religious medals, a bundle of her 'papers' tied together, being her discharges and recommendations from the ladies for whom she had worked when able to do so, a comb, a bit of soap and torn towel, and her few coppers tightly sewn up in a piece of linen. These with a few other odds and ends would make up the parcel, and at night she would go to one of the various Night Refuges for supper and a lodging, while by day she had the Green to rest in, and various 'patrons' to visit. For the winter months she would retire to the building which is designated by herself and her friends as 'St James Hotel'.

Just as Geraldine was sitting down the drowsy man moved and stretched himself at greater length along the bench, thus leaving her about an inch of space. But this was the last straw.

'Would you mind moving a little, please?' she said. 'You can't have all the seat to yourself.'

She spoke sharply, her voice on edge with over-fatigue and nervous worry.

The man turned and stared at her reproachfully.

'Well! it's a quare thing,' he remarked sadly, 'that the swells won't allow the working man to have even the free seats itself! Isn't there plenty of chairs vacant beyond here? Or is it that ye're too mean to pay the penny?'

Rising in disgust he gave himself a shake and shuffled away.

The old woman lifted her dim eyes from the paper parcel.

'Them men do be very contrairy and impudent,' she said. 'They wouldn't let a poor woman live at all if they could help it. Would ye have a penny about ye to spare a poor ould crathur?'

Geraldine, who had refused herself even a tram ride, took out her poor purse and handed the woman a penny.

'I wish it was more,' she said, 'but I—I am poor myself.'

'May God and the Blessed Virgin reward you,' replied the old lady, as she gathered up her parcel, carefully tying it across and across with twine, of which her pockets seemed to be full—and rose to depart—'God bless ye! And may He give ye the worth of this twice over before night!'

'Well! Amen to that!' said Geraldine to herself, as she leant back on the seat, and idly watched the passers-by. They were the usual varied crowd: old and young, rich and poor, the worker, the idler, and the unemployed. The girl was so tired that she had no other wish or desire but just to sit on there and rest and watch—

not the human crowd, of whom she soon tired, but the little feathered creatures who seemed so friendly and cheerful. It gave her an odd sense of rest and peace—almost of contentment—just to sit and look at them living their busy lives, always appearing so full of vitality, so keen about the business of their bird life. How very tame are these citizens of the Green! Two or three left the water and came over to Geraldine, standing looking up at her with bright eyes, and asking quite plainly—'Have you nothing for us? Nor even a biscuit?' One little fellow especially—a queer nondescript-looking chap with a big tuft on his head—pushed in front of the others and stood staring at her, occasionally turning his head from side to side, as if surprised that his blandishments received no attention.

She bent down and spoke to him, echoing her thoughts aloud:

'No; I have nothing for you. I'm sorry, but indeed I have little enough for myself.'

Her eyes strayed across the Green to the south side and she suddenly thought of Jill Devereux.

Jill had been down in the country in Co. Waterford for the past two months, staying with friends, and Geraldine had not heard from her with the exception of two picture post cards with no address. This was just like Miss Devereux, her friend was used to it, but she missed her terribly and had felt her absence more than usual this time on account of her own worry. She remembered now that Jill should have arrived back either yesterday or today, and, feeling a great desire to see her, Geraldine rose to her feet and set off towards the big building at the top of which Jill had her flat.

Very high up it was, too, and poor Geraldine was far from blessing the stone stairs as she toiled painfully up and up, until at last she reached the top and saw Jill's door facing her. On the opposite side of the landing was another door and on it was pinned a card with 'Yvonne Delaunay' inscribed in neat but uncommon characters.

Yvonne, as Geraldine knew, was in England, had been there for several months now, but she kept on her flat as she meant to return to Dublin.

There were movements behind Jill's door, and Geraldine had hardly time to knock before it was flung open and Jill herself stood on the threshold.

'Oh! Jerry, you dear! Come in! come in!' she cried. 'Look at me; I am only just back and still in a state of chaos.'

'I thought you were to have got back last night?' said Geraldine.

'So I was, and so I should have done, but the train was held up by the IRA and we were delayed so long that we missed the connection at the Junction, and had to stay the night in a pokey little hotel. However, here I am safe and sound, for which I should be thankful these times. Now sit down; I have the kettle on the gas and we will have tea in a jiffy.'

Geraldine seated herself rather wearily in one of Jill's comfortable chairs and as she leant back and rested her tired head against the cushion, Jill, who had been flying around setting out the cups and saucers, was suddenly struck with the worn, weary look of her friend, and noticed how much paler and thinner she had become.

'Why, Jerry!' she said, 'what is it? Is anything wrong? You look so—so terribly worried.'

'As well I may,' replied the other, with a sort of sad bitterness. 'I have been out of my job now for two months. You put no address on your post cards, Jill, so I couldn't write, and in any case I would not have bothered you on your holiday.'

'Oh! Jerry, if I had only known. I was sure I put the address all right on the card. But it's just like me. I am a useless beast and no mistake.'

'Ah! don't talk like that, and don't worry yourself.'

'But I do worry when I think of what you must have gone through. Jerry, darling, has it been a very hard time?'

'Well! yes; it has been hard—at least rather'— and then as Geraldine looked up Jill bent down and took her in her arms, and Geraldine's tears broke forth at last—her bitter, tired sobs going to Jill's very heart.

A stiff upper lip is comparatively easy to achieve in the face of adversity as long as we are surrounded by indifferent strangers, but once let us hear the voice of sympathy and feel loving arms around us and all our bulwarks of pride, our veneer of would-be indifference, our pitiful attempts at stoicism are gone. And so it was with Geraldine. She cried till she was too tired to cry any more, and Jill let her do so, knowing that it would only do her good in the end; then while she was preparing the tea Geraldine dried her eyes and unburdened herself of her present worries and her fears of the future, and felt all the better for her tears and her talk.

'Well! now come and get your tea,' said Jill. 'Thank Heaven for Mrs Power's hamper. Sit down, do, and get a decent feed; you look half-starved.'

Jill's friends had sent her back laden with 'Country produce,' and the 'high tea' with cold roast chicken, home-made bread, honey and fresh butter—and real cream in the tea—seemed to put fresh life into Geraldine.

'Oh! Jill; I feel a different being now,' she said, as the meal over they settled down for a good talk.

'Of course you do,' cried her friend, 'an empty stomach would give anyone the hump. Now tell me what chance you have of work and what are you thinking of doing?'

'Well! I am willing to take anything,' said Geraldine, 'and I am answering every advertisement that I can, but you know a trained nurse is not much good at anything else. Times are so bad. Districts that used to keep a nurse or Health visitor are doing without them, and private nursing is very slack. I have spoken to a lot of the doctors, but they mostly have their own regular nurses to whom they are accustomed; and I can't join a Co-op Home, because I could not afford to pay the fee now, besides I might be a long time waiting for a case and would have to keep myself all that time. Oh! Jill; it's very hard. I never was idle before and it—it frightens me. I know that it shouldn't—I know I should have more trust in God, but I have prayed so much and still got no work.'

'Well! don't worry any more than you can help,' advised the other girl, 'you are bound to get something soon, and after all if the worst comes to the worst you will just have to come and chance pot luck with me here.'

'Oh! Jill, as if I could. And be a burden on you.'

'Don't talk rot! Perhaps I will want your help some day. And now have you any news of our mutual friends? I know the Ryans are back from Wormwood Scrubbs. How do they look after the hunger strike?'

'I only say them once since their return,' replied Geraldine. 'They were very thin and haggard, and their eyes were sunken so terribly. Anthony seemed to have felt it less than Desmond, but he has so much more strength of will that I imagine he would not allow himself to feel it like his brother. Tony always seems to walk on such a high spirited plane that the things of the flesh don't trouble him much. Desmond looked worn out—he had such a strained look and was all nerves. It was pitiable to see him. They are down in Co. Wicklow at present trying to pull themselves together again, but I expect they will be back in town any day now.'

'I suppose they will be starting getting into trouble again as soon as they are able?' remarked Jill, rather curtly; 'they won't stop until they are shot, or imprisoned for life.'

'They must continue to do their duty,' said Geraldine, a cold edge to her voice.

'Now, Jerry, don't mind what I say,' cried Jill, quick to read her friend's thoughts. 'You will never make a patriot of me, but you have my sympathies—you know that—even although I cannot but think it is only sheer madness to continue fighting. They are bound to be beaten; in numbers alone England will overwhelm them. And why lose all the best manhood in Ireland to gain—nothing!'

'To gain nothing?' echoed Geraldine, passionately.

'Is it nothing to gain and keep our own self-respect as a nation? To know that our people prefer to die free rather than to live as slaves! How do you know that we are doomed to failure? After Easter Week didn't England think we were smashed; didn't she think that she had ground us to the very dust? And look at us now! For one who was out for Irish Freedom then—how many have we now?'

'Yes; I admit all that is true,' replied Jill, 'but I still believe that there can be only one ending—and it will be a terrible one for Ireland. However, I may be wrong, so let us leave it at that. How is Mrs Ryan?'

'She is in England,' replied Geraldine; 'the desire of her heart is fulfilled at last and now she can tell every one that she has been staying at "My daughter's place in Yorkshire—Hammond Hall, you know".'

Jill laughed at Geraldine's imitation of the poor lady's stilted accent.

'Still true to her type, I see,' she said. 'I wonder will she ever change? You know, Jerry, that lately since Sinn Féin has come so much to the fore it is becoming quite fashionable. Who knows but that we may yet see Mrs Ryan within its ranks—knitting socks for the IRA instead of the British Tommies.'

'God forbid!' replied Geraldine. 'We don't want any of her sort—she would do the cause no good, but harm. But what you say is quite true, Jill. I was visiting a lady a few days ago who had always been a Britisher, although she is of Irish birth and a Catholic. She used to say she was 'loyal' and a 'Constitutional Nationalist'. Ireland within the Empire and all that kind of talk. She had been bitterly—offensively—British during the war, and worked for England and her Allies in every way she could. Well, when I called to see her last week I was very careful, as usual, to keep off everything Irish, when she completely floored me by remarking, "You know, we are all Sinn Féiners here now".'

'How delightful! What did you say?'

'I couldn't answer her for a moment—only sat looking at her with my mouth open. "Since when?" I gasped at last. "Oh! we are Sinn Féiners now by conviction," she replied. "I always like to be quite convinced of the justice of a cause, and so I was waiting to really study the question. I don't believe in rushing at things".'

'After all, perhaps, she is sincere?' hazarded Jill.

'With two sons in the British Army! a likely tale.'

'Did you say much to her?'

'No; I turned the conversation as soon as I could,' replied Geraldine. 'I don't trust her. Not that I mean she would do us any harm at present, but I believe that if England gets the upper hand again she will at once return to the loyal Briton stunt. It's a question of bread and butter—and who can give her the most jam.'

'Yvonne Delaunay returns next week,' said Jill in somewhat irrelevant fashion.

Geraldine froze perceptibly. She did not answer for a moment, and then she said with an effort.

'That will be nice for you. I suppose you have felt lonely?'

'Yes; I have missed her,' said Jill, and was silent for a space.

Geraldine did not speak either; the thoughts of both were with the strange, fascinating personality of the girl who had lived across the landing—the girl with the lovely hair and the inscrutable eyes and mouth, the girl who was returning—for what? For, although Jill was fascinated and Geraldine repulsed, still to both she remained a mystery—a mystery which to Jill was as unsolved now as it had been on that cold January morning over three years ago, when she had heard Yvonne creep up the stairs in the darkness before the dawn. A mystery which she was beginning to wonder would she ever fathom.

She aroused herself with an effort as Geraldine stood up to take her leave.

'And a thousand thanks, dear old Jill. You have made a new woman of me.'

'That's right then. Keep up your heart now and don't get depressed any more. Don't stay away longer than a few days. I'll be out during most of the day, for I have to go round and try and book a few orders—which are very slack just now, but I'll be here in the evenings.'

Geraldine promised, and returned to her modest lodgings, hope springing once more within her heart.

CHAPTER VI

THE TWINS AGAIN

Six weeks later Geraldine met the twins. She was walking up Grafton Street, homeward bound, after another fruitless day, when she saw them swinging along towards her and her face flushed with gladness at seeing them again.

During the past few years they had become her very dear friends, and she had a warm corner for both of them in her honest heart, and if the corner devoted to Desmond was larger than the other—large enough to sometimes hold a queer aching pain—she would not admit it even to herself, for she knew perfectly that in his eyes she would never be anything closer than a friend. A very dear friend, but still only a friend. She had not seen them since they had returned from Wicklow after their release from Wormwood Scrubbs, where they had been on hunger strike, and she could hardly speak when they met now and she felt their hearty handclasp.

'Why, Jerry! we are glad to meet you,' cried Desmond, and Anthony seconded in his quiet way.

'We must celebrate the occasion by having tea together,' went on Desmond. 'Where would you like to go? Have you any particular choice?'

'No! no; anywhere. I don't mind,' she replied happily.

'Well, then, let us cut down Anne Street to the "Sod",' settled Desmond.

Chatting gaily they repaired to the 'Sod of Turf', that quaint tea shop where Irish Ireland goes for tea and talk.

It was getting late and there were not many people there. A young fellow and a girl were consuming scones and tea and talking rapidly in Gaelic at one of the corner tables, and an elderly man with a beard was reading a book intently, while his tea grew cold.

The twins piloted Geraldine to a table and Desmond at once began a chat in Gaelic with the attendant, to whom he was evidently well-known.

With the arrival of tea the three settled down to a good talk and exchanged the news of the last few months.

'So you see here I am, still looking for a job,' said Geraldine, as she ended her recital which the other two had insisted on hearing first. 'And as far as I can see—I can go on looking for it.'

'Ah! not at all,' cried Desmond. 'Something is certain to turn up—probably when you least expect it. But whatever you do, don't lose heart. That's half the battle.'

'Desmond is right,' said Anthony, with his rare smile, the smile that was so charming, seeming to light up his whole face; 'you must not lose heart. None of us can afford to do that at present.'

'You never do, anyway,' cried the girl. 'Now do please tell me about yourselves. Are you getting quite strong again?'

'Yes,' said Anthony quietly, 'we are beginning to feel normal once more. Indeed, I am practically all right, but Desmond'—with a swift, loving look at the handsome face across the table, which was his own replica in all but expression, 'is hardly his own self yet. He is a bit sagged still.'

'I have often wondered what it is like, how it actually feels, to be on hunger strike?' asked Geraldine. 'Do you mind telling me about it? How long were you fasting, and when did you feel worst?'

'We were twenty-three days,' replied Anthony, 'and to me the first few days were the worst, because of the terrible headaches from which I suffered. The hunger was nothing compared to the pain in my head; as a matter of fact I did not feel really hungry after the first two days—only deadly sick, and the awful headache.'

'And later?' asked the girl.

'Well! I just seemed to get weaker and weaker—and the weaker I got the happier I seemed to get, too.'

'Are you in earnest?' she asked. 'Did you really feel like that?'

'Yes; I did really,' he answered. 'When the headache left me in peace I was perfectly happy.'

'But you had no headaches after the first few days?'

'Oh! indeed I had. In fact I suffered from them all the time, but after the fourth day they became intermittent, and during the intervals when I was free of pain I hardly suffered at all until the last week, when my bones began to feel as if they were cutting through the flesh, and my gums became most horribly sore.'

'It must be a terrible ordeal,' said Geraldine, with a shudder. 'I simply cannot think how you endured it.'

'Only for the headaches, which certainly were agonising while they lasted, I did not feel it so terrible. But, remember, we were only twenty-three days; complications arise when the fast is longer which make the suffering harder. All the same, Jerry,' and he shot a strange smile at her from his lovable grey eyes, 'I can understand now the long fasts of the Saints and the ecstasy which they felt at such times.'

He paused for a moment, and then said in a low voice:

'It is as if one had left this earth altogether and had soared to a different plane. But I cannot describe the sensation to you; it was too spiritual for mere words.'

Geraldine felt a sudden contraction of the throat and a mist before her eyes. For the moment it was to her as if the gallant fellow sitting opposite to her and talking so quietly—almost casually—of what must have been a very martyrdom, was typical of the young manhood of Ireland at the time, of their zeal and self-sacrifice, their unflinching heroism even unto death. All done as though it was just part of the day's work. She could not speak for a moment, and then she turned to Desmond with a rather shaky smile.

'And what about you, Desmond?' she asked. 'Did you feel the same way as Tony?'

Desmond flushed nervously, and Geraldine noticed, as she had often done before, how much younger he always seemed than his twin—younger in his ways and his mannerisms, in his very talk.

'No; indeed I did not,' he said emphatically. 'My experience was altogether different, isn't that strange, Jerry? We often speak of it and wonder why, when we are so much alike and there is such an intense sympathy between us, the hunger strike should have affected us in such different ways.'

'Yes; it does seem strange,' she said reflectively; 'but tell me how you felt, that is if you don't mind speaking of it.'

'I felt just wretched. It was—it was Hell the whole time. I was starving with hunger for the first week— ravenous. I had no headache at all, but oh! the desire for food. I used to dream constantly during what little sleep I got—because one cannot sleep much—of all kinds of food. My most persistent dream, or nightmare—for that is what it really meant under the circumstances—was of a rabbit pie with plenty of onions and gravy and a perfect pyramid of mashed potatoes. Oh! it was no laughing matter at the time, although I can smile at it now. But really how I managed to keep from taking food I do not know. And the way they used to tempt one.'

'To tempt you; what do you mean?'

'Why they used to slip in all kinds of food—such delicious food it seemed, Jerry—through the door, and then they would leave it there to tempt us. Even now I sometimes can smell the soup, real good stuff which they slipped us on the second day. But the worst of all to resist was the red herring which they put into my cell in the evening of the third day. Oh! Jerry, the smell of it! It was the day I was the most ravenous, too; after that I got more sick than hungry, although the hunger returned in spasms, but, Jerry, old girl, I don't mind telling you—I had to actually turn my back on the thing and bury my face in the bedclothes to keep out the sight and smell of it. I prayed to God that they would take it away soon.'

'And did they?' asked Geraldine, her voice hardly above a whisper, sympathy shining from her eyes.

'In about half-an-hour—thirty minutes that seemed like thirty years. Oh! but I was thankful when it was gone. I was shaking like a leaf with the force of the temptation.'

Anthony had been listening to his brother with loving eyes. He stretched out his hand now and laid it for a moment on Desmond's and the eyes of the two met in perfect love and understanding.

Geraldine, watching, marvelled again at the sympathy and devotion which existed between these two—so intensely alike and yet so unalike, too.

Then she thought of Sheila, and rather hesitatingly—for she knew it must hurt them—she asked the twins if they had heard from her lately.

'I have only seen Mrs Ryan a couple of times since Sheila's marriage,' she added, 'and she, of course, gave me a perfectly glowing account of your sister, but she would, you know. I often feel anxious about her, you know what friends we used to be, and although I wrote to her again and again, she never answered one of my letters. Oh! I wonder is she happy? Tony, do you think she is?'

'She has as much happiness as she deserves, and that is very little,' said Desmond bitterly. He had never forgiven Sheila, and his whole face became dark with anger whenever her name was mentioned. Anthony's expression did not change in the same way, but a shadow seemed to fall upon his face and a great sadness crept into his eyes.

'Have you heard no news at all about her since her marriage?' he asked.

'No; none,' Geraldine answered, 'except as I told you the few times I met Mrs Ryan, when she gave me such a glowing picture of Sheila and her new home.'

'Glowing balderdash! like the stuff she always talks,' said Desmond angrily. 'Surely you never expected to get the plain truth from that woman.'

Geraldine had to smile as she said: 'I thought I might pick up some news, or something that would give me a clue as to how Sheila really was. Do tell me if you know anything about her.'

'We know very little about her,' said Anthony sadly, 'and what we do know is not very good. Her husband got shell shock in France the last year of the war, and has not been really normal since. Lately, to make matters worse, he has taken to drink.'

'Oh! Tony; how awful!' cried the girl in real distress. 'Poor Sheila. It must be dreadful for her. But how did you hear all this? I thought she did not write to you?'

'And you thought right,' was the rather stern reply. 'We have never had a line from Sheila since her unfortunate marriage, although I wrote several times, and have done so indeed since our release from Wormwood Scrubbs. I knew that—that our mother would have wished it, and I was fretting about her myself. Poor Girlie! To me she is still my little sister.'

'And yet—she never answered?'

'No; not one line. Not that I ever thought that she would,' interposed Desmond hotly.

'Then how did you hear about her husband?'

Anthony smiled.

'That is a question I cannot answer—even to you, Jerry,' he said, 'but you will understand and not think me rude or unkind, for you know enough to comprehend that we have ways and means of obtaining information when we want to do so. But those same ways and means may not be divulged even to our dearest and truest friends.'

'Oh! of course, I understand,' cried the girl hastily. 'Please forgive me for being so curious.'

'You are not curious, Jerry; we know better than that,' said Desmond. 'We only wish we had better news to give you, although, as I said before, she deserves all she gets.'

'Ah! Desmond, don't,' she cried; 'sure you know in your heart that you don't mean what you are saying. Poor Sheila! I wonder is she happy at all—and how she is looking. Quite changed, I expect.'

'I am afraid she is not very happy,' said Anthony, 'especially since the death of her child—.'

'The child!' exclaimed Geraldine. 'Was there a child?'

'Yes; a little girl,' he replied, 'but it only lived a few days, and died—unbaptised.'

'Unbaptised!' she breathed, 'but why, why? Norman Hammond promised—.'

'Promised! English promises to us!' broke from Desmond.

'Now, Desmond, be just,' interrupted Anthony, and turning to Geraldine he continued. 'There seems to have been no Catholic Priest within several miles, and the child appeared a healthy, strong baby. Sheila was given to understand—and believed—that the baptism would take place later, and if the child had lived it would probably have received baptism all right. But the little thing took bad quite suddenly—in fact it died in a few moments.'

'But was there no one—no Catholic? The mother herself?'

'Did not know till it was dead. She was not in the same room with it when it was taken ill—there was no other Catholic in the house—and naturally all was confusion; then it was all over so quickly.'

Anthony sighed deeply—always a sure sign of mental pain with him. 'I believe Sheila felt it terribly,' he concluded; 'she was very ill for days afterwards. But, after all, Jerry,' as she was still silent, 'things may not be so black with her as we fear, and anyway she is coming over next month to stay for a short time at Firfield. You may have an opportunity of seeing her; she may see you even if she wouldn't meet us.'

'Oh! is she really coming home for a time?' cried the girl; 'that is good news indeed. Surely we will manage to get a glimpse of her some way. And now I must be going. I promised Jill to spend the evening with her.'

'We will walk as far as the flat with you,' said Desmond, 'there might be an ambush, you know. Indeed we might as well pay a call on Miss Devereux, too; what do you say, Tony? We haven't seen her since we came from Wicklow.'

'All serene,' replied his brother, and the trio left the 'Sod' behind them, and proceeded up Dawson Street and across the Green. Before they reached the street where stood Jill's flat they had to pass through a populous thoroughfare, which at this hour—just after six—was crowded with cyclists and pedestrians, going homewards from their day's business.

Suddenly behind them came the roar and rush of military lorries, tearing like furies up the street. There were two of them, both packed tightly with Black-and-Tans, and they drew up outside one of the Private Hotels, which they were about to raid. No one took any outward notice of them—the Dublin people knew better, for a glance in the direction of the lorries meant facing a loaded revolver, which might go off accidentally. But each person passing along the street saw with a brief side glance that the raid was about to be carried out in the usual fashion with which every one was so familiar.

The lorries drew up opposite the house, and before they had even time to slow down completely a number of Black-and-Tans sprang to the pavement and with revolver in hand rushed up the steps and in through the open hotel door. Not only had they revolvers in their hands, but at their hip; their Scotch caps crowned their terrible faces—for terrible indeed they were with drink and ferocity. Jerry, as she passed quickly, with Tony's hand slipped protectingly through her arm, saw them in the hall, where she could also see a large panelled mirror and some statuary. But a second later these were gone, a crash of glass and a volley of oaths proclaiming that the raid had commenced, and yet another house in Dublin was learning how the Crown forces restored Law and Order in Ireland during the Autumn of 1920.

Our three friends did not speak until they came to the end of the street, and were walking in the direction of Jill's flat. Then Anthony, after a keen glance at the girl beside him, said in tones of quiet sympathy:

'You don't like these raids, Jerry? They get on your nerves — don't they?'

'Yes, terribly!' she replied with a little shiver. 'I don't really know why they upset me so much. They are such an every day happening now that surely I should have become used to them, and yet somehow I cannot. It is the same, too, at night. When I hear the lorries tearing past I sit up in bed shaking—literally shaking with fear.'

'That is not like you, Jerry,' said Desmond, looking curiously at her. 'You always have seemed so self-controlled and level-headed, and I never would have thought that you knew the meaning of nerves.'

'I never did until lately,' she said miserably. 'I don't know how it is that I have become such a wretched coward, especially at a time like the present when we need to stand firm, and, above all, never to let ourselves become panicky.'

'Ah! well; I don't know,' said Anthony, 'we can only do our best, and the times we live in are enough to try the nerves of the strongest amongst us. I'm certain, too, that there is no fear of you ever really losing your nerve, or getting into a state of panic—the greater the danger, the quieter and stronger you would become. Of that I am convinced, Jerry, because I know you so well.'

In his own mind Anthony was fairly sure that Geraldine was really suffering from the effects of insufficient nourishment and mental worry. He had read the signs in her pale face and harassed expression, and understood what Life meant to the girl just at that time.

CHAPTER VII

YVONNE SHUFFLES THE CARDS

They arrived at the flat, and toiled up the weary flights of stairs, Geraldine, as Anthony was quick to notice, having to rest several times until they reached Jill's door. As they sounded the quaint Egyptian knocker—picked up at a curio shop by Jill herself—they heard laughter and voices at the other side of the door.

'Someone is with her,' said Geraldine, but even as she spoke the door was flung open and Jill stood on the threshold.

'Oh! Jerry dear; but I am glad to see you! Come in!' and then as her glance strayed beyond and she noticed the twins she cried out: 'Oh! it's Tony and Desmond at last! I thought you were never coming to see me again, and you really don't deserve that I should speak to you at all. But I'm so glad to see you that I must forgive you everything.'

While she was talking she was leading the way into the big, untidy room—studio and living room combined. But untidy though it certainly was it still possessed that indescribable picturesque appearance which always caused one to call it a charming room—as indeed it was in its own Bohemian style.

It seemed at first sight to be empty, but a big chair was drawn up to the fire—which was welcome enough as the evening was chilly—and in its capacious depths a small figure was cosily seated. A little person in a bizarre gown of the style known as Jazz, the material of which was of rich, heavy silk, covered with hand-painted designs of birds and flowers—a most exquisite creation. Her tiny feet in quaint sandals with silver straps were stretched out to the warmth of the fire, and her glorious hair was as usual loosely gathered into a huge coil and fastened with the amber pins. Yvonne Delaunay had returned to Dublin.

Geraldine Moore, as her glance fell upon the dainty picture which this strange little personality made, felt a sudden sinking of the heart, and a queer, but very definite premonition of evil.

'You have met before, I think?' Jill was saying to the twins, and the young fellows greeted Yvonne each in his own way—Desmond with that air of delightful homage which he rendered to all women; Anthony with reserved and rather cold civility. As a matter of fact the Ryans knew Mademoiselle Delaunay very slightly, they had only

happened to meet her a couple of times since that May evening—
now more than three years ago—when they had all been at Firfield
House.

She greeted them in her usual fascinating manner, and Jill and
Geraldine, who both knew her so well—one through affection,
and the other through dislike—realised at once that Yvonne was
going to be very charming to the young men. Knowing how
Yvonne's charm affected most men they quite expected to see the
Ryan twins succumb immediately. In this, however, they were
partly disappointed, or relieved. Desmond certainly was her slave
within the space of ten minutes, but Anthony's coldly courteous
manner never changed. In vain did Mademoiselle Delaunay turn
her lovely, inscrutable eyes in his direction with some appealing
question to 'Monsieur Antoine'. The answer would be given to her
with perfect courtesy, and that was all. Her quaint accent and
gestures, her hundred and one fascinating mannerisms, all were
wasted, thrown away on the quiet, rather stern-faced man, whom
Yvonne ever after in her own mind would designate as 'a perfect
bear'.

But poor Desmond was obsessed, he followed her every look
and smile, listened to her every word. His subjection was complete,
plain for all to see, and Jill and Geraldine during a sudden lull in
their conversation with Anthony, both found themselves gazing at
him in a kind of sorrowful wonder. He was very dear to them both,
in their hearts they knew it, but they had always known, too, that
they would never be dearer to him than friends. But now they
realised with dismay that he was not only lost to them, but to
himself, too, for once let Yvonne Delaunay lift a beckoning finger
and the man who came under the spell of her enchantment had no
mind or will-power left to him.

The two girls looked at him, their hearts heavy within them,
until turning they chanced to meet each other's eyes. Both knew
what was in the other's mind, and they flushed almost guiltily as
the looked away.

Jill began to make coffee, and insisted upon them all having
some, although Geraldine and the Ryans declared that they had
tea only about half-an-hour ago.

'At the "Sod," I suppose?' said their hostess with a whimsical
smile.

'Yes, the "Sod," of course,' said Desmond; 'the most Gaelic place in town.'

'Especially when you can show off your fluent Gaelic on ladies who serve you,' returned Jill, and smiled wickedly as she saw Desmond's flush of embarrassment at Yvonne's lifted eyebrows.

Geraldine came to his rescue.

'The Black-and-Tans were raiding Oliphant's Hotel,' she said; 'they had just arrived when we were passing.'

'Oh! they are always raiding somewhere,' said Jill indifferently as she poured the fragrant coffee into the old china cups. 'It's a wonder they don't get tired of it sometimes.'

'They get tired of it!' cried Desmond. 'Have you no sense, Jill? They will never tire of plunder and loot and murder as long as they are left in this country. Why should they? You know, of course, that they are largely of the criminal class—the outpouring and scum of English jails—and they are simply making their fortunes while they are here. Whatever way events turn out in the future, one thing is certain, and that is that the ruffians who compose the Auxiliary forces here will be able to retire and live a life of ease and plenty when they return to their own shores, whenever that may be, and God send it soon.'

'How very dreadful!' said Yvonne's soft voice beside him—that voice which already seemed to Desmond to hold a wonderful music and sweetness in its liquid notes. 'Poor Ireland! My heart bleeds for her, just as it bleeds for my own poor France. Ah! Monsieur Desmond, what do you think of these so terrible times? Will they soon come to an end?'

'God knows!' he answered, in what for him was a very serious voice—'God knows and He alone! But there is one thing of which you may be certain, Mademoiselle Delaunay, and that is that as long as there is one man or woman alive in Ireland we will fight for our Freedom to the last ditch. We will never give in.'

He had risen to his feet in his hasty fashion, while the impetuous words rushed from his lips, and too moved to sit still he began pacing up and down the studio.

'Have we not suffered long enough yet?' he said. 'Is Heaven deaf to our cries that we have to go on losing the best and bravest of our people day by day? Our men shot or hanged, or savagely murdered in other ways, or hunted from place to place as if they were criminals. Our women left to be both father and mother to the children, and to try, too, in many cases to keep the business or farm going in the face of untold hardship and difficulties. If that was all they had to suffer. But just think for a moment of a midnight raid of drunken Black-and-Tans on a lonely house in the country with only a woman or two to face them! Good God! These are things that a man cannot think of without going mad.'

Jill Devereux was standing behind her little table—coffee pot in hand—gazing at him, a sort of puzzled sadness in her face, and when he paused at length in his restless walk, and went over and stood by the fireplace, leaning his head on his hands, she said:

'Oh! Desmond, don't worry like that. It does no good, and—well! it always seems to be so hopeless. England is bound to conquer in the end. All you red-hot Republicans are only knocking your heads against a stone wall. What's the good of it all?'

'What's the good of it?' echoed Desmond, turning round swiftly, his eyes ablaze. 'Why, Jill, how can you talk like that? Isn't it better to die fighting for our Freedom—for our right to Nationality—than to live as slaves? Isn't that what hundreds of our men are demonstrating day by day? Isn't it just for these ideals and principles that Terence MacSwiney and his brave comrades are starving to death in Brixton Jail at this very hour?'

'Oh! that's the way Jerry talks!' exclaimed Jill impatiently, although her eyes were sympathetic. 'She just goes on exactly like that—all in the same high-flown language.'

'Yes; because she feels the same—she's Irish, too,' replied Desmond, and as he turned towards Geraldine they looked at each other in silence for a moment—the sympathy of kindred aspirations, the possession of a common ideal—of the one Faith and Fatherland—held them bound for a brief fraction of time.

And then Yvonne's voice came gently.

'Oh! yes; Patriotism! The love of one's country. Of all the virtues surely it is the most beautiful.'

Desmond smiled at her, his whole face expressing his admiration, and without saying anything more he returned to his seat at her side. Coffee over they all drew near the fire and conversation took a more personal note. They were all—with the exception of Mademoiselle Delaunay—old and tried friends and spoke freely amongst themselves. Yvonne's presence caused some slight restraint certainly, especially with Anthony and Geraldine, but her wonderful manner and rare tact always caused people to accept her as one of themselves, and in most cases she had a most extraordinary way of seeming to identify herself with others when she wished to do so. Even Geraldine presently found herself talking quite freely before her about her unemployment.

'It is a shame!' cried Jill, 'but try and don't worry, Jerry.'

'No; don't worry,' echoed Desmond. 'You are sure to get something soon.'

'Oh! I'm tired of hearing that,' cried Geraldine. 'Here I am now since June and it's the end of September and nothing has turned up, and dear knows I have left no stone unturned. The advertisements I have answered, the people I have interviewed, the long tramps I have gone in search of work. It really seems to me sometimes that it is the people who don't take any trouble to look for jobs that get them.'

'What a pity that your Committee had to give up the work,' said Yvonne, 'and it must be hard to get another position like that. Such work is scarce just now—is it not so?'

'Oh! yes,' said Geraldine wearily. 'A good many of the Government grants have been withdrawn and everything is in a state of chaos.'

'It is so hard for a trained nurse to get other work for which she would be suitable,' continued Yvonne, adding, 'Would you go as a District Nurse, Miss Moore? To do general nursing, I mean, amongst the people?'

Geraldine's face lit up.

'Oh! I should just think so,' she cried. 'I would take any kind of work. I was District Nurse before and would just love to have such a position again.'

'Well! perhaps I can help you,' said Yvonne with a smile.

'Oh! Mademoiselle Delaunay, if you could,' breathed Geraldine, all her soul in her eyes. She would never, never think unkindly of Yvonne again if only she helped her now.

'Eh bien!' said that little person. 'I have a great friend, a Lady Selby Jones, with whom I worked in France; she was a VAD there. Her husband made a big, big fortune. Oh! such heaps and heaps of money she has,' with pretty fingers outspread and eyes wide open. 'I met her in London last week and we had a long talk. She told me then that she was going to start a village nurse for the district in which she lives, and asked if I knew of a really nice nurse who would suit.'

She paused and glanced swiftly around, and although her look seemed to be quite casual, she read as an open book, in that brief second of time, the faces of all those around her.

All the expectant hope was gone from Geraldine. She looked paler and sadder than ever now that those hopes were dashed to the ground.

'But what is it?' asked Yvonne, as though in surprise. 'You do not look pleased and I thought you said that you would like the work?'

'She did not know that it would be in England,' replied Desmond, with a quick look of comprehension at Geraldine.

'Yes; she would not care to work there,' said Jill, adding to Geraldine. 'All the same, old girl, if I was you I would think twice before refusing.'

'No; no,' cried Geraldine. 'I could not work in England. How could I? I would have no interest in my work and no love of it. To be alone there amongst strangers—enemies!'

Yvonne did not reply for a moment, she only lifted her eyes and looked hard at Geraldine, but the girl, although she tried to read the real meaning which she was certain they held, found that now, as ever, those strange eyes were still inscrutable and revealed nothing.

'I could not go to England,' she said again, and then was miserably silent.

'Would you not think it over?' asked Yvonne softly. 'The district is in Berkshire, the salary is £140 a year, and a furnished cottage and garden goes with it. It is a charming old world village—like an old-fashioned picture—and the work would not be hard. Would you not take it until something opens up for you here? I do not want to influence you, but surely for a time—.'

'Yes; Jerry, for a time,' cried Jill. 'Can you not take temporary duty anywhere, and you are supposed'—with a little laugh—'as a Christian to nurse and love your enemies. Surely you are not going to be so insular and narrow-minded as to refuse such an offer?'

Geraldine was silent, gazing before her into the heart of the leaping flames. The temptation to accept Yvonne's offer was very great. £140 a year and rent free. It seemed riches untold to the girl who for the past three months had pinched and scraped and 'done without' until all her happy spirits, all her joyous outlook on life, all her brave independence, were gone. There remained only the sordid problem of food and drink and clothes. Clothes! even as she thought thus she could feel where her shoe was broken at the side.

Broken shoes! That last pitiful signpost on poverty's high road.

She lifted her head suddenly and looked across at Yvonne. 'I'll think it over,' she said, a note of desperation in her voice.

'Bien! bien! But I am glad,' and Yvonne clasped her hands with one of her expressive gestures. 'That is what you people call grand! is it not? And after all, Chérie, you need not stay if you do not like it. A day's journey only. Pouf! What is that? Not worth speaking about.'

'Well! I think it is certainly sensible of you to think it over,' said Jill. 'And if I was in your place I should certainly take it *pro tem*. As Yvonne says, you can leave when you like and a day will bring you home again.'

The Ryans had not spoken, and Geraldine turned towards them. They were both regarding her intently. Desmond in open surprise, and Anthony with a keen, but non-commital look.

'What do you think of it?' she asked.

'Don't go!' said Desmond hotly. 'Good Heavens, Jerry, how could you even be civil to the English now—at this time—after all the happenings we have seen and known about? And as their nurse you would have to be so much with them, so intimate.'

She did not answer him, but her eyes turned to Anthony.

'Think over it well,' was the answer he gave to her mute appeal, 'and pray over it, too, before you decide. Don't let your worries over money or ways and means influence you in the least—we will see that it's put right for you. Don't be in a hurry, and talk it over with me again before you finally decide.'

Yvonne had raised her eyes and was looking at him. For once her feelings betrayed her—an almost unheard of thing with her—so that Anthony glancing at her was surprised, and for the moment puzzled, to catch her gazing at him with an expression that was one of baffled fury. Almost before he could be certain that he had seen aright, she had turned away and was speaking to Jill in her usual gentle voice, and Anthony was inclined to believe that he must have imagined the look which for a second had seemed to flash out at him from her green-grey eyes.

Just then there was a knock at the door and Jill went to open it.

'Peter!' she cried, when she recognised the man who stood on the threshold. 'Come in! Come in! You are a sight for sore eyes. How delightful it is that you came tonight—here are Tony and Desmond before you—I know you are old pals. But now let me see—Jerry, have you met Dr O'Connor?' Geraldine shook her head. She was still feeling too miserably depressed and unsettled to care about anyone or anything, and so glancing at him carelessly she was about to bow distantly when something in the expression of the man arrested her attention, and she found herself gazing at him intently, almost rudely.

Dr Peter O'Connor was a tall, clean-shaven man of about five and thirty. He had keen grey eyes and a clear cut face with a very determined jaw. Iron resolution was written plainly on his every feature, but another quality was there, too, a magnetic personality which seemed to flow from the man and to influence in a greater or less degree all those with whom he came in contact. His eyes, too, had a habit of reading one's thoughts in a manner which at times was rather disconcerting. Those eyes of his were like steel gimlets when he was probing a mystery—a favourite pastime with him—or confronting an evildoer, but they could be very kind at times and were so now when he took Geraldine's hand in his own and gave it a cordial grasp. Not one to stand on ceremony, Dr Peter O'Connor, when he wished to be friends.

'I am glad to meet you, Miss Moore,' he said. 'I have so often heard these boys'—with a backward nod towards the twins—'speak of you that I seem to know you already.'

To her intense surprise Geraldine felt a sudden glow of well-being and hope, it was as though his hand clasp had in some extraordinary way given her help and made life worth living again.

She murmured a reply with shining eyes, and wondered at herself.

But Jill was speaking.

'I don't think you have met Dr O'Connor, Yvonne, have you?—Dr Peter O'Connor—Mademoiselle Delaunay.'

'Pardon me,' interposed the doctor, quietly, 'but Mademoiselle Delaunay and myself have met before. Is it not so, Mademoiselle?'

Yvonne inclined her head, but she did not speak for just a fraction of time, and her face seemed suddenly more colourless even than usual and perfectly expressionless like an alabaster mask. Her eyes were on the ground when she presently replied in a low voice:

'Dr O'Connor is too kind to remember such an unworthy person as my poor self, especially as we met but once, I think?'

Then her eyes were lifted to his face—that face which was just as inscrutable as her own—and Dr O'Connor bowed low as he replied:

'Yes; once only, Mademoiselle, but the occasion as far as I can recollect was somewhat worthy of remembrance.'

Neither had offered to shake hands, and the doctor left her now and went to talk to the twins. The few words between them had been spoken so quietly, and both were so self-possessed and controlled, that only Geraldine had noticed the little bye-play.

The girl's senses that night seemed abnormally acute and it appeared to her almost as if she knew and comprehended the veiled enmity between Peter O'Connor and Yvonne Delaunay. Strange to say, she was not puzzled over it, she accepted it as a fact—a fact that it seemed to her she must have known before in some dim age of the past. She was conscious of one dominant wish and desire at the present moment, and that was to get home and get to bed. She was dead tired—tired physically and mentally, and as she had been drawing for some time now on her reserve forces of strength and will power, Nature was beginning to look for compensation and was presenting her bill of costs—a bill which is always paid.

Geraldine rose to her feet.

'I'm rather tired, Jill,' she said; 'if you will excuse me I think I'll go home.'

'Yes; indeed, and we must follow your example,' said Anthony; 'it's nearly nine o'clock and I have a good bit of work to get through before I turn in.'

The twins stood up and Dr O'Connor with them.

'Ah! Peter; surely you won't go?' cried Jill. 'Why, you have only just arrived. And I wanted you to become better acquainted with Mademoiselle Delaunay.'

'A pleasure which I hope is only postponed,' returned the doctor, his grey eyes darting towards Yvonne's chair with a strange expression in their depths, 'but now I have a case to visit so you must forgive me, Jill, if I run away.'

'Well, if you must, I suppose there is no more to be said.'

'That's right, Jill. You and I are too old friends for you to mind what I do, and as to Mademoiselle Delaunay,' bowing in her direction with almost exaggerated deference, 'as I said before, the pleasure of a better acquaintance between us is but postponed for a short while.'

'And a pleasure I am sure it will be, Monsieur,' replied Yvonne in her softest voice. 'Something tells me that you and I will see much of each other in the future.'

Their eyes met for a moment in cold, expressionless scrutiny, and the doctor bowed again.

'I shall indeed look forward to our next meeting, Mademoiselle,' he said quietly.

Then Geraldine, who had been slipping on her coat—and thinking how badly she needed a new one—said she was ready. Good-nights were said—Yvonne softly whispering to Geraldine as they shook hands, 'You will think it over that, won't you, Chérie?'— and the three men and the girl went down the deep stairway and out into the night. Geraldine's lodging was only about ten minutes' walk from Jill's abode, and they were lucky enough to escape raids or ambushes.

'Take care of yourself, Jerry; you look pretty seedy,' said Desmond, as they shook hands with her at the little gate which opened on to a flagged pathway, a few yards in length, on either side of which were minute flower-beds, railed in, and carefully tended by Mrs Brennan's poor crippled hands when the rheumatism left her any power in them.

'Oh! I'm all right,' replied the girl hastily; 'a bit tired, that's all, and worried.'

'Don't worry,' said Anthony; 'things will come right for you, Jerry, don't despair. Look here, I want you to come to our office tomorrow about eleven and talk everything over—will you?'

'Yes, of course I will, Tony, and thanks a hundred times,' she replied, as she turned to give her hand to Dr O'Connor.

'Good-night, *and sleep well*,' he said. He held her hand for a moment and again she had the curious sense of well-being and peace, and then his footsteps and those of the twins were dying away down the quiet suburban road.

'I hope I will sleep!' thought Geraldine, as she fitted her latchkey in the door, for she was dreading another of her sleepless nights.

'Wipe your boots! Wipe your boots!' screamed Don Juan from the kitchen regions, while Fluff tore along the narrow passage all fussy anxiety to welcome her home. He was a terribly fussy dog, and seemed to imagine that if he did not personally overlook the routine of the household everything would go wrong. 'Home at last! I was really getting anxious about you,' he was now saying quite plainly, and Geraldine, who always understood him, stooped and patted him as she said, 'Yes; I'm back, Fluff, but so tired.'

Mrs Brennan called to know if she wanted anything, or would she come down to the kitchen for a while, but the girl only said that she was very tired and was going to bed.

She literally crawled up to her room, said a prayer, undressed anyhow, and slipped into bed. She was afraid that she would not sleep—she had been suffering terribly from insomnia of late—and tonight, on account of the new problem which confronted her about this English position, she had been sure that her brain would now allow her to rest. However, to her great surprise no sooner was she in bed than she began to feel a drowsy content. Like a gentle but firm whisper she seemed to hear again the words, 'Good-night, and sleep well!' and even as she wondered her tired eyes closed and she slept.

*   *   *

Yvonne Delaunay was sitting before the fire in her own flat several hours later. Her glorious hair hung in two great plaits, and an embroidered kimono was thrown over her crêpe-de-Chine nightdress. She sat and stared fixedly into the cheerful blaze, and so rigidly immovable was she as she sat in the big armchair which, with her usual cat-like love of warmth, she had drawn close to the fire, that she looked like some rare and beautiful piece of statuary.

But if her body was quiet her brain was working—and working at high pressure, for Yvonne had a game to play and the stakes were high, so high that to even contemplate that it might be a losing game was very terrible. It was a game she had often played before, and played with such consummate skill that she was recognised by very great men—men whose names were known in every Court of Europe—as one of their best players.

But tonight when she had made the first move in a game which she had been almost certain of winning she had discovered that it was going to be a very difficult one, for she had not even made the first trick, but on the contrary was in danger of losing it. So she had to shuffle the cards again and plan how she might best play them.

The cards were men and women, and if she could only hold them in her hand and play them herself the game would be hers. But they must not know that they were being played by her, and she must play them, too, unknowingly, against each other. They were a strong hand and if allowed to be played by her enemies she would lose every trick, but if she could only play them as she wished—each against the other, and all for her own ends—then indeed the game was won.

And so she surveyed the cards—those who had been with her in Jill's flat, and looked at them one by one according to their playing value.

First the ace—and that card, strange to say, she allocated at once to Dr Peter O'Connor. His appearance had been a shock to her—she had been told that he was in America, and she wondered if he had felt the same at meeting her. Well! they knew each other thoroughly, that was one sure thing, and so knowing him she called him the Ace.

Then the King was Anthony Ryan, a King whom she detested with all her heart; whom she knew instinctively that she would have good cause both to hate and fear before long, especially if the Ace continued in his neighbourhood.

And the Queen—Geraldine Moore. Yes, she was a valuable card—sincere, true, honest to the core of her loving heart, and in the cause of her country would hesitate at nothing. But she was almost disposed of—she had tried to win a trick with her that night, but had been foiled by the King, and now the Ace was there. How would it go? That Ace again. Yet bah! what could he do? The girl was nearly starving; she would have to take the work in England, and then one of the cards would be gone.

And then—the Knave? Her expression changed for a moment and the stern look relaxed. 'The Knave of Hearts!' she murmured to herself with a little smile. No trouble need be feared from him anyway, the poor Knave of Hearts would always take any trick which it was in his power to win—for her.

And the next and last card—the Ten. Jill Devereux, of course. And in this Yvonne Delaunay showed her acute perception, for in their long talks together Jill had constantly professed her neutrality in regard to the cause of Irish Freedom—and it was an honest profession, for she believed in it herself. But Yvonne, probing deeper with her wonderful knowledge of the human heart knew that Jill's neutrality was only a veneer, underneath which was a very real love for the land of her adoption. Besides there was her affection for Geraldine and the Ryans and other Irish friends. Yea; she was a Ten in value—if not more—and so must be played carefully, but Yvonne's own influence over her would count for much, so that she might not be any trouble. But Yvonne was far from sure about her, one never knew how a personality like Jill's would act under certain unforeseen circumstances.

She sighed and moved in her chair, flinging back her long plaits impatiently.

'With luck the Queen will go almost at once,' she decided. 'The Knave is mine, body and soul, or will be very shortly—the Ten I will play with care. There remains then the Ace and the King—the two strongest cards and most to be feared. If I could remove them from my path the game was won.' She rose and went over to the telephone. It was after two o'clock by this, and there was some delay before she was put on to the number for which she had asked. Then:

'Is that Mr Chester?' and as the answer came through—'Yes; it is I. Yes; very important. I am coming round to your place at six-thirty this morning. I suppose that will be all right?'

The answer came and she rang off, stretching her arms wearily above her head as she turned from the instrument. She looked tired, almost haggard, and suddenly much older than the girlish individual whom Jill and her friends thought they knew so well.

'Eh! bien!' she murmured; 'now to lie down for a couple of hours—and I think the morning will dispose of the King anyway—and perhaps of the Ace, too.'

But the Fates who weave the threads of our destiny knew better than Yvonne, and smiled grimly to themselves as the web passed back and forth through their ever moving hands.

CHAPTER VIII

DR PETER O'CONNOR TAKES A HAND

The Ryans had their offices in one of the streets off Dame Street. They had not only two rooms on the second floor, used as an outer and private office, but they also rented three rooms at the top of the house for a bedroom, sittingroom, and kitchen—in which last apartment, Mrs Pell, the charwoman who 'did for them'—in more senses than one—reigned for several hours of each day.

'Will you walk part of the way with us?' asked Anthony when they had parted from Geraldine, 'or must you go to your patient at once?'

'I have no patient to see,' replied Dr O'Connor coolly, 'but I want to have a talk with you two, and if you don't mind we will take the tram at the corner here and I'll come to Elton Street with you.'

The Ryans and Peter O'Connor were very old friends—a friendship which dated back to their school-days—when Peter, one of the important seniors, had been condescendingly kind to the twins—then very small and junior. The friendship had continued and become stronger and deeper as the years went by, and especially was this so now when common hopes and common danger bound them more closely together, for like themselves Dr O'Connor was deeply involved in the Sinn Féin movement. Tonight the twins had guessed by his manner that it was in relation to something of importance in this connection that he had wished to see them.

'Were you looking for us tonight, Peter?' asked Desmond, as they stood a moment waiting for the tram.

'No; but I intended to call and see you later. It was just a bit of luck that I met you at Jill's studio. I was rather surprised, too—but we will talk of that again—here's the tram.'

Arriving at Elton Street, Anthony fitted his key in the door, and they stepped into the dark hallway. With the exception of the Ryans no one else was in the house at night, but during the day it was crowded, for it was a net-work of offices. It had the stuffy, dusty atmosphere common to such places, but the three men as they mounted the several flights of stairs by the help of Desmond's electric torch, were quite oblivious of the atmosphere—their minds had other things to think about.

Anthony switched on the light in the sittingroom, which was a comfortable, untidy 'man's room,' furnished with odds and ends from Firfield House, and most of the furniture, although shabby and uncared for, was still valuable.

The fire was set in the grate, and Mrs Pell had left the tea things ready on the table, for she knew the twins often sat up late, smoking, talking, and drinking tea—the only stimulant they allowed themselves. The good lady had evidently gone home; her hours 'on duty,' as she would say, were rather erratic—some days she would arrive early in the morning before the twins were awake, when they would be aroused by a noise in the kitchen as though she were engaged in herculean tasks. On these occasions she would get their breakfast and make a great fuss of waiting on them. But on other days they would not see her until evening, when she would enter as quietly as possible and start her work in silence. This meant, as the boys knew well, that she had been 'on it' the night before, for an over indulgence in alcoholic stimulants was Mrs Pell's great drawback. She was a strange character in many ways, and the twins, although used to her peculiar characteristics— she had been their 'char lady' for nearly six years—often found her still an unsolved enigma. She was the widow of a Sergeant in the British Army, whom she had married 'on the strength', as she was very careful to explain, and with him she had been in many parts of the world, and could talk of India and Malta and 'Gib.' with the greatest aplomb. She had a fund of anecdotes but a most unique way of relating them, as she had an extraordinary habit of making use of the wrong word if it happened to resemble, in sound, the one she really meant, and this custom of hers at times made for queer results. Desmond called it—'Mrs Pell's Esperanto'.

She had no pension from the British Government, as her husband, towards the end of his service, had unluckily taken to drink, and had been found out several times robbing the canteen where he was employed. The authorities overlooked it and forgave him as long as they could, but at last he was discharged in disgrace and died soon afterwards. His widow had evidently been deeply attached to him, and considered that he had been very badly treated. She never let the poor man rest, for she referred to him constantly in her conversation—indeed the twins—and Jill Devereux, whom she also 'obliged' with an odd day—felt that they knew 'Mr P,' by which title Mrs Pell always spoke of him, quite intimately, and would hardly have been surprised had he strolled in to see them some day in the wake of his faithful spouse.

Mrs Pell never took any part in the politics of the day, beyond speaking of them in what she described as 'general broad terms,' and her employers did not know what her real opinions were, or indeed if she had any. She had, however, been always faithful to the twins, and during their frequent periods away from the office they always left the key with her, knowing that she would look after the place—for no matter how hard she might be drinking she was strictly honest and always managed also in some strange fashion to keep her wits about her during her sober intervals and to get through whatever work she had in hand. Besides using words in their wrong places, she also never made use of a small word if she could find a long one, and had several pet phrases and proverbs which she brought into most of her remarks. She had a great regard and respect for Anthony, of whom, however, she stood in some slight awe, but Desmond she worshipped with a blind devotion and honestly believed that his equal among young men was yet to be found. It was indeed a standing joke amongst his friends that 'Mr P's' ghost would visit him some evening and demand satisfaction.

'Light the fire, boys,' said the doctor, as he sank into an arm chair, 'this is going to be a lengthy sitting, and in view of the curfew arrangements of our benevolent rulers I suppose you can give me a shake-down for a few hours later on.'

'Of course we can, old chap,' said Anthony as he put a match to the fire; 'only too delighted. We have two beds, you know, and a sofa in case of an emergency.'

Then as the fire blazed up cheerily he sat back in his chair and remarked:

'But I must say I was surprised to see you this evening. When did you return from America, if one may ask so much?'

O'Connor laughed. 'America' was a large-sized cottage, situated on the slopes of the Dublin mountains, and used, as required, by the 'boys' for many purposes, and was especially useful when one of their number wished to retire into private life for a time.

'I only came in last night,' he replied. 'I had to see you two, and some of the others also.'

'But you don't want to get run in—especially now when we have so much in hand,' interposed Desmond. 'Was it wise, Peter, to' show yourself again so openly? I know, of course, that there is no definite charge against you, but that counts for nothing these times. If they want you they will take you—if they can.'

'Ah! if they can!' answered his friend, 'but I don't mean to let them if I can prevent it, as I am wanted where I am at present. But all the same I had no idea when I went to Jill's flat that I would be running straight into the enemy.'

'The enemy! At Jill's. What on earth do you mean?' cried Desmond, while Anthony sat up, and taking his pipe from his mouth stared in wonder at his friend.

'Well! what else but an enemy can I call that Delaunay woman?' said Dr O'Connor. 'For Heaven's sake tell me how long you have known her and is she staying in Dublin, and, if so, where? Tell me all you know about her, for she is a terrible menace to us at the present time.'

Desmond sprang to his feet, his face flushing.

'You are making some great mistake, Peter,' he exclaimed. 'You cannot possibly be speaking of Mademoiselle Delaunay—an innocent young girl like that?'

He was interrupted by the doctor breaking into a laugh—a laugh that was genuine enough although it was tinged with bitterness. But he ceased to laugh when he saw Desmond's expression, and suddenly realised with that wonderful intuition of his—which was as sure as a woman's—that part of the work which Yvonne Delaunay had set out to do was already accomplished. Even as he sat up in his chair and stretched out his hand to Desmond he was wondering if he would be able to undo that work—or was it beyond his power?

'Desmond,' he said, in quiet, serious tones; 'dear boy, listen to me. Do you think I don't know what I am talking about? That woman—.'

'Speak respectfully of Mademoiselle Delaunay,' cried the boy, wrenching his hand away. 'I refuse to listen if you speak like that! Not that I mind what you may say,' he added, 'because I know, of course, that it is all some—some queer mistake.'

'No; I am making no mistake, Desmond,' replied the other. 'That person, of whom you appear to think so highly, is a well-known agent of the British Secret Service in this country.'

'Good God!' exclaimed Anthony. 'And she there—in Jill's flat—her chosen friend. What may we not have unwittingly betrayed to her? Why, we took her for granted—at least I never felt drawn towards her—but the others looked upon her almost as one of themselves, she seemed so sympathetic, so—.'

Dr O'Connor swung round to him.

'What exactly have you talked about before her?' he asked. 'Especially this evening—can you remember?'

Anthony straightened himself, and sat forward frowning, as he tried to recollect all that had passed in the flat, but before he could speak Desmond had interrupted impetuously.

'I don't believe a word of it; not that I blame you, Peter, or mean that you don't think you are speaking the truth, but you are under a wrong impression. It is some other woman—someone like Yvonne Delaunay of whom you are thinking.'

'Are there many like her, do you think?' asked the doctor. 'I, for one, would pray God forbid!' he added in an undertone, and then continuing, 'There is her name, too, the same.'

'Oh! Delaunay is not an uncommon name in France,' replied Desmond, adding angrily, 'Why, man, you must know you are making a mistake. As if that young girl, so lovely, so good, could be a—spy! Oh! God; it is unthinkable.'

'Sit down, Desmond; sit down,' said his brother. 'It is not likely that Peter would make a mistake in such a matter. However, he can tell us how he knows her, and explain matters fully.'

'I don't care a damn what he explains, or what he thinks he knows,' replied Desmond hotly. 'I know that it is all a terrible mistake. But let him tell his yarn,' and he sat back in his chair, puffing nervously at a pipe that had long ago gone out.

'Well! to begin with,' said Peter, 'Mademoiselle Delaunay is not the young girl that you imagine, Desmond. She is older than yourself, being several years over thirty, and she is one of the cleverest spies that the British Government employ. She does the innocent, youthful stunt, and her appearance and wonderful acting are so much in her favour that her methods are nearly always successful. She worked for the British during the war in Europe and is a very clever linguist, although to what nationality she really belongs I cannot tell you. I believe she says she is half French and half Russian and that is very likely one of the few truths which she speaks. I was simply horrified for the moment when I saw her tonight, as I realised at once what her presence in this country meant.'

'Has she ever had any hand in Irish affairs before, do you know?' asked Anthony.

'Yes. Do you remember, Tony, the case of poor Larry O'Brien, who was arrested in London three months ago for carrying seditious literature around?'

Anthony nodded.

'Yes; I knew the chap,' he said; 'quite a boy—about nineteen, I think. Got a long term, didn't he?'

'Yes; several years, an exceptionally severe sentence. Well! I happen to know from one of our agents over there that he owed his arrest to Yvonne Delaunay. He got under her influence, became infatuated, and that was the result.'

'Did you meet her yourself before tonight, or do you only know her through others?' asked Anthony.

'We met in London on one memorable occasion,' was the reply. 'And I reminded her of it, too, although,' with a grim smile, 'she was not inclined to recognise me. But I gave her no option.'

'And when and where was it that you imagined you saw her before?' inquired Desmond sarcastically.

'Oh! I didn't imagine it at all, of that I can assure you, my boy,' returned the doctor quietly. 'I met her in London at one of our meeting places there. She had posed for several months as a friend of Ireland and had so fascinated some of the members, both men and women, that they had trusted her implicitly. I was there for the first time that night, having just arrived from Liverpool. Although I had never seen her before, and knew nothing whatever about her, yet every instinct I possess warned me against her. That very night the premises were raided; some of us, as you know, escaped, including yours truly. But others were taken, a quantity of ammunition and other stuff was discovered—the searchers walking straight to the hiding places—and those who were arrested got penal servitude for long periods. Mademoiselle Delaunay seemed to melt away into air when the raiders entered; she certainly passed out easily and was never seen or heard of again by those whose friend she was supposed to be. I put the affair into the hands of some of our Secret Service people and gleaned the information which I have given to you. You see now that we have already got something for which we have to thank—and remember, Mademoiselle Yvonne Delaunay.'

'It's a lie—an infernal lie!' cried Desmond fiercely. 'I don't—I won't believe a word of it. Oh! it couldn't be true,' he added miserably, and buried his face in his hands.

Anthony and Peter glanced at each other significantly, and for a few moments silence reigned. Then Anthony went over to his twin and put his hand on his shoulder.

'Pull yourself together, old man!' he said, 'and don't be an idiot. What Peter tells us is rather serious and we have to face the facts now and see how they concern ourselves. This woman may prove a real danger and—.'

'Then you believe it, too,' exclaimed Desmond, raising his head. 'It's not like you, Tony, to judge so hastily and without hearing the other side.'

'Peter's word is enough for me,' replied his brother. 'And it ought to be enough for you, too, Desmond,' he added, a rather stern inflection creeping into his voice. 'Surely you are not putting the word of a chance acquaintance before that of a life-long friend like Peter. Just because she has managed to fascinate you with her clever acting and mannerisms.'

'Well! don't argue any more now,' interposed Peter; 'there is your safety to be thought of, and if I know Yvonne Delaunay at all—and I think I have some slight acquaintance with her methods—she will not let the grass grow under her feet. Tell me now exactly, Tony, what matters were spoken about in her presence tonight.'

Anthony told him word for word all that he could remember, while Desmond sat, in sullen silence, gazing sombrely into the fire, perhaps seeing there the bewitching little being who had cast such a spell on him. In his eyes she had seemed so innocent and guileless—so altogether wonderful in her girlish loveliness—and now he was told that she was neither young nor innocent, but a woman of the world and no girl—and most terrible of all, she was that basest of all creatures in the eyes of an honourable man—a Spy!

But the other two were talking and scraps of their conversation fell upon his ears.

'Anyway it is quite evident that she wants Miss Moore out of the way for a while,' Peter O'Connor was saying. 'That explains the offer of work in England.'

'Well! we must not let her go,' said Anthony.

'She won't go,' replied the doctor, 'But neither you nor I will have to move in the matter. She won't go because she won't be able. She is going to be rather ill—and soon, too.'

'How on earth do you know that?' asked Anthony. 'Really, Peter, you are becoming more of a Sherlock Holmes every day.'

'It doesn't need much of a Sherlock Holmes for any kind of medical man to see that the girl is on the verge of a physical and nervous breakdown—a complete collapse,' replied O'Connor. 'She has been half-starved and worried beyond her powers of endurance, and lately she has not been sleeping. However, she will sleep tonight—I saw to that.'

'Your rotten hypnotism again, I suppose,' cried Desmond, as he shot an angry glance at the doctor. 'It's a pity that you couldn't hypnotise some sense into yourself instead of filling your own brain and other people's with a lot of rubbish.'

'Hypnotism—or suggestion—is very far removed from nonsense,' said Dr O'Connor; 'when used properly it is now recognised by the faculty as of great value in the treatment of many diseases. It is likely in the near future that suggestion and psycho-analysis will largely take the place of drugs. However, neither of you want a medical lecture, but there is one bit of advice which you must follow and that is to take a little trip to America for a while until we see how events will shape themselves. You can tell Mrs Pell that you are going down to Wicklow again, and this tale she will, of course, repeat to any callers—undesirable or otherwise. The fewer who know your real destination the better—indeed beyond ourselves and a couple of the boys I would tell no one.'

'I never heard of such ridiculous nonsense in my life,' cried Desmond, impatiently. 'Do you mean to tell me, Tony, that you seriously contemplate running off to the mountains just because Peter imagines—.'

'Be sensible, Desmond,' replied his brother. 'It is always best to be on the safe side these times. And if, as you think, Peter is mistaken—well! it will be no harm to go to the cottage for a week or so. While on the other hand if he should be right—as I must confess I myself believe—then we will probably escape arrest.'

'I don't think that I will go with you at all,' said his brother, his voice full of sullen defiance.

'Oh! yes, you will,' replied Anthony, very quietly. 'Please don't forget that I am your superior officer.'

Desmond had risen to his feet and for a moment he stood looking down at his twin with angry eyes. Then Anthony suddenly smiled up at him—the dear, beloved smile which made his face so charming—and said, 'Go now, like a good fellow, and bring in the kettle; we will all be the better for a cup of tea!'

For a second Desmond stood irresolute, and then he smiled back and raising his hand to the salute—the smile turning to a broad grin—he departed to the kitchen regions to forage for the kettle, which Mrs Pell had a habit of depositing in a different place every night.

'Hard hit,' said Peter significantly, in a low voice.

'Oh! he will get over it in no time,' replied Anthony. 'That is Desmond's way—sure he is always falling in and out of love—it's his greatest failing, and a constant source both of annoyance and amusement to myself. Especially when, as sometimes happens, I meet his temporary best girl when he is not with me, and she, thinking of course that I am he, throws herself figuratively into my arms. The explanations that have to follow are sometimes confoundedly awkward.'

Peter laughed but looked grave almost immediately as he said, 'This is no fleeting fancy, Tony. I'm afraid it's a more serious business than usual, and our only hope is to get him away and keep an eye on him, too. That woman's power when she chooses to exercise it over a man is simply tremendous. Desmond would be wax in her hands.'

'Good Heavens! Peter; you don't mean—.'

'Hush! here he is,' said the doctor softly.

'Found at last!' cried Desmond, entering with the kettle in his hand. 'I ran it to earth at last—in the clothes basket! Mrs P must surely be "on it" again.'

He appeared to be his old debonair self once more but both men found themselves furtively watching him with a nameless fear and dread.

'Come now,' said Anthony; 'and while the kettle is on the fire let us discuss our plans for the morrow.'

*   *   *

'Mr Chester expects me, I think?'

Yvonne Delaunay, closely veiled and wrapped in a great fur coat, stood at the door of 'Mr Chester's' flat a few minutes after six-thirty the following morning.

'Yes, Madam. Mr Chester gave orders that you were to be admitted at once. Please come this way.' And the perfectly trained manservant preceded her along the richly carpeted passage and knocked at a door.

'Come in!' called a languid, rather soft voice, and as the door was flung respectfully open for her Yvonne stepped into the room where the man whom she had come to see at such an early hour was already awaiting her.

'Mr Chester'—or to give him his real name, Ronald Hammond—was sitting attired in a beflowered dressing-gown before a blazing fire in a room which spelt the last word in luxurious comfort. He was a sleek, dark, and rather effeminate young man in the early thirties, with a clever face. He generally tried to hide its cleverness under a mask of lazy indifference, as this particular pose suited his 'profession' better, but at the present moment there was no need of any such pretence, so that the glance he gave Yvonne from his dark eyes was keen enough to almost read her thoughts.

'Coffee—Greggs,' he said then, and rose to greet her.

'Thank Heaven you have such a fire, Ron!' she cried, as she sank into the chair he wheeled forward for her. 'I am half-frozen coming out so early.'

'Yes; it must be something important that would bring a pussy cat like you out of your warm bed at this hour,' said the man; 'but let me unfasten your cloak for you—you will be more comfortable. Ah! here comes the coffee. That is all I shall require, Greggs, and I am not to be disturbed by anyone.'

'Very good, sir.'

The door closed noiselessly after the man, and Yvonne holding out her hands to the blaze gave a little sigh of relief, partly at the warmth which she loved so much, and partly that she could now speak freely. Hammond poured out a cup of coffee and handed it to her, placed cigarettes and matches on the table, then lay back in his chair, and said in his usual soft drawl:

'Eh! bien; ma belle! what have you to report?' For the moment she did not speak—only drank a little coffee and stared at the fire. Then she put down her cup and looked across at the man.

'Ronald,' she said; 'Peter O'Connor is back in Dublin.'

There was silence while one might count twenty—then, 'The devil!' he said, very softly, adding a moment later, 'Go on, where did you meet him? Did he recognise you?'

'I met him at Jill Devereux's. It seems he is an old friend. How is it you did not know this and warn me to be on my guard? And he did recognise me! I knew he would and I tried to bluff—to pretend not to remember him, but he claimed acquaintance at once—you know his way. He can read one's thoughts—even mine! I believe he is the fiend himself sometimes. I have heard so much about him and he seems to have some extraordinary power over people. He is the only man, Ron, that I ever feared.'

Then rapidly, using her hands expressively, and her eyes no longer inscrutable, but wide awake and full of a strange anxiety, she told the history of the previous evening in Jill's flat, and Ronald Hammond sat and listened without speaking while he smoked numberless cigarettes of the particular Turkish blend which he favoured. She had spoken in French, for although she knew English so perfectly, she often lapsed into the other tongue in moments of excitement or mental strain, and Ronald, whose French was excellent, answered her in the same tongue.

'This man O'Connor is, as you say, dangerous,' he said. 'I do not think he is in the Secret Service of Sinn Féin himself—of that I could never make absolutely certain—but if not he is connected in some way with its members and knows them well. Our people have had their eye on him for some time past but have not been able to locate him.'

'But was he not in America—at least so I heard?'

'He was not in America,' replied Hammond; 'he has been in this country since he returned from London six months ago—of that I am assured—but where he was I do not know. They have a hiding place somewhere near Dublin to which they can retire when they like, but we have not been able so far to discover its whereabouts. That would be a job for you, Yvonne; what would you say?'

'I will find out quickly enough for you, my friend,' said the woman, as she lit a cigarette; 'but first you must remove this O'Connor and—and Anthony Ryan from my path. They block my way—they cross me always—always.'

'We had intended to arrest them all, but not immediately,' replied Hammond. 'Have you forgotten the papers, Yvonne, which are in the Ryans' possession? We must obtain those first. Surely you have not forgotten your mission?'

'No; no,' she cried eagerly. 'I have not forgotten—I will get the papers for you—pouf! as easy as possible. But first you must arrest the doctor and Anthony Ryan—they are the ace and king against me in this game and I fear them.'

'As superstitious as ever! But if I give orders for the arrest of O'Connor and the Ryans now how will you discover where the papers are? And those papers will give us very valuable information—names, hiding places, amount of stuff, etc. How then if the Ryans are imprisoned can you get these?'

'Anthony Ryan, I said; Desmond is not to be arrested,' she replied.

The other turned and looked at her, roused for a moment from his languid pose. Then comprehension dawned upon him.

'Oh! so that is your game, is it?' he said, with a lazy smile. 'Samson and Delilah stunt again, eh what? Don't you think it's a bit risky—you know the stuff these bally Sinn Féiners are made of.'

'I am willing to take the risk,' she said. 'Give orders for the arrest of Dr O'Connor and Anthony Ryan and I'll have the papers for you in a few weeks, perhaps sooner.'

'You seem very sure of your power to charm still,' said Hammond. 'Suppose for a change that this Irishman refuses to come into your net?'

She looked at him and smiled—a strange, alluring, and yet evil smile. The man laughed and shrugged his shoulders. 'The same Yvonne, I see,' he said.

'The same, Monsieur,' she replied. 'It will be time enough to talk of failure when I have failed once—and that is not yet.'

'All serene!' replied the man; 'and now when do you want the other two removed?'

'At once—today,' she said. 'That is why I came to you so early. O'Connor went home with the Ryans last night—pretended he had a case to see, but I knew at once he wanted to talk with them and to warn them about me. He will stay the night on account of curfew and if you send early this morning you will have a good chance of finding him there. Can you have it done this morning, Ron? What time is it now?'

He glanced at the clock.

'Seven-thirty,' he answered. 'Would you wish them to be awakened from their morning dreams, or will you give them time to breakfast first?'

'No; no! The earlier the better,' she cried. 'One never knows what card that diable O'Connor will play. Give the order at once—your people know the house in Elton Street—but warn them not to take Desmond, only Anthony. Warn them well about this, Ron.'

'Your ladyship shall be obeyed,' said Hammond, with a smile of amusement at her eagerness, and going to the telephone he sent the message through knowing it would be obeyed immediately.

'Now are you satisfied, ma belle?' he asked.

'I shall not be satisfied till I hear that the arrest has been successfully carried out,' she replied; 'but now, Ron, I must go. It would never do for me to be seen leaving here later. And I want to be back at the flat for obvious reasons.'

'Very well,' he said, touching the bell for his man, and then helping her on with her coat. 'We must have a little dinner together, Yvonne, when you get those papers; they will be worth something to each of us.'

'Ah! bah. As if I didn't know that,' she said. 'And, Ron, I need money badly just now—send me some later—I won't wait now. Yes; I know I am extravagant, but I am worth it and I know that, too.'

'Well! I suppose you are. Get a taxi, Greggs. Oh! yes; you had better have one; it can set you down before you reach the flat.'

'Let me know by code the very minute you hear anything,' she said. 'Don't telephone; send the message by hand.'

'Very well,' he said. 'And I hope I will be able to tell you that the coast is clear. Au revoir!'

On her way home Yvonne Delaunay congratulated herself on having done an excellent morning's work.

CHAPTER IX

YVONNE LOSES A TRICK

When Desmond Ryan had asserted that Mrs Pell must have been 'on it' again he had for once been mistaken. Far from having indulged in stimulants of any kind stronger than tea—which she liked thick and black—the good lady had been particularly abstemious for the last few days. The fact of the kettle having been found sojourning in the clothes basket—fortunately empty of any laundry at the time—was due to Mrs Pell having had a good 'turn out' of the kitchen, during which the various useful articles had played a game of General Post, and the kettle had remained hidden. Accordingly Mrs Pell was as brisk as a bee the following morning, and shortly before 8 a.m. she reached Elton Street. She wished to get her work done early, as she had promised a 'half day' for general cleaning of her flat to Jill Devereux.

Mrs Pell was a woman who might be any age between forty and fifty-five, and was probably nearer to forty, although she looked the latter age. But 'travelling by land and sea'—as she expressed it, and general hardship of later years had combined, with her pet failing, to add to her years. In appearance she was short and very stout, with little beady eyes which almost vanished when she laughed; her cheeks were flabby and of a dark mottled hue, so that when they shook as they frequently did, with rage, excitement, or laughter—Mrs Pell being a most emotional person—they bore a weird resemblance to purple blancmange. She wore a dark skirt and red blouse and the inevitable black 'cabe' of her class, while on her head rested what she called a 'toke'. Her hair was still abundant and only slightly tinged with grey. She had her own latchkey, and opening the door found herself, as she had expected, the first of the 'char ladies' to arrive. There were several others who came daily to 'do out' the various offices, but their rule of life was to arrive late and depart early. There was one exception to this rule—a Mrs Flanagan, who cleaned the offices on the ground floor. She was a very early bird, and as she was a strict TT—flaunting her Pioneer brooch in what Mrs Pell often felt to be a very insulting manner—she was regular in her habits, arriving every day at 8 a.m. to the minute. She was indeed one of the type of whom it is said, 'You could set your watch by her!' Good methodical people no doubt, but sometimes they are not the pleasantest in the world to live with.

On this morning she inserted the key in the lock and stepped into the hall just as Mrs Pell was beginning to ascend the stairs. Mrs Flanagan was a tall, gaunt woman, with scanty, grey hair, drawn so tightly back from her forehead that it gave one a headache only to look at it. A great talker and gossip, she prided herself on knowing all the details concerning the denizens of the various 'floors' in the house. Mrs Pell annoyed her because she refused to be communicative about her 'young gentlemen,' and she annoyed Mrs Pell not only by her inquisitive questions, but also because she spoke as an equal to the sergeant's widow, quite forgetting the social gulf which, in Mrs Pell's eyes, yawned between them. Therefore they were generally in a state of armed neutrality—Mrs Pell priding herself on keeping Mrs Flanagan 'at her distance,' while the latter was determined to show 'that stuck up ould wan that she would take no back chat from her or her likes.'

'Oh! is that yerself, Mrs Pell?' she called, as she came down the hall. 'That's a could soort av a mornin'!'

'Good morning, ma'am,' replied Mrs Pell, with distant politeness. 'The weather, as you observe, is rather insalubrious.'

'Ah! well; sure we must expect it now, and this is the first of October,' replied the other, untying her bonnet strings.

'So it is indeed,' said Mrs Pell, adding as she began to mount the stairs, 'but only that you reminded me of the date, ma'am, I had forgotten, as I had not contained the fact in my memory.'

'Divil a bit av me knows what ye're talkin' about,' muttered Mrs Flanagan to herself, as she turned into her own regions. 'Such a balderdash av words—like some ould professor who was the worse av drink.'

Meanwhile Mrs Pell mounted the stairs laboriously and first looking into the office and opening the windows she went on to the top floor, and entering the kitchen lit the fire there and glanced around for the kettle. She had not waited for her breakfast before coming out and wanted her tea badly.

'It will be in the sittingroom,' she said. 'No doubt they made tea for themselves last night—the poor lambs.'

One of the greatest objections which the twins had to Mrs Pell was her invariable habit of referring to them as her 'poor lambs'.

In the sittingroom she found, as she had expected, the kettle, but found, too—what she had not expected—the fire still burning, although low, in the grate, and the remains of a meal on the table.

Was it a late supper or an early breakfast she wondered as she inspected the table, and then she noticed that three cups and saucers had been used, and putting her hand on the teapot she found it was still warm to the touch.

'Breakfast—and for three!' she thought in bewilderment. 'Heaven protect me this day! What can have happened now?'

The bedroom was off the sittingroom, and as Mrs Pell's glance turned towards it she saw through the wide open door that it was more disordered than usual—drawers pulled wide, the wardrobe open and various articles of clothing lying about. She went in then and searched around and found, as she had feared, that their small suitcases were gone.

'Oh! sure I knew it—I knew it! Me poor lambs! Hunted through the world again they must be.' And Mrs Pell wiped away a tear as she gazed at the disordered room.

'Well! it's no use frettin',' she said then. 'I'll put on the kettle and then I'll tidy up here. As Mr P used to say—it's best to look on the bright side unless ye're a blind man!'

She put the kettle on to boil and returned to the bedroom and then only did she see the envelope addressed to herself which was stuck in the mirror. Hastily putting on her glasses—she was very near-sighted—Mrs Pell sat down and opened it. Only a few words— just to say that they were obliged to leave town again on business and did not know when they would return. She would carry on as usual during their absence, and look after the office and their rooms, but to all inquiries she was simply to say that she did not know where they had gone or when they would return.

'Well! so that's that,' she said to herself resignedly, thrusting the note inside her capacious blouse—where it found itself in the company of a latchkey, a shabby purse, a snuff-box, and a few other articles—she returned to the kitchen and the prospect of tea.

But Mrs Pell's tea that morning was destined to remain merely a prospect for some time longer. The kitchen was situated at the back and perhaps that is why she did not hear the rush and commotion of the lorries as they dashed down the street and drew up at the door. The first thing she heard was someone running up the stairs—gasping for breath—and the next moment Mrs Flanagan stood in the doorway and called to her:

'Mrs Pell! Mrs Pell! It's the military and they're askin' for your young gentlemen. Oh! may God and His Blessed Mother protect us this day!'

Mrs Pell, true to her traditions, tried to maintain her dignity, but her cheeks shook—and this time the blancmange was rather a pale purple—as she remarked with would-be-calm:

'Well! we may be thankful it's not the Tan and Blacks.'

'Black and Tans I suppose you mean?' returned Mrs Flanagan.

'Tan and Black or Black and Tan—I see little to extinguish between them, but—.'

Mrs Pell got no further, as the military were now pouring up the stairs, and entering the room with a rush both she and Mrs Flanagan were held up where they were and not allowed to move.

The officer in charge cross-questioned them both sharply, Mrs Pell especially when he found that it was she who worked for the Ryans, but, of course, she could tell him nothing. So leaving her in the charge of a very young Tommy he proceeded towards the sitting-room and bedroom to commence his search.

Mrs Pell glared at her military guardian for a few minutes in silence and then said in her most dignified tones:

'It's easy to be observed, young man, that you do not comprehend whom I am.'

'That'll do now, mother,' replied the Tommy curtly. 'Keep your mouth shut!'

'Mother!' gasped Mrs Pell indignantly; 'how dare you, young man. If my late diseased husband was alive he would soon make you know your place. He'—her cheeks swelling out and shaking violently—'he was a sergeant-major in the—regiment. Cavalry as you may know—not foot!' with a contemptuous glance at his small dimensions.

This drew no response beyond a slight reddening of the soldier's youthful cheeks, and Mrs Pell's attention was attracted to what was going on in the other rooms. The search was proceeding with vigour and her disgusted gaze had to see drawers and their contents scattered on the floor, tables and chairs overturned, the bookcase dismantled and its volumes flung out, every scrap of paper scrutinised.

'Such scandalous behaviour!' she gasped. 'Oh! Heavens above! If only Mr P was here now to see the way the Army are conducting themselves.'

'Now, then, mother; 'old yer gob. We don't allow no gas 'ere, yer know!'

Mrs Flanagan, who was held up near the door by a very stout little Tommy, was quite speechless between rage and fright. The former, however, predominated when she saw the grin on his face.

'Don't dare look at me like that!' she cried shrilly. 'I s'pose ye think that ye're a great fella! But let me tell ye that ye're greatly mistaken.'

'Now; now, mother! That'll do!' replied the fat Tommy with a broad wink at his comrade on guard over Mrs Pell.

'Don't dare mother me, young fella!' cried Mrs Flanagan. 'Mother, indeed! God knows if I was mother to the likes av yous I'd drown myself.'

At this moment the officer in charge came back to the kitchen followed by the men who had been engaged in the search, and they now proceeded to continue their work there. Nothing was spared—the dresser was opened and its contents flung out on the floor, pots and pans taken off their hooks and thrown down, the table overturned and its drawers ransacked, the very window curtains torn down as they had been in the other room—even the tea-caddy opened and the tea spilt on the floor. Poor Mrs Pell! Her eyes seemed to become smaller and smaller and her cheeks bigger and bigger until Mrs Flanagan began to have uneasy visions of seeing her suddenly burst into space on her way to rejoin the 'diseased' Mr P.

But for all this search nothing was found—not a word or scrap of incriminating evidence could be produced. After what he designated as a warning to Mrs Pell and a threat of a probable speedy return, the officer clattered down the stairs, evidently in a very bad temper, his men following him noisily.

'Well! Glory be!' ejaculated Mrs Flanagan as the noise of the departing lorries grew fainter. 'Did ever ye see the like of that, Mrs Pell? What is the world comin' to at all when two dacent married women can be held up for an hour at a time be bits av Tommies!'

'Well! Mrs Flanagan, ma'am,' replied Mrs Pell, her voice taking an added dignity to make up for the slight she had sustained; 'all I can say is that if my dear departed Mr P is looking earthwards now Heaven will not be Heaven to him this day.'

'Well! let us get a cup of tea in God's name,' replied the other, who as usual began to feel 'fed up with old P' as she would have said herself, 'and then I'll help you to clean up the mess they've med. God help us! The place is a fright.'

Over the tea cups they became quite friendly.

'My poor lambs!' sighed Mrs Pell; 'my poor lambs! Little did I think, Mrs Flanagan, when last night I was arranging the table for their repast that I should arrive in the morning and find them fled. Oh! if only Mr P was here to contain and condole me!'

Mrs Flanagan did not grasp that the speaker meant to sustain and console, although she knew that she meant differently from her spoken words, but it would have taken Desmond to comprehend Mrs Pell's esperanto when she was at all upset.

The two women remained talking over the tea cups for some time longer, until a clock striking ten recalled them to the work-a-day world once more.

'Heavenly Powers! Can that be ten o'clock that's after striking?' exclaimed Mrs Flanagan; 'and the offices below never touched. But what can they expect considerin' the times we're livin' in. Anyway I must go down and explain things if any of them are in yet. I'll come back later, Mrs Pell, and give ye a hand, so don't be killin' yerself workin'.'

Mrs Flanagan hastily departed to her own regions, while Mrs Pell began to clear away the breakfast things in preparation to starting her work. For work indeed it was to try and get any kind of order out of the terrible and complete chaos left behind by the military.

At the end of half-an-hour she had accomplished so little that she paused for a moment and stood gazing around her, wondering when she would be able to get straight again. As she stood thus, she heard a light footstep coming up the stairs, but although the footfall was light, it was coming slowly enough, as if it found the many flights very wearisome. The next moment Geraldine Moore stood on the kitchen threshold regarding Mrs Pell and her chaotic surroundings with wide open eyes.

'Why, what is the matter, Mrs Pell?' she asked. 'Is Mr Ryan not at home? He asked me to call this morning, and as the office door was shut I came on up, as I know I am rather early.'

'Oh! Miss Moore, is that you?' said the charlady. 'You find us in a state of devastation—a state almost of siege. As for me I am prostrated—collapsed. Oh! what I have gone though this day!'

'But what is it?' again asked Geraldine. 'Where are Mr Anthony and his brother? Will they be here soon, and what in the world has happened?' gazing around her in astonishment.

'Where the two gentlemen? Oh! me poor lambs!—are gone, I know not,' replied Mrs Pell, folding her arms with a dramatic gesture; 'also when they will return—if ever!—is beyond my power of repression. Enemies are on their tract! I know no more!'

She paused and surveyed Geraldine's puzzled face for a moment before she added slowly and tragically: 'The military—two lorries of them—have just gone. This' with a sweep of her hand—'is their work.'

'The military!' echoed Geraldine, her voice hardly above a whisper. Then the room seemed to be going round and round in some horrible way and she felt Mrs Pell guiding her to a chair.

For a few moments she could not speak and heard, as in a dream, Mrs Pell's voice going on and on. Then her mind began to work again and, sitting up straight in her chair, she began to piece things together.

She remembered in detail the previous night in Jill's flat, and especially did she remember Dr Peter O'Connor. She seemed to realise now—it came to her in a lightning flash of comprehension—that he had known of some threatened danger and had prevailed upon the Ryans to leave town again. How right he was in his deductions—whatever they may have been—the raid by the military that morning had amply proved.

'Oh! Mrs Pell,' she said, 'thank God they were gone in time.'

'And indeed, Miss, you may well say that,' replied the sergeant's widow emphatically, 'for if ever I beheld a man look real savage it was the officer when he found they were not here. Someone must have given the poor lambs the tip to be off, and may God bless whoever it was.'

Geraldine was silent, staring miserably into space, and looking, as Mrs Pell now noticed, very pale and weary.

'You don't look well, Miss,' she remarked. 'I'll put on the kettle and wet you a cup of tea. I'm not long after some meself—me nervous system was shattered beyond compare. As I said to Mrs Flanagan—a well-meaning woman, but very ignorant, not having travelled—as I said to her, such behaviour from the Army was lamentable. Ah! it's very changed from my time, I can assure you, Miss. I do believe if Mr P happened to be looking down here on this blessed day that he would not rest even in his bed in Heaven.'

Geraldine had a fleeting vision of Mr P recumbent on a feather bed, somewhere in the clouds, and her lips twitched in spite of her troubled mind and general wretchedness.

'Thank you, Mrs Pell,' she said. 'I would be thankful for the tea, I am so thirsty. But I couldn't eat anything—my head aches terribly.'

She drank the tea feverishly when it was ready, shivering as she did so in spite of the warm fire.

'I suppose they left no message of any kind?' she asked suddenly.

Mrs Pell dived into the bosom of her capacious blouse and brought forth the note, which she handed to Geraldine, who read it through rapidly. It was in Anthony's handwriting—one great difference between the twins was their handwriting; it was totally dissimilar—and just contained the brief instructions to Mrs Pell.

'They must have expected a raid,' thought the girl; 'this note is so guarded. That, too, is the reason why they left me no word, they were afraid it might have been found during the search, as this note would have been only Mrs Pell was so early this morning.'

Before leaving she went with Mrs Pell into the other room and gazed around at the general chaos, while the charlady expatiated on the amount of work before her.

Geraldine's glance was suddenly arrested by a large oil painting which hung over the fireplace. It represented a beautiful woman of early middle age, the expression of the face very sweet and gentle, and it bore a vivid resemblance to Sheila—Sheila as she might become when some of the sorrow of the world had touched her.

'Why, Mrs Pell,' Geraldine cried; 'that must be the first Mrs Ryan, the boys' mother. Do you know if it is?'

'You are right in your conductions, Miss Moore,' replied the other with dignity; 'that is indeed me poor lambs' dear mother that was. They got that painted from a small picture they had; it was only finished a few weeks ago, and they think the world of it. They hung it up there themselves when no one else was here with them—you'd think it was sacred—the Shrine of a Saint no less, and no one dare touch it only themselves. I darn't so much as put a duster near it on dread of me life.'

Geraldine remained for a few moments looking at the sweet face which seemed to be gazing down on her; then she said good-day to Mrs Pell and went downstairs. The door of the Ryans' office on the floor beneath was now open, and looking in she saw a similar scene of disorder to that which reigned above, while Mr Dillon, the clerk, stood surveying it, his hands in his pockets, his lips softly whistling. Mrs Pell had told Geraldine that some of the military had been searching the office while the others were in the room above.

'It's well that I had opened the office on my way upstairs, as I always do, to let down the window to air them or the doors would have been smashed in,' she had added.

Geraldine toiled slowly homewards. Although it was still early in the day she felt too utterly weary and tired to do anything else. She was terribly disappointed, too, the Ryans' forced departure had come upon her as a great blow. She had built so much upon her interview with Anthony; he had seemed a tower of strength to the tired girl, and she had allowed her hopes to rise so high that now she felt doubly stranded and desolate. Dr O'Connor, too; Mrs Pell had told her about the third cup on the breakfast table, which pointed to his having spent the night and probably gone away with them in the morning. Would he stay away? she wondered. After all, what would be danger for them would most likely mean the same for him. So they were all gone—fled no one knew where—and it might be many a long day before they could come back to Dublin with safety.

In the meantime she was literally at the end of her resources. Nothing remained for her except to go and live with Jill Devereux and be a burden on her friend, who was already feeling the pinch of the present hard times, or to take the position in England offered by Yvonne Delaunay.

But when at last she reached her lodgings—and it seemed to her that she had been walking miles and miles before she arrived there—she was feeling really so ill that she simply crawled up the stairs and flung herself, fully dressed as she was, on her bed, for once not caring, and indeed not capable of caring, what became of her or what the future held in store for her. She was conscious only of her throbbing head, and poor, pain racked body.

About five o'clock Mrs Brennan—who had called up to her several times and got no reply—came stiffly up the stairs to investigate matters. She found her favourite lodger lying on the bed, still dressed in her outdoor things, for she had only removed her hat, tossing restlessly from side to side and moaning now and then as though in pain. She recognised Mrs Brennan and tried to talk to her, but the talk was not very sensible and the woman saw at once that she was seriously ill. She lit a fire and dispatched the little girl from next door who went with her messages to Miss Devereux's flat asking her to come over as soon as she could. Mrs Brennan had no regard for the 'mad French hussy,' as she called Jill, but she knew that she was devoted to Geraldine, and knew, too, that the sick girl would rather have Jill beside her than anyone else. The two were singularly alone in the world, neither of them possessing any known relatives nearer than cousins, and for many years now they had been real comrades in the best meaning of the word. Mrs Brennan had shown her good sense in sending for Jill. She happened to be at home and came at once, and between them they got Geraldine properly undressed and into bed.

'I'll stay with her tonight, Mrs Brennan,' said Jill then; 'I must go back to the flat for a few things I need, but I won't be long, and I'll call on my way and leave word with Dr Manly to come and see her.'

She returned to her flat feeling very worried and anxious about her friend. She was pretty certain that Geraldine was in for a sharp attack of influenza and knew that in her weakened condition she was a bad subject to resist its onset. Jill was worried also over the financial outlook. Sickness meant a lot of expense; Geraldine's exchequer represented nil, and Jill herself was in very low water just then. Orders for work had been slack and the cost of living, even for one person, very high. Still she was determined to do her utmost to get everything that was needful for Geraldine, and well— if the worst came she had several articles which she could sell or pledge.

Thus thinking she was fitting her key in the door when that of the flat across the landing opened and Yvonne Delaunay, in her coat and hat, came out. It was the first time that Jill had seen her that day, and she noticed that the other seemed quiet and rather unlike her usual fascinating self. However, when she saw Jill she came across to her with a smile and asked if she was going out.

'I have only just come in,' replied Jill, 'but I am going out again in a short time. Geraldine is very ill—the influenza, I think—and I am going to stay the night with her.'

As she spoke she was surprised to see an expression of real concern cross Yvonne's face—that strange little face that was generally so inscrutable. Fascinated as she had been by her queer neighbour, and fond of her in a way, Jill had yet hardly given Yvonne credit for much feeling where Geraldine was in question.

But now thinking that she was really interested she told her all she could about the girl's illness, and the other listened with grave sympathy.

'Oh! but I am sorry; so sorry,' then said Yvonne's soft voice, 'and how unfortunate that she should be ill just now when I was so hoping that she would be able to take that post in Berkshire. But perhaps she will be better shortly, and then it would be the very thing for a change of air for her—would it not?'

'Well! perhaps, but I don't know,' replied Jill rather doubtfully. 'I am sure it will be some time before Geraldine can take up duty again. She is just worn out.'

'Oh! but the work in Berkshire would be very light—just a small village you know. The country air and good food would work wonders with her. Ah! well,' with a quick glance at Jill's rather dubious face, 'we will talk about it later when Miss Moore is better. If I can do anything—anything to help her now, please tell me. But I must run now as I have an appointment about some work. Give your friend my dearest love and best wishes for her speedy recovery.'

As Mademoiselle Delaunay ran gaily down the iron stairway her face became blacker and blacker as she descended. The news of Geraldine's illness was another set-back to her plans, and she could ill bear it patiently when she remembered the disappointment of the early morning.

On her arrival home from 'Mr Chester's' she had spent a restless couple of hours, expecting every moment to hear news of her great coup. She was almost certain that it must be successful, for even if Dr O'Connor suspected her he would still never dream that she would act so quickly. Yes; she was sure that she would foil them, the hated Ace and King, those two whom she dreaded and feared would be put where they could do no harm, where they would be unable to interfere in any way with her well laid plans.

And so when a knock came to the door and a boy handed her a letter she almost snatched it from him. She knew him, of course, as he knew her.

'There's no answer,' he said briefly, and clattered down the stairs.

Yvonne entered her flat and turned the key softly in the lock, and going through into her bedroom she locked that door also. Then standing in the middle of the room she opened the envelope. It contained only a half sheet of paper with a few words in code inscribed on it—a code which she knew so well that she could transpose as she read. But well as she knew it she almost doubted at first that she had read aright when she made out the following message:-

'All three birds had flown and no evidence of any kind was found.'

Yvonne Delaunay ground her little white teeth viciously as she tore and re-tore the note into minute fragments.

She had lost the first trick—and she knew that the Ace had taken it.

CHAPTER X

MR SHORTALL PAYS A VISIT

Jill Devereux had been correct in her diagnosis of Geraldine's illness, and for a week the sick girl had a hard fight against the influenza fiend. But although weakened by the last few months of poor living and anxiety, Geraldine had a strong constitution, with youth and hope on her side, and at the end of a fortnight was over the worst, and a few days afterwards she was able to be moved to Jill's flat.

All that Jill had been to her during her sickness Geraldine could never forget—a thousand times over had she proved herself 'the friend in need'. Not she only. Mrs Brennan also had turned up trumps, and during the hours when Jill, of necessity, had to be out seeing about her work, the landlady would toil stiffly up the stairs and sit beside her lodger, ready to do all she could for her. As for Fluff, that fussy little animal was constantly in and out, coming to her bedside and gazing at her with inquisitive, puzzled eyes that asked so plainly—'What is the matter? Why don't you get up?'

Thomas, the huge black cat, paid an occasional visit of ceremony to her, but like all his tribe was only coldly polite. Mrs Brennan asked her one day would she like 'Don Juan' for company, and Geraldine had to refuse the offer very diplomatically, as his mistress considered the parrot 'as good as any Christian for talk!' Like all very sick people the question of ways and means had not troubled Geraldine at first; she took whatever was given her in the way of medicine and nourishment and thought no more about it. It was not till she was at Jill's and able once more to take an intelligent interest in the every day life around her that she began to think over her financial position. She had wanted for nothing during her illness; not only had everything which the doctor ordered in the shape of medicines and nourishment been provided, but many unnecessary luxuries and dainties had always been at hand. These had continued up to the present moment, when sitting by the fire in Jill's armchair she allowed her glance to rest on the fruit and biscuits placed on a little table by her side.

She looked across at Jill stooping over a drawing outspread on the table.

'Jill,' she said then, 'I have been thinking about my illness and the—the expense it must have been. How did you manage at all? You must be terribly out of pocket?'

Jill left her drawing and came over to the fire.

'I have been expecting this question for some days now,' she said with a smile, 'as I have noticed that the patient is now able to sit up and take notice. I knew that the next thing would be that you would be worrying yourself over these matters. But, Jerry, my dear old girl! take my word for it, you have no need to do so.'

'No need!' cried Geraldine. 'Oh! but, Jill, how can I help it, knowing what my illness must have cost you. You have been an angel; but how did you manage?'

Jill laughed.

'Well! if I have been an angel it was because another angel in disguise helped me,' she said. Seeing Geraldine's puzzled look she drew forward a chair and sat down. 'I'll tell you all about it,' she announced then, 'and you will hear what a wonderful piece of luck has fallen to me. It really seemed, Jerry, as if your illness had proved to be my mascot, for it was just a few days after you were taken sick that I got my first order from Mr Ferdinand Shortall. I may as well confess that I was more than a bit anxious about our finances, your exchequer being empty and my own very nearly so, and it suddenly seemed as if orders for advertisement pictures had gone out of fashion altogether, when one day I got a typed letter asking me to call at 24, Rose Street, which—as you probably know—is one of those small streets in the South Circular Road direction. The letter just said briefly that the writer could put some advertisement work in my way and I was to call to see him between four and five o'clock.'

'Yes; and you went?'

'Of course. On arriving there I was shown into a tiny sittingroom by a young girl and almost immediately Mr Shortall entered. He was a tall old man, very stooped, with a long, white beard and longish hair. He was rather shabbily dressed and wore blue glasses. He was a bit shy and stiff in his manner at first, but soon became quite friendly. He began to tell me then that he had invented a new patent for rolling umbrellas quickly and neatly— did you ever hear of such a thing, Jerry?—and he wanted it well advertised. I was to design posters on the subject, showing, of course, all kinds of people and all kinds of umbrellas, and illustrating the tidily folded umbrella and the reverse. I was to draw all classes, all weathers, all costumes, and so on. I saw at once that it would mean a splendid opening for me and would also mean steady work for a long time, and Jerry, I was awfully glad of it, but——.'

'But what?' asked the other. 'Were you afraid of the old man?'

'No; not afraid, but doubtful if he was quite sensible and if he had the money to pay me.' She paused for a moment, and Geraldine laughed.

'I don't wonder you were so doubtful,' she said; 'but go on, Jill, and tell me if the old fellow was what business men call solvent or not?'

'He was indeed—very solvent,' replied Jill. 'He first gave me an order for two large posters which would be suitable for a hoarding, and for these he paid me ten pounds each. And ever since he has kept me supplied with advertisements for the papers and magazines. I am earning at the rate of six pounds a week from him.'

'And he pays all right?' asked Geraldine with open eyes.

'Oh! yes; always,' replied her friend. 'I have to leave the drawings at his house sometimes; at other times he gets me to post them. He always tells me which to do and he is a very kind old man and quite interested in you, Jerry.'

'In me!'

'Yes; I happened to mention about your illness and he was so kind, quite fatherly—or grandfatherly indeed I might say—and he wants to call to see you when you are stronger.'

'I must say it all sounds rather strange,' said Geraldine; 'but I suppose he is all right. Do you think that he has really invented that patent?'

'Oh! yes;' promptly replied Jill. 'Its rather an ingenious device, too. I'll show you some of the advertisements and then you will understand it. But I don't believe for a moment that it will ever bring him fame or fortune. I would scruple taking the old chap's money only I honestly believe he has plenty, and if I didn't take it someone else would.'

'But why then does he live in those pokey little lodgings?' very sensibly asked Geraldine.

'Oh! I suppose he is just an oddity,' said Jill. 'Look, Jerry, here are some of the designs for his advertisments.' And she showed her several very clever drawings which she had just completed, showing how beautifully finished and smart an umbrella would appear when folded according to the old Mr Shortall's idea.

'There is only one thing that really puzzles me about him,' she said suddenly, 'and that is the persistent idea that I have seen him somewhere before. I cannot locate where or when, but I am constantly obsessed with the notion. His voice, too, at times has such a familiar sound—and—oh! in several ways he reminds me of someone, but I cannot think who it is. However, I suppose it is just one of those chance resemblances of which we hear so often. Oh! Jerry, but I was glad to get that work. If I had been an orthodox Christian I would have said that it was sent straight from Heaven.'

'As it was,' said Geraldine softly.

Jill did not answer, but she slipped an arm round Geraldine and they kissed in silence.

From that on Geraldine picked up strength quickly, and she soon began to think and plan what she would do in the future. The more she thought the clearer it seemed to her that she had better take the position offered her by Yvonne Delaunay.

That little person was a constant visitor, running across from her own flat several times a day, very often bringing flowers and fruit or a book for Geraldine, offerings which the girl could not well refuse, but the acceptance of which was strangely repugnant to her.

About a week after Jill had told her about the queer Mr Shortall, Geraldine was sitting alone by the fire one afternoon. Jill was gone out and would not be back for another hour or so, and Geraldine, as she sat by the firelight, thought of many things.

She was thinking of her country, its terrible sufferings, and the agony and torture through which so many of her fellow-country men and women were now passing. It was inevitable that her thoughts should fly to Brixton Gaol and the last act of the awful drama which was now drawing to a close, for the day of which we write was October 24th, 1920, and the whole of Ireland was keeping watch in spirit by the deathbed of Terence MacSwiney.

Geraldine, like many another, was praying for the end to come, the torture and suffering had been so long drawn out that it had seemed to her sometimes as if it would never end. 'Surely he has suffered enough,' she thought; 'take him, dear Lord. Oh! take him to his eternal rest and end his agony.'

While the shadows deepened and only the glow of the fire lit the room, she passed her Rosary beads through her fingers as she prayed for him and all those who were suffering with him.

Her prayers finished, she leant back in her chair and began to think of herself and her own affairs, and above all of the fact which troubled her most—that she was not able to do any work for Ireland. Not only that, but that now circumstances over which she seemed to have no control pointed to her having to leave her country and work in England, to spend and be spent in the nursing and care of the enemies of her land. Her whole being revolted against the idea. Yet what else could she do if she was to obtain work for which she was fitted, and for which she would receive a living wage, which would enable her to pay back to Jill a little of the big debt she owed her.

Not, of course, that Jill wished such a thing, or cared whether it was ever paid or not, but Geraldine's independent spirit could not brook that she should be under such an obligation—even to her dearest chum. Not only that, but she knew that Jill could not really afford it. Also the work with Mr Shortall might not continue—he was evidently an eccentric and might change his mind about the advertisements any minute. As Yvonne had said, she need not stay in England any longer than she wished—only just long enough to save a little money and get strong and well again. Afterwards she could return to her own country if she could get work there.

'Yes; that's just it,' she thought desperately; 'the want of work here. If I got something to do I would take it at once, even if the pay was much less that what I could get in England. I would take anything which would pay me enough to exist upon, and trust to be able to repay Jill later. But I cannot get it, and I know I am not strong enough to begin again that terrible nightmare search for employment. As to this offer. Am I justified in refusing it because it is not in Ireland? Why do I feel as if I should not take it, as if it was not right for me to go?'

That was exactly how she did feel—just as if her conscience forbade her to leave Ireland.

'It must be sheer sentiment on my part,' she argued. 'If I had money or influence, or if I was engaged in any definite work that could help on the cause, why then, nothing would induce me to leave. But as I am situated it would not only be foolish, but it would be wrong for me to refuse such an offer. The next time that Yvonne Delaunay comes in I will tell her that I will accept, and start for Berkshire as soon as I can travel.'

It seemed to be almost in answer to this resolve that Yvonne knocked and entered a few moments later.

'Why, Chérie, you are alone then?' she cried, and crossing over to the fire she sank into a chair opposite to Geraldine and stretched her pretty hands to the blaze. 'It is cold, is it not?' she continued. 'How are you, petite? You are looking better today—I am so glad.'

'Yes; I feel a lot better and more like myself,' replied Geraldine. 'I hope to be able to work soon again.' She was not looking at her visitor as she spoke or she could not have escaped seeing the strange look which flashed for a second from behind the lowered lids.

Geraldine, however, was gazing into the fire, and it was a moment before she turned and looked across at Yvonne with clear eyes and lips that tried to smile.

'I have been thinking, Miss Delaunay,' she said, 'about your—your kind offer. I—I have decided to accept.' For one brief fraction of time Yvonne Delaunay kept her eyes downcast; she was afraid that Geraldine would catch the look of triumph which she knew she had not been able to conceal. It meant so much to her just now to get this tiresome young woman out of the way, and it had seemed at times as if she was going to fail. Oh! how often she had almost lost patience with the imbecile. But now! She smiled across at Geraldine in her most fascinating manner.

'I am so glad!' she cried. 'I know that Jill will be glad, too. How often she said to me that she hoped so much that you would be sensible about this.'

Geraldine was silent. Some strange feeling kept her from mentioning any of her real objections to Yvonne, although as far as she knew the French woman was very sympathetic to the Irish cause. But Geraldine had really never been able to trust her.

Yvonne was speaking again.

'I may write then to Lady Selby-Jones?' she asked. 'She has been so kind keeping the position open for you. When I wrote and told her about your illness she was so sorry. She loves the

Irish, too; she will be charmed to welcome you. Of course you cannot say how soon you will be able to go? You will hardly be ready for a little time yet?'

Geraldine pondered for a moment.

'I think I should be ready to travel in about ten days' time,' she said slowly, 'that is if I go on getting stronger every day as I have been doing for the last week.'

'You will, of course,' cried the other. 'Ten days—that will be delightful. I will write to Lady Selby-Jones tomorrow, as I know she would like to have the cottage ready for you. It is so pretty. I saw it when I was on a visit last year—all covered with roses. The country around, too, is lovely and so peaceful. The people have such dear little houses and they keep them is such order. There are plenty of rich farms also. Oh! you will get quite fat there with the cream and butter and fresh eggs.'

Something seemed to rise in Geraldine's throat and threaten to choke her. She could not speak, but sat silent while her heart told her what she had known all along—that she would rather have one poor room in a Dublin slum, or one bare half acre of bog in the country, with a crust or a dry potato, and be here in her own land and amongst her own people, than to have the daintiest fare and the prettiest house over there.

But she said nothing, and before Yvonne could speak again they heard Jill's footsteps outside, and with her were other footsteps—slow and heavy.

'Here is Jill,' cried Geraldine; 'she has someone with her.'

Even as she spoke the door opened and Jill appeared with a tall, bent old gentleman beside her.

'Geraldine!' she cried; 'this is Mr Shortall. We met just outside and I have brought him in to see you.'

He was so like the description which Jill had given her of him that Geraldine felt that she would have known him anywhere. She came to meet him with outstretched hands.

'I really feel as if I know you already,' she said with a smile, 'we have so often spoken of you.'

'I, too, have heard of Monsieur Shortall,' said Yvonne's musical voice with the faint foreign tones as the old man bowed in her direction. He seemed, as Jill had remarked, rather shy with strangers, but took a chair near the fire gratefully, sinking down amongst its cushions with the stiffness of old age.

'Rheumatism, my dear young ladies; rheumatism!' he said apologetically. 'I suffer much from it at this time of the year.'

Then he turned his blue spectacled eyes towards Geraldine, peering at her in his short-sighted manner, while he said with old-fashioned courtesy:

'I trust that you are feeling better, Miss Moore, and I must beg you to pardon me for intruding upon you so soon.'

'I think it is very kind of you to come,' replied the girl, looking at him with frank friendliness. 'I am much better, thank you. Indeed I hope soon to be at work again.'

'That is good hearing,' he said; 'but take an old man's advice, young lady, and don't be in too great a hurry to get back to harness.'

'Oh! no; I will have another week at least before I start.'

Jill looked at her quickly and asked:

'Why only another week, Jerry? What do you mean?'

'I mean,' replied Geraldine slowly, 'that I have just been telling Miss Delaunay that I accept her kind offer of the district in Berkshire and will take up duty there as soon as I feel able.'

There was silence for a moment, as Jill was so taken aback by this sudden decision on her friend's part that she was too surprised to say anything.

Then old Mr Shortall coughed, and rubbed his hands together over the fire as he said:

'Are you going to Berkshire, did you say, Miss Moore? A lovely spot—a lovely spot! I once spent a summer there and I am sure it will be the very place for you now. A change of air and climate. Nothing could be better.'

'I certainly think you have decided wisely,' said Jill then; 'but I wish you would take a longer rest before going. Surely,' turning to Yvonne, 'there is no need for her to rush away so quickly? Would not your friend wait a little longer?'

Yvonne appeared to hesitate as she said in a regretful voice:

'I am afraid she will not wait very much longer. You see she has already waited a good bit. Of course she could have got heaps of nurses before this. But she wished to oblige me.'

'I am sure the change will only be beneficial to our young friend,' here interposed their visitor; 'once she gets over there she will feel a different being.'

They talked for a while longer, chatting in a friendly way over the tea which Jill had prepared, and still the old gentleman sat contentedly and showed no disposition to move homewards. At last Jill glanced at the clock.

'I have to go to a lecture tonight at seven o'clock,' she said, 'on Futurist Art! But I promised to be there, so, Jerry dear, I'll have to leave you.'

'I, too,' said Yvonne. 'I am also going to the lecture. May I come with you, Jill?'

Yvonne was really a fairly good artist and she made a point of going on with her studies. Indeed the more she was involved in her real work so much the more did she, apparently, study her art.

'So you ladies are going out?' remarked Mr Shortall, adding, rather timidly, 'I wonder if I might be permitted to stay and keep Miss Moore company for a short while longer? Although I am such a stupid old fellow I fear I won't interest her much. Except indeed that she would care to hear about my patent; that would certainly prove of great interest.'

Jill threw a whimsical look of sympathy at Geraldine as she said gaily:

'Oh! Mr Shortall, how kind of you. I'm sure Geraldine will be delighted.'

'Yes, indeed,' said the latter; 'it is very good of you to think of it.' But in her inmost mind she was thinking he would be rather a bore.

Yvonne ran across the corridor for her hat and coat and a few moments later they were off—old Mr Shortall insisting on opening the door for them and politely bowing them out.

Geraldine, from her chair by the fire, heard their footsteps descending the stairway and gradually dying away in the distance. Then she heard another sound which made her turn around with a start. It was the click of the key as old Mr Shortall turned it in the lock, and then—as the girl gazed spellbound—he drew the heavy portière curtains across the door.

He turned then and faced Geraldine, no longer old and stooped, but tall and erect, with vigour and strength in every movement. As for her, she sat for a moment paralysed, and truth to tell, extremely frightened. She was still weak after her illness, and she put out her hand and grasped the arm of her chair with an almost pitiful gesture. Then a voice she had heard before—a vibrant voice which had seemed once before to bring her courage and hope—cried out: 'Don't be frightened. Oh! what an idiot I am. Miss Moore, don't you know me?'

He swept off the patriarchal beard and wig and blue glasses as he spoke, and Geraldine found herself looking into the keen eyes of Dr Peter O'Connor.

'Dr O'Connor!' she gasped.

'The same at your service.'

'But——.'

'Oh! but me no buts and I'll tell you all about it,' he answered. 'May I sit down?'

'Oh! yes—yes. Please do; and—and how are you?' And she reached out both her hands in greeting.

He took them both and before releasing them he raised them for an instant to his lips. We will presume that Geraldine thought he was still acting the part of the courtly old gentleman who had so suddenly disappeared.

Sitting opposite to her he took her completely into his confidence, first explaining that he spoke in perfect secrecy, and she was to repeat to no one what he was about to tell her. Geraldine promised quietly. One word from her was enough, as Peter O'Connor, keen student of human nature, quite understood.

He told her that he was using his present disguise—which had proved useful on other occasions—to get into touch with her without either Jill Devereux or Yvonne Delaunay guessing at his identity. 'Not that I mistrust Jill herself,' he said. 'None of us do, but she is as yet very much under the influence of the other woman, and we cannot be too careful where she is concerned. I know you don't like her,' he added, 'but I don't suppose you ever suspected that she is nothing more or less than a paid spy in the service of the England.'

While Geraldine listened open-eyed, hardly believing the evidence of her own ears, he explained the whole matter to her and let her see that Yvonne had been responsible for the raid on Ryans' premises, and that she was certainly seeking their arrest.

'That is Anthony's arrest—and probably my own,' he said; 'but I heard from a sure source that on the day of the raid there was to be no arrest of Desmond.' Geraldine looked at him, not comprehending.

'But I wonder at that,' she said, 'for Desmond is quite as much involved in the movement as his brother, and he is if anything more extreme—the hotter—of the two.'

'Well, he's the bigger talker anyway,' replied the doctor curtly, 'but he was not to be arrested—and the reason is plain. Miss Moore, did you not think that Desmond was rather—interested in Mademoiselle on the night they met here?'

Then the girl understood, and she flushed scarlet.

'Oh!' she said; 'but—but surely Desmond won't—won't make a fool of himself?'

'Well! we hope not, but he is an added anxiety at the present to both his brother and myself because he wants to return to Elton Street now, and we both consider it would be better to wait a little longer before we slip back.'

Then he told her about the homely cottage on the Dublin hills—the 'America' of the boys—where the twins and a few others had taken up their quarters.

'I stayed a few days with them,' he said. 'By the way, we only got away half-an-hour before the raid that morning—lucky, wasn't it?—but I returned to town then and heard about your illness.'

'Oh!' cried Geraldine with flaming face—she had suddenly remembered—'It was you then who—who——.'

'Supplied Miss Devereux with work,' he said with a kind look in his piercing eyes. 'Well! a few of us did it between us, because we wanted you to get well soon as we have work for you.'

'For me?'

'Yes. The Ryans want you to go to their office every day and keep an eye on things. You see Dillon is all right—he is one of ourselves—but he hasn't much brains, and we want someone with quicker wits, or, may I say, a woman's instincts, to be there on the spot and watch everything. See who calls and on what business—even Mrs Pell is to be watched in case the enemy tries to meddle with her—not that she has any information to give. But still we want to test her.'

'Oh! but I am sure she would be loyal to the twins; she adores her "poor lambs"!' cried Geraldine.

O'Connor smiled.

'Yes; I know,' he said, 'but she has her failing and *in vino veritas!* But now will you do this for us? That is when you feel strong enough, and needless to say you will be in receipt of a decent salary. You will, of course, be employed outwardly as a clerk.'

'But,' said Geraldine with half a smile, 'you said earlier this evening that I was to go to England for a change of air.'

'Old Ferdinand Shortall said that!' Peter said as he smiled back, 'and he is a blithering old fool. But I say that you are to stay and work in and for your own country.' Then he added in a softer voice, 'Don't you want to do something for Dark Rosaleen?'

'Oh! don't I?' cried the girl. Then clasping her hands, with shining eyes she said, 'Dr O'Connor, I think—I believe that God must have sent you to me now. Only this very day when I was sitting alone here I was wishing that I could do something—no matter how small it was—for Ireland. I was thinking of—of Terence MacSwiney and all that he and his brave comrades are suffering. The others, too, working and planning and suffering. And I—I could do nothing—not only that, but it seemed that I must even go away and work amongst the persecutors of my race! And now—now you come and offer me—oh! its too good to be true—I can't tell you——.'

Her voice broke suddenly and she covered her face with her hands.

The man sat in silence for a moment, and then he leant forward and placed his hand gently on her shoulder.

'Miss Moore,' he said, 'or may I say Geraldine? You and I are going to be friends, so let us have done with formalities. Geraldine, listen to me. Ireland wants her sons and daughters at home now, except those whose special work may be across the sea. But you are not one of those; we want you here; and do you not know—have you not understood—that our enemies want you away? Tell me, who got you the position in Berkshire?'

Geraldine lifted her head and gazed at him.

'Yes,' he said; 'I see that you understand now. Your removal was desired by Yvonne Delaunay—she feared your influence with Jill and she thought, too, that you might prove useful to us in some way like this—hence the convenient Berkshire post. Remember, in dealing with her we must meet guile with guile— therefore let her think for the present that you are going—let even Jill think it, too. I know this will go against the grain, but it is only for the present. We trust Jill absolutely herself, and later on we may be able to take her into our confidence.'

'Very well,' said Geraldine. 'I will not like deceiving dear old

Jill, but you know what is best.'

'That's right,' said the doctor. 'I wonder could you come to Elton Street next week for just a couple of hours during the day—come so that neither Jill nor the other will know about it? If you cannot manage every day, come when you can. I want you to be there; I will be able to meet you sometimes, and besides there may be certain of the boys calling for instructions and so on which I am afraid to entrust to that stupid Dillon. Then in a fortnight's time you could come openly as clerk from ten till five. The Delaunay woman would have to know then, but that will give us two weeks without her guessing where you are. Good Heavens! but she will be gnashing her teeth when she knows the game of getting you away is all UP!'

'If only she knew who was the old man to whom she was so charming this evening!' said Geraldine. 'And Jill, too. How in the world did you manage to hoodwink her when she knew you so well?'

'I was a bit nervous about her,' he replied; 'but after all I had done this part before and was fairly sure of myself, and then she had no reason to suspect me to be any other except Mr F. Shortall.'

'Well! I must say you are splendid,' replied the girl. 'How lucky that you should have called tonight when they were going out.'

'Oh! that was no mere luck!' replied the doctor. 'It would waste too much valuable time to leave such occasions to luck. No; I knew that the lecture was on tonight and that most probably they would be going. Now, Geraldine, is all arranged and can you do what I have asked? If so drop me a P.C. to Rose Street just saying on it—"Seeing about posters today"—and I will know that you will be in Elton Street that day. Mention hour on the card.'

'Yes; that will be all right,' replied the girl eagerly. 'I'll do anything you say—just tell me always what you think best and I'll follow your advice.'

'That is the right spirit,' said the doctor. 'You know, Geraldine,' he added, as he looked into the fire with grave intent, 'I believe that every Irish man and woman is, as it were, going through the crucible during these terrible times, going through the crucible emerging from it either as pure gold or—dross. For surely these days in which we live must so purify our nation that those of us who remain after all is over—and how many or how

few they will be only God knows—should be tried of metal, the
real gold from which our glorious future will spring.'

He paused and sighed, his keen eyes still fixed on the leaping
flames as if he would read the future in their depths.

Geraldine spoke then.

'Dr O'Connor——.'

'Peter, please!'

'Well! Peter; I was going to say would it all ever end—except
indeed in our extermination. We are so few and so weak in
comparison with them that surely they must conquer in the end.'

'Never!' cried the man, drawing himself upright, and striking
his clenched fist on the arm of his chair. 'Never! They can go on
with their persecutions and tortures; they can leave our women
widows and our children fatherless; they can destroy our
industries and sack our towns and leave thousands homeless; and
they can kill our bodies, but, Geraldine, the Soul of a nation
cannot be slain, and through our spirituality we will survive—aye,
and live again amongst the nations of the earth, long after the
British Empire has fallen from power and become as nothing in
the eyes of the world.'

She looked at him with shining eyes.

'God grant it!' she breathed softly. 'Oh! you give me courage
again—courage and hope as you did before!'

'I leave it with you again,' he said, as he rose to go. 'Good night
now and—sleep well.'

Geraldine laughed.

'Do you remember saying that to me before?' she asked.

'I do. Did you sleep that night?'

'Like a top,' she answered. 'I was so thankful to you. Good-
night and remember me to Anthony and Desmond and tell them
that they can depend on me absolutely in any way they like.'

'I will,' replied the doctor; 'and now I must resume my disguise
once more.'

In a couple of moments Dr Peter O'Connor had disappeared
and old Mr Ferdinand Shortall, bent and white-bearded, had
come back again. Certainly O'Connor acted the part well—even
to the voice and shaky movements of a rheumatic old man.

Then he was gone and Geraldine sat motionless staring at the
fire with food, and to spare, for thought.

When the others returned Yvonne came in for a moment to say

good-night. She was especially affectionate and full of kind inquiries.

'Did he bore you dreadfully, that so dull old man?' she asked, with one of her charming pouts.

'Yes; he was rather a bore!' assented Geraldine; 'he can talk of nothing—absolutely nothing—but his old umbrella patent!'

'Poor Jerry,' sympathised Jill laughingly.

'Ah! well; he did not stay long, that was one comfort,' said Geraldine, and wondered, with a mental gasp, if the Recording Angel quite understood that such slight prevarications were not to be entered against her name.

CHAPTER XI

JILL BEGINS TO THINK

Jill Devereux could not sleep that night. Not that that was anything new or out of the common, for like all artists—let their creative work be what it may—she often suffered from insomnia, and knew only too well what it was to toss from side to side striving in vain to woo the fickle spirit of repose.

Geraldine had her own bed and a few other articles of furniture, and these had been moved to Jill's flat with her trunk and suitcase, for it had been considered best by all that Geraldine should give up her room at Mrs Brennan's until she knew what her future plans would be. So she was quite at home at Jill's and was, at this moment, fast asleep in her bed on the other side of the room.

There was no light, but above the girl's head shone a luminous crucifix, and Jill found her eyes turning in its direction every now and then while she tossed about and envied Jerry her placid sleep—the recuperating sleep of convalescence.

But for Jill there was no sleep and her brain became alive with that diabolical activity with which the insomnia fiend can always imbue it. She was compelled against her will to go over and over again all the things that had been troubling and puzzling her lately. First there was Geraldine, and Jill's eyes softened as they sought the little bed under the crucifix. She remembered the long years during which they had been friends—real friends and comrades. Both of them were without parents or near relations and both had their own way to make in the world, so that they had much in common in spite of their acutely divergent temperaments. And the love between them was very real and binding. Men sometimes say there is no real friendship between two women. They are wrong. Women can be true and leal to each other, and their friendship, too can be lasting, while a so-called friendship between a man and a woman cannot remain such. We all know the inevitable ending of 'Platonic friendship'.

So Jill Devereux, full of love for her comrade, was tossing restlessly on her pillow, and wondering if she had done right in advising her to go to England. Common-sense said Yes, but her woman's intuition, which is so seldom wrong, said No, and said it with no uncertain voice.

'But why? Why should she not go?' Jill reasoned, and was astonished to find that her mind gave back the answer—gave it back in spite of herself in some strange, sub-conscious way— 'Because Yvonne Delaunay is anxious to send her—Why?'

Suddenly, clearly, she seemed to hear again the stealthy footstep on the iron stairway and the click of the opposite door as Yvonne stole in on that dark January morning over three years ago. Why had that episode remained so engraven on the tablets of her memory, so engraven that no effort of her own could ever wipe it out? She had tried—aye, again and again—to put it away— not to think about it—to forget it. But always in vain. It remained as though it was to be a warning finger—beckoning—beckoning to her to be careful—had so remained for the last three years.

Now she did not need its reminder, because she had heard on two occasions, since Yvonne's return a month ago, the stealthy footstep and the click of the lock as her neighbour opposite went out or came in during the small hours of the morning. Little did Yvonne know what a light sleeper Jill was, and yet even if she had known it she could hardly have made less noise than she did. But lately Jill's ears were strained like many another woman's at the time—strained as she listened for the tear and rush of the lorries, for the savage blows as doors were battered in.

As to her real feelings towards Yvonne, Jill could not analyse them. At first she had been attracted in some extraordinary way— obsessed as it were—by the quaint and charming personality of the other. But lately for some reason or other, the fascination was still there to some degree, and there were times when Yvonne could still cast the old spell over her, yet she knew that she was beginning to sift and analyse her little neighbour as she had not done before. To some extent the scales were falling from her eyes—to the extent anyway that she did not trust Yvonne—and that she knew, too, that she did not always speak the truth. Sometimes lately when she was with her a strangely repellent feeling had come upon her and she had felt as if she could not bear the other's presence near her. She could not explain the why or wherefore of this even to herself—it seemed a hopeless tangle—but now as her eyes sought Geraldine in the darkness she knew that she was afraid to trust her in England on Yvonne's recommendation, and she determined to tell her so in the morning and advise her not to go.

Then her mind wandered to the twins. Of Anthony she thought with true regard and affection; he was one she could honour, a man to be depended upon for help and advice, of him indeed she knew it might be said that 'Nature could stand up and say to all the world—this was a man!' But when her thoughts drifted to Desmond they were different; indeed she did not seem able to think very coherently, and she buried her flaming cheeks in the pillow and hated herself for the moment because she felt like this, and nearly hated him, too, because he was the only man in the world who could make her heart throb one extra beat. But her love of justice and common-sense made her acknowledge that it was not the man's fault—he had treated her no differently from other girls—in fact he had not even flirted with her as he did with many others. No; it was just 'Desmond's way'—a way that caused many a feminine heartache. She realised, too, that just because she happened to be one of those 'One man' women and could never find consolation elsewhere like some of his other victims—well! that was not Desmond's fault either. But it did not ease the heartache, and to try to forget him for the moment she began to think of Peter O'Connor.

She and the doctor had been friends off and on for some years when she was very young. He was indeed a distant connection of her mother's family, and used to insist laughingly that as an elder cousin he must look after her occasionally. But of late years she had not seen much of him, and had known that he was engaged in work for Ireland—work in which he risked life and liberty. Then she had heard in some vague way that he had gone to America, and remembered now that she had mentioned the fact once when talking about him in a casual way to Yvonne and Jerry. The latter had never happened to meet him, but had often heard Jill speak about 'my cousin Sherlock Holmes O'Connor.' Was it imagination, or did Yvonne seem especially interested on this one occasion when she mentioned his name before her? An interest, too, which she had tried to hide immediately, but which caused Jill to say very little about the doctor, except that she had heard he was in America, where he would probably stay for some time. 'Even then—some months ago—I suspected her,' she thought sadly; 'and now—Oh! I am getting just hatefully suspicious.'

Had Jill known of the 'America' on the slopes of the Dublin hills she might have wondered at the coincidence which had made her speak of Dr O'Connor as being in America.

'Oh! will I ever get to sleep this night,' she groaned, louder than she meant, and Geraldine, hearing the sound in her sleep, turned and murmured 'Jill'.

'Are you awake, Jerry?' and Geraldine muttered what was meant to be an assent.

Impulsive Jill slipped out of bed and running across the floor in her bare feet she knelt beside Geraldine and cried quickly, but in a whisper as she remembered the watching door across the landing, 'Don't go to England, Jerry! Oh! don't go. I was wrong to advise you; promise me that you won't go.'

'Why, of course I'm not going,' murmured Jerry, not properly awake. 'Don't be afraid of that,' and she gave a sleepy little laugh.

Jill stared at her in surprise for a moment—Jerry had spoken as if the English business was over and done with—she must be still dreaming!

'Wake up for a moment, dear; do please,' she said. 'I want to talk to you.'

Sleepily Geraldine pushed back her hair and sat up, and then noticing for the first time that her friend had left her own bed and was kneeling beside hers she said in puzzled tones:—

'Why, Jill, what is it? Is anything wrong?'

'No; at least nothing in particular,' replied the other; 'but I want you to promise me not to go to England.'

Geraldine's mind groped through the mists of sleep for the meaning of Jill's words. Then she remembered—remembered, too, the need for discretion and secrecy—she must be careful what she said. Leaning upon her elbow she slipped her other arm round Jill's shoulder.

'Don't worry, Jill,' she said; 'it will be all right. I'll promise not to do anything in a hurry.'

'Oh! Jerry, promise not to go at all,' insisted the other frantically.

Geraldine was fully awake now and Jill's words puzzled her. What had happened to change her friend like this so quickly? She wished that she could allay her fears completely by telling her the whole truth, but she had given her word to Peter O'Connor not even to tell Jill, so her lips were closed. She dare not even give her a hint of how things were, so all she said was: 'Go back to bed now like a dear; you will get your death of cold like that. Don't worry— there's a darling! I'm not going to run away at once, and I'll promise to think well over everything.'

With that small comfort Jill had to be content. As for Geraldine, she was wishing that she could have taken the other entirely into her confidence and made up her mind to ask Dr O'Connor's permission to do so. She would get into communication with him as soon as possible and arrange it, for she knew that she could trust Jill absolutely.

Silence fell upon the flat then and both girls slept after a while, and no sound disturbed the quietness until morning—for Yvonne Delaunay, too, was sleeping in her dainty room across the corridor, as no special work called her abroad that night.

That morning the post brought a letter to Geraldine which surprised her, while it pleased her, too. It was from Sheila Hammond, now staying for a while at the home of her girlhood— Firfield—asking Geraldine to go out and see her. 'Come early and spend the day,' she wrote; 'for I want to talk to you, Jerry.'

Geraldine handed it across the table to Jill, who read it and then said quietly: 'You will go, Jerry, I suppose?'

'Oh! yes,' cried the other; 'of course. I'll go today. I am just longing to see Sheila again, and I'm so glad she wrote. I was afraid she was going to cut all her old friends.'

'You will find her changed, I expect,' said Jill, and added, 'Don't tire yourself, Jerry; do you really feel quite equal to it?'

'Oh! yes; of course. Why I will enjoy a day in the country,' replied Geraldine gaily. And then she said hesitatingly, 'Jill, what did you mean last night when you woke me that time?'

'I'm sorry I woke you,' replied her friend; 'but you spoke in your sleep and I thought you were waking. As to what I meant, I told you, Jerry. I don't want you to leave Ireland just now.'

'But you were so anxious for me to go,' said Geraldine in puzzled tones. 'What has changed your opinion, Jill? There must be some reason for it.'

'Oh! I—I just wanted you to stay here longer. I thought——,' but as she spoke Jill's eyes had turned towards the door leading on to the corridor, and she had instinctively lowered her voice. Geraldine's quick brain jumped at once to the right conclusion.

'It's Yvonne!' she said, and even although she spoke softly Jill murmured 'Hush!' and placed her finger on her lips.

'You mistrust her, too?' whispered Geraldine then. 'Since when?'

'I don't know really. Lately, some way, I have known—I have felt that she is not to be trusted. And then last night when I couldn't sleep I began to wonder why is she so anxious—for she is terribly anxious—for you to be out of Ireland just now?'

Poor Geraldine! What would she not have given to be able then to take her friend into her complete confidence and tell her all. But her given word held her dumb, she could only try and hedge a bit until she had seen Peter. 'Well! don't worry, Jill,' she said. 'I'll not do anything rash. We can talk these things over again. And—' as an afterthought—'you can keep your eyes and ears open about our neighbour and tell me if you notice anything strange or unusual.'

Later Jill had to go out about some designing work. She was not absent long, but on her return Geraldine was struck by the expression on her face.

'What is it, Jill?' she asked quickly.

The other put her arms round her and Geraldine was surprised to see the tears in her eyes—it was so seldom that Jill cried. But even as she wondered Jill spoke:

'Terence MacSwiney has got his release, Jerry,' she said, and Geraldine, as she looked at her, realised the meaning in her words.

Yes; he had got his release—his eternal release from pain and suffering. His martyrdom was over at last.

Her own eyes filled, yet not so much in sorrow as in relief.

'Oh! Jill,' she said. 'Thank God that his sufferings are over. For so long I have had to think of him on his bed of torture—racked with pain and dying by inches. Oh! it was a picture always before my mind. Now, he must be so happy, meeting all the others, too, and talking about Ireland.'

Jill looked at her in tender amusement that yet was tinged with sadness.

'What faith you have, Jerry!' she said. 'One would think your Heaven was just round the corner.'

'It has seemed very near and real to me lately—more so than ever,' said Geraldine. 'I don't know what we Irish would have done without our faith during these times. Oh! Jill; if only you had it, too!'

'Oh! well; you can pray for me,' said the other. For a moment she seemed inclined to say more, but suddenly changed her mind and dismissed the subject with a characteristic shrug of the shoulders.

'You had better get ready if you are going to Goatstown early,' was all she said.

The other with a stifled sigh went into the bedroom to put on her outdoor things.

CHAPTER XII

THE CRUCIBLE AT WORK

Geraldine reached Dundrum soon after one o'clock. It was a delightful October day, clear and crisp, and she thoroughly enjoyed her walk to Firfield along the fresh country roads which were strewn so thickly with the autumn tinted leaves.

Arrived at Firfield House, a smart parlourmaid admitted her and showed her into the library, where a cheery fire was blazing.

'Mrs Hammond will be down in a minute, Miss,' she said, and Geraldine was left to herself in the lofty book-lined room.

Her gaze went to the window, where old Mont Pelier seemed to be lifting his head in welcome, and then she glanced at the garden, which was making a brave show with dahlias and chrysanthemums. But Geraldine's thoughts were all with Sheila—with the friend of her girlhood whom she was soon to meet. It was over three years since she had seen her—not long as we count time perhaps—but long in changes and happenings for both of them. It seemed so strange to Geraldine to think of Sheila as married; she could only think of her as the lovely, golden-haired girl, the rather spoilt little beauty, who had captured all hearts so easily. She who had been the very idol of her brothers' hearts. How she had treated them in the end. Fond as Geraldine still remained of Sheila, she had never been able to forgive her for her behaviour towards the twins. But she was very anxious to see her—how she wished she would come!

Even as her fingers drummed impatiently upon the low window seat the door opened, and, turning, she saw a woman on the threshold.

A very lovely woman, slight and fair, and perfectly dressed and groomed from the crown of wavy hair to her dainty shoes, but a woman with hard lines around the mouth, and with tired lines round those sweet violet eyes which looked at the world with weary disdain.

For a moment Geraldine stared at her in bewilderment, very much as the twins had once gazed at the girl Sheila standing on that very threshold on a summer's night three years ago. She hardly recognised her. Could this cold-looking woman of fashion be the laughing girl she remembered? But even as she hesitated a change passed over the face of the other— a sudden softening and breaking up—a veritable thawing of the ice of reserve, and Sheila, with a little inarticulate cry, ran across the room, and the next moment Geraldine was holding her in her arms and kissing and petting her as if she was still the little spoilt Sheila of long ago.

But only for a moment—the tired, weary look, the hard expression, returned to Sheila's lovely face, and she drew away from the encircling arms and looked up at Geraldine with a weary sigh.

'I wonder you can still care for me, Jerry,' she said then, 'but it was good of you to come and see me. 'I hardly hoped for it. Come and sit down by the fire; we have time for a little chat before lunch. You can stay till evening—can't you?'

'Oh! yes,' replied Geraldine, 'if you really want me to do so, but as to lunch, well! I am not very well dressed as you can see, so if you have visitors——.'

She glanced down at her well-worn tweed skirt as she spoke and thought of the plain knitted jumper under her coat. Her shoes, however, were new and good—a present from Jill, in spite of her protests. She had thought little of her dress until she had noticed Sheila's lovely gown, which had accentuated the difference between them so acutely.

Sheila glanced at her indifferently.

'Oh! as if it mattered what you have on,' she said wearily. 'One gets so sick of clothes at times. But we have no visitors at present—no one is here besides Mums—except, of course, Norman.'

'Oh! is your husband here?' said Geraldine. 'He is Captain Hammond now, I believe?'

Sheila nodded.

'Yes; he got his Captaincy just before he was gassed the last time. Then he had shell shock and has never really got over it—he drinks, you know, when he can get it, but we have a man to look after him and he keeps it from him as much as possible, although, of course, he has to be allowed a little.'

Geraldine stared at her aghast, the weary indifference, the utter unconcern with which she spoke of her husband appalled the girl.

'But, Sheila,' she said—speaking almost in spite of herself—'you—you were so fond of Captain Hammond. You left your home—and the twins—and everything for him.'

A spasm of pain crossed the other's face.

'Yes; I suppose I did,' she said. 'We are all mad at times, but oh!

Jerry, I have paid dearly for my madness. But tell me now about yourself, for we have not much time before the gong will ring, and after lunch I want you to come to my room for a serious talk.'

So sitting before the cheery fire, and surrounded by what to her was the essence of comfort and luxury, Geraldine told the story of the past few years, and Sheila listened quietly, very seldom interrupting but drinking it all in as if she had been thirsting for the news.

Geraldine told her not only her own story, but told all she knew about the twins also, glancing curiously at Sheila's impassive face as she did so. Would she never speak? Was she as indifferent to them as she seemed to be to most things now? At last she could bear it no longer.

'Oh! Sheila!' she cried. 'Don't you care for them any longer? Have you forgotten them?'

'Care—Forget!' said the woman opposite lifting her dark violet eyes and looking at Geraldine with a word of anguish in their depths. 'Oh! Jerry! if you knew—if you knew! But later I will explain better to you. I don't want to talk about these matters at present. And now, Jerry, don't be vexed; but won't you let me help you a little until you get another position? Let me, for the sake of old times. I have more money than I know what to do with—and nothing to spend it on. If you won't take money let me buy you what you need. Come for a day's shopping with me; we will have a day in town together. Ah!'—in a changed voice—'I see you won't.'

Geraldine looked at her sadly.

'How could I, Sheila?' she asked quietly. 'I would always be remembering how you got your money. It is English—for it you gave up——.'

'No—no, Jerry; be just!' interrupted the other. 'I did not give up my country and ideals for money. I was not so base as that—bad as I was. I gave up all that I should have held dear for the love of a man, and'—her voice became exceedingly bitter—'I have reaped my reward. A man—a sot!'

'Oh! Sheila! Surely it is not so bad as that,' said Geraldine in real distress. 'Surely Captain Hammond is not always—he used to be so devoted to you.'

'You are right, Jerry. I am not quite just. Poor Norman! Circumstances, I suppose, have really made him what he is—a physical and mental wreck. He is not too bad just at present, although you will see a big change in him, but please don't pretend to notice anything, he always tries to pull himself together when strangers are here. But there's the gong. Come up to my room and take off your hat and coat; you will have plenty of time for we are not very punctual people here.'

The luncheon that followed was rather like a bad dream to Geraldine.

Mrs Ryan received her with cold indifference, and Geraldine perceived at once that the elder woman was changed very much. She looked much older and care-worn and seemed like a woman who had hidden troubles of her own. Her would-be society manner of the past was gone—she seldom troubled to make conversation, but was very quiet and silent, although when she did speak she did so with the stilted accent which she had acquired so painfully. But although the woman was undoubtedly not the same, still the girl could not fathom in what the change really consisted, but her instinct told her that Mrs Ryan was not happy. As they were sitting down to lunch she asked her stepdaughter in a rather timid manner if Norman was not coming?

'I don't know I'm sure,' was the indifferent reply; 'but I rather think that Andrews has taken him for a walk.'

Mrs Ryan glanced quickly at Geraldine, but Sheila said carelessly:

'Oh! Jerry knows about him.'

A few minutes later there was a footstep, which, however, resembled a shuffle, outside the door. It was thrown open by his attendant and Captain Hammond entered.

'Can you manage all right, sir? Shall I stay?' inquired the man as the Captain shuffled on into the room.

'No, no; of course I'm all right—damn you! Why shouldn't I be all right. Why——.'

Then he noticed Geraldine and tried to pull himself together.

'This is Miss Moore, Norman—I expect you remember her?' said his mother-in-law in rather embarrassed tones, while Sheila never lifted her eyes from her plate.

Geraldine shook hands with him—noting the shaky flabbiness of his with some disgust—and he subsided into his chair muttering—'Oh! yes, yes—to be sure! Just so! What's for lunch?'

His blood-shot eyes swept the table and then he called to the waiting parlourmaid, 'Here you! Bring me a drink!'

Although she did not want to look at him, Geraldine found her gaze drawn to his face in spite of herself, and she was astonished to observe the difference which the last few years had wrought in the man. She remembered him at the time of Sheila's ill-fated marriage and he was then a well set-up young fellow of splendid physique—more physique than brains certainly, but he still had been strong and athletic, a fine specimen of manhood, very different indeed from the poor degenerate who now faced her across the table and whose shaking hands spilled both soup and wine, and whose sagging lips made his eating a repulsive sight.

He tried at first to join in the conversation, but after a few more or less incoherent attempts he gave it up and applied himself to his lunch.

Geraldine was thankful beyond words when at length the meal was over and she accompanied Sheila upstairs to her own pretty room, the same room that had been hers when as Sheila Ryan she had dreamt her innocent dreams inside its walls.

'Have you learned to smoke yet, Jerry?' she asked, as she wheeled forward two easy chairs to the fire.

'No; nor never will,' replied Geraldine with a smile. 'My Lady Nicotine has no charms for me.'

'So much the better for yourself. Now, Jerry, I want to talk to you very seriously.'

She glanced round the room as she spoke, and then going over to the door turned the key in the lock.

'We are fairly secure here,' she said, in reply to Geraldine's surprised look, 'but Norman has a horrid habit of wandering all over the place, and if he once got in here it might be hours before we could get rid of him. I must speak to you privately.'

She sank into a chair and idly stirred the fire, and for a few moments remained silent, gazing into the flames with her lovely, sad eyes.

The she said softly:—

'So Terence MacSwiney is gone!'

Geraldine looked at her with wide eyes.

'Why, Sheila!' she cried, 'do you care. I thought that you—you——.'

'That I was Irish no longer!' interposed the other bitterly. 'No wonder you thought it—I don't deserve that you should have any other opinion of me. But you are wrong—I am more really Irish now after my years in England than I ever was before. I am going to prove it to you.'

She paused for a moment and then she lifted her eyes and looked long and steadily at her old friend.

'I am going to trust you, Jerry,' she said; 'to trust you as I would trust Tony or Desmond—the dear, dear boys—if they were here. What I tell you now you are to carry to them as a message from me.'

'Sheila! what do you mean?'

'Listen, and I will explain. I don't know if you are aware of it or not, but Yvonne Delaunay is an agent of the British Secret Service. Oh! you do know it. How?'

Briefly Geraldine told her, and with a nod of comprehension Sheila continued: 'Another agent—the one who works with her hand in hand in this country—is my husband's brother, Ronald Hammond; but his professional cognomen is "Mr Chester". He has a flat in town near where Yvonne is and she can see him easily and quickly. It was she who caused the raid to be made on Elton Street; she wanted to arrest Tony and Peter O'Connor.'

'And not Desmond?' asked Geraldine. She was anxious to learn whether Sheila had come to the same conclusion as Peter O'Connor.

'No, not Desmond,' was the reply. 'She gave most definite instructions that he was not to be arrested.'

Geraldine sat looking at her almost stupidly.

'Oh! Jerry, can't you see?' cried the other. 'Oh! don't be so slow. She means to ruin him another way; to fascinate him and learn all she can from him; to destroy him utterly.'

Geraldine stared at her in frozen horror.

'How do you know all this?' she asked faintly.

'By listening! By acting the part of a spy myself. I was hidden behind those great curtains in the library for hours one night when Yvonne was here.'

'Yvonne—here!'

'Yes; she comes here sometimes to meet Ronald when they want a long conflab together and she doesn't care to go to his rooms. She has wound poor Mums round her little finger, and when the household has gone to bed she slips down to the library and meets Ronald. Of course he is often here, being Norman's brother. Poor Mums would get a fit if she ever came upon them—she would think it was some terrible scandal. It is purely business with them, but oh! for us, Jerry, if you could hear their plans and their talk! It has almost driven me mad at times!'

'How did you first guess anything about it?'

'From my unfortunate husband. They have some hold over him—something he did in France long ago at the very beginning of the war. I don't know what it is, but he thinks he is in their power and I believe he used to help them at times, but now, of course, he is quite useless for that kind of work. He sleeps in a room off mine and the door is left open between, because he won't have the man in his room at night, and sometimes he takes a notion to get up and wander around, and then I have to call Andrews. He talks in his sleep and I heard him say something about Ronald and Yvonne that made me suspicious. Then one day when he was drunk I got more information from him—it was he told me then that I would find the two of them in the library at night. So I went down fairly early one night and hid behind the great velvet curtains and waited. And they came.'

'Oh! Sheila! if they had discovered you.'

'What would it matter? Except that I would not have been able to warn you, but now when I have told you all I don't care what happens to me.'

'Don't talk like that, dear old Sheila. Why, just think how valuable you will be to us now that you are staying here. Tell me all you know—all you have heard, and then I will explain our position to you.'

'Well! they are looking for some special papers of very great importance which it seems Tony and Desmond have in their possession, and these papers would give them full details of names and localities, especially of one hiding place where a lot of stuff is stored. They want the names on the list, too—there are lots of "wanted" men amongst them.'

'I daresay,' said Geraldine ironically, 'but I don't fancy that they will ever see that list.'

'Do you know where it is?'

'No, but I know the twins have it—that's all.'

'Well! give them this warning, won't you? And oh! Jerry, above all else do impress on Tony to keep Desmond away from that woman.'

'Oh! but that is unnecessary, Sheila,' said the other. 'Surely you don't believe for one moment that Desmond would be such a fool as to give away or even to speak of such a matter at all to an outsider like Yvonne.'

'Jerry, I am afraid!' was the answer. 'She boasted here—sitting there—about her power over Desmond. Ronald agreed with her that he would be easily fooled.'

'But he has gone into hiding again, you know that?'

'Yes; but she says he will come back—to her.'

'Oh! rot!' cried Geraldine with a laugh. 'She thinks too much of herself. They will both venture back after a while, of course, but to think that Desmond is going to run after Yvonne—why it's absurd even to think of it.'

'Well! I hope you are right. But tell the boys what I heard about the papers they have and speak privately to Tony and tell him that I say he is to look after his brother. And give them both my love— my dear love—if they will take it, and tell them, too, that there is nothing—nothing—that I would not do to help them—and Ireland! But I suppose you won't see them for some time, or could you send a letter safely?'

'I won't see them for a while, but I can send any message quite safely by Dr O'Connor.'

'Oh! yes. Of course, I remember him. And I know he is to be trusted,' replied Sheila. Then she noticed for the first time that her friend's cheeks had flushed as she mentioned his name—and drew her own conclusions. 'I used to think she was one of Desmond's victims,' she said to herself with a wistful smile.

They had a delightful tea by the fire in the cosy little room and then Sheila drove Geraldine to the station. She had a little two-seater of her own and drove well. It was not till she was in the train that the girl had a few minutes to think quietly over what Sheila had told her. When she tried to do so her brain got quite confused, and it was no wonder, for between Dr O'Connor's revelations of the preceding night and now Sheila's confidences she hardly knew where she was standing. But her first and foremost feeling was one of joy and thankfulness that Sheila had returned to them again— and returned to them in every way.

'How pleased the boys will be,' she thought, and then she remembered the warning about Desmond, and although she would not admit to herself that it was serious, she could not but remember that Peter O'Connor had been of the same way of thinking.

'Oh! if it should prove true. That dreadful woman!' she thought with a shiver as she alighted at Harcourt Street Station.

It was not yet seven o'clock and on her way home Geraldine called at the house of a boy scout whom she knew well and could absolutely trust. By him she sent a message, and the result was that towards eight o'clock Mr Ferdinand Shortall, spectacled and bent, and crippled with rheumatism, arrived at the flat. Jill admitted him, somewhat surprised at his visit, but it was nothing to the surprise she felt a moment later when the door locked, and the heavy curtain drawn across it, Dr Peter O'Connor suddenly stood before her—minus all disguise—and with hand outstretched in greeting, his keen eyes twinkling with amusement at her astonishment.

'Oh! Peter! You—you horrid Sherlock Holmes,' was all she could gasp.

His first serious question was about Yvonne. She was gone out it appeared, and Jill thought she would be late back, as she was dressed for dining out, probably going to a restaurant or hotel with some of her admirers.

Then the three sat down as friends in Council and discussed everything fully, Peter having first spoken to Jill and received her promise of secrecy. Geraldine told about her interview with Sheila to the amazement of the others, and Jill listened thunderstruck while Peter unfolded to her a few details about the fascinating Yvonne. She learned, too, about Geraldine's future arrangements with delight, and could smile now at the remembrance of how the latter had been compelled to put off her importunities of the previous night.

'You wretch!' she said. 'And I was in such a state. If only you could have given me a hint.'

But Geraldine shook her head.

'I have given my word,' she said, and Jill understood.

Dr O'Connor could not stay very long for obvious reasons, but before he went they understood each other thoroughly, and had all their plans and arrangements made for watching Yvonne and at the same time cheating her into the belief that they knew nothing of her real work, but accepted her, in all simple faith, to be what she wished them to think her. They also had settled what to do in the event of certain emergencies, and Peter had promised to see the twins on the following day and to give them the various messages from their sister. He promised, too, that he would speak seriously to Anthony about Desmond.

'Although I have already done so,' he added, as he rose to go, and began putting on his disguise again.

'But you don't really believe that Yvonne has the power to influence him—do you?' asked Geraldine, and was dismayed in spite of herself when she got the same answer that Sheila had given her earlier in the day.

'I don't know, of course,' said Peter; 'but—I am afraid.'

CHAPTER XIII

MRS PELL SAYS 'NO'

For the next three weeks both Geraldine and Jill 'lay low' according to instructions, and Yvonne suspected nothing. She came in and out of their flat as usual, always fascinating and full of kind care and thought for Geraldine, above all very anxious that she should pull up her strength quickly so as to be able to take up the position in England. Geraldine was no actress and often found it hard to play the part assigned to her, but Jill met guile with guile and her acting was splendid. Geraldine, in the meanwhile, went to Elton Street on several occasions for a couple of hours at a time and got to know the clerk and some of the more confidential callers there. Dr O'Connor had spoken of her to young Dillon and explained her real work there, and also to as many as he wished her to know in connection with work for the cause. She was already engrossed at the thought of the work before her and only wishing that she could be there regularly.

She was therefore delighted when at the end of two weeks Peter thought it would be best to mention casually to Yvonne that Geraldine considered that she would not be strong enough for district work in England, and that she had decided not to go.

Both she and Jill were more than a trifle nervous when the time came to speak. Yvonne had run in to visit them one evening as usual and was sitting by the fire talking to them, and when Geraldine announced her decision the look of baffled rage which showed for a moment in the strange eyes opposite to them made them—as they afterwards confessed to one another—nearly shake in their shoes. But Yvonne's feelings only showed for a brief second, so brief was it indeed that if the others had not been watching her so closely they might not even have noticed it. She pulled herself together immediately, and seldom had she been so clever an actress.

'Ah! but I am sorry—so sorry!' she said, and her wonderful voice was as sweet and musical as ever; 'and I know that Lady Selby-Jones will be desolated! She does so love the Irish and was longing to see you. But have you really made up your mind quite?'

Geraldine nodded.

'Yes,' she said; 'I have thought everything over very fully,

Mademoiselle Delaunay, and I am sure that I would not be able for the work over there, and besides I have got work here.'

Yvonne's eyes narrowed and she glanced swiftly to where Jill was standing—to all appearance intent on some drawing designs which she was holding out before her while she studied them critically.

'Yes?' said Yvonne in sweet interrogation, 'and if you will not think me too rude, dear Miss Moore, might one ask more particulars?'

What Yvonne was to be told had already been settled and Geraldine therefore had her answer ready.

'Oh! yes,' she said; 'a friend of mine at Clontarf wishes me to go every day from ten till five and help her with the children and the housework. I will have my lunch there and the salary will suit me for the present.'

'So!' Yvonne's eyes narrowed still more, but nothing was to be learned from the tone of her voice, and so whether she suspected anything or not the others could not tell. They talked it over together after Yvonne had left the flat.

'Well! it can't be helped if she does suspect,' said Jill. 'It was the best yarn we could think of, and you do know Rose Kelly out at Clontarf. Besides there is very little likelihood that Yvonne will go to the offices in Elton Street—what would take her there? You don't even have to go out for your lunch, you can always make it in the rooms above, so you won't meet her in the street.'

'All the same I hope she won't ever come to the office,' said Geraldine. 'I think I would faint if she took me by surprise some day.'

'What nonsense!' cried Jill. 'Why, Jerry, I believe you are half afraid of her. Besides what could she do to you?'

'It's not myself I am thinking about,' was the reply, 'but she might take her revenge on others.'

'Don't meet trouble half way,' advised Jill the philosopher, 'and whatever we do, Jerry, keep a cool head, for Heaven knows we all need courage and self-control these days.'

Poor Jill! She often needed all her own courage and self-control when she remembered the danger, the danger that was two-fold, hanging over one beloved head.

So Geraldine entered regularly upon her new duties and attended the offices in Elton Street each day. She had plenty to do—learning to type and understand other details of office work from Frank Dillon, who soon became her willing slave, besides her secret duties which Peter O'Connor explained to her from time to time. She had a quick brain and a true woman's intuition, and, as Peter had foreseen, she soon proved very valuable to them in taking and passing on various messages and dispatches. It was very long since Geraldine had been so happy. She felt she was at last doing something for Ireland, and in spite of the Terror all around her, so that she never knew, when she left Jill's flat in the morning, whether she would be alive or able to return to it in the evening, and despite, too, her anxiety for dear friends and comrades she thoroughly enjoyed her work and her life just then.

Speaking to Peter one day—the doctor came openly to the office 'as himself,' keeping the Ferdinand Shortall impersonation for other purposes—she remarked that she was so thankful that Yvonne Delaunay had not discovered where she was really employed during the day. Peter had looked at her rather curiously for a moment, and had been about to speak, but seemingly he thought better of it and with some non-committal remark changed the subject.

The truth was that he knew perfectly well that Yvonne was aware of where Geraldine passed her days, and that she also had a shrewd guess of the kind of work for which she had been specially engaged. Yvonne had had her shadowed as soon as she began to go regularly to Elton Street, but Peter thought that the longer Geraldine was in ignorance of this fact the better it would be for her nerves. But he knew that it could not be for long, she would have to know one of these days, as Yvonne would be almost certain to play another card in the game very soon.

He was right. The week before the Croke Park shooting Geraldine was bending diligently over her typewriter with Frank Dillon beside her; when she heard a step entering the office and swung round on her seat, to see Yvonne Delaunay crossing the threshold. She was wearing a fashionable jade coloured coat with black fur, and on her lovely head was an undescribable hat with 'Paris' written all over it. She made a very beautiful picture and it was little wonder that young Dillon gazed and gazed in stupid wonder.

She came towards Geraldine, who rose to meet her in dazed bewilderment, for what could she say or do? She felt as if she was caught in a trap.

'So!' said Yvonne, 'what a naughty girl! Or what is it you say in Dublin—bold, is that it? A bold girl!'

Geraldine was silent, she felt unable to speak, but Dillon came forward with a chair—which he reverently placed as for a goddess.

'I may sit?' and as Geraldine nodded dumbly Yvonne took the chair in her usual graceful way, with a fleeting smile at poor Frank—he might be useful some time.

'So this is where I find you then,' she went on, in well-feigned surprise; 'I could hardly believe it.'

She glanced swiftly round the office as she spoke, noting every detail with rapid thoroughness, although to all outward appearance her survey was but very casual. Geraldine felt that she must speak—she must say something.

'Did you want to see me?' she asked, almost stupidly. 'Or did you call here on business?'

Yvonne must have smiled to herself as she thought of her real business there, but she only lifted her perfectly gloved little hand in gentle protest.

'Ah! no; but listen, just listen how it happened,' she said, her eyes raised in apparent innocence to Geraldine's puzzled face; 'I met a friend of mine just outside, in Dame Street, and she said to me, "So your little companion has got employment now—office work I suppose?" I asked her of whom did she speak and she then said that you came here every day. How astonished I was.'

Then she lowered her voice and leant forward as she said: 'But why deceive me, Miss Moore? I, that have always been your so fond friend.'

Geraldine was terribly embarrassed. She was so essentially honest and open herself that she was at a great disadvantage at a time like this. What was she to say? 'Oh! it was more of a—a joke than anything else, my coming here I mean. We did not think it would last and probably it won't.'

She felt even as she was speaking what nonsense it must sound to the other.

Yvonne laughed, showing all her pretty teeth— a laugh that Geraldine did not like to hear.

'So!' she said; 'it was just a joke. Well! I suppose I must forgive— I am fond of jokes myself.' And she laughed again.

To Geraldine's relief at this moment two men—one of them a solicitor—entered the office in reference to a case which Anthony had been compelled to hand over to others. They wanted certain papers in connection with the business, and as there was some difficulty in finding these it gave Geraldine the excuse she wanted of saying to her unwelcome visitor, 'Will you excuse me?'

Yvonne with a polite little smile rose to her feet, just saying:—

'Eh! bien; I'll see you tonight ma chère!' and left the room gracefully—three pairs of masculine eyes watching her to the very last as she disappeared through the doorway. But Yvonne did not go straight down the stairs and out into the street. She remembered that the Ryans' private rooms were on the top landing of the building, and the born instinct of the Secret Service Agent sent her up the remaining stairs.

She reached the top landing and went softly along until she came to the open door of the sittingroom. She slipped within noiselessly, and standing in the centre by the table took a rapid survey of the room and furniture. It was homely and comfortable and in good order, and Yvonne remembered that Geraldine Moore did not leave the building during the day—this had been reported to her with other details—and she concluded that she would use this upper part at times, and would in any case like to keep it ready for 'the boys'. Her attention was now arrested by a large portrait in oils which hung over the mantelpiece. She guessed at once that it was the mother of the twins from the place of honour it held and from the resemblance to Sheila. She stood looking at it for a few moments. The eyes gazing back at her seemed as though they were reading her very soul, and although Yvonne was, as a rule, impervious to any feeling of that sort, she now turned away quickly and went back to the table.

'I wonder by any chance would there be any useful papers lying around?' she thought, 'but it is not likely, they are too clever for that.'

Still she went across to a bureau by the window and softly pulled on the brass handle of its drawer.

It yielded to her touch, and she was just about to draw forth some papers which she saw within when an indignant voice from behind her caused her to swing round swiftly.

'And might I ask, young lady, what might be the subject of your visit here? You seem to be quite at home anyway, and although in the position of lady housekeeper to the Mr Ryans for many years I don't remember having encountered your profile previous to this.'

Mrs Pell stopped for breath while she stood by the door leading into the kitchen and surveyed Yvonne with her beady eyes, which were almost lost behind the shaking blancmange of her cheeks.

It was nearly four o'clock in the afternoon, and Mrs Pell had not long arrived to do 'a bit of cleaning up.' She had been sitting by the fire and had not heard Yvonne until she made the slight sound at the bureau, and truth compels us to admit with sorrow that Mrs Pell had been 'on it' the night before. She was practically sober now, but the after effects were there all the same; she was cross and irritable and out of sorts, and in fact suffering acutely from the life's not worth living feeling of 'the day after'. Yvonne rose to the occasion at once—Mrs Pell would surely be easy fish for her net to land— and she might prove of great use. She came across the room with her sweetest of smiles and outstretched hand and without a shade of embarrassment.

'Now I am sure that you must be Mrs Pell?' she said. 'I have heard so much of you, both from Miss Moore and Miss Devereux, and from my old friends the Ryans, too. I am so glad you have come, for perhaps you can help me to find the address of a Mr Rossiter? He is an artist on whom I wish to call and Mr Desmond promised to leave the address here for me.'

It was the first excuse that entered her head and it went down with Mrs Pell all right as she had foreseen. That good woman was quite flustered when she took a better look at Yvonne and noticed her stylish appearance—and then she had been so gracious, such a real lady! Mrs Pell almost curtsied as she began to make her apologies.

'I beg your pardon, I am sure, madam,' she began in her most grandiloquent manner; 'my eyesight lately has not been so good and ——'

'Oh! please say no more,' entreated Yvonne prettily, 'but have you any idea where Mr Desmond would have been likely to put that address? I know that he had to go away in such a hurry that he might have forgotten to leave it for me.'

'Ah! indeed, my poor lamb, hunted and worried.' Mrs Pell was now all regret that she did not know where it was and neither of the young gentlemen had mentioned such a name to her—it would indeed have been hard for them to do so. 'As for papers or letters, nothing was kept up there. The papers in the bureau were only accounts—bills for coal and light, etc.'

'Ah! well; it does not matter; it is of but little consequence,' replied Yvonne; 'but I am so tired and rather cold. I wonder, Mrs Pell—indeed I hardly like to trouble you—but would you let me sit by your fire and warm myself for a little while?'

Mrs Pell was charmed and wheeled an easy chair to the kitchen fire, into which Yvonne sank with her usual languid grace, while the other watched her admiringly. To Mrs Pell she resembled the 'officers' ladies' who used sometimes to chat to her when she was doing their laundry in the days of long ago—that happy time when she was travelling round the world 'on the strength'. Oh! those were the days of style and grandeur.

'You are very comfortable here, Mrs Pell,' said Yvonne's voice; 'it is very nice for you to have this, is it not? And with your Army pension I suppose you are able to live quite nicely?'

She knew perfectly that Mrs Pell had no pension, and knew the reason, too, as she had heard all the particulars from Jill before the latter's suspicions had been aroused.

Mrs Pell, standing respectfully at the other side of the fire, threw an appealing glance upwards to an unjust Heaven.

'I am not in deceit of any pension, Miss,' she replied, and Yvonne rapidly translated deceit into receipt—for she had heard of Mrs Pell's Esperanto. 'My late sainted husband Mr P knows that I speak but the truth.' And the widow threw another glance towards the ceiling—doubtless this time directed towards Mr P's heavenly bed.

'No pension!' echoed Yvonne, in well-feigned surprise. 'Oh! what a shame. Do sit down, won't you, and tell me all about it—if it will not distress you too much.'

Her quick eyes noticed that the woman was not altogether herself, and she determined to see of what stuff she was really made and to find out if she could make any use of her or not.

Mrs Pell willingly seated herself, although still at a respectful distance, and Yvonne was soon listening to what she knew was a perfectly fictitious story of the late Mr P's unjust treatment at the hands of the British military authorities. Yvonne listened and sympathised—she even shed a few tears to the memory of the 'diseased' Mr P.

Mrs Pell was completely subjugated—seldom had she met such a tender-hearted young lady. Very different indeed from Miss Moore and Miss Devereux, who were wont at times to cut short her reminiscences of the late Mr P in a rather abrupt way.

'If I might make you a cup of tea, Miss?' she ventured to ask. 'I would carry it into the other room for you and——.'

'No; no please, Mrs Pell—not in the sittingroom. But if I might have it here, by your so lovely fire and in your so clean kitchen. How do you keep it so beautifully?'

Later, as she was sipping her tea, Yvonne thought the time had come for her to lay a few cards on the table.

'I have some influence with the military authorities,' she said; 'perhaps I could get them to look up your case again.'

But Mrs Pell knew only too well that the more her case was investigated the less chance she had of obtaining anything.

'Ah! no, Miss,' she replied sadly, 'pray don't incommode yourself; it would not be of any prevail.'

'But, Mrs Pell, my—my influence is fairly strong, and you must let me speak for you. It seems such a shame that you should be treated like this.'

Mrs Pell shook her head and lifting her apron to the corner of her eye she wiped away a tear.

'I don't mind informing you, Miss,' she said then, 'for you are of such a sympathising preposition, that poor, dear Mr P—well, he took a little drop on a few occasions, and they have it against his name.'

'Oh! that's too bad!' said Yvonne. 'Why nearly all soldiers are sometimes like that. I will speak for you, and I believe—indeed I know—that I can get you a pension, and also the arrears since the time your husband died.'

Mrs Pell gazed in a dazed way at her; she did not believe that she could do as she said, of course. But still supposing that this lovely little lady was a daughter or sister of some 'big-wig'? Stranger things had come to pass. But no—it would be too wonderful.

'Ah! Miss; you will have your little joke!' she said, with a polite but wistful smile.

'It is no joke—no joke really,' replied Yvonne. 'I can get you what I have said. Will you let me do it, Mrs Pell?'

'Let you do it? Why Miss I—I—Ah! don't raise false hopes within my breast.' Even in her excitement Mrs Pell spoke in her usual theatrical style.

'They are not false hopes,' said Yvonne. Something in the way she spoke—an air of authority—almost of power, told Mrs Pell that she was speaking only of what she could perform. 'I can get you what I promised, and I will do so if you wish, but——.'

She paused for a moment and looked at Mrs Pell keenly. The latter caught her breath.

'But what, Miss?' she asked, almost faintly in her excitement. 'Are you afraid you won't be able to manage it after all?'

'No,' replied the other quietly. 'I can do all I have said, and can do it at once. But if I do this for you, will you do something for me?'

Mrs Pell looked at her in puzzled wonder.

'And what could I do for you, Miss?' she asked. 'But you need not ask would I do it, sure it would be queer if I wouldn't after all your kindness to me.'

But Yvonne did not reply at once. She sat looking into the fire, the flames of which were dancing and flickering on her lovely hair where it peeped from beneath her hat, and on her pretty, soft frock, from which she had slipped off her coat. Then very gently and sympathetically she inquired:—

'I suppose Mrs Pell, that you are very much attached to Mr Anthony and Mr Desmond?'

The woman's face lit up, although she was apparently rather puzzled at the change of subject.

'Fond of them!' she cried. 'Why, Miss, they are the very apple of my eye. And as for Mr Desmond—the darling boy—Mr P used to say sometimes of his Colonel, he is indeed a perfect gentleman, the glass of fashion, and the very symmetry of form!'

'Yes; but they are both rather foolish. Don't you think so?'

'Foolish? Did you say foolish, Miss?'

'Yes, foolish. Surely, Mrs Pell, you have not been with them all these years without knowing that they are taking part in very dangerous affairs. They have already been in prison, and were in Frongoch before that as you know, and I am very much afraid that they will soon be arrested again.'

'Ah! no, Miss; don't say it. My poor lambs!'

'Yes; I am afraid they will get into trouble, Mrs Pell, and serious trouble this time. It might even mean the death penalty.'

Mrs Pell, with a smothered exclamation, crossed herself devoutly.

'Yes; it is dreadful, isn't it?' asked Yvonne. 'But we must try to prevent it—and you can help in this.'

'Me? did you say me, Miss?'

'Yes, Mrs Pell, you. You can help quite a lot to prevent these foolish boys, for they are little else, from running their heads into a halter.'

'How can I help them? Sure, Miss dear, there is nothing I wouldn't do for my poor lambs.'

'Well! listen now, Mrs Pell. I want you to keep your eyes and ears very wide open and to watch carefully and take note of any callers that come here, especially if they are in conversation with Miss Moore, for she, poor child, is foolish, too, and does not understand the harm she may do. And then if any letters come for either Mr Anthony or Mr Desmond—by post or delivered by hand—you must bring them at once to me.'

She stopped, arrested by the look of horrified incredulity on the other's face.

'What did you say, Miss?' Mrs Pell asked. 'I cannot have heard aright!'

'Yes, you did,' said Yvonne sharply. 'I told you to bring me all the letters that came here for your employers during their absence.'

'And that's a thing I refuse to do, Miss,' was Mrs Pell's answer in her most dignified tones. 'I would not so far demean myself as to touch any correspondence belonging to another.'

'But, Mrs Pell, when it is for their good. You said yourself that you would do anything for the Ryans.'

'Yes, Miss, I did; but not that kind of thing. And it looks to me,' she went on, with a curious glance at the lovely figure opposite to her, 'very queer that a lady like you would even suggest such a thing to the like of me. Ah! no, Miss, I could not think of it—Mr P would not approve of such at all.'

'And what about your pension and the arrears? It would be a great—oh! such a great lot of money—when you got the arrears. And all in one big sum, Mrs Pell.'

There was no answer. Mrs Pell was staring straight in front of her nervously biting a corner of her apron. She was trying to understand, to sift the matter, but her intellect was not at its best that evening and she knew it, and knew the reason, too.

'God forgive me!' she thought. 'When I should be keeping all my senses about me why did I go and muddle them?'

Yvonne was still speaking, her soft, persuasive accents dropping gently into the quiet room.

'Now, please don't be foolish Mrs Pell,' she was saying. 'I only want to save those heedless young men for their own sakes, and you can help me a little. Why will you not do so and get your fine pension? You would be able to have such a good time, and there is your married daughter—your only child, isn't she?—she is so badly off and look how you could help her.'

It was here that Yvonne made one of the biggest mistakes of her career. She should not have offered to bribe Mrs Pell. If she had come to her and asked her as a favour to do what she wanted, putting it all on her anxiety about the twins, it is very likely that Mrs Pell—especially in her rather fuddled condition—would have consented. Not perhaps as to the letters, but in various other ways Yvonne might have been able to get information from her. At least the woman would have continued to regard her as a friend of the Ryans. But the Sergeant-Major's widow was no fool and her brain was now working as rapidly as the mists of alcohol would allow it, and she began in her own words to 'smell a rat'.

But she let Yvonne talk on and did not at once reply, for there is no doubt that the temptation was very great. A pension for life— the pension of a Sergeant-Major's widow, and all the money for the years since he had died—twelve years of arrears! The very thought made her almost giddy and she moved uneasily in her chair. After all this lady—whoever she was— might be right, perhaps it was her duty to do as she was asked. She tried vainly for the space of a few moments to reason that way, but her instinct told her that it was wrong, and she knew that her instinct was right. Common-sense, too, of which she had plenty under all her queer ways, asked plainly why she was bribed so heavily to do this, for that it was a bribe which she was offered she saw clearly now.

'Well! Mrs Pell, what do you say?' Yvonne was asking a trifle impatiently.

'What did she say?' The poor woman lifted a shaking hand and made the Sign of the Cross.

'Oh! God direct me!' she prayed. 'Our Blessed Lady and St Patrick help me now!' She felt somehow that she was not able of herself to withstand the temptation, and to turn her back upon the glittering vision opened up by the lovely woman who was leaning forward and speaking so nicely, and who was apparently so innocent and good. And then suddenly before her eyes she seemed to see a picture of Desmond—her adored Mr Desmond—as he had looked one night when he had only just returned from Frongoch, nearly four years ago now. He had sat there on the kitchen table— her glance went to the very spot—had sat there in the winter firelight like this, and had told her a lot about his imprisonment and camp life, making her laugh and cry in turns. But when she would have been sorry for him he had gently brushed away her sympathy.

'Why, Mrs Pell!' he had cried, with his boyish smile, 'I am glad I went through it. What does it matter what we suffer or for how long if we can help Ireland? And every little sacrifice counts when it is for the cause. Oh! Mrs Pell, don't you wish you could do something for the old land?'

How strange that the picture of that evening—almost forgotten—should have come back to her so vividly just then.

'Well! Mrs Pell?' And now Yvonne's voice held more than a shade of impatience. She wanted to get away before there was a chance of Geraldine's coming upstairs. 'Well! Am I to write for the money?'

'No, thank you, Miss!'

'No? Is it possible that you can be so foolish as to refuse?' Yvonne's eyes flashed angrily as she spoke—for the moment she was raging.

'I don't think it is foolish,' was the reply, 'although of course I may be mistaken. I'm not very clever. But as for you, Miss, whoever or whatever you may be, angel or—or the other thing, God help me for I don't know—all I have to say is that I won't touch a letter or a note or a scrap of paper that's not belonging to myself, and neither will I be getting any keyhole information for you! No; not for all the pensions the British Government could give me!'

There was silence for a moment while both women sat and looked at each other. And then Yvonne, who knew that she had failed, spoke:—

'Anyway you will hold your tongue about what has passed between us this evening?' she said. As the other did not immediately reply, she added, with a deadly quietness that struck more fear into Mrs Pell's heart than any loud threatening could have done, 'If you do not it will be worse for yourself—and for some others.'

Then putting on her coat and gathering her furs round her she went softly down the stairs and passed out into the busy street— unseen by Geraldine or anyone else in the building.

CHAPTER XIV

FRIENDS IN COUNCIL

Needless to say Geraldine gave Jill a very vivid account of Yvonne's unexpected visit to Elton Street, and Jill listened, partly anxious, partly amused. Although less obsessed by fear of the woman than Geraldine, she still realised that Yvonne was a very real danger, and the fact that she should happen to be in the same building with them and, as Jill phrased it—'doing the friendly stunt'—made her powers for mischief all the greater. For Jill knew perfectly that both she and Jerry would be but infants in a game against Mademoiselle Delaunay.

The two friends were interrupted in their low-toned talk—for they did not know whether Yvonne was out or in her room across the landing—by a visit from Mr Ferdinand Shortall, bent and old as ever with creaky voice and shaky limbs, until the door was safely locked and the curtain drawn across.

Geraldine was delighted to see him; he had not been at the office for several days, and it was nearly a fortnight since he had visited the flat. When he had listened to her story about Yvonne he told her that he had been fully aware of the fact that 'the Delaunay woman' had had her shadowed some time ago.

'Oh! Peter; you might have let me know. I would have been prepared then for what I might expect,' she said reproachfully, adding, 'You knew, too, how I dreaded her coming.'

'I considered the matter both ways,' he answered, his keen eyes softening as they rested on her flushed cheeks, 'and I thought it would be better for you not to be always watching, and expecting every footstep you heard was made by the dainty shoe of Mademoiselle Delaunay. You know she has got on your nerves to some extent and you are only pulling round after your illness.'

'Oh! I know she has got on my nerves, but I can't help it. I always feel that some horrible trouble will come to us through her.'

'Well! try and don't think about it,' he advised; 'and now I must say what I came to see you about as it is best for me not to stay longer than I can help. Anthony and Desmond will be at Elton Street tomorrow evening—yes, they are really returning back about some important business—and they would like to see you both. Jerry can remain on after the office is closed, and if you, Jill, will manage to join us about six o'clock we can have our chat together.'

'Oh! I am so glad,' cried Geraldine; 'but I suppose they will be going away soon again?'

'Yes; they will both return to "America" the following evening. I want you both not to mention what we know about the plans of the Delaunay woman. Anthony knows all, but both he and I agreed that it would be better not to mention even her name before Desmond. We have told him nothing about what Sheila found out.'

'But, Peter,' cried Jill. 'Surely that is very foolish. If Desmond knew all that we know about her———.'

'It would not make the slightest difference. He's obsessed, bewitched! I hate to tell you this, but I must, so that you can understand how matters are. The infatuated boy believes firmly that she is innocent, or that we are mixing her up with some other woman, and nothing we can say will convince him to the contrary, or make him see the woman for the base thing she is.'

Jill and Geraldine were silent, dumb with misery. Peter glanced at them and ran his fingers several times through his hair, a sure sign of disquiet with him.

'Tony and I have talked it over,' he said after a few moments, 'over and over again. We have decided that the only course to take is to ignore the matter to all appearance, so far as Desmond is concerned, and not to speak of her at all before him. The affair may blow over if they don't meet, and for that reason it was really a godsend that he had to go to "America." Well! now I must go, and don't forget tomorrow and all I have said to you.'

So the next evening about six o'clock our five old friends were sitting round a good fire in the sittingroom at Elton Street and enjoying a cosy tea. Mrs Pell had just departed, having first, so to speak, left her benediction to the whole assembly. She had been truly glad to see the twins, and to see, too, that they were safe and sound. She was still suffering from the effects of her interview with Yvonne, but had not 'touched a drop' since, and her mind was at present made up to keep 'off it', in fact she had very serious thoughts of enlisting as a Pioneer Probationer, but the thought of Mrs Flanagan glancing down at her from her superior position as a full Pioneer of many years' membership discouraged her. She would have dearly liked to have taken the boys into her confidence about the preceding evening, but fear, stark fear of Yvonne's unknown powers, tied her tongue. Had she known how much the others already knew about Mademoiselle Delaunay she would not have hesitated to tell them, but she thought they knew nothing. Many and many a tear was she to shed in the days to come for her silence now.

Geraldine had to tell the twins again and again all about her visit to Sheila, how she looked, what she said; and she told all she could without mentioning Yvonne's name. They listened eagerly, each in his own characteristic way, Desmond standing on the hearthrug and looking down at her with shining eyes, and now and then interrupting with a question or exclamation, Anthony sitting very quiet and silent in his chair but following every word.

Geraldine had to pull herself up short once, when she had almost forgotten Peter's warning and nearly said something about the night when Sheila was in the library listening to Yvonne and 'Mr Chester'. Peter, however, noticed her sudden confusion and covered it adroitly, so that Desmond did not notice anything. Anthony, of course, understood. It was Anthony who spoke presently in a pause of the conversation.

'We must not keep our visitors too late, Peter,' he said, 'so I think we might tell them now what we want them to do for us—if they will.'

'If!' cried the two girls together, and Geraldine added, 'Why, we would do anything to help you.'

Desmond laughed as he said, 'Wait till you hear first.'

'The fact is,' said Anthony then, 'we have our uniforms here—mine and Desmond's—and we don't want to leave them in these rooms for several reasons. The friend who was keeping them for us is no longer able to remain in his own house and they have to be removed. So we were wondering if you two could manage to hide them in your flat? Would it be too much to ask you to do? Because, of course, you know that if you were raided and they were found it would be a very serious matter for you.'

'Of course we will take charge of the uniforms and I know how we will hide them, too,' said Geraldine eagerly. 'We will make cushions of them! I knew a girl in the country who did that, and when the house was raided the uniforms were never found. She covered them well with padding wool and then with plenty of chintz and frills, and no one would guess what the cushions contained.'

'And a jolly good idea, too,' cried Desmond. 'I'd back a woman's brain for strategy any day.'

'Have you got them here with you now?' asked Jill.

'Yes; and we thought that Jerry would be able to get them to the flat by degrees—as not too large and quite inconspicuous parcels you know.'

'Oh! but we will take them tonight,' said Jill. 'They can make up into two or three parcels if you tie them tightly and we can take them at once—the sooner they are away from here the better.'

They talked of much that evening short as their time together was, and it was an evening that was destined to live in their memory ever afterwards.

In the course of conversation Anthony, who had a very real regard for Jill, far more so than Desmond, who although he was naturally delightful to all women, would never really give a second thought to one who was not pretty, asked her, half in jest, half in earnest:——

'I suppose that Jerry here has not converted you yet?'

Jill shook her head, but a serious look crossed her face—that speaking face of hers, which although plain in Desmond's estimation was yet so mobile—so alive.

'No,' she said, 'and I am afraid she never will. I say afraid,' she added after a brief silence which none of the others had broken, 'because I would gladly believe in the Christian Faith if I could. Ever since Terence MacSwiney died I have been drawn towards that Faith as I never was before. But someway or other I am so hard to convince and I could never dope my soul and pretend to believe any doctrine that my reason could not accept. I sometimes really think,' she added, with a slight laugh that held a tinge of sadness, ' that it would take a message from the dead—from one who had gone on to the next world—if there is a next world, to convince me.'

Her friends said nothing, only looked at her in silence. Desmond stared at her, too, for a minute, then he threw back his sleek dark head and laughed lightly.

'You are a hard case, Jill, and no mistake,' he cried. 'But never mind, if I ever get a chance after my departure from this vale of woe I'll come back and see if I can convince you.'

The others laughed at him, it was just Desmond's nonsense, but

Jill shivered involuntarily.

'You·are cold, Jill,' interposed Anthony, 'and it is time for you and Jerry to be getting home—I don't want to seem inhospitable, but you know the times in which we live. Come along, Des, and we will see if these uniforms can be made up into fairly small parcels.'

They managed to put it up into three parcels which were not too large, and Peter O'Connor, who had also retired into the bedroom, from whence he emerged as old Mr Shortall, put one of them under his great coat. The two girls said goodbye to the twins with brave cheerfulness, although none of them knew would they ever see each other again, but that fact had become so commonplace and so much a recognised factor in their lives that it really affected them but little.

'We are returning to "America" tomorrow evening,' said Anthony, as he took Geraldine's hand in his.

'God be with you!' she answered quietly.

But Jill, as she turned towards Desmond, found herself saying suddenly, and saying it in spite of herself, 'Oh! Desmond. Take care of yourself, I am afraid for you.'

He laughed at her in his old careless manner, and then suddenly stooped and carried her hand to his lips.

'Be not in fear for me, oh! lady fair!' he said lightly with a dramatic gesture, and then added in his everyday voice, 'Sure I can always take care of myself.'

She felt the touch of his lips for hours afterwards, but it was not until she was in bed that night, when the flat was silent and Jerry sleeping, that she put her own lips to the spot that he had kissed, and baptised it with the burning tears of renunciation.

CHAPTER XV

DELILAH

From his early boyhood Desmond Ryan had always suffered at times from severe headaches. He would awake some morning conscious of a dull, heavy feeling across his forehead and eyes, which he knew only too well would develop into agonising pain later on. This was how he awoke on the morning following the evening of which we have been speaking.

He turned in his bed and groaned aloud at the thought of the pain-racked hours which stretched before him, and Anthony hearing him called from the other bed:——

'Have you got one of your bad heads, old chap?'

Desmond groaned again as he said, 'It's coming on anyway. I think I'll ask Mrs P for a cup of tea—that sounds like poetry doesn't it, Tony? But I don't feel like a poem—I know that.'

He shouted for Mrs Pell, who being on her good behaviour was already banging around in the kitchen, and she was immediately all sympathy for her poor lamb—and this her pet lamb, too.

'Oh! don't make a sheep of me,' said Desmond irritably, 'but bring me a cup of tea.'

In a few minutes he was sipping a cup of Mrs P.'s strongest concoction—the kettle having been as she had announced—'conveniently on the boil'.

He rose and dressed then, trying, as he always did, to shake off the coming headache, to baffle it, and force it away by strength of will. He always tried and always failed, and today was no exception, the pain increased hourly until Anthony said, 'I'll go and get you that powder—it's no good trying to do without it any longer.' It was then about five in the afternoon. Peter had given him a prescription for a certain powder which always stopped the pain. He would fall into a heavy sleep about half-an-hour after taking it and when he awoke the pain would be gone, but he would be in a stupid, dazed condition of mind for some time after. Dr O'Connor had warned him not to take this medicine except when the pain was very severe. The ordinary headache remedies had no effect whatever when the headache was really bad.

He assented dully when Anthony spoke, but when the latter returned with the powder he asked him, 'How am I to go with you this evening, Tony, if I take this now? You know I'll be dead asleep when I ought to be on my way to "America"?'

He tried to smile as he spoke, but his brows were drawn together with pain.

'I've thought of that, dear boy,' replied his brother, as he unfolded the powder, 'and it will be best for you to remain here for the night and come on tomorrow—you might manage it early in the morning if you feel all right. It's a bit risky, but it can't be helped, as you certainly can't get out to the mountains this evening.'

When Anthony left later for 'America' his brother was lying down on the couch before the fire just beginning to feel drowsy.

'You are sure you will be all right, Des?' asked Anthony, as he tucked a rug around the other with a touch as tender as a woman's. 'I hate to leave you alone like this, but you know the others will expect me about that affair which we have to discuss.'

Desmond reached out his hand and grasped his brother's.

'I'm all right, Tony,' he said. 'Good-night, dear old chap.' Yet Anthony felt strangely loth to leave him. He turned at the door and looked back; there was no light but that of the fire, the daylight had gone on this November evening, for it was nearly six o'clock, and Desmond could not bear any artificial light. He lay on the couch with closed eyes, very pale and still, but it was not the boy's physical condition which worried Anthony; he knew these headaches of Desmond's and knew that tomorrow would see him himself again. It was something else—some undefined feeling of danger which he felt and yet could not understand. He turned away with a sigh— for his duty called him very clearly—and in the kitchen he was waylaid by Mrs Pell.

'Oh! Mr Anthony, my poor lamb. How is he now sir?'

'He has taken the powder, Mrs Pell, and is going asleep,' replied Tony. 'He will remain here for tonight, but I cannot.'

Mrs Pell then informed him that although she had to return to her own house at six o'clock as her married daughter was waiting there to see her, that she would be certain to come back to Elton Street later on and see how Mr Desmond was.

'He might be wanting a cup of tea, and I'll put a hot jar in his bed—the poor lamb.'

'Thanks very much, Mrs Pell,' replied Anthony gratefully; 'that's awfully good of you, but you always are kind to us,' and he took her hand and shook it cordially to her mingled embarrassment and delight.

At a few minutes after six o'clock she looked in at Desmond and saw he was sleeping soundly. Very gently she put more coal on the fire, and then turning the gas low in the kitchen she went downstairs. The whole building was silent, the offices were shut, all the staff were gone home, and Desmond was the only one there now. Mrs Pell let herself out and shut the door after her ; she had, of course, her latchkey to enter the house later.

It was nearly eight o'clock when Desmond awoke. For a few moments he lay motionless, trying to remember where he was. It all came back to him then and he gave a great sigh of relief as he realised that the agonising pain was gone, but the next moment he had raised himself on his elbow and was searching the firelit room with a puzzled expression on his handsome face. That strange sense which we all possess told him that he was not alone, and at the same moment he became aware of a faint but very lovely perfume which seemed close to him. It was familiar, too, but where had he noticed it before? Then suddenly he remembered—it was the rare Oriental perfume which always seemed to cling to the beautiful garments of Yvonne Delaunay. He turned round and glanced swiftly towards the door. Just then a coal dropped noisily from the grate, and the fire flared up, and by its flickering light he saw Yvonne standing on the threshold looking at him.

He flung aside the rug which covered him and sprang to his feet.
'Yvonne!'

For as such he had thought of her—as such she had been in his dreams by day and night for these past weeks.

'Monsieur Desmond!'

Quickly she came across the room with outstretched hands, crying again:—

'It is Monsieur Desmond. Oh! how glad I am to see you. I thought the house was empty; I came in for shelter, for I have had a fright—such a fright!'

By this Desmond had somewhat recovered himself. 'Come over to the fire,' he said, wheeling forward one of the shabby but comfortable armchairs, and pushing away his couch. 'You must excuse me for being like this, Mademoiselle Delaunay, but I was lying down with a bad headache. Oh! yes, thank you, it is quite gone now.'

Yvonne took the chair and looked up at him as he searched for a match to light the gas.

'Oh! please, don't mind the gas!' she cried prettily. 'The firelight is just lovely! Won't you sit down until I tell you about my so terrible fright?'

Obediently he drew forward another chair and sank into it, feeling rather dazed still, as he stared fascinated at the lovely vision seated opposite. A lovely vision it certainly was—Yvonne had seen to that! Not for nothing had her underspies brought her word of Anthony's departure earlier in the evening, and not for nothing had she a duplicate key of the hall door in her possession for the past week. She had planned and thought out the present interview in detail and was now ready for the part which she was about to act.

She was wearing an evening gown of old gold charmeuse, a most exquisite thing, over which was a theatre wrap of black and gold brocade. A lace scarf was wound carelessly round her little head with its wealth of hair.

'Listen, Monsieur Desmond,' she was saying; 'I was going to dine tonight at Jammet's with friends of mine from Paris. I had come by tram to Nassau Street and then I thought I would get out and walk down Suffolk Street. But it was very quiet and rather dark and I had only gone a few minutes when I saw two men following me. Oh! I know they were following me and I was so terrified. I just walked on and on as quickly as ever I could until I noticed I was passing your door, and how surprised I was to see that the door below was not quite shut.'

Desmond started and swore mentally. Naturally he blamed Mrs Pell and yet he had to acknowledge that it was not like her to be so careless. But Yvonne was still speaking, 'So when I saw it was not closed but left as you say, ajar, I slipped in and shut it tight to keep out those dreadful men.'

Desmond looked at her with the smiling tenderness which we would feel for a frightened child.

'But are you sure they were following you?' he asked.

'Oh! mais oui! It is certain! They saw I was dressed for dinner perhaps and thought I would have jewels. And then the hall below was so dark—and not a sound in the whole place—I could not stay downstairs, so I came up hoping that I might find Miss Moore or Mrs Pell, but never thinking to find you. Oh! Monsieur Desmond, you will forgive my intrusion—will you not?'

'Why ask me to forgive that which you know is a pleasure, Yvonne?' said Desmond softly, as he stooped to put more coal on the fire.

'I must go soon,' she said. 'My friends they will be waiting and wondering. But I may stay just a few minutes until I think those horrid men are gone?'

'Why do you ask such a question? Don't you know that every moment you stay is joy to me?'

Then Yvonne very gently laid her first card on the table. 'But to your friends, Monsieur Desmond,' she murmured tentatively, 'my presence, I think, is not always so welcome?'

The young fellow flushed and dropped his eyes—he felt suddenly ashamed that this girl, so innocent and so lovely as she seemed in his sight, should have felt the veiled hostility of his brother and friends.

'You must not mind them,' he said; 'they do not understand you, and so make mistakes.'

'Ah! yes; I know,' was the reply in the soft voice that was music itself to the ears of the listening man. 'But why—why do they mistrust me like that? What have I done—poor little me—that they do not like me? Perhaps you can tell me?'

Desmond raised his eyes and looked at her. She had let her cloak fall on the back of her chair, and her beautiful shoulders gleamed like polished ivory above the dead gold of her gown, while her great mass of hair shone like hot ashes when they are stirred. He could only look and look again—all his heart in his eyes, and he, who was always so self-possessed, so perfectly at home when talking to the opposite sex, now felt as tongue-tied and gauche as any schoolboy.

'Don't mind them, Yvonne!' was all he could say again. 'They are mistaken.'

'But how mistaken? For who or what then do they take me?'

He was silent, for how could he even hint to her the vile insinuations of Peter O'Connor.

'Ah! you do not answer,' she went on. 'But it is not necessary, for I know. I know that they think that I am an English spy—what one calls a Secret Service Agent! Is that not so?'

Too ashamed to answer her, he remained silent, and she continued:—

'Ah! yes—I guessed it all—and I will tell you why, Monsieur

Desmond. It is because I have a cousin who is very like myself and has the same name also, and she—ah! but I am ashamed to say it!— is employed in the Secret Service of England. Oh! is it not terrible? How can she do such work? So base; so underhand! And your friends will have heard of her—Dr O'Connor, I think, met her, or saw her, once in London, and so they think it is I—because we are so much alike.'

Desmond listened to her with a great joy flooding his whole being. He had never believed that the facts which Peter had told about her were true, but all the same he was delighted now that she had herself, and without being asked, explained the matter so plainly. He thought, too, with intense satisfaction of how easily he could now 'shut up old Peter when he started yarning again!' He was still gazing at her in a sort of adoring silence when she suddenly leant forward and held out her little hands to him.

'But you—you did not believe this, Desmond?'

He sprang from his seat and knelt beside her, and taking both her hands he crushed them to his breast.

'Yvonne!' he cried, and again, 'Yvonne!' and stooping he kissed the hem of her satin frock.

'You silly boy! Do you think that I am a princess, then?'

'Yes, my princess!' he answered with passion, 'and my queen! Yvonne, don't you know that I adore you?'

His arms involuntarily reached out to her, but she gently drew back from their grasp.

'You say you love me,' she said with gentle sadness—while she mentally played another card—'Why, then, do you not trust me?'

'But I do trust you!' he answered vehemently. 'I never mistrusted you, Yvonne—it was the others. I never believed what they said.'

'But what was it that they said?' she asked with a laugh. 'Do they think I am a very terrible person?'

After a momentary hesitation he decided that it would be only fair to let her know what was being said about her, especially now that she could explain everything so fully. So he sat at her feet and told her what Peter had said and she listened with such perfectly feigned surprise and indignation that he almost repented having allowed himself repeat the doctor's false accusations. Inwardly the woman was seething with rage. Apparently Peter O'Connor knew more about her than she had imagined and while she listened to

Desmond and acted her part she was resolving that she would make the doctor suffer as he had never suffered before in his life.

'And you—yourself? You never believed any of this!' she asked.

'How can you ask me that, Yvonne?' cried Desmond. 'As if I could think such things of you.'

'And do you trust in me—believe in me absolutely?'

'As I trust and believe in Heaven!'

'Ah! Desmond—you so dear boy!'

'Yvonne! Do you—could you love me?'

She smiled and threw him a smile from her strange eyes that sent blood rushing to his head.

'Love? I do not know! But I—I like you very much, Desmond.'

'But will you try to love me, Yvonne? It is your love I want—not only your liking.'

'Ah! but I could never really love anyone who did not trust me.'

'But I do trust you, Yvonne. Good God! Haven't I told you so again and again?'

'But I would want proofs of that love.'

'Proofs?'

'Yes; you would have to trust me with all your secrets, and tell me everything about your work, just all those very things which your friends think I want to find out. And then indeed if you did that I would know that you trusted me entirely.'

Just for a moment Desmond was dumbfounded, her request was so unexpected. He looked at her in perplexity, but the lovely piquant face, the innocent laughter in the eyes, and the frank expression with which she returned his glance, put his latent doubts to flight. He knelt beside her and gathered her, this time unresisting, into his arms.

'And if—if I tell you, Yvonne,' he said hoarsely, 'what reward will I have?'

Smilingly she lifted her vivid red mouth, and as he stooped and laid his lips on hers everything in the heavens above and earth beneath was blotted out for Desmond—and nothing mattered but the one thing alone—the woman he held in his arms.

So Yvonne played her trump card—and won.

And yet this woman, she who had looked upon all men as her lawful prey—to be used for her own ends—was amazed and almost frightened to find that the clasp of this man's arms and the touch of his lips made her feel as no other man's caresses had ever done.

Perhaps for one second of time her purpose looked almost base to herself, and her desire for ill-gotten gains grew faint. Who knows? She banished the unwanted sensation almost immediately; she who had never allowed sentiment of any kind to interfere with her work was not going to do so now when so much was at stake. She was a perfect mistress of such a situation as the present, and with her soft, caressing fingers she smoothed Desmond's dark head, and drew it down to rest against the soft satin of her gown.

'Talk to me now!' she whispered, and kissed him lightly on the cheek. But his arms tightened round her and he crushed her lips fiercely to his.

'Ah! no; Desmond! You hurt me.'

She pronounced Desmond in a quaint foreign way that was very delightful to hear, on her tongue it sounded like 'Desmoond'.

He was all contrition instantly for his roughness and, of course, she forgave him prettily. Again drawing his head against her breast she laid her soft cheek against his and said, 'Tell me all your secrets now.'

Incredible as it may seem, he told her—told her what he would, in his normal condition, have hesitated to tell an angel from Heaven. For that is the only excuse which can be offered for Desmond Ryan on that fatal night—he was not normal either in mind or body. The drug contained in the headache powders always left him dazed and somewhat stupid. Yvonne's presence and his overwhelming passion for her had swept him entirely off his feet and left him altogether at her mercy—he was literally as wax in her hands. If history tells true he was not the only one of his sex who behaved in the same way under the same circumstances.

In half-an-hour's time Yvonne Delaunay knew all those things for which she had worked, and planned and schemed for so long, and her heart exulted within her as it had seldom done before. She had learned all about 'America' and about the twenty other volunteers who were there now with Anthony discussing the disposal of a large amount of ammunition which was hidden near. She pretended great stupidity about the locality of the cottage and laughingly declared 'if she was a volunteer she could never, never be able to find it.' Whereupon Desmond drew her a rough sketch with pencil and paper, showing very clearly the various roads and mountain tracks which led to 'America'. And with a gay little laugh she slipped it inside her frock. She heard, too, about the papers for which the British were looking—those papers which would mean the hunting down and death of so many of Ireland's gallant sons—the papers, too, which, when found, were to be the occasion of a 'little dinner' for herself and 'Mr Chester'.

'And you have them hidden?' she breathed eagerly. 'Are they quite safe, do you think? Where are they?'

At this Desmond hesitated. Even to her could he tell this? His conscience answered no, with no uncertain voice; only too well he knew that to no one had he the right to reveal their hiding place.

'Ah! I see. You do not trust me, and I was right to say that you did not. But why then do you say you love me?' And she was withdrawing from his arms, but they tightened around her like steel bands.

'No; no, Yvonne, don't say that! Love you? My God! I adore you!' and he rained kisses on her upturned face.

'And the papers?' Very soft was her voice, hardly above a whisper—almost indifferent, too, in its casual note, as if it was but a fancy, a passing whim, that caused her to ask.

Desmond raised his eyes to the oil painting above the mantelpiece, and the woman followed the direction of his glance.

'That is my mother's portrait,' he said, a tender note of reverence in his voice, 'and the papers are—behind it. There is a sliding panel over a recess in the wall, Anthony and I fixed it ourselves and put the papers there.

There was silence for a few seconds, for Yvonne could not trust herself to speak; afraid that he would catch the note of triumph which she was sure her voice would contain.

Desmond's gaze was still on the pictured face of the mother he had loved so dearly, that mother who was the sweetest memory of his boyhood's days—the mother, too, who had been the first to teach him love and devotion to his Fatherland. He moved uneasily, and Yvonne glanced at him swiftly.

'What is it?' she asked.

'Nothing—nothing!' he said. 'I thought for a moment that her eyes were alive, they—they seemed to be looking into my very heart! It's the firelight, I suppose.' But he still kept his gaze on the painting, and Yvonne, remembering how she herself had felt about those pictured eyes on the occasion of her other visit to that room, shivered a little and spoke hastily.

'I should be going now, I suppose? Although I fear I am too late for that dinner party.' And she laughed deliciously.

But Desmond caught her to his heart again and kissed her wonderful perfumed hair as he whispered:

'Ah! no. Don't go yet; it is not nine o'clock. Wait for another half-hour and I will see you home.'

But for many reasons this did not suit Yvonne's plans and she would not hear of such a thing.

'No; no, indeed!' she cried. 'You must not come out with me and run into danger on my account. Desmond, my dear, how could I ever forgive myself if anything happened to you? No; no. I will stay another half-hour if you really want me, but I will go back to the flat by myself. There is a garage which I know quite close and I will take a taxi and will be home in a few minutes.'

So with that assurance he had to be content, and they sat in the firelight, cheek against cheek and hand in hand. But even as she listened to his vows of love and suffered his caresses, Yvonne's mind was busy with plans. She had the immediate future to think about—for her work was not yet finished.

'Are you going back to that cottage, I forget its name—ah! yes, of course, "America"—how stupid I am. Are you going back tomorrow? And will you have to go in the morning early?'

'Well! I think I ought to get away as early as possible,' he replied. 'I should have been there tonight you know.'

'Ah! well; it is no use then for me to ask you for a favour—a great favour?'

'A favour? What is it, darling? If I can grant it—it is yours.'

'Oh! it is not much after all. Only just that I wanted to spend one whole day with you. We have seen so little of each other, Desmond, and—and'—with a sigh 'who knows how little we may be together after this?'

'We will be together all our lives please God!' the man answered, 'for I mean to marry you soon, Yvonne. Why should we wait? Let us take our happiness while we can.'

He did not see the queer smile that twisted her lips for a moment as he went on, 'But how could we manage to spend tomorrow together, sweetheart? Where could we go?'

'To Bray,' she answered; 'to the Dargle. I know it is a queer time of the year to want to go there—but there will be no one to interfere with us. Let us go, dear Desmond, and spend one long day together.'

She held up her mouth for his kiss as she spoke. They arranged it then, he would meet her at the station at ten o'clock and they would go to the Dargle and spend the day there. They would come back early in the evening, so that Desmond could return to the cottage that night. He could send word to his brother by a boy scout who was thoroughly known and trusted—the message would just be to say that he would return to the cottage about eight at night instead of in the forenoon, for, needless to say, he would give no hint of what was detaining him. The infatuated boy was only eager to do what Yvonne desired—far, far more than that would he have done for a smile, or a kiss from her vivid red mouth.

She left him about a quarter to ten, whispering softly, 'Until tomorrow,' as they kissed good-night. She would not even let him come downstairs with her, but insisted on saying goodbye on the top landing. 'There might be some clerk doing overwork in the office below,' she said, 'and I do not want to be seen. I can go softly—but you!'

He laughed and let her go, turning back to the sittingroom as he heard her reach the hall below. But just as she was about to let herself out a key turned in the lock and the door opened to reveal Mrs Pell's portly figure, the light from the street lamp shining on her well known 'cabe and toke'.

Of the two she was more astonished than Yvonne, as Desmond had mentioned that she was returning, a bit of news which had somewhat precipitated Yvonne's departure. She laughed very softly when she saw the charlady, and murmured, 'Good-night, Mrs Pell!'

Mrs Pell could only stand and stare. Poor woman! She looked not unlike a gasping codfish just brought to land, for her fat cheeks were blowing in and out in her efforts to understand what Yvonne was doing there at that hour. But Yvonne had no intention of enlightening her; she gave another light laugh and slipped into the street, leaving Mrs Pell still standing—'flabbergasted' as she would have said—in the narrow hall way.

At length she pulled herself together and went upstairs to see how Desmond was. She found him standing by the fire with flushed cheeks and shining eyes—a transformed, glorified Desmond who was walking, for the time being, on air.

'And is the headache better, sir,' ventured Mrs Pell from the doorway.

He looked at her without seeing her at first, until she spoke again.

'Oh! the headache!' he said then. 'Yes, of course, I had a headache—I had forgotten. Oh! Mrs Pell, bother headaches; bother everything. Nothing matters except I am the happiest creature on God's earth tonight.'

She only stood and looked at him as comprehension began to dawn upon her. Her face reflected none of his gaiety as she remarked, 'Then I may go home, sir?'

'Go home? Yes, of course, Mrs Pell. I'm all right and thanks for coming back. But I won't sleep. Oh! I couldn't sleep I'm so happy. I'm only afraid it's too great a happiness to last.'

'Well, good-night, sir,' she said. As she went down the flight of stairs she cried to herself over and over again, 'Oh! my poor lamb—my poor lamb,' and Mrs Pell carried home a very heavy heart that night.

CHAPTER XVI

SHEILA MAKES REPARATION

Desmond Ryan would have been considerably astonished if he could have followed Mademoiselle Delaunay when she left Elton Street. She had spoken the truth when she said that she was known at a garage near the Ryans' offices—in fact at that garage so well known was she that a particular car and a particular chauffeur were both at her services at any hour of the day or night. She went there at once now, and as soon as she was seated in the car directed the man to drive to Firfield House. As a matter of fact, Yvonne was staying there for the next few days—over the weekend, and this was Friday—the weekend, let it be remembered, of the Croke Park reprisals.

She had arrived at Firfield that afternoon about three o'clock and had been intensely curious when Mrs Ryan happened to mention at tea that Geraldine Moore had spent the earlier part of the day with Sheila, and had lunched there. Naturally Yvonne dare not seem to be very interested or surprised, and the most adroit questioning on her part elicited nothing. Mrs Ryan knew nothing—therefore she could tell nothing—while Sheila was both warned of and prepared for her visit.

Geraldine had given her all the news up to date that morning; had told her about the twins and how delighted they had been to hear about her and to receive her messages. She told Sheila, too, that they were both returning to 'America' that evening, and Sheila smiled half sadly, half tenderly, for she knew the cottage that now went by that name, and many a picnic had she and the boys had on the mountain slope on which it stood long ago, 'in the dear, dead days beyond recall.'

'An old man used to live there,' she said to Geraldine; 'he often boiled our kettle for us, but I suppose he is gone?'

'Yes; I think I heard the boys say that he was dead,' replied Geraldine. 'It was empty when they got it, but in fairly good condition, and they have really made it quite comfortable.'

They discussed all those matters which were uppermost in their minds as they sat together in Sheila's cosy room, and the latter told Geraldine that Yvonne Delaunay was coming out that evening to stay till about Tuesday. 'That means,' she added, 'that

Ronald will be certain to come also—he will probably arrive for dinner. Poor Mums thinks it is going to be a match between them. Oh! dear God!" she broke off suddenly, 'if it was only that which brought them together here.'

'You will be able to do a bit of Secret Service work yourself, Sheila, while they are here,' suggested Geraldine.

'Yes, and I mean to do so,' replied the other earnestly. 'I will not let a single opportunity slip of trying to learn some of their hateful plans. The best of it is, you know, that they never for a moment suspect me. They think I am rather empty headed and shallow, and on account of my marriage to Norman they believe that if I take any part at all in the present state of affairs I must side with the British. Mums also thinks that I am "loyal" and I take care not to disabuse their minds, as it makes it all the safer for me and easier to find out their plans.'

'Yes; but don't get into trouble or danger—don't be too reckless,' warned Geraldine.

'No; I won't. I will be very careful,' replied Sheila. 'Not indeed for my own sake, because I would willingly suffer anything now to help my country, but because if I was found out I would not be able to stop any of their bad work.'

Geraldine, who, at Peter's suggestion the night before, had taken a morning from the office to see Sheila and give her all needful information, went back to town directly after lunch and so missed Yvonne. That fascinating little person arrived later in the afternoon and told Mrs Ryan that she was desolated—quite, but she would have to return to town that evening to have dinner with some tiresome people at Jammet's. She would go up by train and they would motor her back. No; she would not be late getting back to Firfield—very probably she would be home by ten o'clock so that Mrs Ryan need not be anxious about her.

The truth was that Yvonne was returning to the flat, there to wait until those who kept constant watch on Elton Street came and reported how matters stood. Every evening now for nearly a week she had been waiting for this one chance which was to fall to her that night as we know now.

Later in the evening Ronald Hammond telephoned to know if Mrs Ryan could possibly put him up for the weekend—he was feeling a bit seedy and would like a change from the city. She was charmed, of course, and asked him to come that night for dinner, to which he agreed. Sheila, listening to the talk over the phone, smiled bitterly to herself, yet was glad that she had work to do now which might prove of use to her country.

Ronald Hammond arrived at seven-thirty, after Yvonne had left for her mythical dinner at Jammet's, and he was, needless to say, very surprised to hear that Mademoiselle Delaunay was spending the weekend there also. Sheila, watching him, could not but admire his consummate acting—it was simply perfect, so natural, and not at all overdone. He turned to greet her with his usual charming manner—the manner which caused Mrs Ryan and others of her class to designate him as 'a perfect gentleman,' but which, as Sheila knew while he bent gracefully over her hand, was simply that of the trained Secret Service Agent. To him Sheila was a perfect nonentity, and never for a moment entered into his scheme of things.

When, at about ten-thirty, Yvonne's motor drove up the avenue, Ronald and Mrs Ryan were together in the drawingroom. Norman, under protest, was being put to bed by his man, and Sheila had also retired, complaining of a troublesome headache, which she said would never leave her until she could get a good sleep.

Mrs Ryan was glad to see her guest back again— Yvonne had fascinated the good lady to suit her own purpose—and asked about her evening.

'Oh! yes; the dinner was quite good,' was the reply. 'Jammet's is the one place in Dublin, dear Mrs Ryan, where the food is a little like that of my dear Paris. But oh! I am so tired. You will forgive me if I go straight to bed—will you not? And Mr Hammond, too?'

And she sent him a 'wireless' from her strange eyes as she spoke which was perfectly understood by the man to mean, 'In the library, later!'

Then saying goodnight with all her usual grace she went to her room.

Mrs Ryan shortly afterwards said goodnight to Ronald, he having announced his intention of having a read by the library fire, giving his hostess to understand that he was interested in some book of diplomacy which he had discovered there.

And so silence settled down on the old house by degrees as the servants also departed to their rooms—a few doors opened or shut—someone went upstairs or across a corridor, and then complete quietude reigned, broken only by the loud ticking of the grandfather's clock in the wide hall.

*   *   *

The same old clock had struck the hour of midnight, some fifteen minutes and more, when Ronald Hammond sitting by the library fire lifted his eyes from the book which he was reading—not any deep work on diplomacy, but a very modern French novel—and stared in front of him as one listening.

The next moment the library door opened noiselessly and Yvonne Delaunay entered; she was still wearing her dinner frock but had thrown a warm coat over it. And closing the door as gently as she had opened it she came over to the blazing fire and sank into a chair opposite the man. He offered her his cigarette case and lit a match for her before he spoke, and then it was only to say—'Well?'

Yvonne looked across the room at him and smiled through her cigarette smoke. 'You may indeed say well, mon vieux,' she said then; 'for it is well—and very well!'

His eyes lit with sudden interest, but all he said was, 'Pray proceed, ma belle!'

Yvonne smiled again while she continued to watch the spirals of smoke which she was blowing ceilingwards.

Then:—

'You may order that little dinner, mon ami!' she said.

'What!' The man sat up in his chair as if electrified—for once shaken out of his habitual languid pose.

'What! Have you the papers then?'

'I know where they are; you can have them in your hands tomorrow.'

'Where are they then?'

'In the Ryans' rooms at Elton Street. They are hidden in a recess in the wall over the mantelpiece—behind the oil painting of the first Mrs Ryan, the twins' mother, you know. A sliding panel conceals them and—Ron! what noise was that?'

'Noise? What do you mean? I heard nothing.'

'Did you not hear a sound like—like a moan of someone in pain?'

The man raised his eyebrows.

'Are you by any chance developing nerves at this time of your career?' he asked derisively. 'Who would have expected it?'

'I am sure I heard something,' persisted the woman.

'A noise—a creaking chair—you know the noises one hears at night. Go on, Yvonne, with your tale; your news is stupendous!'

She then told him all the information which she had gained during her interview with Desmond—not a word that might be of use was forgotten, and in the end she drew forth the little sketch or map which showed the direction that led to 'America' and handed it to him.

He studied it closely and then laughed softly.

'By Jove! Yvonne,' he said, 'you are simply—it! I'll order that little dinner for—what night shall we say?'

'That is for you to decide,' she said; 'but I must tell you that I have left you tomorrow clear for the raids on Elton Street and on 'America'. I have arranged that Desmond Ryan is to take me to the Dargle for the day—we will not be back in town until about six in the evening and you will have all your work finished by then—the papers will be in your possession and Anthony Ryan and the rest of those at the cottage will have been arrested. You will also have found the hidden stuff.'

'And Desmond Ryan?'

'Desmond is not to be arrested. I have made that a part of my bargain with you, Ronald, and you know it. He is not to be touched—not to be arrested on any account even if he walks into your very hands. If he is,' she added vehemently, 'you will regret it. I, Yvonne Delaunay, tell you so.'

The other laughed lazily.

'What! Hard hit—eh, Yvonne?' he asked.

But she took no notice of his question. Rising to her feet she said, 'You know all now and can make your own arrangements for tomorrow. Desmond and I meet for Bray at ten in the morning. I only ask that all will be over when we return to town. I will send Desmond Ryan to Elton Street alone and I will return here. You can let me know then how matters have gone. To Mrs Ryan I will say that a friend in Bray is ill and wants to see me. One more thing, Ron—and this is a personal favour. If that diable O'Connor is at the cottage let them take him dead or alive—he must not escape!'

'All serene; I'll give the order. Will we settle Monday for our dinner—what do you think?'

'As you will,' was the indifferent reply.

'What is wrong, Yvonne? Are you tired? You might give a fellow a goodnight kiss, just to celebrate the occasion, you know.'

But she flung aside the arm he was putting round her and with a cold 'Goodnight' left the room as softly as she had entered it a short while back.

'Mr Chester' remained to smoke a final cigar—a smile of satisfaction appearing now and then on his handsome, clever face. This was a big coup indeed—thanks to Yvonne Delaunay. What a clever little baggage she was. He would have to give her something for a memento—a ring or a bangle—although he knew that she would be well paid from official sources for such a fine bit of work.

'But I could never have managed alone—I must admit that!' he thought; 'and now to turn in, for tomorrow promises to be a busy day.'

He gathered up his book and cigar case, switched off the light, and went upstairs to bed.

Ten or fifteen minutes later the heavy curtain at the end of the room which hung over a recess in the wall where at one time a large bookcase had stood, was drawn apart and a woman came out, and crossing to the fire bent over the blaze to warm her cold hands. It was Sheila Hammond—Sheila who was now deathly pale with cold and fear.

She had been hidden behind the curtains since half-past ten; fortunately for her there was a low chair and cushion in the recess, so that she had been able to sit down during her long vigil, but she had been literally afraid to move and was cramped and half-frozen. She had heard every word that had passed between the other two. When she had heard Yvonne telling where the papers were hidden—which, of course, she did not even know herself—she had indeed allowed a little moan of anguish to escape her lips and was terrified when Yvonne heard her, fearing that the curtains would be swept apart and she would be discovered in her hiding place.

Her work that night lay straight before her—the work of getting as quickly as possible to the cottage on the mountain side and warning Tony and the others of the intended raids. She would take her motor; she knew every inch of the way and with careful driving she could take the car to within a mile or less of the cottage, after that she must walk the rest of the way over mountain paths and tracks. She wished that she could go at once, but commonsense and prudence told her that she must give Yvonne and Ronald time to get soundly asleep.

'I'll give them an hour,' she thought. 'That will be two o'clock—I should be able to get off safely then.'

So at two o'clock she made her preparations. In the hall was a big leather-lined motor coat belonging to her husband; this she put on with a cap to match, and on the hall table were her own motor gloves. Then as softly as possible—Yvonne herself could not have made less noise—she slipped out of the house by a side door. As luck would have it, the garage was simply a big shed which was built in a field a little way from the house—the one small stable being occupied by the fat pony. From this field a lane led to the main road, so the danger of discovery on account of any noise made by the motor was not very great.

At two-fifteen a.m., she was on the road outside the gates of Firfield heading as hard as she could go for the mountains. It was not a dark night—the moon showing now and then from behind the clouds, and the lights of her car were good, so on she rushed with only one thought—one idea obsessing her body and soul—to get to Anthony as quickly as was humanly possible. There is something strangely exhilarating in flying along a lonely country road at night, especially if one is racing against time, with a definite object in view—when speed is the essential thing, when one cares for nothing in the world but just to race—on—on with hedges and trees flying by and the wind moaning in the telegraph wires. The 'wine of sensation' some writer has called it, and when one is in such a mood it becomes indeed a kind of intoxication, so that we fly along as though driven by unseen forces.

So when Sheila saw in the distance several forms stepping into the middle of the road—as if they had suddenly arisen from the earth—and the challenge to 'Halt' rang on her ears she did not really comprehend what it meant; she did not understand that it concerned her.

Again, more insistent—came the command:

'Halt! Hands up!'

Then it dawned upon her that the words were addressed to her and that there were men in uniform trying to block her road.

Now Sheila had only arrived from England a couple of months ago and during that time she had seldom left the near neighbourhood of Firfield House, although she had heard a lot of talk about raids and ambushes and the general behaviour of the Crown forces in Ireland she had hardly believed it. When she left the country three years before things had been bad enough, but the real reign of terror of late years had not properly begun. So she had simply taken it for granted that these tales she so often heard were exaggerated, and none of those at Firfield House were likely to enlighten her on the subject. Geraldine—who could have opened her eyes—had been so busy talking about personal dangers that she had said little about the state of the country in general, thinking, no doubt, that Sheila knew all about it. But it so happened that on this night of which we write she knew so little that she never thought for a moment that there could be any real danger to her—a young woman alone, and unarmed. On the contrary she still held to the belief that British soldiers would not fire on a woman—a belief that is now gone finally from all Irish minds—and her only feeling at their challenge was one of annoyance at the delay, but she had not the slightest intention of stopping the car. She would only have to tell untruths if they questioned her, and they would naturally wonder where she was going to at this hour. So calling out at the top of her voice: 'I'm in a hurry! Mind yourselves!' she put on speed and raced forward. It takes time to tell this, but it all actually occurred in a few seconds—she had not even slowed down the car.

The soldiers—petrified at her audacity—had only barely time to spring aside as she tore past them.

'Fire!' shouted the officer furiously, and pit-pat came the bullets racing round the car.

Sheila hardy noticed them at first, and she certainly did not realise her danger until she felt a sting in her arm, and immediately afterwards another bullet sent her cap spinning in the air. Her lovely hair then came tumbling down over her shoulders and the wind blew it across her face, so that she could hardly see the road in front of her, but when she tried to lift her hand to brush it aside she found that she could not do so, and at the same moment she became conscious of something warm and damp trickling down her arm. She knew then that one of the bullets had gone home. But she was thankful that it was no worse, and in her excited state she felt no pain at present.

She had now left the military some distance behind her;

fortunately they were a detachment on patrol and had no motor with them. She knew every twist and turn of the mountain roads and if she met no others would surely reach the cottage in about an hour's time. She met no more of the Crown's forces, indeed she saw no trace of a human being as she raced on her way. There was nothing to hinder her now, and she could not understand at first when she found her car behaving in a strangely erratic manner, zig-zagging from one side of the road to the other. Her head, too, was giddy and light, and her hands, which still clung to the wheel, were cold and clammy. But she exercised all her will-power to keep her brain clear and not to faint, for she knew that if she gave way to this deadly feeling of weakness which was trying to overpower her that she would never reach her journey's end and would fail in carrying the message which meant so much. She had planned to take the motor to a certain spot about a mile from the cottage and then to proceed the rest of the way on foot—the path from that on being unfit for a car. But she found now that she was not able to drive any longer—her hands refused to guide the motor and she knew that she would have to leave it. She pulled up and got out—almost falling on the road as she did so. She sent up a wordless prayer for help, and went on, determined not to give up while she had any power at all left to her. It was an untold blessing that she knew all the country around from her childhood's days, and that knowledge was to stand her in good stead tonight. She was now on the road to Kilmashogue, and she suddenly realised that if she could only manage to climb up part of its bulky side and down the other it would be a short cut to the cottage, and save her nearly a mile round the road at its foot. She determined to try the ascent, and slowly but steadily she made her way onwards. Presently glancing at her wristlet watch by the light of a match she saw that it was now nearly four o'clock. What a time she had been getting even this far, and how slowly the motor must have gone for the last hour—she could hardly have been driving it at all. And she wished now that she had got out of the car sooner, she would get on better walking. But it was weary work; her head was light, and her left arm heavy and useless, while her frock was sticking to her with the blood which was still trickling down her wounded arm. Doggedly she kept on, stumbling over loose stones—sometimes falling—but always pulling herself together again and keeping on her way. She had not thought of changing her footwear before leaving the house, and her thin evening slippers were soon cut to pieces on the rocky mountain road. As the ascent began to stiffen she had at times to lie down and crawl, now and then pulling herself along by a stone boulder or a clump of furze. At last she reached the highest point and began her descent down the other side. She was not, of course, even half-way up the mountain proper, but had come around its side by a way known to her from long ago. Once down the other side now and a bare quarter of a mile or less would take her to 'America'—if only she could hold out so long. It was just like a journey one takes in a nightmare, on and on, struggling and fighting against terrible odds. But in our dreams we never get any nearer to our journey's end, while Sheila knew that she was gaining—slowly, very slowly, it was true—but still she was making progress by degrees.

She almost tumbled down the last part of the descent and then the remainder of her journey lay before her. Along a narrow mountain track that ran around the mountain slope, and then up a narrow little lane and she would find the cottage. Find the cottage and deliver her message—and rest! Oh! dear God! if she could lie down and rest—she thought that she would never ask to rise again.

Slowly and painfully, literally inch by inch, she dragged herself along, having perforce to stop every few minutes to try and ease her difficult breathing. The pain of her wound, too, which could no longer be overlooked, was very sickening.

Was it really only a quarter of a mile to the cottage? Or was it ten—twenty—thirty miles, she wondered dully.

Her last bit of strength seemed gone, and just as she felt that she could not crawl one step further the moon shone out for a last look at the world before retiring, and by its light Sheila saw the big furze bush and the turning that led up to the cottage.

With a supreme effort she dragged herself along on her hands and feet and started to crawl up the lane. Yes, just a few yards away was a flicker of light—someone was up then—and she tried to grasp the fact that her journey was really over—just another yard or so—Oh! Merciful God! if she could but reach to it. As she came nearer to the cottage the dragging movements which she made were very audible in the silence of the enveloping darkness, and now and then also a little moan escaped from her parched lips. For almost it seemed to her that she never would get there.

Only a couple of yards—and yet it might as well have been miles—aye, or the rolling ocean itself that stretched in front of her, and with a heart-broken sob she sank down on the ground—beaten at last.

Young Paddy O'Driscol was on guard outside the cottage, and for a couple of minutes he had been standing—rigid and motionless—trying to make out what in the world was coming up the lane? He was very young and new to his work, and he did not want to rouse the others without cause, for he knew how tired they were. The noise might only be caused by a wandering donkey or goat. But why did it moan—for it was a moan that he heard then? Some animal in pain? Or could it be a ruse of the enemy to draw them out?

As soon as the bare idea of such a thing entered his head he rushed into the cottage. His entry aroused Anthony Ryan and several of the others who were light sleepers—among them being Dr Peter O'Connor, who happened to be there that night.

'Well! what is it?' asked Anthony curtly, springing up as he spoke. Like the rest of them he had only taken off his coat and waistcoat before lying down.

Young O'Driscol saluted hurriedly.

'There is something in the lane, sir,' he said. 'I thought I had better report it to you.'

'Something?' repeated Anthony. 'What is it?'

'I don't know, sir,' was the reply; 'it is crawling along and moaning—I think it must be a sick animal. I was going to look when I thought it might be perhaps a stunt of the enemy to get us out.'

Anthony waited for no more.

'Come on boys!' he said tersely, and slipping on their coats and taking their revolvers in their hands they went out. They did not venture to bring out a light with them, but they heard the pitiful moaning distinctly, and then a voice that was trying to call for help.

'It's a woman!' said Peter, and ran forward, the others close behind him.

And just a few yards down the lane they almost stumbled over her—she looked like a boy in the big motor coat, only for the glory of her hair which was lying around her—one tress of it turned from gold to red where it had been soaked in the ominous flow which had made its way over the collar of her coat.

'It's a woman all right,' said one of the men; 'but who is she?'

Even as he spoke Anthony had brushed him aside and had flung himself down on the ground beside her.

'It's Sheila!' he cried. 'Oh! Peter! My God! My God! It's Girlie—my little Girlie!'

At the dear remembered word she opened her eyes and looked at him.

'Tony!' she said faintly, 'at last!'

They carried her into the cottage and laid her on her brother's bed and Peter came forward to examine her. She shook her head protestingly.

'Wait a minute,' she protested. 'Afterwards. Tony!' he was beside her, his arms around her. The other men were about to withdraw, but she stopped them with a little movement of her right hand.

'Listen all of you!' she said, slowly, painfully, every word an effort of will. 'The military will—raid here—early morning—and Elton Street—for papers behind—mother's picture.'

There was dead silence for a moment, the men standing beside her and gazing down at her in stupefied wonder.

She turned to Anthony alone then. 'Stoop down!' she whispered, and he bent his head so that only he could hear what she had to say.

'Desmond told Yvonne,' she breathed—for she could not speak of her brother's shame to the others.

The her head sank against his shoulder and she was swept away into the silent regions of unconsciousness, but the work which she had set out to do that night was accomplished.

CHAPTER XVII

THE PICTURE

Half-an-hour later there remained in the cottage besides the wounded girl only Peter, Anthony, and young O'Driscol—the latter to keep watch outside. The rest would gladly have remained if they could have been of any use, and indeed freely offered their services. But Anthony as their superior officer issued his orders without delay. Only he and the doctor and Paddy O'Driscol would stay at the cottage—the others were to scatter immediately to the various hiding places near, of which they knew.

And so they had gone, not without several backward glances at the unconscious girl who at the risk of her own life had probably saved theirs.

The wound in Sheila's arm was a nasty one, the bullet having ploughed its way through the flesh of the upper arm and become embedded near the shoulder. Driving the car afterwards, and her long and painful walk, had increased the hæmorrhage very greatly, and she had lost a considerable amount of blood. But the First Aid equipment at the cottage was very good, and the doctor had all he wanted to hand, so that he had extracted the bullet and cleaned and dressed the wound in a short space of time—allowing the girl to remain in merciful unconsciousness while he did so. It was not until Peter was finishing off the bandage that Anthony spoke.

'Well?' he said then. 'What do you think of her?'

The doctor looked up and smiled cheerily—he knew the terrible anxiety which was consuming his friend.

'I think she will do all right,' he replied. 'It's a nasty wound—and has been irritated a lot by her journey here. But if no septic trouble starts it ought to heal well.'

He paused and looked down at the pale, flowerlike face on the rough camp bed. Her brows were drawn together and an anxious harassed look overspread her countenance—it was as though in her unconsciousness she was again living through the past few hours.

'I wonder how she got wounded?' said Anthony with a catch in his throat.

'Oh! she must have met some of those devils!' replied the doctor. 'But how in the world she escaped from them, or how she heard the news which she brought to us—well! that is a mystery which we must only wait to hear from her own lips. But one thing is certain, Tony, old man, that you may be jolly proud of your sister!'

Anthony's stern face, so lined now with worry and anxiety, lit up for a moment.

'Yes,' he said softly. 'Thank God for that! I do thank Him, Peter, that she has—as you would say—gone through the crucible and proved herself to be true metal. This night has blotted out her past foolishness.'

'Ah! well; she comes of good stock,' said the other. 'After all the girl is a Ryan, so what else could you expect?'

A spasm of acute pain crossed Anthony's face at these words, and the doctor, noticing his expression, looked at him in surprise. There was silence for a few moments—a miserable silence for Anthony, who knew that he would have to take Peter into his confidence about Desmond. This was necessary, and Anthony knew that it must be faced, but that did not lessen the agony of shame which he felt in every fibre of his being. He glanced towards the door, outside which O'Driscol was keeping vigilant watch, he and Peter were practically alone, he had better speak and get the thing over.

So in a few halting sentences he told O'Connor what Sheila had whispered to him. Only just three words! But he knew that Peter, like himself, could fill in the sordid, shame-laden tale of a boy's mad infatuation and an unscrupulous woman's wiles.

As he spoke Anthony had covered his face with his hands—he could not look even at his dearest friend, while he stumbled over those words of terrible import. He and Desmond had always been as one—they had never seemed to have had a separate existence apart from each other until this unspeakable thing had come between them. And so Anthony felt just as if it was his own treachery to which he was confessing as he stood there like a guilty man before Peter.

Peter saw it all, understood it all, too, and his heart went out to his comrade. Coming to his side he laid his hand on Anthony's shoulder, as he had often done long years ago when he was a senior boy, the twins only humble juniors, and his willing slaves.

'Now, don't be foolish, Tony,' he remonstrated with quiet commonsense. 'A boy's foolish obsession!—why it is an everyday story! But we have got to act—and to act at once so as to prevent the mischief which his madness would have caused. It is thanks to your sister that we can prevent it. Don't forget that.'

Anthony nodded silently, but he said nothing, waiting for the other to continue.

'Now let us think what is best to be done,' said Peter; 'for we must not lose any time. We don't even know what hour the military will come here, or to Elton Street. Our hope is that Sheila knows—I see she is stirring now.'

The girl moved and asked for a drink, for she was feeling the terrible thirst which always follows loss of blood. Peter first mixed her a restorative, which she drank obediently, then gave her a little weak, half-warm tea which revived her greatly, and shortly afterwards, to their great relief, she was able bit by bit to tell them all that they were so anxious to hear. She described the interview between Yvonne and Ronald Hammond in the library at Firfield House, and while she told in halting sentences all that she had heard from Yvonne relating to Desmond, her face, like Anthony's flushed with shame, and her eyes avoided Peter's pitiful gaze.

Then she told of her resolve to bring the warning to the cottage, of her meeting with the military, her reckless driving past them, which had been followed by the shots, one of which had wounded her, and after that of her long wearisome journey until at last she had just managed to crawl to the lane outside, there to sink down in utter exhaustion, fearing that no one could see her or hear her poor little moans and cries for help.

Anthony listened while tears which were no disgrace to his manhood filled his eyes. He stooped and kissed her, gently brushing back her thick hair from her forehead—he took her two little cold hands in his strong ones, and kissed them, too, and rubbed them gently to warm them.

'Girlie!' he said softly, 'I am proud of my sister tonight.'

'And more than you will be proud of her, too, I'm thinking,' broke in the doctor. 'But now to practical matters. What are we going to do? What would be best to arrange under the circumstances as we now know them?'

'I am going to Elton Street at once,' said Anthony, 'to get those papers before the raid takes place. As Desmond is not to meet that woman before ten he will not leave the place before nine-thirty, and we may be sure that the raid will not begin until they believe that he is safely away en route for the Dargle. The Dargle. My God! Ah! well, it's no good saying anything more. Now, Peter, I know that you will take Sheila·over to the Byrnes' place, where she can rest in safety as long as is needful. It's a good job that we have a stretcher here; I'm sure that you and Paddy can carry her between you.'

After a little more consultation it was decided that this was indeed the best plan. From a medical standpoint the doctor did not care to leave Sheila just then, besides that Anthony, for obvious reasons, was the proper person to go to Elton Street to save the papers.

That this was no easy undertaking, but one beset with danger on all sides, both men realised, but although they made light of it before the girl they did not succeed in throwing dust into her eyes, and she clung pitifully to Anthony when he was ready to start. She had been made comfortable on the stretcher, well covered with rugs, while the doctor had packed up all he could carry of the First Aid dressings and bandages. Paddy O'Driscol had hidden all the other stores in a hollow under a rocky boulder behind the cottage, over which hiding place a great furze bush threw its thorny protection. Then they kicked out the fire, and dismantled the cottage as much as possible, leaving nothing of the slightest value—nothing that could give the least clue of any kind to the expected raiders.

'Now, don't worry yourself, Girlie,' said her brother as he tenderly loosened her hands from his shoulder, kissing them lovingly as he did so, 'I will be able to mind myself—never you fear. Keep up your heart, and do all that Peter tells you, and you will hear from me as soon as I can possibly manage to get a message through.'

With that he set out for his walk to the city, while Sheila and her escort moved cautiously across the hills to the friendly shelter of the Byrnes' homestead.

It was just six o'clock, and the dawn beginning to show on this dark November morning, when Anthony Ryan turned his steps Dublinwards. He had to keep a sharp look-out for any of the enemy en route and he had to walk quickly, as he wanted to reach the office before Desmond had left. He must see the infatuated boy and tell him all. That Desmond would be horrified beyond words when he realised the trap into which he had fallen, and understood how nearly he had been the cause of a terrible blow to the whole organisation, Anthony never doubted for a moment. Knowing his twin as he did, he realised how terribly the other would feel all this, and what unspeakable agonies of shame and humiliation would be his. That was why Anthony was glad that he himself would be able to break it to his brother, and to guard against any rash act which Desmond might contemplate when the full measure of his folly was brought home to him.

He knew from Sheila that Yvonne was to meet Desmond at the railway station at ten o'clock, and he guessed that the latter would leave Elton Street about nine-thirty or nine-forty, while he himself should easily be there about eight-thirty, or even sooner if he had the luck to get an early tram when he reached the suburbs. So thinking he swung quickly along, moving rapidly and easily down the rough mountain path, but making as little noise as possible, keeping vigilant watch into the surrounding mist, and his hand on the revolver which was in the pocket of his overcoat.

Perfect silence was all around him, except where here and there a sleepy bird called to the dawn, and probably wished in his little feathered heart that it was the summer sun, and not the mists of winter, which were awaking him. Furze bushes, and great spaces all bracken covered—the brown, rusty bracken of winter—passed by, and then hedgerows loomed up to meet him, and fields and occasional houses. The light was clearer now and he would soon be on the outskirts of the city—once there he would pass for an early worker going to his daily toil. Anyhow the nearer the city the less he thought the risk to his safety would be, and pulling his hat low down on his brow he strode on quickly. But suddenly the silence was broken by a sound which he recognised only too well—a sound with which he had good reason to be familiar—and to dread. Out of the distance towards him came the rush and throb of military lorries.

Anthony immediately realised his danger, but he did not lose heart nor his presence of mind. A deep ditch ran along the roadside, from which it was divided by a grassy incline, and in a fraction of time Anthony was in this ditch, lying down flat and straight in the cold slimy ooze which struck so deadly chill to his limbs. There he stayed, as motionless as though there was no life in him, waiting till the lorries should pass and the noise and clang of them should die away in the distance. He only grumbled mentally as he thought of his wet and discoloured clothes in which he would have to walk to Elton Street.

Nearer and nearer came the lorries, but instead of rushing past as he had so confidently expected, he realised with a quick sense of dismay that they were slowing down—they came to a halt in fact just beside his hiding place. Wonderment was mixed with alarm and he realised that the lorries had actually come to a standstill, for he could not believe that they could have 'spotted' him before he had taken refuge in the ditch. He was sure such a thing was impossible, for he had not been able to see the lorries at the time he had taken cover—only their noise had proclaimed their nearness to him. However, the mystery was solved in a few minutes when scraps of their conversation were carried to the listener's ears. Something had gone wrong with the first lorry and they had pulled up for whatever slight repairs were needed, and Anthony breathed a sigh of relief as comprehension dawned upon him. Motionless he lay and listened. The men had evidently dismounted and in their extraordinary and lurid language were discussing whatever was wrong, and going over the various parts of the lorry. Anthony could see absolutely nothing of them, but he knew by the sounds that there were two lorries, and he judged by the voices that there were a fair number of men and one officer.

The men in the second lorry did not get out; they amused themselves with throwing jibes and taunts at their companions who were overhauling the other lorry, and partaking of refreshment—there was a great popping of corks and food of some kind seemed to be handed around. From which Anthony came to the conclusion that they had visited—and raided—some country public house en route. In this lorry, too, was a dog—evidently one of those mascots which the Auxiliaries were so fond of—and its shrill bark joined now and then with the men's laughter and oaths.

To Anthony, lying in the cold ditch afraid to move even a hair's breadth to ease his cramped limbs, aeons of time seemed to have passed, but in reality it was barely twenty minutes before the lorry was ready to proceed on its road. Doubtless it would have gone on its way immediately only that the men who had been engaged in fixing it up declared in choice terms of their own that they were both hungry and thirsty and didn't see why they shouldn't have refreshments as well as the others. A short halt was evidently agreed upon and Anthony had perforce to continue lying motionless in the ditch, praying that they might soon go, and that he might not be suddenly seized with a desire to cough or sneeze. He was chilled to the bone and enduring a misery of discomfort, but he hardly felt it, so terrible was the mental anxiety which was consuming him.

In the meanwhile talk and laughter of the usual loud and ribald style proceeded from the men, interspersed with the shrill barking of the dog, which seemed to be anxious to get out of the lorry.

Presently a voice from the lorry which had caused all the delay called out:-

' 'Ere, let Ginger down; 'e wants a share of our grub too.'

The dog was let out of the lorry, and ran to the others, who amused themselves with throwing scraps down to him, and then as he became quiet they soon forgot all about him, and continued to shout and laugh amongst themselves, while the dog, delighted with his temporary freedom, was soon foraging around on his own account.

After the manner of his kind he went nosing about everywhere and after a few minutes Anthony, to his intense horror, heard a rustling of the dead leaves near his hiding place, and turning his head saw two bright canine eyes regarding him with puzzled surprise. For a moment neither man nor dog moved, but only continued to stare steadily at each other. Then the dog drew a little nearer while Anthony still kept quiet and immovable. He realised only too well the danger he was in, for that the dog would bark and raise the alarm was almost certain, and for one second his hand went out towards the animal. It was wearing a big collar and his momentary idea was to grasp this collar with one hand and with the other hand fell the dog to the ground with the butt end of his revolver—or even to strangle it. But Anthony had always loved dogs as they also loved him, and now all his old dog friends of a lifetime seemed to rise before him and plead, in their dumb way, for their comrade. He couldn't do it, even though he knew that it might be his only chance—he simply could not, in cold blood, strike cruelly at the brown doggy eyes which were gazing at him, while their owner's stumpy tail wagged tentatively.

'After all,' he thought rapidly, 'even if I did kill the poor little beast the men would be sure to miss him and to look for him before starting off, and probably they would find his body here, and then what good would I have done myself?'

The dog was a nondescript sort of mongrel, but very likeable and evidently both friendly and intelligent. Anthony's sole hope now was to keep him quiet. He addressed the animal in a soft whisper:

'Good dog! Poor old boy!' But unfortunately this had the very opposite effect to what he desired, for the dog now quite charmed with his new acquaintance gave several short barks of delight, and then springing into the ditch jumped around Anthony, endeavouring to lick his face and wagging his tail energetically.

''Ere, I say! Wot's come over Ginger? There must be something in that bloomin' ditch.'

Anthony laid his hand lightly on the dog's shaggy head.

'I'm afraid you've done for me, old boy!' he murmured; 'but you didn't mean it.'

He sprang to his feet as he spoke, for the Auxiliaries were pouring out of the lorries and rushing straight towards his hiding place, and he determined to make an effort—desperate and reckless though it seemed—to escape from them. Had it only been a question of his own arrest and nothing more he might have surrendered to such overwhelming odds, but the thought of those papers, which must not reach the enemy's hand, made him a determined and desperate man.

So when the first Auxiliary sprang on the ditch Anthony's revolver rang out and the man fell—shot through the brain.

There was a perfect howl from his companions, cries and oaths and execrations as they came tumbling up, and before Anthony could even attempt to make a bolt for it, which had been his mad idea, his revolver was wrenched from him, and he was knocked down with a crashing blow on the jaw from the sledge-hammer fist of a drunken-looking giant.

Meanwhile the rest were examining their comrade's body where it lay sprawling across the ditch.

'By Gawd! 'E's gone west! Willis is shot! You blasted Hirish swine you'll pay for this!'

Unspeakable language followed, and it looked very much as if they were about to take summary vengeance at once for their dead companion. Indeed Anthony, sick and faint, and only partly conscious—for several more kicks and blows had followed the first one—had given himself up for lost, and was trying to say an Act of Contrition, when the officer strode forward and looked closely at him.

'By Jove!' he said, after a prolonged scrutiny; 'I believe this chap is a badly wanted man! Wanted alive, too! Bind his hands and put him in the lorry. We will deliver him over to the military. Oh! don't be afraid,' as some of the men seemed inclined to dissent, 'he will get all he deserves. You may be sure of that.'

Anthony was pitched headlong into the lorry, bruised and dazed, with blood flowing freely from his head and face, the lorries turned back towards the City—that suffering City which was just awaking to more scenes of horror and bloodshed.

*   *   *

Just at this same hour Desmond Ryan, in his bed at Elton Street, suddenly awoke, and sat up listening intently. He thought he had heard Anthony's voice calling to him, an urgent, insistent call— 'Desmond! Desmond!' Then as he awoke fully and realised where he was he knew that he must have been dreaming. Yet the sound, the echo of the voice as it were, remained in his ears in a strangely persistent manner. Could Tony want him. Or be in trouble of any kind? He was almost inclined to spring out of bed, dress himself, and set off for the cottage on the slopes of Kilmashogue. And then as he hesitated his mind suddenly conjured up the memory of the previous night, and he saw again Yvonne's lovely mouth held up for his kiss, the firelight dancing in the meshes of her wonderful hair.

'Why, of course!' he thought as he sank down again amongst his pillows, 'I am to take her to Bray—to the Dargle. We are to be together for the whole day. And here I am getting into a fever over a silly dream about Tony.'

It was only a little after seven o'clock and he tried to settle himself for another sleep, but soon found that he was compelled to give up the attempt. He remained tossing and turning in his bed— always seeming to hear his brother's voice calling to him, and feeling absolutely and completely wretched both in mind and body. Although he would not admit the fact to himself, he knew in his heart and soul that something was wrong with Anthony.

The brothers possessed that strange affinity which is sometimes found amongst twins, of feeling each other's pains and troubles. As children they always suffered physically together; if one had the toothache or a headache, or even a cut finger, his twin would affirm that he felt the pain also—and to all appearances seemed to do so. Although of late years this had not been so marked in small matters, still in the case of any big happening, or of much pain or suffering to either of them, the other would always suffer to some extent. Therefore Desmond understood the warning, but would not give into it, even though his head was aching and he felt sick and tired and wretched in every way. Only for his appointment with Yvonne he would have been on his way to the mountains before Mrs Pell arrived that morning. As it was she found him up and trying to dress himself with extra care. He looked so ill, however, that she exclaimed at the sight of him, and was immediately all fussy anxiety, advising him to go back to bed and allow her to bring him some strong tea and toast, 'for it's plain to be seen, Mr Desmond dear, that you haven't got over your headache yet.'

Her well-meant words only made matters worse, and Desmond, turning upon her furiously, spoke as the poor woman never remembered to have heard her favourite speak before—telling her to hold her tongue and get his breakfast quickly. She retired precipitately to the kitchen, breathing deep maledictions on Yvonne's lovely head as she set about her work, for she was quick enough to be able to put two and two together as she remembered her meeting with Mademoiselle on the preceding night. Just once, while she was frying bacon—which Desmond was to leave untasted—the thought came to her to tell him about her own interview with Yvonne. But she was afraid to do so, afraid of angering her 'poor lamb' further, and still more afraid of the warning and threats of Mademoiselle Delaunay. Afterwards she was to nearly break her heart because she had not done so, but it is very unlikely that Desmond, in the condition of mind in which he was that morning, would have even listened to her.

In the meantime he had finished dressing, and had left his bedroom, to walk restlessly to and fro in the sittingroom, trying to shake off his feelings of mental and physical suffering. His eyes suddenly chanced to rest on his mother's portrait, and his gaze remained, arrested, in some queer way, by an expression on the pictured face with seemed new and strange to him, which seemed, indeed, almost to change the portrait into one he had not seen before.

It was as if his dead mother was trying in some inexplicable way to speak to him—as if she had a message to give him. Involuntarily he took a step forward and nearly found himself saying—as if he was a small boy again and she had called to him—'Yes, mother. Do you want me?'

He tried to shake off the feeling, but all through his pretence of a breakfast it remained with him and every time that he raised his unwilling eyes—drawn by some strange force which he was powerless to resist—and looked at the picture, the eyes seemed to be still appealing to him, urging, remonstrating, pleading with him.

'What can it mean?' he thought miserably. 'Am I becoming an imbecile, or what can be wrong with me this morning?' Then the thought of the all-important papers in the niche behind the portrait crossed his mind, but, believing as he did that they were absolutely safe, he thrust the thought from him. Indeed the papers only brought closer to him the remembrance of last night and Yvonne—Yvonne who would be waiting for him soon now, waiting with her alluring red lips and her inscrutable eyes. Hastily swallowing his cup of tea he sprang up and seized his hat and coat; it was only nine o'clock, but he felt that he could better pass the time of waiting in walking about the streets than by remaining in his rooms. He would not admit the fact to himself, but in his inmost heart he knew that the haunting appeal of the pictured eyes was driving him out.

'I'll be back about half-past six or seven this evening,' he called out to Mrs Pell, 'but you needn't be here; I can look after myself.' And he ran downstairs two at a time.

'Look after yourself indeed!' muttered Mrs Pell, as she entered the sittingroom to remove his breakfast things, 'And that's just what you can't do, me poor lamb! I wish to God you could—you wouldn't be eaten up and devoured by wolves dressed like fashion plates.'

Thus soliloquising she started to clear the table, and then she, too, found herself looking up at the portrait over the mantelpiece.

'The artist that painted that must have been a real good one,' she thought. 'God knows but the dear lady looks as if it was alive she was this blessed minit!'

She turned away, but a few moments later she again found herself compelled to look at the picture, and this time the eyes seemed indeed to be speaking—to be asking something.

Mrs Pell remained for a short while gazing across the room at the portrait, and then making the Sign of the Cross devoutly she went and stood by the mantelpiece and gazed up at it. Still the eyes gazed into her own—gazed with a look of unspeakable yearning, as though pleading for help.

'Yerra, ma'am dear, what's on you at all?' Mrs Pell suddenly found herself saying aloud, 'What is it you want, you poor soul?'

Again she made a determined effort to turn her back on the picture, but again felt constrained to turn and look at it.

'Now I must be going balmy—a little bit off the thatch! as Mr P used to say,' she muttered. 'Bother take the thing! Sure it's only a picture anyway.' And as if to prove this to herself she took a duster, and—what she had been strictly forbidden to do so by the twins— began to dust the portrait. Not only did she dust the face, but she turned the oil painting round and dusted carefully behind it in case of cobwebs. There were none, but Mrs Pell continued to dust and rub, and in doing so she knocked her knuckles against the wall, and noticed the peculiar hollow sound which followed. Her suspicions were aroused—she remembered the Ryans' strange care about this painting—she determined to find out if there was any hidden mystery. After about ten minutes she discovered the ingeniously contrived recess in the wall hidden by the sliding panel. This was worked by a clever spring arrangement, and as far as Mrs Pell was concerned it was, as she herself would have said, 'more be chance than good luck' that she presently saw it slipping open before her eyes. A square opening in the brickwork was before her and in this was a bundle of MSS papers tied together. Mrs Pell looked and pondered, slowly but surely piecing things together. This then was why the twins had hung the portrait themselves and forbidden her ever to touch it; this was why they had told her that some bricks had fallen down and they had a bit of work to do over the mantelpiece—work that had taken nearly a week, which was always done at night when she had gone home, and of which there was never any trace.

These papers then must be very precious, very important. They were probably there during the military raid and had escaped. That was a good job anyway! But there was that dangerous hussy— if she found them out, and she coming to the flat as bold as brass while Mr Anthony was away, and poor Mr Desmond—the innocent lamb!—just like a child in her hands. If she should get her hands on them! Mrs Pell, although, on principle, taking no apparent part in Irish affairs, still knew enough to hazard a pretty accurate guess at the contents of the package facing her.

'I wonder will he bring that she-wolf of a vampire back with him his evening?' she thought. 'God knows but he might. Sure he's that infatuated with her that it's plain for all to see. If only Mr Anthony was here—or if I knew where to find him!' Then a daring idea flashed across her mind. Why should she not take the papers and keep them safe for Mr Anthony? Her house would never be suspected—she, the widow of a Sergeant-Major, and her daughter married to a Navy man—not that he was much good as a son-in-law! She would give them back to Mr Anthony as soon as he returned, and she would have to tell him then all about Mademoiselle Delaunay and her suspicions of that lady. He might be furious with her, and Anthony's cold rage was more terrible in her eyes than Desmond's quick passion, but she knew—she knew—that the papers would be safe with her, and something—instinct, intuition—what you will—told her that they were not safe where they were.

So she lifted them from their hiding place, and although she was the widow of a British soldier Mrs Pell kissed them reverently, as though they were a Scroll of Honour, before thrusting them inside her blouse, where she fastened them securely with safety pins.

She pushed back the panel, put the picture in place again, and dismounted heavily from the chair on which she had stood to investigate, duster in hand. Then as she looked once more at the pictured face of the twins' mother she actually started—for she had for a moment imagined that the sweet, serious eyes were smiling down at her.

'God between us and all harm!' she said, crossly to herself. 'But that was surely what the poor lady wanted.' And aloud she said, 'Yes, indeed, ma'am, I'll mind them safe—with me very life if needs be.'

She finished her work quickly, and in half-an-hour had left the offices. As she reached the corner of Dame Street she met two military lorries tearing past. Looking back she saw them turn into Elton Street and heard them drawing to a standstill. She knew then that she had done right, and she breathed a prayer of thanksgiving that she had been in time.

'I've done me bit anyway, as Mr P would say!' she thought. Then remembering the need for caution and discretion she went on her way calmly, and looked neither to the right or the left until she had reached her own two-pair back in Mercer Street.

CHAPTER XVIII

THE BEGINNING OF THE END

The Dargle in November is certainly not seen at its best—the very opposite in fact is the case, and on this particular day in late November it seemed especially dreary and dismal—a nightmare of damp and ghostly mists—to those two who had looked forward on the previous evening to spending within its gates some happy hours together. What then had happened to change their whole outlook of glad anticipation? Not the weather or the time of year—dreary as these were—for such details make no difference to lovers, they are oblivious of them.

Many years ago a picture was exhibited in the Royal Academy in London portraying a young man and a girl. She was attired in the dowdy-looking dress of the period, and was shabby and poor into the bargain; he was like a badly paid City clerk. The rain was coming down in torrents, splashing on the railings of the City park behind them, and shining on the glistening pavements, drenching them through their clothes, for neither of them had a good coat or waterproof. But he was holding his umbrella over her, looking down at her pale, rather pretty face in a manner that told plainly how gladly he would have sheltered her from all the world; and she, her hand within his arm, was gazing up at him with all the love of her heart shining from her eyes. To these two the rain and cold, their apparent poverty, the unsympathetic crowds passing, the long, dreary tomorrows facing them—all these things were as if they existed not. And the title of the picture was: 'The Garden of Eden.'

It is a garden that most of us walk in at some period of our lives, and let the time we pass there be long or short we can never forget it, for flowers are always growing there no matter what the time of year may be, or how harsh the outside weather is, and the soft winds of that garden waft to our ears the sweetest secret ever told. There is no other place just like that garden, so dear and sweet and altogether beautiful. When after a while the common fate of mortals overtakes us and we are thrust out from its gate and can enter it no more we feel the stinging blasts and bitter storms of the outside world cutting us to the heart; and our feet, used to the soft flower-bespangled grass of the delectable garden, stumble painfully over the rough roads and stony pavements of the world outside its gates.

But we become acclimatised again, and the time we spent in the Garden of Eden becomes more and more like a dream—a half forgotten dream of long ago. Only sometimes when we meet a couple like those in the picture we remember, and we catch our breath quickly as if something had hurt and turn away from them, for we know that they are in the garden which we can never enter again.

But there can be no Garden of Eden without love, and there was no love between Desmond Ryan and Yvonne Delaunay—only a mad infatuation on the one hand, and on the other sordid, mercenary plans, combined now with a passing fancy for the man—the nearest feeling akin to affection of which the woman was capable.

From the very beginning the day had been a failure. Even when their hands met in greeting at the station something had seemed to come between them, like an intangible wall of separation. Desmond felt it, and tried to shake off the impression, even as he tried to shake off the feeling of general physical and mental misery. But it was all in vain. Yvonne, too, had realised at once that things were out of gear and wondered why it was so. Had anything happened since last night? Had he by any chance heard or guessed anything? Well! she would make it her business to find out. So as the train ran through the suburbs and sped along towards the coast she leant forward and placed her hand on his. They were alone in the compartment and Desmond was sitting in the corner seat opposite to her; he had not offered to kiss or touch her, indeed had hardly spoken since the train started.

'Desmond! What is it?' she asked.

He turned from his weary gazing out at the flying landscape and looked at her, and his eyes softened for a moment; indeed Yvonne just then was a sight to make an old man young. Her tantalising little face under the fur cap which only partly hid the glory of her hair, the soft black furs round the white throat, the beautifully finished coat, and arched foot in a perfect shoe, all made a delightful and fascinating whole. She had slipped off her gloves and her little manicured hand lay like a spot of white on Desmond's brown one. He laid his other hand over it and smiled at her as he replied:

'Nothing is the matter, or rather I don't know what is wrong with me really, except that I have got a rotten headache. Have had it all morning.'

Yvonne gave an inaudible sigh of very real relief to find, as she thought, that Desmond's behaviour was due to merely physical causes. She had been fearful of some other reason for his strange depression, but now she strove to turn his thoughts away from his headache and was particularly sweet and charming. But as far as her companion was concerned she might almost have remained silent; he did try to respond indeed, tried to smile and talk, even to make love. But it was useless—the attraction of the woman was gone, and not the slightest desire for her burned now in the heart of Desmond Ryan.

Thinking that it must be his physical condition and feeling vexed that Yvonne's day should be spoilt for her, he suggested, when they reached Bray, that they should only stay a short time and go back to town early.

'For I am fit for nothing today—whatever is wrong with me,' he said, 'and I would only spoil the day for you, Yvonne. I feel like a bear with a sore head. Let us go back to town and we can arrange another day for our outing.'

But, needless to remark, this suggestion did not suit Yvonne; she was aghast at the idea, and actually frightened for a moment for fear that Desmond would insist on returning. She brought forth all her powers of persuasion and after a time succeeded in gaining her own ends. They strolled along the Promenade for a little while, and Desmond tried to imagine that the sea air was making him feel better. Then they had lunch, a meal which, like his breakfast, was a mere pretence for Desmond, and after that they took a car to the Dargle.

There they strolled around for an hour or so, but so dreary and dull did everything seem that they were glad to leave it. Yvonne glanced curiously at her companion from time to time, for she was frankly puzzled by him, and in her astute brain she was convinced that a headache would not account for the extraordinary change in his manner towards her. Yet it was not that he wished to be cold to her; he tried several times to act a lover's part, but always failed in the attempt. The truth was that Desmond on that day was a haunted man. Always in his ears he heard his brother's cry of 'Desmond! Desmond!' and always before his vision seemed to come the

pleading eyes of his mother as she had looked down on him from
her picture over the mantelpiece in Elton Street—that picture
which was the guardian and custodian of the hidden papers. And
then the thought of those papers would force itself upon him. It
was strange, he thought, how these thoughts tormented him and
would not be banished. Again and again he tried to brush them
aside and to smile and make love to the fascinating woman beside
him—as she so plainly expected him to do—but all in vain. And he
felt so deadly ill into the bargain. Poor Anthony! wherever he was
he must be suffering—Desmond was convinced of that now, and
admitted the fact to himself. At last he could endure his
wretchedness no longer and suggested a return to town although
it was much sooner than they had originally intended to go back.
However, Yvonne, who was tired and disgusted with the day, was
quite ready to assent and they arrived back in town shortly after
four o'clock.

Yvonne wished devoutly that she could have left the train at
Dundrum when it had reached that station, but for various reasons
she thought it better for Desmond not to know that she was staying
at present with his stepmother, and with all her cleverness she did
not know that Sheila had any means of communicating with her
brothers. Sheila was to her an absolute nonentity and of no account
in the game. So she went on to Harcourt Street with Desmond, but
they said good-bye at the station—she going her way to the flat to
see if any message had arrived, although she knew she would get
full details later from Ronald at Firfield: Desmond going his way to
Elton Street.

As he walked through the familiar streets he began to feel more
like his normal self; the headache, too, was better, and his brain
clearer, and as he strode swiftly along he planned to give just a hasty
look in at Elton Street to see that all was as usual, and then to set off
at once without any further delay to the cottage in the mountains,
for by this time he could no longer blind himself to the fact that he
was anxious, terribly anxious, about his twin. He was also
experiencing certain qualms of conscience that he had not put off
his day with Yvonne—he could have telephoned her early in the
morning—and gone instead to ascertain if all was well with
Anthony. And after all what a dismal failure the day had been—a
complete fiasco from beginning to end. Why it had proved so he
could not understand, he had painted it to himself in such roseate

colours only the previous night, he had hardly been able to sleep thinking of the happy hours which he and Yvonne would spend together. And how different the reality had been! It was not Yvonne Delaunay's fault—she had been the same as ever—just as fascinating and bewitching, but her wiles had had no effect on him that day. He had to admit to himself that if she had been withered and old and hideous, he could not have felt more utterly indifferent towards her. Something had come between them— something over which he had no control. He only knew that every time she spoke to him he seemed to hear instead of her soft accent the cry of Anthony as he called to him—'Desmond! Desmond!' and every time her inscrutable eyes met his they seemed to change to those of his mother pleading with him from her picture.

'What a day it has been!' he groaned. 'Thank God! it's nearly over.' He gave himself a mental shake as he turned into Elton Street and fitted his latchkey in the door.

It was just five o'clock and some of the offices were already closing—he passed several clerks in the passage and on the stairs, who looked at him curiously, but he never noticed them as he hurried on. Arriving at his own office landing, however, his attention was arrested immediately, for through the open door where he paused in dismay, he saw the place was in disorder, with every evidence about it of having been subjected to another raid. Frank Dillon was sitting in a chair at the table, with his head in his hands and looked the picture of despondency.

Desmond stood aghast, silent for a moment, as a quick touch of fear smote him.

'Dillon!' he cried then, his voice sharp with anxiety, 'What is it? What has happened?'

The boy raised his head and looked stupidly at Desmond, who was struck by the haggard expression on his face. He continued to look at Desmond for a moment without speaking, and his eyes seemed to harden. He had not the slightest idea of the other's real share in this terrible thing which had happened, but he had heard from Mrs Pell that Desmond had gone off for the day somewhere, and poor young Dillon had had to bear alone much which he justly considered Desmond should have helped him to share.

'Where were you all day?' he asked, his voice toneless and weary from grief and fatigue.

Desmond flushed angrily.

'That is no concern of yours,' he said. 'Answer my question, please. What has happened? Has there'—with a glance around—'been another raid?'

'Yes.'

'The military? When did they arrive?'

'At ten o'clock this morning.'

'Then why haven't you put the place to rights again?' asked Desmond irritably. 'Or are you waiting for me to help you?'

Then as the other did not answer he went on: 'After all there is no harm done. You know there is nothing here for them to find. So what are you worrying about? They can raid here as often as they like. Pull yourself together, Dillon, and don't be a fool. I'll be down to help you to clear up this mess in a few moments, but I can't stay long, as I'm off to America this evening. I'm just going to see if all is right upstairs—I suppose they have left the usual work for poor Mrs P!'

And before Dillon could bring himself to say anything more Desmond was racing up the stairs, eager to see if all was right in the upper regions. Not that he felt anxious, he believed so firmly in the safety of the hiding place that he did not anticipate anything more than the usual raid, with the accompanying disorder and extra work for Mrs Pell.

So he entered the sittingroom confidently enough, and met as he had half expected, a scene of disorder and chaos—only half expected, because he had thought that probably Mrs Pell would have tidied the place by this hour, and he was certainly surprised that she had not done so.

'I suppose she must have been gone before they arrived,' he thought. 'I told her not to bother coming back this evening.' His glance swept the room, and he noticed that it was not so generally upset as on the occasion of the previous raid, except in one part of it, and then as he raised his eyes to the mantelpiece he stood there on the threshold as though suddenly turned to stone, gazing in awful, frozen horror at the dismantled wall with the bricks torn out and scattered around, with dust and mortar over everything, and in the centre, facing him, the recess—empty!

For several moments he remained immovable—only staring—staring in front of him. Then his lips twitched.

'The picture is not on the wall! Where is it? Where is it?' This was the first coherent thought that came to him, it was the question which hammered for an answer even before that of the fate of the papers.

Stumbling like a drunken man he crossed the room and came to a halt near the fireplace. No fire was burning in the dismantled grate and he had not lit the gas, but the daylight was still bright enough for him to see that there, on the floor at his feet, lay what once had been the oil painting of the mother who had been the very idol of his boyhood. It had been wrenched from its frame and lay there, face upwards, or what had once been the face, for brutal, sacrilegious hands had slashed and torn and stabbed at that dear remembered countenance; both the eyes had been gouged out; the face had been slashed across and across, and ribald fingers had drawn a mock moustache round the sweet mouth. They had done their work so well that Desmond found himself gazing down at a horrid caricature in place of the picture of his beloved mother.

Just at first he could not realise it—he thought he must be dreaming. This thing—this awful thing—could not be true, it must be a nightmare from which he would thankfully awake. But there was no awakening. The deepening shadows gathered around him as the daylight got less and dusk drew its dark veil over all, but that which had once been his mother's picture only seemed to shine more clearly before his anguished eyes.

'Mother!' he cried then, with a terrible cry—the cry of remorse than which there is none more awful—the cry which Judas made when he flung back the thirty pieces of silver—'Mother!'

He flung himself face downward on the floor beside the defiled fragments of her pictured face, the poor sockets wanting eyes, the twisted, mockingly decorated mouth.

How long he remained there he did not know, but he found himself gradually returning to consciousness of what was passing around him by hearing the sound of weary, monotonous sobbing close at hand.

Rising to his feet he pushed open the door leading into the kitchen and paused for a moment on the threshold, dazzled by the bright light of the gas after the darkness. Then as he looked within he saw Mrs Pell sitting by the fire, with her apron over her head, rocking herself to and fro, and sobbing with the bitter tears of middle age. She did not seem to have heard him coming in for she did not lift her head.

'Mrs Pell!' he said then, and his voice sounded strange in his own ears, so harsh and strained was it.

The woman dropped her apron and looked around, and when she saw who it was she gave a cry and ran forward.

'Oh! Mr Desmond, dear! Oh! thank God ye're back. Sure I knew you would come! And have you seen him? I suppose you wouldn't be let speak to him?' He stared back at her stupidly.

'Have I seen him? Seen whom?' he asked then. He moistened his lips as he spoke, for a great horror seemed to clutch him with an icy hand.

'Seen who?' the woman echoed shrilly. 'Why Mr Anthony, of course. I thought you might have been up at the Castle, but I suppose—.'

'Mr Anthony! The Castle!'

Gropingly he put out a hand and held the table to steady himself.

'What are you talking about?' he asked then. 'What do you mean?'

But Mrs Pell, aghast to discover that he knew nothing of what had taken place during his absence, and trembling at the idea of breaking it to him, could only stand and stare at him.

'Can't you speak—or are you dumb?' he said, and placing his hands on her shoulders he shook her angrily, 'Oh! for God's sake speak—before you drive me mad!'

'All right, Mr Desmond, dear, I will—I'll tell you all. But sit down—oh! me poor lamb—sit down!'

She pushed him unresistingly into a chair and began to speak quickly. She felt that if she must tell him she must get it over at once without pausing to think or she would never be able to tell him at all. 'Mr Anthony is arrested,' she said. 'It seems there was a raid on where he was hiding and they—they got him.'

'How do you know this? Where did you hear it?'

'From Mr Dillon below. He was here when they raided and he came round to my house afterwards and told me and I came back here with him. Miss Moore was here, too, when the raid was on, but they held her up in the hall below. She went home afterwards. Mr Dillon told me that the military were searching behind the picture for—for papers and—.'

'Go on—go on!'

'While they were still here a lorry full of Black and Tans drove up and they had Mr Anthony with them a prisoner and they brought him up here and—.'

'Were you here then?'

'No, Mr Desmond, I was gone home. It was Mr Dillon told me.'

'Call Dillon up here.'

When the latter came and found that Mrs Pell had already broken the ground for him he told Desmond all that he had witnessed and all that he knew about the day's events. He had arrived at the office a few moments before the military, and on their arrival they had held him up in the office and made a perfunctory search there, but the majority of them had dashed straight upstairs and had evidently made straight for the recess over the mantelpiece, for he heard the sounds of crashing masonry and falling bricks and mortar. 'They called me up then,' he said, 'and asked me if I knew anything about certain papers which they seemed to expect to find in the recess which they had broken open behind the—the picture of your mother, Mr Desmond.'

Desmond looked up in quick surprise.

'But they would have found the papers by then,' he said. 'They must have been bluffing you, Dillon—looking for more information.'

'No; they had not found them,' was the reply. 'The picture was down off the wall and the recess open and all the wall around it ripped up, but they had found no papers.'

'Not found the papers!' echoed Desmond; 'but they must have done so. The papers—as I may as well tell you both now—were hidden in the recess.' Young Dillon stared at him in bewilderment.

'Well! all I know is that they did not get them,' he repeated.

'But I tell you they must have got them,' cried Desmond. 'Good God—man! Do you think I am a fool? The papers were there—and they are in the hands of the military now except—except someone else was here before them. When did you leave, Mrs Pell?'

'It was almost ten o'clock, Mr Desmond—indeed I passed the lorries in Dame Street, but of course I had no idea where they were going.'

Mrs Pell was taking no chances with Desmond. She had fully made up her mind not to give him the papers. She knew that he had proved himself untrustworthy already, and she dreaded Mademoiselle's influence over him. All day she had weighed the matter over, and although Anthony's arrest complicated matters for her she was still resolute to hold on to the packet she had taken from the recess until she could hand it over to one whom she knew could be entirely and absolutely trusted. The one she had in her 'mind's eye', as she would have said, was Dr O'Connor. But she had not the faintest notion where he was to be found, so all she could do was to hold on to the papers until she chanced to meet him. It cost her a lot to stick to her resolution not to tell her beloved Mr Desmond; her heart ached to let him know that they were safe, but she could not do that without revealing their whereabouts, which she was determined not to do. He must suffer—at least for a short time—for his folly.

'Did you see Mr Anthony?' Desmond was asking young Dillon.

'Yes,' was the reply. 'I was up here being cross-questioned about the papers, of which, as you know, I was absolutely ignorant, when the lorries with the Black and Tans arrived and Mr Anthony was with them. They brought him up here and questioned him about the papers.'

He hesitated for a moment, looking perfectly wretched, and Desmond threw him a quick searching glance as he asked:

'Did they ill-treat him? How was he looking?'

'Ill-treated?' here interposed Mrs Pell, unable to remain silent any longer. 'Was he ill-treated, is it? Oh! wait till you hear. Oh! Mr Desmond—Mr Desmond! What will we do to save him at all?'

'Be quiet!' cried Desmond, turning on her savagely, in the madness of his grief and anxiety. 'Dillon! for God's sake tell me quickly all you know.'

'Well! I couldn't get a word with Mr Anthony,' replied the other; 'they kept us apart, of course, and when I looked at him he only smiled back as—as sporting as you like. But he could not even make me a sign, because his hands were tied. He was very disfigured; his face was covered with blood, and there was a bad looking wound on his head. He had certainly got brutal treatment, but that's not the worst of the affair. Mr Desmond, I—I don't know how to tell you—.'

'Go on! Go on!'

'Well! from what I heard from the Black and Tans it seems that he had—had killed one of their fellows; shot him dead, before his arrest.'

'My God!'

There was silence for a few moments and then Desmond lifted his haggard face.

'Are you sure of this, Dillon?' he asked. 'It's so unlike Tony to take life that way.'

'Yes; that's what I thought myself, but they said he did anyway, and I believe, from the way he looked—his expression—when they spoke of it before him, that he did shoot the man. Very likely though he did not shoot to kill.'

'Anthony is such a splendid shot,' said Desmond, 'that he would hardly make a mistake.'

'I followed the lorries to the Castle afterwards,' went on Dillon; 'they let me off for a wonder—I quite expected to be arrested, too, and I am surprised that they did not take me. Indeed I hardly cared at the time whether they did or not—I was so desperately anxious about Mr Anthony. I actually went to the Castle and asked to see him, but, needless to say, I was not allowed. Miss Moore tried also, but with the same result. Oh! Mr Desmond—we are afraid for him! The military were so furious that they did not get the papers, and they believe that he knows where they are. God only knows what they will do to him. But he doesn't know where the papers are either, because I noticed his look of astonishment—he was thunderstruck—when he saw that the others had not found them.'

'But where are they?' cried Desmond. 'Who in Heaven's name can have got them?'

And to this there was no answer. Only Mrs Pell knew and she was determined not to speak.

Presently Desmond said huskily.

'Who did—that—to my mother's picture?'

'One of the Black and Tans,' averting his gaze from Desmond's face. 'They were a terrible crew. The military had only flung the picture down on the floor while they tore open the wall, but when the others came—oh! I can't tell you what they said and how they went on. And before Mr Anthony, too. I could not even look at him having to stand there and look on—powerless—a bound prisoner.'

Desmond rose to his feet.

'I'm going to see Miss Moore,' he said; 'and later I'll try and get to the cottage and see what has happened there. You had better go home—both of you. I'll hardly be back here before some time tomorrow—if then.'

'Don't forget Curfew, Mr Desmond—it's getting late,' warned Mrs Pell.

'Oh! damn Curfew! What do I care for it?' And he raced downstairs and out into the night, white faced and haggard.

The two left behind did not speak for a few moments. Then Frank Dillon said, 'He takes it hard.'

'And why wouldn't he?' asked Mrs Pell. 'Sure Mr Anthony and himself were like one person—there was no separating them. Oh! me poor lambs! Me poor lambs! What will become of the both of you at all, at all?'

'I wonder where the papers got to anyway?' said Dillon. 'Do you know anything about them, Mrs Pell?'

'Ah! for God's sake have sense, Mr Dillon. How would I know? Is it likely that they would take me into their confidence? Not that it would have been the first time that I had a hand in affairs of State—poor, dear Mr P often consulted me about certain matters which I can reassure you, Mr Dillon, he would not have shouted from the top of Nelson's Pillar.'

'Well! I wonder where they are—I know it's a perfect mystery to me.'

'Time will reveal all!' remarked Mrs Pell sententiously, as she drew her 'cabe' around her ample shoulders; 'and now I must be getting home. I feel both collapsed and contracted after such a day.'

She hesitated for a moment when she was ready to depart and then asked:

'I suppose you don't know where Dr Peter O'Connor is to be found, do you, Mr Dillon?'

'Why do you ask? Do you want to see him?'

'Oh! it doesn't matter,' she said hastily. 'Of course, if you don't care to tell me his residence—.'

'Oh! it's not that, Mrs Pell, but the truth is that the doctor is here today and somewhere very different tomorrow. I don't know for certain where he is just now, but I should say he is probably arrested with the others who were taken in the raid on the mountains. (I wonder, by the way, why Mr Anthony is on his own, and where are the others?) But there is a house where you could call and ask for Dr O'Connor with perfect safety, or leave a message for him if you cannot see him.' And he gave her the address of Mr Frederick Shortall, adding as he did so, 'I wouldn't tell you that much, Mrs Pell, only I believe that you are the right stuff and that I can trust you.'

'Your trust shall not be displaced, Mr Dillon,' replied Mrs Pell with much dignity.

CHAPTER XIX

DE PROFUNDIS

Geraldine Moore and Jill Devereux were sitting by the fire in their flat, and although the fire was a good one they shivered involuntarily from time to time, but more from misery and dread of they knew not what than from the cold. The day upon which they were looking back seemed so long and dreary. And then the suspense which they were now going through was very trying. They really knew so very little of what had actually taken place—just that there had been a raid at Elton Street and presumably also on the cottage, and that Anthony had been arrested. If any more had been arrested with him they had not heard. They were puzzling over this, and also over the fact—the unaccountable fact—that the papers had not been found. Perhaps they had not been hidden in the recess behind the picture after all? And yet it was evident from Anthony's astonishment—as described to them by Dillon—that he had thought they were there. If he had put them there who could have removed them? Could Desmond have had anything to do with it? Then the thought of Yvonne would descend upon them like a black shadow. But above all—and this thought they feared to voice to one another—would Anthony be tortured in the Castle to make him tell all he knew about the papers? The military, too, might believe that he was cognizant of their present hiding place. That the raids were probably due in some way to Yvonne Delaunay both the girls were positive, but did she know anything about the papers or not? She had come back to the flat about five o'clock that evening after being away for most of the day, but she had not remained long, leaving again almost immediately, presumably on her way to Firfield.

'I must go and see Sheila early tomorrow,' said Geraldine, breaking a rather long silence. 'Perhaps I should have gone today, but I really hardly knew what to do—I have been stupid since morning.'

'Sheila will not be likely to know anything more than we do ourselves,' said Jill, 'except that she might have picked up some information from Yvonne or Ronald Hammond. But if it had been anything urgent you know, Jerry, that she would have managed some way to let us know.'

Just then they heard footsteps on the stairs, evidently coming up the long, iron stairway leading to the top flats. Jill glanced at the clock and she saw that it was a quarter to eight, and she wondered who it could be, and whether it was a visitor for them or for the door across the corridor.

The footsteps came up rapidly and a knock at their door—a loud, imperative summons—made the two overstrung girls start and turn pale. But Jill went swiftly across the room and flung open the door. As she did so she drew back a step and said, 'Desmond!' She spoke very softly, only just above her breath, but Geraldine heard her and ran forward, and as she saw Desmond standing on the threshold, something in his attitude—for he stood as one not sure of his welcome—made her take his hand and pull him into the room.

'Shut and lock the door, Jill,' she said, and as the other obeyed Geraldine pushed forward a chair towards the fire for Desmond, and he sank into it without a word.

'I see you have heard the news,' said Jill. 'Oh! Desmond, we have had a terrible day—especially Jerry. I suppose you have heard nothing further?'

'No; I have only just heard about it all from Frank Dillon and Mrs Pell,' he replied. 'I was in Bray,' he went on, 'and only got back to town a short while ago. It was a terrible shock! I had no idea, I never thought—Jerry, will you tell me how Tony was looking this morning?'

But she had little to add to what he already knew, and could hardly bring herself to speak of Anthony at all; the fleeting glimpse she had had of him as he was jostled past her on his way to the lorry was one of the things which she would have liked to be able to blot from her memory.

'But he saw me, thank God!' she said, 'and I was able to give him a smile to cheer him.'

Desmond rose suddenly from his chair.

'I am just going across the corridor to see Mademoiselle Delaunay for a moment,' he said. 'I will come back here before I leave.'

'Yvonne Delaunay!' echoed Geraldine, while Jill grew slightly pale and her fine eyes dilated, 'You won't see Yvonne now, Desmond. You are just too late; she has already left for Firfield.'

'For Firfield?' he said. 'Yvonne gone to Firfield! What do you mean?'

'Why—didn't you know?' replied the girl. 'She is staying there for a few days. She slept there last night and will probably stay till Tuesday. She only ran into her flat here for a moment this evening—we did not see her—only heard her coming up.'

Desmond stared at her stupidly.

'Are you sure she is gone to Firfield?' he asked.

'Why, yes, of course we are sure,' interposed Jill. 'She is often there. She and Mrs Ryan are very friendly. As Jerry says, she was there last night.'

'Last night!' repeated Desmond dully.

He was trying desperately to think—to piece things together so as to make a logical whole. Why, if Yvonne had been staying at Firfield had she not told him? Why make a mystery of it? Why had she pretended—as she had done that very day—that she was sleeping at the flat?

He swung round towards the door.

'Are you going, Desmond?' asked Geraldine.

'Yes; I'm going to Firfield.'

'But will it be safe for you? If Anthony is arrested they are surely looking for you, too.'

It was evident that Geraldine had either forgotten or did not trust to Yvonne's power to protect him.

'Even so I must risk it!' he said. 'I want to see Sheila and Mademoiselle Delaunay. And afterwards I must try and make my way up to the cottage and find out who was taken when they raided it. Peter O'Connor is sure to be one of them. I must make sure anyway of how things are going.'

Geraldine had suddenly flushed and then turned pale at the mention of the doctor's name, but Desmond did not notice it. He paused on his way to the door, however, to put a question to her.

'I suppose you do not know anything about the papers which have so mysteriously disappeared?'

'Oh! no, Desmond. Why you know that I did not even know where they were. But the military were furious at not finding them—they seemed so certain of finding them there immediately. Someone must have given them the information.'

'Given them the information?' echoed Desmond. 'But that is impossible. No one knew where they were except Tony and Peter besides myself—.' He suddenly stopped and flushed scarlet and then turned quickly towards the door.

'Give my love to Sheila,' said Geraldine, 'and tell her I will try and see her tomorrow—and God speed you!'

He promised to give her message, and the next moment he was gone—leaving two very anxious hearts behind him, and in one of them a very bitter pain that was hard to bear.

Desmond was fortunate in securing a taxi, and during the ride he sat huddled miserably in a corner trying—trying to reach down to the bedrock of all this mystery which seemed to have suddenly surrounded him. But trying in vain, for no matter how he thought and reasoned and wondered he still found himself baffled. In the midst of his cogitations the taxi turned into the lodge gates and the next moment drew up before the big hall door of Firfield House, and Desmond jumped out. He paid the man and told him he need not wait, as he would not be returning to town that night. Then he sprang up the steps and rang and knocked loudly.

The door was opened immediately, it was as if the inmates had been on the watch, as indeed they were, but not for him.

Even as the maid flung open the door with another behind her, and Norman's man anxiously hovering in the background, his stepmother came rushing out of the diningroom.

'Is that Sheila?' she cried. 'Oh! who is it?'

When she saw Desmond she stopped and stared at him in mingled resentment and surprise, and then a gleam of hope lit up her haggard face and she came forward quickly. 'You have news of her?' she asked. 'Oh! Desmond, do you know where she is? Where is Sheila?'

Desmond stared at her in astonishment.

'What do you mean, Mrs Ryan?' he asked. 'Is Sheila not here? I want to see her. Where is she?'

'Where, indeed! That is what we do not know,' answered Mrs Ryan, the tears starting to her eyes. 'My poor child is missing since last night.'

'Sheila missing! What in God's name do you mean?' Desmond asked blankly, and for a second wondered could he have heard aright or was his brain giving way under these horrors which seemed to be overwhelming him.'

'Come into the library,' said Mrs Ryan.

'Then you hadn't heard,' she continued as they entered the big, comfortable room which held so many memories for the man.

'And you don't know anything about her? I thought when I saw you, Desmond, that you might have some news for me.'

'Not about Sheila. Anthony was arrested this morning.'

He added no more, for he hated to talk about his twin to their unsympathetic stepmother, and indeed to Mrs Ryan the fact of Anthony's arrest meant very little. He had been arrested several times before and she looked upon it as quite an ordinary occurrence where her stepsons were concerned.

'So Anthony is arrested again?' she said. 'Well! it is only what may be expected as long as he is so foolish. But how was it you were not taken, too?'

'Never mind now!' was the reply. 'Tell me about my sister. Do you mean that she is really actually missing—that you don't know where she is?'

In a very short time he knew all that Mrs Ryan knew herself, which was the bare fact that Sheila had been missed in the morning and not seen since. She had not been very strong lately and did not always come down to breakfast, so that when she did not appear at the table that morning no one minded, but took it for granted that she was breakfasting in her own room. It was not till Mrs Ryan went up to her room later that she found Sheila was not there and that her bed had not been slept in. Later still the empty garage told that the girl had taken her motor with her. 'Mademoiselle Delaunay is staying here at present,' went on Mrs Ryan, 'but she had to go to Bray early this morning to spend the day with an old friend of hers who is ill.' Desmond winced. 'She only got back a short while ago. She and Ronald Hammond, who is staying here, returned to town an hour ago. They thought that perhaps Sheila might have gone up to see Miss Moore and had been detained in town—the times are so terrible!'

'No; she is not there,' said Desmond dully. 'I have just come from the flat and Jerry was saying that she would come out tomorrow to see Sheila. Where can she be?'

'Ah! Desmond, what would I not give to know,' replied Mrs Ryan. 'And I don't know even where to begin to look for her. Her husband, too—poor, dear Norman—is still suffering from shell-shock and—.'

'Oh! I know all about him,' interrupted Desmond impatiently. 'But now don't worry about Sheila. I will find out where she is or what has happened to her. I promise you that. I must be off now,

Mrs Ryan, and I'll send you word as soon as I have any news.'

'But surely you are not going away at this hour,' cried his stepmother; 'nearly eleven o'clock—and in these times. You had much better stay the night here, Desmond.'

'No; I must go—thanks all the same,' he replied; 'but I am not going back to town. I have some friends near here to see.'

And with a hasty good-night he left the house. Once on the road he began to make his way by well-known and secluded paths up towards Kilmashogue. He felt as if he was groping in a mental maze and was not able to find a way out. His visit to Firfield had only complicated matters for him; his interview with Yvonne Delaunay must be put off, and he had somehow imagined that she would be able to help him, although he did not know how or in what way. And there was the strange disappearance of Sheila. Everything puzzled him, for the key to the whole problem—which was Yvonne's perfidy—was still unknown to him.

He had not met a soul during his long, lonely walk, but when he was within half-a-mile of the cottage he thought he heard a rustle in the furze bushes near him. He halted for a moment listening intently, and a few seconds later a voice called softly in Irish, 'Who is there?'

Desmond answered in the same tongue, and the next moment young O'Driscol was clasping his hand.

'Oh! Mr Desmond. Is it yourself?' he said. 'Isn't it lucky I saw you. I thought it must be one of ourselves, but I was a bit doubtful at first. Is it to Byrne's that you are going?'

'To Byrne's farm? Why? Is the cottage done for?'

'Well! it's in a bad state since the raid! But the doctor and your sister are all safe and sound beyond the field there at Tim Byrne's house, and the rest of the boys got away all right. Have you news of the captain, sir? He said he would send us word as soon as he could.'

It took Desmond a little time before he was able to take in the news of Sheila which Paddy told him—the whole story seemed almost incredible, while O'Driscol on his part was overwhelmed with grief when he heard of the arrest of his adored captain.

When they reached the Byrnes' homestead his escort brought him into the little sittingroom off the big farm kitchen and went to find 'the Doctor'. Having done so he went back to his sentry duty, and a few minutes later Dr O'Connor and Desmond Ryan stood facing each other in silence. Then Peter spoke—his icy, curt tones cutting the quiet of the room like a knife.

'Well! Desmond,' he said. 'What do you want?'

'I want my sister,' replied the other, up in arms at Peter's manner. 'I suppose I will be permitted to see her.'

Then suddenly forgetting all anger and resentment— remembering only his grief and anxiety for the little sister of long ago, he broke down and cried out:-

'Oh! Peter. How is she? Is she very ill? How did she get wounded—poor little Girlie?'

But Dr O'Connor's stern look did not soften as he replied in cold, measured tones:

'Your sister received her wound from the military as she was driving in her motor in the early hours of the morning. She was trying to reach the cottage and to give us warning of the coming raid, and to tell us also of the intended raid at Elton Street to get the papers which were hidden there.'

'But how did she know of all this. How did the enemy know about—about the papers? My God! Peter. Am I going mad?'

'It would be small wonder if you were,' was the reply. He paused a while, his eyes still holding Desmond's in a merciless look. Then he went on, speaking in quiet, cutting accents—every word falling like a knell on Desmond's listening ears.

'The military knew all about the papers and their exact hiding place from their paid spy—Yvonne Delaunay. From whom she heard it—you know but too well. Your sister, who knew the Delaunay woman for what she was, and knew, too, that Ronald Hammond was another British Secret Service agent, had been working on our behalf for some weeks past. Yvonne Delaunay when she returned to Firfield after her sentimental and delightful evening with you at Elton Street met her fellow-spy in the library after midnight and recounted all that had taken place between you. She also handed him the rough map which you had so carefully drawn of the route to the cottage. Sheila was hidden behind the curtains at the end of the room and heard all. When they had retired for the night she took out the motor and started to find us.'

He then told Desmond about her encounter with the military and her subsequent painful journey until she had dropped exhausted in the lane outside the cottage, her footsteps and moans having been luckily heard by Paddy O'Driscol.

'She saved us all that night,' he finished. 'We may thank your sister that we are all alive and safe now. The rest of the boys made their escape, and Anthony, I hope reached Elton Street in good time to save the papers. He thought he would be there before you left for your pleasant outing. But as you are so ignorant of all that has happened I suppose he must have missed you?'

'Tony was arrested this morning before he reached Dublin,' said Desmond, speaking mechanically in the dull, lifeless tones of a human machine. Then as Peter did not immediately answer he added in the same indifferent way, 'He shot a Black and Tan dead before he was arrested.'

'My God!' cried Peter, and putting out a hand for a chair he sat down heavily. 'Where is he?'

'In the Castle.'

'And the papers? Desmond—the papers? They got them then? The military have them?'

Desmond shook his head.

'No; the papers are gone, no one knows where,' he replied, 'but they are not in the enemy's hands.'

'What do you mean? Desmond! for God's sake tell me quickly all you know.'

Desmond recounted in his dull voice, from which all life seemed to have gone, the events of that day—everything from the moment he had awakened, wretched and ill, until he had met Paddy O'Driscol on the mountain roadside.

When he had finished neither spoke for some time. Dr O'Connor's keen brain was at work to see if he could find any loophole by which Anthony might be saved, while Desmond, incapable just then of coherent thought or reasoning power, remained standing with his elbow on the mantelpiece staring straight before him in a frozen, wretched silence.

Peter's professional eye was caught by his unnatural strained attitude, and for the first time that night he felt something like a wave of pity for the boy.

'Come; pull yourself together, Desmond!' he said, not unkindly. 'What is done—is done. We must only try and see if any of the harm can be lessened in any way. Do you want to see Sheila?'

Desmond shook his head.

'No—not now,' he said.

'Ah! well; later you can go in to her,' replied the doctor. 'She is sleeping now. Stay here for a while Desmond; I will be with you again later on—you can lie down on that sofa and try and get a sleep.'

He went upstairs to take a look at Sheila, who was still sleeping, and then went on to the room which the Byrnes had so cordially given up for his use. He paced the floor for several hours, but think and search his brain as he might he could neither think of any way in which to reach Anthony, nor to discover the whereabouts of the papers. As to the latter he was absolutely—but mistakenly—sure, that they were in Yvonne's possession. 'She fooled that poor boy and got them some way or other—that's certain!' he said. And then feeling deadly tired he threw himself on the bed for an hour's sleep before dawn.

Meanwhile Desmond, left to himself, made no attempt to do as Peter had suggested. On the contrary he remained as though in a trance until actual physical exhaustion compelled him to drop into a chair, and then covering his face with his hands he gave himself up to the unspeakable bitterness which was flooding his soul.

For he understood at last what a pitiful dupe he had been in the hands of the woman whom he had placed on a pedestal, and against whom he had refused to hear one word of warning or advice, even from those whom he knew to be his best friends. As he realised the result of his folly he wondered would he have the strength to face it. Black remorse spread its dark wings over his spirit, shutting out every ray of hope, and for the space of hours Desmond wrestled with the agony of mind which threatened to overwhelm his sanity. The Catholic faith alone that night kept him from putting a revolver to his head and going forth into everlasting darkness.

When, later on, he began slowly, but surely, to recover his mental balance he strove pitifully to think clearly and to plan out his future course of action. He resolved to set out early for Dublin, and to go first to Elton Street to see if there was any news, and then endeavour by every means in his power to see Anthony. He valued his own life now so little that the fear of arrest was simply nothing to him.

So towards morning he roused himself and prepared to start on his journey. But first he must see Sheila. He did not want her to see him—how could he ever look her in the face again—but if he could manage to get a peep at her unseen? Friend of the Byrnes since his earliest boyhood, he knew the house well, and O'Connor had told him the room where Sheila was sleeping.

Cautiously he made his way upstairs through the sleeping house. Peter was the only one, however, that he half expected might be awake; the rest of the household he knew were hard workers and would probably be sleeping soundly, while O'Driscol would be on guard outside. He reached the door of Sheila's room, which was next to O'Connor's. Both doors were ajar, and peeping into Peter's he saw that he was lying on the bed, evidently asleep, and then glancing into Sheila's he saw that she, too, was sleeping.

Very gently he stepped to her side, and looked down on the girl who had been the petted baby sister of his boyhood, and whom he had not seen now for over three years. She was changed—older looking—not so girlish, and just now there was a drawn look about the lovely face and black circles under the eyes which went to Desmond's heart. He remembered that it was through his insensate folly that she was wounded. She had given her very blood for the Cause which he—a sworn soldier of the Republic—had so basely betrayed. He recollected, too, how hotly and bitterly he had spoken to her when she married Norman Hammond, and since then how frequently had he spoken of her in anger. Well! she had redeemed the past—and redeemed it nobly—but he could never redeem it. Nothing—not even his very life itself—could undo what he had done now. Sheila's hair was lying like a golden cloud on the pillow, and stooping he pressed his lips again and again to the soft tresses. His heart felt at that moment that it must break, and afraid to stay longer he turned and left the room and the house—setting his face towards the city in the grey of the November dawn.

When Mrs Pell arrived at Elton Street at eight o'clock she found him there before her, sitting in the cold, chilly sittingroom and staring in front of him at the empty recess and dismantled fireplace with haggard eyes and drawn face. Everything was as he had left it, except that Mrs Pell had removed the fragments of the defaced picture before she had left on the previous night.

She exclaimed now at the sight of him—so wretched and pale, unshaven and unwashed, his hair tossed any way. She clasped her hands dramatically as she cried:-

'Mr Desmond! Oh! where in the world have you been? You do look bad, sir!'

And then as he did not answer she asked hesitatingly:

'There's no news of Mr Anthony, I suppose, sir?'

'No; none. But I am going up to the Castle to see if I can get in.' Desmond rose to his feet as he spoke. 'I'll be off now,' he said. 'I was tired and sat down for a little.'

Mrs Pell stared at him aghast.

'But you are not going out like that, Mr Desmond,' she said, with a sudden remembrance of the normal Desmond—particular to the point of vanity about his clothes and person.

'What way?' he asked now, indifferently.

In reply Mrs Pell brought a small mirror and held it out before him. He gazed into it, dully at first, and then as he realised the sorry spectacle reflected in it a half smile curved his weary lips.

'You are right, Mrs Pell,' he said. 'I suppose I had better have a wash and change. Get me some shaving water.'

'What about your breakfast, sir?'

'Oh! I don't want any—don't bother about it.'

'Now, Mr Desmond, you must eat something. When had you your last meal, if I may ask?'

He wrinkled his forehead in thought.

'I don't remember really. I think it was in—Bray—some time yesterday.'

'Heavenly powers!' ejaculated Mrs Pell, and fled to the kitchen.

No one could work quicker or better than Mrs Pell when she wished to do so; therefore when Desmond presently emerged, washed and shaved in another suit, he found an appetising meal just ready.

'You must take it in the kitchen, Mr Desmond dear—it's too cold entirely for you in the sittingroom,' said the good woman, drawing up the table near the range, in which the fire was cheerily burning, while on the gas-stove fizzled a pan of rashers and eggs.

'Come now and eat something—that's my poor lamb! Oh! Mr Desmond—don't refuse me. Besides if you contemplate seeing Mr Anthony you must fortify yourself with sustenance.'

Desmond knew that Mrs Pell—under all her usual veneer of queer talk—spoke sensibly, and although the first mouthful of food threatened to choke him he persevered and managed to eat a little; he was thankful, too, for the tea, which he drank feverishly.

Just as he was finished they heard quick footsteps outside and immediately afterwards a knock at the door. Mrs Pell opened it and a small boy confronted her with a note in his hand.

'For Mr Desmond Ryan,' he said, 'but I am to give it into his own hands or not leave it at all. Is he here now?'

'You impudent young puppy!' said Mrs Pell, indignantly. 'Hand me that note this minute and be off about your business!'

But the boy shook his head.

'I am to give it to himself!' he insisted.

Here Desmond called out impatiently:

'What is it Mrs Pell?'

And when she had explained he told her to send the boy in.

When he had delivered the letter and gone Desmond sat for a moment holding the unopened envelope in his hand, and as he did so a faint but familiar scent assailed his nostrils—a scent which seemed now to almost sicken him. He knew then from whom the letter came.

His first unreasoning instinct was to fling it unopened into the fire, but prudence prevailed, and conquering his repugnance to even handle it he opened the envelope.

'Mon ami,' wrote Yvonne, 'I have but just heard of the arrest of Monsieur Antoine and the so strange disappearance of your sister. What a terrible happening! What can be the meaning of it all! Also I heard about the loss of those hidden papers of which you told me. This must all be dreadful for you, but I think—and do not you also?—that Monsieur Antoine must know where they are. He will have moved them lately and perhaps not told you. In that case he had better tell you now where they are and between us we will find a safe hiding place for them. I happen to have a friend in Authority and so I am able to enclose you this permit, which will gain you admission to see your dear brother at any time. Be sure and learn all from him—it is so important for you. When you have news drop me a line and I will arrange a meeting. Till then, adieu—and think sometimes of your

YVONNE.

He grew white with rage as he read. Think of her sometimes. Would to God he could forget her! He clenched his hands at the thought, while Mrs Pell watched him furtively from the other end of the kitchen. Instinct told her that the note was from that 'bold creature,' and she would have given a good deal to know just what it contained.

Meanwhile Desmond was thinking. 'So she thinks that I can still be duped and fooled! She hasn't given up the game yet. Good God! If she only knew! She wouldn't have sent me this,' and he examined the permit curiously. It was only a few lines and the name which signed it was unknown to Desmond—although probably it might not have been so to Dr O'Connor. However, he determined to try its effect on the Castle authorities at once, and after consigning the letter to the fire he carefully placed the permit in his notebook and rose to his feet.

'I'm off to the Castle now, Mrs Pell,' he cried. 'If I see Mr Anthony—and I think I will—I will tell him that you are praying for him.'

She smiled at him through very misty eyes.

'Will you get Mass first, sir, or afterwards,' she asked.

Desmond paused as he was leaving the room.

'Good Lord!' he cried. 'But, of course, it's Sunday. I had quite forgotten. I'll hear Mass now in Clarendon Street and go on straight then to the Castle, for dear knows how long I may be delayed there. Thanks for reminding me, Mrs Pell, and don't forget to pray for me.'

He was gone then, and Mrs Pell, very anxious and lonely, sat down to a belated cup of tea.

She had barely finished when Dr O'Connor raced up the stairs and, not waiting to knock, burst in upon her meditations. Never had she been so glad to see any one, and when after a hasty explanation she placed the lost papers in his hands—warm and strongly smelling of snuff from their recent resting place—she felt as if a great responsibility had dropped from her shoulders.

His joy and relief can be better imagined than described. He could hardly speak for a moment, but when he took her work-grained hand in his and said quietly, 'Mrs Pell, I can never tell you all you have done for us, and the lives you have probably saved, but in the name of Ireland—I thank you!' then Mrs Pell felt repaid indeed, and wondered if Mr P from his heavenly bed could hear the praise she had earned.

The doctor was in a hurry or she would have told him then and there all she knew about Yvonne, but she only mentioned now about the letter Desmond had received that morning and which she believed to be from that lady. What its contents were she could not tell him—only that Desmond had gone to the Castle to try and see his brother.

'That's rather risky, Mrs Pell,' remarked the doctor. 'Although,' meditatively, 'he may be safer than others. But there has been some shooting of British officers this morning and the Crown forces are seeing red all over the place. However, I must be off—I want to see Miss Moore particularly,' he rushed away leaving Mrs Pell to go on her knees and pray for the safety of the twins.

Desmond, meanwhile, had heard Mass, and vainly tried to pray without distraction, and then had made his way up Dame Street and boldly presented himself at the Castle. Here all was noise and confusion in the Castle Yard. He could not have come at a worse hour, and there is no doubt but for certain orders which already had been given, and the permit which he held, he would have been arrested on sight. However, as it was he was bandied about and kept waiting an unconscionable time before he at last found himself, with a guard of two soldiers, awaiting the appearance of the officer who could give him information about Anthony. That individual looked Desmond all over and up and down when he at length arrived, and he was wishing devoutly in his own mind that he might arrest this tall young fellow with the haughty bearing and fearless look. But for certain diplomatic reasons he had been told that he could not do so.

'You came to inquire about your brother. What is his name? Ah! yes; Anthony Ryan,' he said superciliously.

'Yes,' replied Desmond curtly. 'I wish to see him.'

'Indeed! Well! he is not here at present.'

'Not here?' And in spite of himself Desmond paled. 'No; he is not in the Castle. He was courtmartialled early this morning and has been removed to Mountjoy. He is to be hanged tomorrow for murder—Hello! Tomkins, the chap is fainting! Who would have thought he'd be so chicken-livered—probably one of the murder gang himself—a bally Sinn Féiner!'

CHAPTER XX

'PASSING THE LOVE OF WOMAN'

It was six o'clock that same evening before Desmond Ryan stood face to face with his brother in Mountjoy Prison. No one knew where he had spent the intervening hours since he staggered out of the Castle at noon. But now at last he was with Anthony, and by his special request—and the strange power with which Yvonne's permit seemed to endow him—he was allowed to visit him in his cell. They were alone except for the warder who stood just inside the door—a kindly, sympathetic man, who kept out of earshot as much a possible. Now and then he would walk up and down the cell for a few minutes and would hear them speaking of their sister or their friends, but if he had been able to hear their conversation when he stood by the door he would have been none the wiser, for it was entirely carried on in Gaelic, only changed rapidly into English on his near approach.

There was little perceptible change in Anthony, he was just as collected and self-possessed as ever, and his rare smile was just as winning. Desmond had realised at once that his brother meant to go to his death—even though it was the shameful death of the scaffold—as bravely as if he was giving up his life in battle. His joy at seeing Desmond had been very great.

'Dear old Des,' he said, 'I was getting afraid that you would not be allowed in to see me. I have so much to say to you—so many messages to give you for the others.'

'Don't, Tony—don't.'

'But, dear boy, I must; our time together is only short, and I have so much to speak about.'

'Let me speak first then,' cried Desmond. 'I want to tell you everything, Tony—to confess. Listen!' And he rapidly sketched for him the whole story of his own folly through his infatuation for Yvonne, the events of the past night and day, and finished by telling him of the letter she had sent him enclosing the permit.

'And there is certainly some magic about that same permit, Tony,' he said. 'I have only to show it and I am not only safe, but even treated with some sort of civility.'

Just then the warder drew close, and Desmond started to take off his overcoat, leaving it on the chair with his soft hat.

'I feel quite warm,' he said distinctly in English. 'I walked here very fast.'

Anthony raised his eyes in slight surprise, and the man passed out of earshot again and took up his position at the door. Desmond lowered his voice and relapsed into rapid Gaelic.

'See here, Tony,' he said. 'You are not going to die—you are going to escape! Don't look like that! Speak naturally—seem indifferent while I explain.' While Anthony did his astonished best Desmond quickly unfolded his plans.

'We must change places first,' he said; 'the next time the warder looks away change chairs with me quickly. Then when our interview is ended you will stand up and quietly put on my hat and coat and pass out of the prison. You will be perfectly safe. The permit is in the inner pocket of the coat—just produce it if anyone questions you. I came in with my coat buttoned up tightly and my hat jammed down on my head on purpose; you must do the same. It will hide the wound in your head, and look here,' and with a deft movement Desmond quickly parted the thick hair at the side of his head and disclosed a very artistically got up 'wound'. He grinned across at Anthony.

'You see I have thought of everything,' he said. 'When you are gone my hair can be ruffled enough just to let the wound be seen. But anyway they will never suspect us if you play your part all right. It's so easy, Tony. You simply have to be me for tonight. Try and imagine it and you will manage to carry it through. No one here knows us very well; we are so alike that strangers as you know can never tell us apart, and certainly when you pass out in my things and with the permit in your pocket no one will ever suspect you.'

'That may be so,' replied Anthony quietly; 'but what about yourself, Desmond?'

'Oh! as to that!' and Desmond smiled in his old light-hearted manner and winked gaily at his brother. 'I will be all right! All arrangements are made for me to be out of this before eight o'clock tomorrow morning.'

'You will have to give me more definite information than that,' replied Anthony gravely.

'Ah! now, Tony! Can't you take my word for it when I tell you that I will be free and out of this in the morning? For certain reasons I cannot give you full details—certain persons are involved in the matter and I promised not to reveal their names. Oh! hang

it all, Tony! Time is passing and you must not lose such a chance—
why it means your life—your life spared to work for Ireland. Don't
forget that!'

Anthony was thinking rapidly.

'It's Yvonne Delaunay, of course,' he concluded. 'For her own
ends she will get Desmond out of here. He must be trading upon
her influence and pretending to her that he is still her dupe.
Probably he has said he will look for the papers again and give
them in return for my release! It is quite evident that he believes
his plan is safe. But suppose something should happen at the last
moment to prevent that woman from carrying out her
arrangements? In that case! No! no! Desmond,' he said aloud, 'I
cannot do it! I will not. You must not take such a risk for my sake;
if anything should go wrong or—.'

'I tell you nothing can go wrong,' replied his brother in a tense
whisper.

Just then a knock came to the door and the warder turned to
open it.

'Quick!' breathed Desmond, and almost before Anthony knew
it he was in Desmond's chair, and his twin was smiling at him from
the other.

'Now listen, Tony,' he went on; 'we have only a few moments left
and for God's sake don't hesitate. Everything is in our favour. You
have a warder to guard you instead of a Black and Tan, who would
never have let us talk like this, but they are all out rushing round
the city like devils after shooting all before them at Croke Park. Go
straight home to Elton Street; you will find Mrs Pell there
according to my instructions, and, Tony, you are to be me to her.
Don't forget for a moment. All I want you to do is to write a note
to Geraldine Moore and tell her that Anthony will be out of prison
in the morning—that you have seen him and it is all arranged. Sign
your name Desmond, and make the writing as like mine as you
can—scrawl it carelessly as if in a hurry, that will be best. Tell her
to expect Anthony about seven-thirty tomorrow morning, and go
to her flat at that time yourself. You will then hear news of me
almost immediately.'

'Will you join us at the flat?' asked Tony.

'That I can't tell you just yet. Perhaps not, but you will hear. I will
be safe wherever I go, and remember, Tony, you are to be
Desmond Ryan for as long as is necessary for your safety.'

'I don't like this, Desmond,' said Anthony in a puzzled tone. 'There is too much mystery about it for me. Are you sure—perfectly sure that you will be able to get out of this early tomorrow?'

'Absolutely!' was the reply. 'The plans are already arranged—certain officials in the Castle have agreed to them. In any case I am safe. I swear to you, Tony, that I will be a free man by eight o'clock tomorrow morning!'

Anthony looked at him keenly, but Desmond's voice seemed so sincere—he seemed so certain about what he was speaking that the other brother was convinced almost in spite of himself.

'If you are sure, Desmond?' he said. 'But, oh! dear old man—if there was the least doubt—.'

'But there is not, Tony! You need not have the slightest hesitation in doing what I say as far as my safety is concerned. Now remember you are Desmond for tonight in Elton Street, then be at Jill's flat at seven-thirty tomorrow and wait for news from me. And, afterwards continue to be Desmond and use the permit for as long as you think fit. I need not tell you, Tony,' flushing deeply, 'to be careful of Yvonne Delaunay—don't meet her at all if possible. Well! now you understand all and—.'

'Time is up, sir,' said the warder coming forward. 'I'm sorry, gentlemen, but—.'

'All right, warder,' replied Desmond at once, 'My brother is just going. We had better say good-bye now, Desmond.' He glanced significantly at Anthony, and then flung an appealing look at the warder. The man understood and turned his back to them.

'Now!' breathed Desmond.

And Anthony, almost before he realised it, found himself donning Desmond's coat and hat. Then they clasped hands in silence for a space of time that could be measured by seconds, or by years.

'Until tomorrow then?' whispered Anthony, still half hesitatingly.

'Until tomorrow!' replied Desmond.

Their hands fell asunder and Anthony followed the unsuspecting warder to the cell door, but he turned there for a last look at his brother. Desmond was standing at the salute—tall, straight and fearless—every inch a soldier—and with a smile on his lips. Slowly Anthony raised his hand and returned the salute, and then swung round and stepped after the warder into the bleak corridors of Mountjoy.

He had not the slightest difficulty in leaving the prison and went straight to Elton Street. The streets of Dublin that evening were very quiet; a tense feeling was in the air, for the people were terrified at the shooting in Croke Park, and all who could manage it were within doors. Anthony, however, arrived safely at his rooms, and, as Desmond had said, Mrs Pell was awaiting him and had a substantial tea ready. He was rather chary of passing her sharp, button-like little eyes without detection, for she had known Desmond so well and been so fond of him. To tell the truth, Anthony was already chafing at having to deceive her—or anyone else. Deceit in any shape or form was abhorrent to him. But Desmond's instructions had been so emphatic that, thinking there must be very urgent reasons for them, he had resolved to follow them to the letter.

‘Oh! Mr Desmond, dear, thanks be to God that ye're back! And did you see him, sir? Oh! have you any news at all?’

Anthony had no choice but to push hurriedly past her into the sittingroom and to stand at the table with his back towards her.

‘Yes; I saw him, Mrs Pell,’ he answered then, and as the twins' voices, unlike their handwriting, were absolutely alike he had no fear in speaking.

‘And he is all right and will be out of prison tomorrow.’

‘Out of prison tomorrow,’ echoed Mrs Pell. ‘Oh! thanks be to God! But, Mr Desmond, dear, how in the world did you manage it? Oh! but that's great news. And how is he looking, sir?’

‘Not too bad,’ replied Anthony evasively; ‘but you will see himself in the morning. He expects to be released by eight o'clock. But now I have an awful headache, Mrs Pell, and I think I'll go to bed at once. You need not stay after I have written a note which I want you to take to Miss Moore before you go home—if you don't mind.’ Going to the bureau he hastily scribbled what Desmond had directed was to be written, and fastening the envelope handed it to Mrs Pell.

‘Here you are, Mrs Pell,’ he said—she noticed in some surprise that he had kept on his hat and coat all this time. ‘Take it round to the flat at once for me, please. Then get straight home. The streets will not be very safe tonight.’

‘But your tea, Mr Desmond? If you have a headache can I not

procure you something? The chemist's beyond is open—it is now,'
with a glance at the clock, 'their stimulated (stipulated) hours for
Sundays.'

'No; thanks, Mrs Pell. Please don't bother. I see you have left me
everything I need, and the kettle is on—so I'll just make a cup of
tea and lie down. Thanks so much for taking the note for me. I
want Miss Moore to get it early.'

'Mr Desmond is very queer and quiet in himself,' thought Mrs
Pell as she went down the stairs. 'His head must be bad—poor
lamb! But thank God that Mr Anthony is to be released. And what
a wonder that he is. One thing is sure—he couldn't have killed that
Tan and Black anyway.'

She went at once to Jill's flat and toiled heavily up the stairs—
glancing askance at the door opposite while she knocked at Jill's.
Both the girls were within and insisted upon her coming in and
sitting down for a rest while they read the note.

'Anthony to be released! Coming here early tomorrow
morning!' exclaimed Jill; while Jerry stared back at her with open-
eyed wonder.

'But, Jill!' she cried, 'how can he be released when he shot that
Black and Tan? They will never let him off unless it was all a
mistake.'

'Who gave you this note, Mrs Pell?' asked Jill.

'Mr Desmond himself, Miss—he's just after getting back from
the Castle and Mountjoy. Out all day he was, the poor lamb! He
must have been busy over Mr Anthony all the time. He ran into
Elton Street about five o'clock this evening and says to me, "I'll be
back about seven to tea, Mrs Pell; have it ready and be here
yourself, like a good soul." He was rushing down the stairs then
when back he came on a suddent and shook hands with me, "God
bless you, Mrs Pell," he says, "you've always been a good friend to
me!" I wondered at him after he telling me that he would be back
at seven to his tea. However, I thought he might be thinking that
he wouldn't get there safe or something. But he was back all right
a little after seven as he said. He has a bad headache, poor lamb,
and is gone to bed. Sure he must be wore out with walkin' the
streets all day.'

'He says here, Mrs Pell,' said Geraldine, 'that Mr Anthony will be
released early tomorrow, and that we may expect him here before
eight o'clock.'

'Yes, Miss; so he told me,' replied Mrs Pell. 'It is, as you say, very strange, but it must be the case.'

'Well! it's most extraordinary!' said Jill, 'and I cannot make it out.'

They sat over the fire discussing it in all its pros and cons after Mrs Pell had taken her departure. Peter O'Connor had been with them that morning, when he had astonished them with the news about Sheila and had promised to come back that evening if possible, but since then the Croke Park shootings had taken place and the city was in such a state that they doubted if he would manage to come.

Just before the early Curfew he came—as Mr Ferdinand Shortall.

'I couldn't get earlier,' he said. 'I have had a hot time dodging round, nothing but failure all along the line. I couldn't get any information at all about Anthony, and although I managed to slip into Elton Street, Desmond was not there. He was out nearly all day, Mrs Pell told me.'

But Jill had already locked the door and drawn the curtains, then pushing the doctor—now divested of his disguise—into a chair near the fire she handed him the note which Mrs Pell had brought.

'What do you think of that?' she asked.

Peter read it through once—twice, frowning in perplexity as he did so.

'From Desmond?' he said, then in a questioning tone adding:

'It's not like his writing. More like Tony's.'

'Oh! the note is from Desmond,' interposed Geraldine, 'but he is terribly tired and has a bad headache, Mrs Pell told us. It seems he has been out all day seeing about this business of Anthony's release.'

'But how in Heaven's name did he manage it?' asked Peter. 'I would have expected them to shoot or hang Anthony—not release him. The thing is incredible.'

If any of them had known that Anthony's execution had been fixed for the following morning they would have been still more puzzled.

'There is only one solution that we can think of,' said Jill; 'and that is that Yvonne Delaunay is helping Desmond in this.'

Peter was silent for a moment considering. 'Have you seen her today?' he asked.

'No,' replied Jill. 'She has not been here all day as far as we know. She came here on Saturday night about five o'clock for a few moments and then went on to Firfield. In a couple of hours she returned and told us about Sheila's disappearance. It upset us terrible—especially Jerry—because we had not heard the truth about it from you then and we didn't know what to think. Yvonne thought that Sheila might be here. She left the flat again then, although it was getting late, and we don't think she has returned— we have neither heard nor seen her. Where can she be?'

'Then it very probably is the case that she is working this affair of Anthony's release,' replied the doctor. 'Desmond is using her now without her knowledge. She thinks that there is still a chance of getting possession of those papers—very likely she believes that Anthony knows where they are. Desmond may have promised to try and get them in return for her help in Anthony's case. It seems a risky game for him to play. However, we can't interfere now; even if we thought we should we are powerless till morning. As it's after Curfew, ladies, and even old Mr Shortall might not be safe outside, may I seek repose on your hearthrug here?'

'Oh! you needn't immolate yourself on the hearthrug,' said Jill; 'you will find the couch very comfortable, and I can give you plenty of rugs.'

'My dear cousin, you are indeed a friend in need!' was the reply, while he added more seriously, 'But you know, Jill, that I wouldn't bother you like this only that necessity—and our benevolent rulers—compel me to do so.'

'Oh! shut up, Peter,' was Jill's undignified reply.

Here Geraldine, who had been silently thinking, asked suddenly:

'I wonder will the papers ever come to light again! How I wish I knew where they were!'

The doctor smiled.

'The papers are all right, Jerry,' he said, 'and in a safe hiding place this time.'

'Oh! of course, Sherlock Holmes again!' cried Jill sarcastically. 'We might have know that you would ferret them out.'

'You are rather wide of the mark this time in your conductions— as a certain worthy lady would say,' he replied, and to their astonishment told them about Mrs Pell.

'Good Heavens! who would have thought that she had it in her?' cried Jill. 'We will have to be careful of our char lady and her conductions in future.'

'How often have I told you, Jill, not to judge the book by the cover,' admonished the doctor with mock severity.

'Oh! hold your tongue or I'll give you no supper!' said Jill.

They had quite a cheery little meal, for the very thought of Anthony's release—although still puzzling—was very comforting.

'I suppose that Desmond will come here with him in the morning?' said Geraldine.

'Well! he might not think it would be wise for them both to come together,' replied Peter; 'but we will know all in the morning and must only have patience till then.'

They were all up and dressed before seven the next morning—so excited were they, and the breakfast was set and the fire burning cheerily—all ready to welcome Anthony. It was barely a quarter past seven when he knocked at the door to their delight and relief.

'Why, Peter, old man!' he cried, on seeing the doctor; 'this is great! I didn't hope to find you here.'

'I certainly didn't hope to see you a free man today, Tony,' replied the other. 'Come on now and tell us all about it—we are just dying to hear. But first, what about Desmond? Will he be here soon, do you think?'

'Well! I don't really know,' replied Anthony. 'He was a bit uncertain about what his movements would be this morning. I suppose it would depend upon circumstances. You see he did not take me fully into his confidence last evening, and I quite understood that he might have had certain reasons for not doing so. However, he seemed absolutely sure that he would be released from prison by eight o'clock this morning.'

Dr O'Connor stood and stared at him—as did also the two girls—open-eyed and puzzled.

Jill was the first to speak, in a queer, strangled whisper.

'Is Desmond in prison then?' she asked.

'Yes; but I was not to tell you anything about it until this morning,' replied Anthony. 'He told me to come here about this time and explain everything that he had arranged last night. We were to wait then for news of him, which he promised we would have early. I asked him if he would be with us himself, and he only said that he couldn't say.'

Then he gave them full details of the previous evening, and ended by saying:- 'It must be through that Delaunay woman that he is working this. But I am not anxious about him now as far as her influence is concerned, for I believe he has had a lesson that he will never forget. He is, I imagine, determined to use her for his own ends—to get some of his own back, as he would say himself.' He glanced at the clock and saw that it was only just half-past seven.

'Do you know I feel extraordinarily happy this morning!' he said, looking at the others with one of his rare smiles. 'As if something very great and beautiful was about to befall me! I wonder what it can be? I am quite uplifted as if I was walking on air, and going forward to some great and glorious adventure. That is one reason why I believe that dear old Des will join us very shortly— I feel very close to him.'

Just then quick, light steps were heard coming up the stairway and a sharp knock came to the door. It was Yvonne Delaunay, and as she came forward into the room Peter stepped quickly behind a screen.

'Is there any news of Sheila?' she asked. 'I just ran in to inquire— I was staying with a friend last night who is sick. But I was anxious to know if you had some news.'

Anthony was standing with his back to her, and she had spoken so far before she caught sight of him. She gave a little cry when she saw him, and going to his side placed her hand on his arm.

'Desmond!' she exclaimed. 'At last! Where have you been? I was searching for you everywhere.'

Anthony turned round slowly and looked at her without speaking. For a moment she stood without moving—like a woman of stone—staring back, horror struck, into the steady cold eyes bent upon her.

'Mon Dieu!' she cried hoarsely, then 'Mon Dieu! who is it? Ah, Monsieur Antoine! You—you! Where then is Desmond?'

It was Peter O'Connor who answered as he stepped forward and confronted her.

'Desmond Ryan remained in prison last evening instead of his brother,' he said. 'We understood, Mademoiselle, that you knew about it—that indeed the whole affair was arranged with your connivance. Anthony has only just told us that his execution had been fixed for eight o'clock this morning. Desmond took his place in order to save him, and he assured his brother that he need not feel the least anxiety in changing places. He, Desmond, would be a free man this morning.'

There was dead silence for a few seconds, and then Peter spoke again, his voice suddenly strained and tense with a nameless dread.

'I never thought to ask anything from you,' he said, 'but I ask—I beg you—in God's name to tell us what you know.'

'I—I had nothing to do with it! I know nothing about it!' she cried then. 'I was looking for Desmond all yesterday and could not find him. Oh! you fools! You fools! Desmond has taken his brother's place, you say? Yes! and he will lose his life this morning—he will be hanged at eight o'clock. And for you!' turning upon Anthony like a fury—'for you! Diable!' And lifting her clenched fist she struck him across the mouth twice with all her strength. Her rings cut his lips and she stared at the blood on her hand with a shudder, and then lifting her eyes glanced at the clock like one demented.

'Nearly a quarter to eight!' she said, speaking to herself alone, the others now forgotten. 'Oh! will I be in time? Will I be in time?'

And still like one possessed she turned and fled from the room, rushing down the long stairs with lightning speed. Those left behind were stupefied; they were only struggling yet to understand this terrible thing which had come upon them. It was still almost beyond their comprehension. But could it be true?

Jill had collapsed suddenly in a heap on the floor and Geraldine was kneeling beside her trying to speak, to say something—anything, but trying in vain, while the two men faced each other in horrified silence.

Anthony was incapable of speech, he only looked at Peter with such agony in his eyes that the other involuntarily turned away his head.

At last came a hoarse whisper—'If I had known! Oh! God; if I had known!' And he turned towards the door, but Peter stopped him.

'Don't go, Anthony!' he said. 'You can do nothing now, and would only be arrested yourself. Our one hope lies in Yvonne Delaunay, and for her own sake she will do her utmost to save him. The time is everything. God grant she gets a taxi near.'

In the meantime Yvonne was rushing wildly through the streets in the direction of the nearest garage, which was only a few yards round the first turning. She had felt that she would reach it quicker than if she had telephoned from the flat—the very idea of waiting at the receiver in her present state of mind was unbearable. Her only idea was to run, and run she did with all her might, but the early November morning was foggy and the streets greasy and slippery, and Yvonne's high heels were not meant for such rapid going. But she flew on and turned the corner towards the garage— there is was, just across the street. She started to run across, panting and breathless, never looking round or heeding anything, and just at that very moment two military lorries came tearing down the street. They were nearly on her, looming suddenly like giant vehicles out of the fog, before she realised it. She tried to quicken her steps still more, but slipped and fell, going down with terrible suddenness in the centre of the road. And when at last the lorries managed to pull up a few yards further down the street the men went back to find a bundle of torn and bloodstained clothes, which mercifully hid from sight the mangled body they covered. But the face was not covered, and even the soldiers—used to terrible sights as they were—averted their eyes from the awful thing that had once been the lovely head and face of Yvonne Delaunay.

In Jill's flat the clock ticked on and on remorselessly, getting nearer and nearer to eight o'clock. Geraldine had a senseless desire to stop the hands, but then the thought of not knowing how the terrible minutes were passing was too awful to contemplate. That quarter of an hour left its mark for all time on those four who passed through it that morning.

At last the hour struck—the tiny silvery little strokes falling on the silence like claps of thunder, and as the last stroke fell Anthony put up his hands to his throat, and then tore at the air as though he was choking—he became black in the face, and his eyes, wild with pain and agony, seemed to be starting from his head. Aghast the others watched him, too petrified to move, then as Peter with an effort of will came to his side Anthony gave one terrible gasping cry and dropped in a dead faint at his feet.

CHAPTER XXI

THAT NIGHT

It was a couple of hours later when the priest who had attended Desmond to the scaffold came to Jill's flat and tried to bring a ray of hope and comfort to the little group of stricken mourners, who were at first almost too stunned and stupefied with grief to understand what he was saying to them.

'I celebrated Mass in his cell this morning,' he told them; 'having first heard his confession. It was then I found that he was Desmond Ryan, and not his brother Anthony, as I had naturally believed. He told me only in Confession so that I could do nothing to prevent his sacrifice. He asked me to come and see you afterwards, as soon as possible, and to tell you everything. I was to tell you also that he had gone to his death gladly, without fear or hesitation.'

He paused for a moment and glanced round at his listeners. The two girls were sitting together on the couch, Geraldine openly crying, but Jill was perfectly quiet, with a face of stone, and eyes which had lost the power of shedding tears. Peter was standing by the fireplace, his hand over his face, and Anthony was leaning back in an armchair, with drawn, haggard face, and eyes which seemed to hold within their depths the very bitterness of death itself.

'He sent his dear love to you all,' Father Maher went on, speaking slowly and with deep feeling, 'and asks that you will remember him in your prayers. To his brother he sent a special message—"Tell him from me, Father, that Ireland needs him. He can do more work for the cause and do it far better than anything I could do, especially now. I do not deserve to be allowed to lift a finger again to help my country, but if my life can be given for Anthony's, then I will have done one last service for the land I love".'

There was silence again for a space, broken only by the sound of Geraldine's pitiful sobs. The others made no movement and presently the priest continued, his voice shaking as he spoke:

'I need not tell any of you who knew him so well that he went to his death as a soldier and a brave gentleman. He appeared to be— and I believe he was—perfectly happy, and he stepped on the scaffold with a smile. That smile, so brave and gay, is the last thing that I remember of him. And I shall remember it all my life.'

He stayed a short while longer with them, trying to ease a little the weight of this almost unbearable cross—this terrible and unlooked-for blow which had fallen upon them. He endeavoured especially to rouse Anthony from his stupor of grief, but with no success. He was too crushed, mentally and physically, the shock had been too severe to allow him to rally so soon. The priest knew this and said a few words privately to the doctor, asking him to put aside his own grief for the sake of the greater sufferer, and to be to him both a doctor and a friend.

Peter promised, but with a heavy heart, and without much hope of being able to bring consolation to his friend just yet, for he knew that such a grief would only be eased by time. Forgotten or altogether cured it would never be. On the other hand Anthony's strong unwavering faith would come to his aid, he had a Rock to which he might cling during this time of storm and stress, the Rock which never yet failed anyone—for 'that Rock was Christ'.

The medical man knew, too, that Anthony's life had given him a sound mind in a sound body, self-control, and a strong will, and clear reasoning powers. All these would help him at the present hour and enable him to bear his grief as a Christian and a man.

When the priest had left them Peter glanced at the two girls. Geraldine was still crying, but softly now, and he knew that her sorrow, although sincere and real, was still infinitely less than that of the other two. Something in Jill's set face arrested his attention; she seemed even more dazed and stupefied than Anthony. Going across to Geraldine, Peter said to her, 'I wonder, Jerry, could you make us some strong coffee—really strong? I want to try and make Tony drink some.'

It aroused her as he had intended, and presently when the coffee was ready he persuaded Anthony to have some. The other drank mechanically, evidently only to escape the trouble of having to refuse it.

But Jill dashed aside the cup which Geraldine, with the best intentions, offered to her. It fell on the carpet smashed into a dozen places, while Jill, roused at last from her unnatural quietude, cried passionately:

'Oh! what do you mean? How could you expect me to eat or drink while he—while he—Ah! don't forget that I have no faith—no belief in a life after death! I will never see him again! Never—

never!'

She gave a little cry, half sob, half moan, and rushing into the bedroom closed the door after her.

'It's all right—leave her alone,' said Peter quietly, as Geraldine got up to follow her. 'She will have to go through with it, and it's best for her to be alone—for the present anyway.'

Somewhat to the surprise of the other two Anthony sat forward in his chair and glanced at the shut door while he said:

'She seems to feel it very much.'

'Yes,' replied Peter. 'But didn't you know that Desmond was very dear to her? Her love was not returned—I don't know if he was aware of it, but I have known for some time that he was the one idol of her heart.'

Geraldine found herself thinking with a kind of sorrowful amusement that if poor Jill knew that Peter had read her secret she would have another reason for calling him Sherlock Holmes.

Gradually the three left in Jill's quaint living room began to talk together softly. Bit by bit they gathered up the pieces in the puzzling drama just played to its finish, and they saw how each fitted into its place until all became clear to them. They realised that Desmond's sacrifice had not been in vain—he had given complete freedom to his brother, and left him free to work for Ireland. For that end he had died. For that, and also to make reparation for his unconscious, but criminal, betrayal of his country. To one of Desmond's sensitive and chivalrous nature such a blot on his escutcheon could only be wiped away by his life blood.

As for Anthony, he could now go where he liked without let or hindrance, for in the eyes of the enemy Government he was, to all intents and purposes, Desmond Ryan. As far as they knew, Anthony, his twin brother, lay in a 'murderer's' grave in Mountjoy. They believed from Yvonne Delaunay that for certain reasons Desmond was to be left alone. She had given them to understand, for her own ends, that he was valuable to them in many ways and even now when she was dead 'Desmond' would be safe for some time. The news of Yvonne's tragic end had reached the flat just before the arrival of the priest, and although those whom she had tried so hard to injure might forgive her and endeavour to feel sorry for her as a woman—still could not but feel relief at the thought that the spy was taken from their path. And with her went the present danger for Anthony.

They finally decided that after a few days in Elton Street as 'Desmond' he should go down into the country and in beautiful Wicklow take a few weeks' rest, so that he might become strong again and able to work for the cause once more.

'For that was his wish!' he said; 'and for that he gave me my life.'

He left very soon to go to Elton Street, where he had a harrowing scene with Mrs Pell, who, of course, had to be taken into his confidence and told all. Her grief for his brother made Anthony break down and sob like a woman, so that Mrs Pell had to put her own grief aside and comfort him. But she never forgot Desmond, and was never the same woman again, her abundant brown hair becoming rapidly grey and her face lined and older looking. She had loved him from his boyhood days and lavished on him all the affection of her queer old heart. But in one way she was a better woman. She took the pledge and kept it—in honour of his memory.

After Anthony had left the flat Geraldine and Peter were alone together, standing opposite one another on the hearthrug. Neither had spoken since Tony closed the door after him, and Jerry, lifting her eyes to Peter's face, found his eyes gazing into hers, and she read there something which made her drop her own again, while she suddenly flushed scarlet.

He did not speak for a moment, and then it was only to say the one word—'Jerry.' But as he spoke he held out his arms, and Geraldine, without a word, went straight into them and shed her last tear against his shoulder.

A little later when he had gone Geraldine went into the bedroom to see what Jill was doing, for there had been no sound or movement of any kind since she had entered the bedroom and closed the door after her.

The girl was lying across the bed, face downwards, her hands clenched on the coverlet.

'Jill!' cried her friend softly, 'Jill!'

'Go away, please, Jerry,' came the muffled reply. 'You can do nothing. Oh! please leave me alone!' Nothing else would she say; it was the same every time that Geraldine ventured near her. She lay there rigid and motionless, and neither food nor drink passed her lips, although the other brought her a cup of tea twice she would not touch it.

At ten o'clock Geraldine, who was fearfully tired after her day of sorrow, went to bed, first asking Jill if she would allow her to help her to undress and get properly into bed, and begging her to have some hot milk and to try to sleep. But Jill would neither take off her clothes nor touch the milk.

'Just leave me, please, Jerry,' she said, in tired, hopeless tones which went to the other's heart; 'leave me alone, and put out the light when you are ready. Don't mind me.'

And so Geraldine had to do as she wished, and was presently in bed and asleep—worn out with the day's happenings—her eyes heavy and sore with weeping.

Shortly afterwards Jill slowly raised herself on the bed and looked around. The room was in darkness except for the faint light from the luminous crucifix over Geraldine's bed, and as it met her eyes Jill's lips curved half scornfully.

'I suppose it is well for those who can dope themselves with such legends,' she thought in bitterness of spirit. 'They think that they will meet him again. But! for me there is nothing but the certainty of the grave—the Great Silence, from which there is no awakening.'

All that day she had been in a veritable Hell of torment. Again and again she had seen the rope tighten round Desmond's throat, and seen his face blacken, and his eyes staring horribly—just as his brother's had done during the few seconds in which he had suffered with that inexplicable sympathy which had existed so strongly between the twins. She had followed her beloved, too, into the very grave itself—seen the dear body shovelled hastily in and covered with quicklime—to be followed later by the inevitable dissolution which would end in a few ghastly bones and a handful of dust. And that was all that would remain of that gay and handsome personality, that fascinating and beloved being—the Desmond who had made the romance of her life. For poor Jill believed firmly in the words which tell us that:-

> 'Imperious Cæsar, dead and turned to clay,
>   Might stop a hole to keep the wind away.'

To one who has no other belief than this the thought of death is very terrible, and when they lose a beloved one they taste of its very bitterest dregs.

> 'O Death, where is thy Victory?
>   O Grave, where is thy sting?'

can be said only by the Christian, for to him alone 'Death is swallowed up in Victory.' And for this, 'Thanks be to God who has given us the victory through Our Lord Jesus Christ.'

For Jill there was no such hope—no such word of cheer and comfort. At last she raised her tired, weary body and slipped to the floor very softly so as not to waken Geraldine. She was stiff and sore and worn out after hours of silent agony, but she was unconscious of everything except just her one overwhelming desire and longing for Desmond's presence—for the sound of his beloved voice—for the sight of his dear face.

Gropingly but surely she walked across the room, and kneeling down beside a basket-chair laid her head on a cushion there. There were two of these cushions, one in the other room, and this one lying on the bedroom chair; they were gay, chintz covered, frilly cushions in appearance, but sewn inside them were the uniforms which the twins had handed over to the care of Jill and Geraldine that night in Elton Street—a night which was destined to be never forgotten by Jill. The cushion in her hands now contained Desmond's uniform, and obeying some strange impulse she felt on the dressing table for a scissors and rapidly began to undo the stitches that held the coverings together. In a few moments she had drawn out the well-remembered tunic and laying her weary head down upon it she pressed her lips on the green cloth. She held it in her arms, straining it to her breast, and talked to it softly and tenderly as if it could hear and understand her anguish. It had been his—his hands had touched it—it had lain near his heart. That gay, brave heart of his that now was stilled for ever in the dust of the cruel grave. The room, as has been said, was in darkness, save for the glow from Geraldine's luminous crucifix, and Jill now suddenly noticed that the light from that crucifix had seemed to become stronger during the last few moments, for the room was certainly lighter and the objects in it were more distinct. Turning her head in that direction she started violently, and then remained staring straight in front of her, rigid, as if turned to stone, with the green tunic still clasped in her arms.

Standing near the crucifix, a few paces away from it, was the figure of Desmond Ryan. He was as she had seen him that night in Elton Street, and was wearing the very uniform which she still held in her hands. Tall and straight and fearless looking he stood there before her, a smile on his lips and in his eyes.

'It will pass—it is an illusion—some figment of the brain,' she thought, and turned her eyes away for a moment. But when she looked again he was still there, clear and distinct, just as she remembered him—as she always would remember him.

Then at last she breathed his name 'Desmond!' in the softest of whispers, but with what a wealth of love and longing in her voice.

He seemed to answer her with a smile, and then he raised his hand and pointed to the crucifix over the bed where Geraldine was so quietly sleeping. Jill followed the direction of the hand and understood. She remembered immediately the night in Elton Street when she had said that it would take a message from one who had gone on to the next world to convince her that there was such a place. And she seemed to hear again the words he had said to her then:

'If I ever get the chance I'll come back and see if I can convince you!'

She turned her eyes to him now and nodded her head and tried to smile at him. An expression of joy and happiness passed over his countenance and he raised his hand to salute, his smiling eyes looking straight into her own, which were dim with sudden tears. The next moment he was gone, and the room was in darkness again, save for the light of the Crucifix—Lumen Christi, which will never cease from shining and which will never be quenched.

CHAPTER XX11

SUMMER AT FIRFIELD

The last days of July, 1921, were slipping by, and for the past couple of weeks a temporary peace had come to Ireland. On this summer day of which we write the heat was still intense, and although the clock pointed to six-thirty p.m., the sun still shone as if it was but five o'clock. At Firfield House, on the lawn at the back, upon which the French window of the morning room opened we find some old friends.

The tea-table had been placed under the shade of the big cedar—as it had been once before on a certain May evening four years ago. And today, as then, Mrs Ryan poured out the tea for her visitors, who were grouped around her chatting and laughing.

But three of the old group are missing—and the others are more or less changed.

Mrs Ryan herself is quieter; she speaks but little, and never now professes to be a 'loyalist'—indeed she seems to take no interest whatever in the burning questions of the day. The truth was that she was frankly puzzled and bewildered by recent events, and found herself confronted by problems beyond her comprehension. Desmond's execution, too, had been a very real grief and shock to her. So she now very wisely affirms that she is 'neutral'. She has also partly returned to the ways and accents of her younger days, and is in consequence a much pleasanter and more natural person.

For this reason, too, Anthony and she are better friends, and he is often surprised to find how well he is now getting on with his stepmother. He has spent the last seven months in strenuous work for his country, and is looking very thin and worn as he stretches his long length in a wicker chair. But at the present moment he is feeling at peace with all the world, for the knowledge that one can come and go freely, and lie down in one's bed without fear of being dragged from it to be tortured or murdered before dawn is very pleasant after years spent in fighting or imprisonment, or 'on the run.' Sheila is sitting on a low seat beside him, and his hand is holding one of hers as he talks to her. She is wearing a black dress, which only increases her fair loveliness, and her face has lost the look of weariness and discontent which it had worn during the last few years.

Norman Hammond had died two months ago, and Sheila is a wealthy widow, young enough to live her life again in a better and wiser way.

Her wound had healed well, and after a month at the Byrne's house she had returned to Firfield and remained there quietly, helping to look after the sodden wreck whom she had once thought to be a very god amongst men.

Anthony is at present staying at Firfield, and Mrs Ryan has also two visitors for the weekend. They are a newly-married couple who have just returned from a short honeymoon—Dr and Mrs Peter O'Connor.

Geraldine is looking so happy and so pretty—there is no beautifier like Happiness!—that one wonders could she be really the same Jerry as the shabby girl who only a year ago was tramping the city 'looking for a job'. The doctor also seems to be in splendid condition, and they are both rejoicing in the Truce, which at least gave them time to get married.

'But will it last?' Sheila was saying, 'and what will the result be? What has the future in store for us?'

'God alone knows that!' replied Anthony. 'But of one thing I am certain, and that is, that as long as we Irish hold together and show a united and solid resistance to the enemy we are impregnable. But let us once disagree amongst ourselves and black chaos will follow!'

'But why should be disagree?' asked the doctor, with a smile. 'That is not likely to happen now, Tony, after all we have gone though together. What makes you talk like that?'

'Oh! I don't know!' was the rather weary reply. 'But the enemy is so diabolically clever—so absolutely Machiavellian in cunning that they may think of some plan, some offer, that would cause disunion amongst us. The recent regime of terror has failed, therefore they will try different methods. We have always been foolishly credulous in our dealing with England, again and again they have fooled us! So why not once more?'

'Why not?' echoed the doctor. 'Because we have learnt our lesson, Tony—that's why! We know now that we have but to stand firm, to heed neither their cajolery nor their threats, but to go on as we have done for the past four years, and the fight is won! Do you think for a moment that we are such consummate fools as to give in now? Why, Tony, only madmen would do such a thing.'

'Well! I hope you are right, Peter,' replied his friend. 'But all through the story of our unfortunate country History has a maddening way of repeating itself, and always in the same way.'

Just then a woman stepped out of the French window and came across the lawn.

'Oh! it's Jill!' cried Geraldine, and jumping up she ran across to meet her.

'We thought you were not coming,' she said. 'What kept you so late?'

'I was working on a design which had to be finished this evening,' replied Jill, as she shook hands with Mrs Ryan, 'and I could not get away sooner. Oh! how lovely it is out here after the dust and heat of town!'

'Have you had tea?' asked Mrs Ryan, and when Jill told her that she had had tea before leaving the flat she said, 'Then you must stay for dinner. Dr and Mrs O'Connor are staying and you can go back to town with them.'

Jill sank into a seat with a sigh of relief. She was looking pale and tired, for she was working hard and seldom got a holiday. But she did not look unhappy; her vivid little face was bright and contented enough, and there was a look of peace in her big eyes which was not there some time ago. Jill had been received into the Catholic Church a month before and was walking amidst the green pasture where converts always find themselves at first, before God in His all-seeing wisdom leads them by stony ways and thorny paths to the arid desert where their Faith must be tried and their soul strengthened.

'Come into the rose garden, Jill,' said Anthony after a while, 'the roses are lovely still; you must get some to take back with you.'

Together they strolled along the fragrant paths, past the very rose-bushes amongst which Sheila Ryan and Norman Hammond had stood on the fatal evening when she had promised to marry him.

Anthony's eyes turned very frequently upon the slim figure at his side. Jill was smartly dressed in white which always suited her, and her little French shoes were a joy to behold. Altogether she made a pleasant picture, and the man who was strolling by her side certainly thought so.

A silence had fallen between them, but it was the silence of two people who understand each other. For these two had become very real and dear friends since that November day when a common sorrow had drawn them together. They had managed to keep in touch with each other since then and Anthony had always tried no matter where he was to get news through to Jill. And she had looked after his comfort whenever she could, with parcels of food and clothing when needed, and cheery letters which helped him in his trouble and loneliness. It almost seemed as if the spirit of the dead boy who had been so dear to both of them was trying to draw them nearer to each other.

Anthony broke the silence presently, looking at Jill where she stood beside him under an arch of crimson ramblers.

'Jill!' he said. 'There is something that I want to say to you— something that I want to ask you.'

She glanced at him in surprise, for the usually cool and self-possessed Anthony seemed to be decidedly nervous.

'Yes?' she said.

And then something in the expression of his face, in his honest grey eyes, enlightened her, and a wave of scarlet as vivid as the roses under which she stood flushed all over her pale face.

He saw that she understood.

'Yes, Jill,' he said then, 'that's it! Could you—will you—marry me?'

She gazed at him in silence, and having found his voice he went on, speaking now with more ease.

'I know that you can never give me the love that was his, but we are both lonely, and we both loved him—we have so much in common, too! Ah! Jill, do you think you could?'

She continued to look at him gravely, taking note of the tired lines about his eyes and mouth, the sprinkling of grey in the black hair. How much he had gone through—how terribly he had suffered for the land they both loved so well. He could never take Desmond's place in her heart; could never enter within that Holy of Holies where the dead boy reigned alone. But Anthony knew this, and was willing to take her on those conditions. Surely Desmond would have wished it? Desmond who had given his very life for his beloved twin. Could she not also give what was left of her life to make him a little happy—a little less lonely?

And Anthony, watching her in tense silence, saw a smile creep round her lips, as she lifted her hand and placed it on his arm.

'Well?' he asked, almost in a whisper. 'What do you say, Jill!'

'I say—Yes, Tony, if you care to have me!' she replied.

And stooping he laid his lips on hers, while a great peace seemed to fall upon them, as they stood there together in the dear old garden, with the scent and beauty of the roses all round them.

Peace was in Ireland, too, at last, but—for how long? Was the fight over—the battle won? Or must our people again go through the Crucible of suffering and temptation, to come forth from that fiery trial either as worthless dross—or pure gold?

The answer—like the future—lies in God's Hands.